THE FIGHT AGAINST THE DARK

BY

PETER WACHT

Kestrel
Media Group, LLC

BOOK 8 OF THE SYLVAN CHRONICLES

Copyright 2021 © by Peter Wacht

Cover design by Ebooklaunch.com

Published in the United States by Kestrel Media Group LLC.

ISBN: 978-1-950236-14-5
eBook ISBN: 978-1-950236-15-2

Library of Congress Control Number: 9781950236145

Also by Peter Wacht

THE SYLVAN CHRONICLES

THE RISE OF THE SYLVAN WARRIORS

THE TALES OF CALEDONIA

YOUR FREE SHORT STORY IS WAITING

Through the Knife's Edge

The Shadow Lord's Dark Horde is descending upon the Kingdoms. Two Sylvan Warriors charged as scouts form a reluctant alliance in order to survive. Not only must they learn to work together to stay alive, but they also must confront Malachias, the warlock tasked with killing them.

On the run from hunting Ogren and avoiding the Dragas that are scouring the skies, Rya Westgard and Rynlin Keldragan race to escape the Charnel Mountains to reach the leader of the Sylvana and warn her of the approaching army about to flood the Kingdoms with dark creatures – before it's too late.

Note to Readers

This short story, a prelude to the events in *The Sylvan Chronicles*, is free to readers who receive my newsletter. Sign up and get your free copy here: www.kestrelmg.com

CHAPTER ONE

DREAM OR REALITY?

The tendrils of black mist snaked their way around Thomas Kestrel, whipping about as if each one had a mind of its own. The inky cords probed, testing for a weakness, twisting around one another as they sought to latch onto his body, then rearing back rapidly as the Dark Magic tried to escape the killing stroke of the Sword of the Highlands. Each time Thomas' brightly glowing blade, infused with the Talent, slashed through a strand of corrupted sorcery, the formless dark creature that towered above the Sylvan Warrior howled in pain, its tentacle dissolving as it was cut free from the beast. Yet even with the suffering that its quarry inflicted upon it, the churning mass of darkness continued its assault, a dozen new tendrils taking the place of each tentacle sliced off much like the mythical Hydra. Thomas fought with a will, his movement economical and lightning fast as he cleaved and cut through the threads of black that shot toward him time after time and gave him no chance to take a breath. But even he, his actions so quick that they seemed to blur, couldn't keep up with the speed and ferocity of the dark creature's attack.

Dozens and dozens of tendrils flailed and snapped around him, seeking a path through the shield that he wove with his brilliantly shining steel. Sadly, despite his best efforts, he was doomed to fail, and he knew it. The Shadow Lord's servant was too much for him. First a cable of black slipped past his blade and wrapped itself around his right leg, holding him in place. He tried to cut it off, his fear growing as the cord became darker and more solid, anchoring him to the ground. Each time he slashed down with his blade more and more strands of Dark Magic got in the way, blocking his attempts and allowing that single thickening cable to maintain its tight grip. While he was distracted, another inky cord found purchase, winding its way around his waist. Before that thread could tighten its grip, Thomas cut it off. But that obstruction permitted two more black threads to curl around his left arm. He tried to slash down with his steel, but he couldn't. His sword arm wouldn't move, held tightly by another thick strand of black that had threaded its way past his defenses. He strained against the solidifying cords, desperate to free himself, but the strands only tightened their hold, constricting around him as if he were caught within the coils of a giant snake. His alarm grew. Unable to move, his rising terror threatened to engulf him.

With its prey locked in place, the billowing cloud of evil sent tendril after tendril shooting toward Thomas, curling around him tighter and tighter, compressing his sword arm against his chest and encircling his body. The seething mass of sable tentacles then began to pulse a deep black. Thomas continued to struggle against the threads that were as strong as steel, but as the cords darkened in color, he began to weaken, his strength slowly ebbing away. He imagined that what he experienced now was similar to having his life drained from him by a Shade's kiss. That thought only served to increase his panic all the more. Unable to break free, his head held tightly in place, Thomas could only stare into the two pinpricks of blood red that burned brightly in the center of the swirling mass of black. As the darkness closed around him, his body growing heavy, his thoughts drifting away, his vision blurring, all he could focus on were those points of red blazing in the encroaching shadows as his consciousness faded away …

Thomas didn't know how long he floated through this world of inky black, but slowly, ever so slowly, a new image began to form in front of him. As his senses and memories returned to him, he recalled being in the Highlands, fighting on a plain of long grass that stretched off into the distance, imposing, snow-capped peaks surrounding him. But no more. That had all disappeared. Somehow, he had traveled to a place where the bright sunlight of the day had been replaced by a thick, grey gloom. Thankful that he could move once again, he turned around slowly. He could make out very little in the murk, seeing nothing but a wispy grey except for the two blood-red eyes that still burned brightly in front of him. He should have felt shock, surprise, terror, but he didn't. Rather, he felt whole, as if he were exactly where he was supposed to be. As Thomas' bright green eyes adjusted to the darkness, he picked out more of the cowled figure standing in front of him, still black robes hanging in the air, not even rippling at the touch of the wind.

The seconds stretched into minutes as Thomas studied the figure before him, the silence deafening, the stillness arresting. A faint disturbance in the air was the only sign that gave away the fact that something had changed. Thomas raised his sword above his head, not realizing that he still held it in his hand. His brightly shining steel caught the black sword before it cleaved him in two. Not done, his shrouded adversary flipped his blade around in a backhanded swing that targeted Thomas' midsection, but again he countered, sword sliding down to push the strike away from his body. And so it went for the next few minutes, the light-eating sword of black slicing through the gloom while Thomas danced around his attacker, deflecting each lunge, cut and slash. Each time the two swords met, sparks illuminated the blackness with a flash as the Talent and Dark Magic repelled one another. Thomas wanted to attack, to seek the advantage, to change the trajectory of the duel somehow, but it was all that he could do to defend himself, the black steel weaving around him often no more than a whisker away from slicing into his flesh.

Then just as abruptly as the cowled figure's attack began, it came to an end. The shadowy figure glided backward, the black steel disappearing. Thomas took a few steps back as well, sword still held warily in front of him, not convinced that the fight was truly over. For some strange reason, he suspected that it actually had just started.

"You fight well, boy," rasped the robed man who faded in and out of the gloom, the only constant his blood-red eyes. "But not well enough."

"Well enough to hold you off." Thomas said the words with a confidence that he didn't feel. Although he had defended himself from each of his opponent's attacks, it had been more of a struggle than he had anticipated. His adversary filled him with a fear that almost paralyzed him, slowing his ability to react.

"Believe that if you want, boy. But you know the truth."

Thomas stared into those blood-red eyes, doubt seeping into him as the two orbs burned brightly, flaring in the murk. The shadowy figure was right, though he didn't want to admit it to himself. The duel had felt more like a test rather than a fight.

"What do you want?" Thomas was pleased that his voice was steady, strong, and didn't reveal what he was actually experiencing as his emotions roiled within him.

"Isn't it obvious?" asked the cowled figure. "I want you."

"Why?"

"Don't play the fool, boy. It doesn't become you. You know why."

Thomas' eyes hardened, the rebuke angering him. His hand flexed on the hilt of his sword. For just a moment, he considered lunging for his opponent, his brightly glowing blade pulsing in response to his emotions. But he tamped down the impulse, knowing that it would lead to little good.

"I'll never serve you."

"We'll see, boy," replied the cowled figure, the quiet sibilance of his voice reminding Thomas of a bloodsnake. "We'll see very soon." The blood-red eyes sparked, giving the dark gloom a red haze. "Be ready, boy. I'm coming for you."

"Not if I come for you first."

Then in a blink of the eye the figure was gone, and darkness settled over Thomas once again.

The squawk of a kestrel flying high above the Marcher encampment broke through the fog that surrounded Thomas, waking him. He shook his head, trying to clear the cobwebs from his mind. He felt as if he hadn't slept at all. The sun still a distant thought in the early morning, Thomas rolled out of his blankets and followed the large shadow of the raptor with his eyes as it soared above him. The kestrel shrieked again, and Thomas smiled in return. He had been dreaming. He was still in the Highlands. The dark creature that had almost emptied the life from him was dead. Only a bad memory. Thomas closed his eyes and breathed deeply, enjoying the crispness of the air. A bolt of fear ran through him. His eyes popped open, and he looked down at his right hand, the Sword of the Highlands firmly in his grip. He didn't remember pulling the blade free from its scabbard when he woke. Had he done so in his sleep? An unnerving realization shot through him as he stared at the inscription that ran down the length of the steel: "*Strength and courage lead to freedom.*" The fight against the dark creature had been a dream, of that he was certain, but what of the duel against the cowled figure? Had that been a dream as well? Or had it been real?

Thomas turned his gaze toward the north and the Charnel Mountains, which were only a smudge far off in the distance. Within those ash-covered peaks lay the Shadow Lord's lair. Blackstone. The seat of his adversary's power. He could feel the pull. It was growing stronger by the day, more insistent. He would need to go there one day soon. But not yet. Thankfully not yet. He needed to do something else first. If his plan worked as he hoped it would, he could do as he said when he spoke to the shadow with the blood-red eyes. Something that his enemy wouldn't expect.

CHAPTER TWO

RUMBLING DISSATISFACTION

A tall figure covered in misty, pitch-black robes stood in the center of his throne room lost in thought. If not for his fiercely burning blood-red eyes, he would have blended in perfectly with the natural gloom of the chamber. The symmetry of the alternating black and white tiles, all as large as a man's stride, usually pleased him, giving him a feeling of control. That everything could be put in its proper place. But not now. Not in this moment. Not when his mind drifted elsewhere. At first, fixated on the future, on what was yet to come, then just as much on the past, on what had come to pass. Finally, it was the present that drew him back from his mental wanderings.

The Shadow Lord listened to the roars that drifted into the circular room through the open doors. Normally the sound would have filled him with a sense of his own power, of what he could achieve when the time was right. Now it only reminded him of his failures. He glided out onto the balcony and looked down upon the immense courtyard below. Ogren raiding parties formed into ranks on the square, destined for the Highlands with the goal of creating an avenue into the Kingdoms that would allow his dark creatures to avoid the Breaker. The Shadow Lord was certain that, if necessary, his Dark Horde could break through the Kingdoms' primary defense, scaling the massive wall built to keep him and his servants in the Charnel Mountains after the devastating conclusion of the Great War. But why take an unnecessary risk? Why not circumvent the inevitable delay that breaching such a barrier would create? Why not put in place a better strategy that would allow him to gain his objectives more quickly and easily?

With all that in mind, he had done so, cultivating and corrupting the current High King. The Shadow Lord had aided Rodric Tessaril during his rise to the throne of Armagh and the honorific of High King that went with the title. He had helped that inept scoundrel remove the uncle and cousin, giving that insipid yet temporarily useful fool a clear path to power. And with Rodric as High King, the Shadow Lord could use him to weaken the other Kingdoms, bringing to his side those willing to sell themselves for the riches and power he offered, and isolating or eliminating those foolish enough to ignore his entreaties. At first, the move had proved effective. Yet in the last few years, despite the time and effort that went into every single detail of his plans, the strategy, so long in the making, had begun to unravel.

As a result of the defeat of the Armaghian army in the Highlands, the High King Rodric Tessaril was on the run, risked losing his Kingdom, and had threatened the Shadow Lord's plans with collapse. With Rodric no longer a threat, the Marchers could turn their attention to protecting their northern border, making it harder for his Ogren raiding parties to gain control of the territory that he needed that would allow his Dark Horde, when the time was right, to avoid the Breaker and sweep into the Kingdoms unopposed. All his planning and scheming appeared to have been for nothing, his plan decades in the making now laying in tatters, thanks to an incompetent High King and an upstart boy. A boy who should have died a decade ago, but didn't, escaping the assassin's blade. A boy who should have died multiple times since then, but still lived.

Rodric, Killeran and Chertney all had been in a position to stick a knife between the boy's ribs, but failed to do so. Every Nightstalker and Shade sent against him had been defeated as well. Even Malachias had been found lacking in his efforts to eliminate the boy, and he was the most powerful of the Shadow Lord's servants. The one who had served him the longest and with the greatest success. Even the Wraith, the most dangerous of his assassins, had fallen short, at least initially. Perhaps the Wraith would succeed in time, only bested by the boy but not destroyed. But was it wise to count on the dark creature to complete its task having already failed once? Time and time again the boy had made a fool of him and his minions. That seemed to be the only constant.

The Shadow Lord's blood-red eyes burned like a raging fire as his fury began to consume him. So much at stake, all of it at risk, because of a boy. And now the boy was growing stronger and more dangerous by the day. The boy needed to be eliminated, yet he was surrounded by fools and incompetents and nothing he had tried in the past had proven successful.

As he drifted back into the chamber and came to a stop in its very center, the Shadow Lord struggled to control his temper as a tremor of unease flitted through his thoughts. Was he the boy of the prophecy? The one destined to stand before him on this very spot and engage him in a duel that would decide the fate of the Kingdoms? Maybe so. Maybe that was why the boy continued to escape the traps set for him. Maybe only he, the Shadow Lord, could kill the boy. If such was the case, then so be it. He would take great pleasure in sliding his blade into the boy's heart, for the Shadow Lord had no doubt how the duel would end. He was too skilled, too powerful, too treacherous to lose.

But it should never have come to this. It should have ended long ago. Needing to release his anger, the Shadow Lord shot a bolt of black energy through the gloom, shattering the skylight that enclosed the top of the circular chamber. The Shadow Lord watched without emotion as the broken glass rained down around him, the sparkling shards covering the disc set in the very center of the hall and surrounded by the alternating black and white tile. Unexpectedly and much to his annoyance, a beam of sunshine blasted through the hole at the top of the chamber and shined down on the glass-covered stone disc just seconds after he had destroyed the skylight, the light revealing the intricate design carved into it.

Two figures emerged from the cuts in the block, done with such excellent workmanship that they appeared lifelike. The first resembled a young man with a blazing sword of light. Opposing him was a tall man with a cruel face wielding a sword that swallowed the light. They were locked blade to blade, their faces no more

11

than a finger's breadth apart. The boy wore a look of determination, the man a grin of arrogance and sure victory. As the sun met the stone it grew warm, the light touching the broken glass and igniting a kaleidoscope of colors. A rumble began in the room, drifting out to the very edges of Blackstone, an occurrence that had become much more common in the Shadow Lord's city over the last few months. An event that suggested change could be coming. A happening that still worried the Shadow Lord despite his confidence in the likely result of the prophesied duel.

As the rumbling intensified so did the brightness of the beam of light, the dazzling colors dancing irregularly across the chamber's halls. Gaining more and more strength with each passing second, the sunlight blasted away the scraps of darkness and gloom that inhabited the throne room until the Shadow Lord had no choice but to turn away, the glare of the blazing, white light too strong even for him.

CHAPTER THREE

Another Demand

The tall man walked silently along the mountain trail, cloak drawn tightly across his shoulders, cowl pulled down to cover his head in a failed attempt to ward off the biting cold. Although it appeared that he wasn't paying attention, his senses were extended in all directions, attuned to everything around him. Dark creatures haunted the crevices, crags and shadows of these peaks, so his hand never strayed far from the short sword on his belt. Touches of darkness, of things terrifying and unnatural, of things better left in the jet-black of night, flitted across the extreme edge of his perception, but he knew that he wasn't in any immediate danger. If he hurried, he could reach the grotto that would offer him some protection and peace of mind as he settled in for the night.

Most people refused to enter the Charnel Mountains, and those who did rarely returned. Any who traveled within ten miles of the forbidding crests shrouded in ash could feel the evil lurking there, hidden away from the sight of man, but always present. Always watching, always lurking, always waiting for just the right moment to strike.

Some said that the Charnel Mountains were an abomination, caused by a tremendous magical battle between the forces of good and evil. Those who followed the light had won, but they could not destroy the dark, they could only hold it back. So instead they imprisoned their enemies in the mountains, sealing them away for eternity, or so they thought. Before the Shadow Lord came to be, the Charnel Mountains looked very much like the Highlands, the landscape defined by hidden valleys and lakes, the wind-swept peaks, towering evergreens and other conifers, and brambles and thickets hiding innumerable glades. But when the Shadow Lord took up residence there and began creating his servants — the Ogren, Shades, Fearhounds, as well as other beasts that were even more frightening and deadly — the mountains slowly transformed into what they are today. Barren. Desolate. Dead. Dark grey stone formed the stone spires, the very tips of the monstrous peaks a sooty black. What trees that remained were stunted and twisted, struggling to survive with their roots in an earth covered by a thick layer of ash and cinder.

The tallest of the mountains could not be seen completely, as fully a third of its mass rose up into the grey clouds. Known as Blackstone, that single peak had an even older name. Shadow's Reach. On certain winter days, when the sun was in just the right position, the shadow of Blackstone reached out across much of the Northern Steppes, turning day into night and, for those travelers caught in that empty land, life into a horror.

No one in their right mind scouted the Charnel Mountains on their own. Not if they wanted to live. Yet that was his task, so here he was, wandering the ravines and gullies, staying out of sight, tracking the dark creatures that sought to raid across the flat grassland to the south into the Highlands and perhaps into the Kingdoms beyond.

Having reached a steeper part of the narrow trail, the tall man began to pick his way carefully, wary of the scrabble beneath his feet. He reached out to the rocks lining the path, pulling himself up the more difficult sections. As he finally attained the level part of the path, he stopped short, his hand whipping the short sword out in front of him.

The blade glowed brightly as the scout infused it with the Talent. A mysterious man wrapped in black robes stood before him. Bald, his features sharp, he appeared almost skeletal. His sunken, dark eyes gave away no emotion. There was nothing in his eyes but a flinty hardness, a malevolent spark dancing within that sea of black and sending a shiver of fear through the scout.

"There are easier ways to arrange a meeting, Malachias. You don't need to play your games."

The Shadow Lord's servant examined the man before him, noting that the sword remained within his grasp, its white light pulsing along the length of steel. He ignored the comment.

"You dare to challenge me?" questioned Malachias with a smirk, his raspy voice sounding like metal sliding across stone.

The tall man stared at Malachias a moment longer, then sighed, acknowledging the power that he faced. Releasing his hold on the Talent, he sheathed his short sword. He knew that he didn't have the strength to defeat the Shadow Lord's right hand, so there was no point in continuing the show.

"I have another task for you."

The man shook his head in frustration. "I have done enough, more than enough. I have done everything that you have asked of me. This has to stop. No more tasks. No more assignments. I want to be free of this."

For the first time some little fragment of emotion drifted behind Malachias' eyes. He appeared to be amused.

"You believe that you can break the contract that you made with our master?" A scratchy laugh erupted from Malachias. "You knew full well the bargain you made, and what you were getting in return. Once you struck your bargain, the terms were set. Your fate was sealed. Your life was no longer your own. You belong to the Shadow Lord."

"I have done everything he's asked!" shouted the tall man, Malachias' words cutting to the very bone. He had been such a fool, thinking that he could find some way to escape the deal he had accepted. The compact that bore down on him like a ten-ton stone. "Everything. And many of the things I've done I'm desperate to forget, but I cannot. They stay with me, always there in the back of my mind. Please, I need to be free of this. I can't do it anymore."

Malachias' laughter died quickly, his eyes resembling granite once more. "Once you have committed yourself to the Shadow Lord, there is no turning back. There is no release, not even in death. You will do as commanded. Remember, there are always worse tasks that can be given to you. Tasks that will make the ones that plague your memory now seem pleasant in comparison."

The tall man closed his eyes in resignation, desperate to be free of the bindings on his soul, but acknowledging reluctantly that he had no power to remove them. Knowing that his one moment of weakness had turned his life into a waking nightmare.

"What would you have of me?"

Malachias stared at the man before him a bit longer, confirming for himself that the traitor understood the strength of the cage within which he had placed himself so long ago, a cage that would continue to hold him no matter what he tried to do to escape.

"Multiple plans have been set in motion to remove a thorn from the side of the Shadow Lord. But this thorn has proven most resilient and continues to prick our master, as you well know. This thorn has prevented us from using the Highlands to enter the Kingdoms. That cannot continue. We must be able to avoid the Breaker. Yes, the Kingdoms are weak. We can surmount the barrier. But it would cost us time and resources. Better to make the Highlands our staging point. If the Dark Horde can march through the Highlands, the Kingdoms are doomed before the battle even begins."

"And my role?"

"Put yourself in a position to remove this thorn, as you've done in the past. You should have no trouble getting close to him if circumstances demand it. But this time do what's required of you. Remove this thorn. Otherwise, the consequences will be severe."

"Who am I supposed to kill?" the tall man sighed with weariness, knowing the answer already but still needing to ask the question. A bolt of fear sent a shiver up his spine and jolted him from his growing melancholy. He had tried once before and failed, barely escaping with his life. His hand unconsciously moved to his chest, touching the silver amulet hanging around his neck, the silver amulet carved into the shape of the curled horn of a unicorn. It felt like an icicle against his body.

"The Highland Lord."

CHAPTER FOUR

TAKING FLIGHT

Thomas Kestrel stood atop the Breaker wrapped in a thick, dark green cloak, ignoring the harsh, cold wind that buffeted him, seemingly trying to knock him from his perch on the battlements. Carved from massive blocks of granite, the Breaker rose well over three hundred feet in height and was one hundred feet wide, extending from the western Highlands to the coast and the Winter Sea. Its broad expanse gave the soldiers of the Kingdoms the space they needed to repel an attack by the Shadow Lord's dark creatures. But there were no defenders standing atop the parapet now, and there hadn't been for centuries. Because the Shadow Lord had faded from reality to myth in the minds of most in the Kingdoms, the Breaker was no longer viewed as a barrier, but rather just as an obstacle.

The first time the Shadow Lord had tried to conquer the Kingdoms, one thousand years in the past, the rulers of the different lands didn't perceive his evil as a serious threat then either, since he was far to the north and the Northern Steppes stood in the way. Consequently, only a small contingent of troops from the eastern Kingdoms went into the Northern Peaks to fight. They did all that they could, not knowing what they truly faced until it was too late, as they were heavily outnumbered by the Ogren, Shades, Fearhounds and other hideous beasts that formed the Dark Horde that sought to invade the Kingdoms. The soldiers fought valiantly, yet could only disrupt the Shadow Lord's inevitable advance and hope that help would come.

The other Kingdoms finally realized the great threat presented by this new danger, that hard-earned wisdom built on the lives lost because of that initial ill-conceived stratagem, but it would take weeks for those Kingdoms to call together their armies and march to the north. At that time, druids still held sway over the land, and often served as advisors in the courts of the different monarchs. The chief druid, a woman named Athala, suggested that the Kingdoms send their best warriors to her, and under her leadership they would fight the Dark Horde until the massed armies of the Kingdoms could take the field … or her small fighting force was destroyed.

The unprepared and rattled rulers balked at first, but several unexpected events finally convinced them to move forward with the proposal, and the greatest warriors of that time met Athala on the Northern Steppes in order to counter the Dark Horde, which was pushing hard for the south and would soon break out of the Northern Peaks onto the grasslands. When that happened, the Kingdoms would have little chance of stopping the dark creatures from flooding the Kingdoms. Athala called those who made up her small host of only several hundred Sylvan Warriors, naming these coura- geous fighters after a mythical band of soldiers who, the stories told, appeared in times of need and fought for those who had been wronged or protected the land when danger threatened.

The Sylvan Warriors met the Dark Horde at the southern border of the Northern Peaks, and there at a place called the Knife's Edge they battled for three days and three nights. The Sylvana fought desperately to hold back the Shadow Lord's advance. In the end, after untold sacrifices and a bravery rarely seen on the battlefield, they succeeded. The small band of warriors forced the Dark Horde to retreat to the north. Before the Shadow Lord could recover and send his dark creatures south once more, the armies of the Kingdoms arrived and pushed him and his minions even deeper into what was then already being described as the Charnel Mountains.

But despite their best efforts the Sylvan Warriors and the combined might of the Kingdoms couldn't destroy the Shadow Lord. They could only defeat him. So the rulers of the Kingdoms again followed the advice of Athala and proclaimed the Sylvan Warriors a permanent fighting force with no ties of allegiance to any Kingdom. The sole purpose of this elite company was to fight the Shadow Lord and his servants, and they had done so ever since.

Yet even with the formation of the Sylvana and trusting in their skills and power, at the conclusion of the Great War the Kingdoms still feared the Shadow Lord's return, knowing that if their armies had not appeared when they did to aid Athala and her intrepid troop, the Dark Horde would have overrun the Kingdoms. Therefore, the monarchs of the Kingdoms banded together and built the Breaker and formed the First Guard, soldiers from the different Kingdoms charged with serving a year on the massive wall, watching, waiting, and preparing for the next attack so that when the Shadow Lord once more tried to conquer the Kingdoms, and all assumed that he would, the Kingdoms would be better prepared to defend themselves. But as time passed no attack had come, and the Kingdoms began sending fewer and fewer soldiers to serve in the First Guard until eventually no one stood atop the Breaker, leaving only the Sylvana to guard against the return of the Dark Horde.

Now, in a replay of events a millennium gone, many of the Kingdoms failed to recognize the danger or willingly ignored it, more worried about the happenings in their own Kingdom thanks to the machinations of the High King rather than, at least to their own eyes, a yet to be confirmed threat to the Kingdoms as a whole that appeared to remain more story than substance. Such shortsightedness could prove costly, Thomas knew, as it had in the past. Not very tall, the Lord of the Highlands still radiated a power and presence that few could project. Deep in thought, his green eyes flashed brightly as he stared to the north at the dark smudge of the Charnel Mountains that rose above the flat expanse of the Northern Steppes. He had needed to clear his mind, to get away, if only for the afternoon, from the crush of business that had fallen upon him now that the Marchers had expelled the High King and his army from the Highlands. Finally, after a decade of terror and anguish, of servitude and misery, his homeland was free. But for how long?

Attacks by the Shadow Lord's dark creatures continued in the northern Highlands. At first the raiding parties had predominantly been Ogren led by Shades, but now packs of Fearhounds and Mongrels also were attempting to carve a path through the peaks of his mountain homeland. The increased pace of these incursions could mean only one thing. Time was growing short. The Shadow Lord was stirring, and the Dark Horde would come again. But Thomas couldn't focus on that task just yet with the High King still running free.

Rodric Tessaril seemed to be able to slither out of closing traps with ease. Every time Thomas thought that he had the man responsible for his grandfather's murder within his grasp, he slipped away. Admittedly, the last time, just a few days before, Rodric's hidden ally had come to the fore and helped him, allowing the High King to flee back to Eamhain Mhacha, capital of Armagh, with his tail between his legs. Thomas couldn't let the High King enjoy his freedom for much longer. Rodric would only create more problems and intrigue, which would distract from what needed to be the primary focus – defending the Breaker and defeating the Shadow Lord. No, before anything else, the issue of the High King had to be addressed, once and for all. Rodric Tessaril needed to be removed from the playing board. Permanently.

Thomas turned to the northeast, facing Blackstone. Although he couldn't see the dead city situated among the Charnel Mountains, he could feel its pull. It was growing more insistent, more demanding. He knew that the prophesied time that he feared the most approached faster than he would have preferred. Just not yet, but soon. Very soon. Unable to take his mind away from that fact, his grandmother's favorite saying ran through his mind: *You must do what you must do.* Even if doing what you must came at a cost you didn't want to pay. Forcing that depressing thought from his mind, he turned to the west. He felt another pull, a fainter pull, very faint, but with each passing hour it was becoming more irritating, like an itch between his shoulder blades that he couldn't reach. This very vague tug reminded him of the time before he joined the Sylvan Warriors, when the pull of the Pinnacle had grown increasingly stronger as time went by. The same thing was happening now, this strengthening need for him to travel to the western coast of the Kingdoms. He wasn't certain, but he suspected that this new sensation was connected to the task that he dreaded. Should he follow it? Would whatever he discovered at the end of this nagging feeling give him a chance, however slim, of surviving his encounter with the Shadow Lord? He could think about it all he wanted, but there was only one way to find out.

The Shadow Lord. The High King. Two problems that continued to plague him. Separated, these two opponents tested him constantly. Combined, they could prove overwhelming. So better to cut away the High King and eliminate that threat as quickly as possible. When he returned to the Highlands, he would convince the other rulers of the course that needed to be taken.

That decision made, his mind began to wander. Was Kaylie Carlomin another issue that needed to be dealt with? The Princess of Fal Carrach had made her anger known when he had stepped within the dome of energy his grandparents had constructed with the Talent as they sought to contain the Hydra-like dark creature the Shadow Lord had set upon them during the final battle for the Highlands. Just thinking about her punch to his arm after he had destroyed the monster set his arm aching. The vehemence of her words continued to play through his mind: "Don't ever do that again." He could understand her anger, but what she had done next had left him stunned. Why had she kissed him after hitting him? Her action had surprised and confused him, leaving him standing there not knowing what to do. But the more he thought about the incident, the more he realized that there was more to her words and actions than met the eye, and that worried him. What was he to do? And knowing what his future held, should he do anything at all?

A shrill squawk that reverberated off the Breaker pulled his thoughts back to the present. The large kestrel settled itself onto the battlements just a few feet from Thomas, its sharp gaze seeking him out. Its strong wings spanned seven feet, and the white feathers speckled with grey on the bird's underside blended perfectly with the sky. When visible, the raptor was a dangerous predator. When hidden, it was deadly, shooting down through the thin air like an arrow, its sharp claws outstretched for the kill. The Highlands was the raptor's domain, now its only home. Once, not too many years before, raptors lived in every Kingdom from the Western Ocean to the Sea of Mist. But no more. Nobles and wealthy merchants paid dearly for the feathers of the mighty bird. Rumors of their magical powers abounded. Some believed the feathers, when ground down and mixed with a few select ingredients, served as an aphrodisiac. Others insisted that drinking the strange brew gave wisdom. Still others thought it brought riches. Though no one had ever proven the truth of these myths, the old beliefs died hard. As the years passed, so did these majestic birds, until none remained except those in the Highlands, protected by the harsh weather, the rough landscape and the High-landers themselves, for the raptors held a special place in their hearts. Moreover, the kestrel was the namesake and the symbol of the Highland Lord.

Thomas knew this raptor, having met it several times before. It appeared almost as if this kestrel looked out for him. And with that knowledge, strange as it may seem, came a sense of comfort. Looking up into the cloudy sky, he picked out the four other raptors that circled above. Not a day went by that he didn't have four or five kestrels flying above him now, ever vigilant. Watching. Waiting. Protecting. The massive birds enjoyed the strong current of air gusting off the Charnel Mountains and flowing toward the Breaker, twisting and turning at the whim of the wind. He realized that circumstances had changed drastically when they dipped their wings at the same time to curl toward the blackened mountain peaks to the north.

Dots appeared in the sky, appearing larger with every heartbeat. The raptor that had landed on the Breaker nodded to him, then used its sharp claws to push off the weathered stone, beating its wings fiercely to catch up to its brethren. Thomas watched intently, a sense of dread settling in his stomach as those dots materialized into monstrous beasts. More than four times the size of the raptor, the Dragas was a significant threat. The flying dark creatures enjoyed a clear advantage over the kestrels, their scaled hides offering them additional protection though it did cost them the speed that the raptors put to such good use.

Five Dragas approached, roaring in fury upon seeing the raptors. Normally, the kestrels would work together to take on just one of these massive dark creatures, seeking to dig their sharp claws into the soft underbelly of their mortal enemies. But they couldn't do so today. There were simply too many to fight. Yet that didn't stop the predators. The raptors dove from above, hurtling down toward the Dragas and trying to catch them by surprise. Although several of the kestrels did succeed in slicing into the unprotected undersides of a few Dragas, most failed, their sharp claws simply skittering off the hardened scales as the Dragas avoided the attack. The battle quickly denigrated into a game of cat and mouse, as the kestrels used their speed and tighter maneuverability to avoid the chasing Dragas, understanding the penalty if they were caught by the dark creatures' long, spike-like claws and sharp teeth.

Thomas watched the fight in the air begin, his anger growing, as he saw several of the raptors barely escape the Dragas, which were emboldened by the knowledge that though the dark creatures did not have the speed of the kestrels, they enjoyed greater stamina and strength. The longer the battle continued, the greater the chance of success for the dark creatures. Keeping all that in mind, Thomas took hold of the Talent. In a flash of bright white light, he took the shape of a kestrel, rapidly winging his way toward the aerial fray.

Quickly gaining height, Thomas surveyed the sky around him. One kestrel flew to his left, darting about, desperately trying to escape a Dragas that flew just a few feet behind its tail feathers. Tipping his wing, Thomas banked down and to the right, curling toward the raptor that struggled to dodge its pursuer. With a final burst of speed, Thomas shot right below the chasing Dragas, extending his claws and slicing across the dark creature's belly. The Dragas extended its wings, stopping its flight and hovering in the air, its attention now focused on Thomas as its black blood flowed freely from the long, deep gash that scored its underside. Ignoring the pain of its injury, the Dragas prepared to launch itself toward Thomas, who had flown back around in a tight circle with the hope of lining up another strike. The Dragas viewed his attacker as the primary target, realizing too late that Thomas had become the bait. Not sensing the danger, before the Dragas could propel itself toward its new quarry, the raptor it had chased slammed into it from behind, its deadly claws tearing through the Dragas' wings until the thin, loose skin had been shredded into a bloody mess. With a screech of anger and fear, the Dragas dropped from the sky, its broken and torn wings no longer able to support its weight.

Thomas and the other raptor didn't bother to watch the dark creature slam into the ground far below. Instead, they turned their attention to another Dragas, this one also pursuing a kestrel, so intent on its prey that the dark creature missed what had just occurred. Working together, Thomas and the other kestrel quickly dispatched the next Dragas in a similar fashion, Thomas focusing on the belly, the kestrel on the wings, both raptors so quick in their attack that they didn't have to worry about the Dragas' teeth or claws. Thomas and the kestrels built on his strategy, and as each Dragas fell from the sky, plummeting to the grassland far below, the kestrels, which had at first been the prey, quickly had become the predators. In just a few minutes, the skirmish came to a satisfying end for the kestrels. The sky clear of Dragas, the raptors screeched in triumph, exultant in their victory.

Thomas turned to the south and began winging his way toward the Highlands. Four of the raptors took up positions around him, much like points on a compass, while the fifth kestrel, the one that had tracked him since his time living in the Crag, dipped down from a higher altitude to fly next to him, its pride obvious in its sharp eyes. As Thomas and his escort neared the Highlands, the snow-covered peaks became more distinct as the raptors' powerful wings drew them ever closer. Thomas resolved that he'd keep this latest incident to himself. Remembering her reaction to his taking on the dark creature sent by the Shadow Lord, he didn't want to risk angering Kaylie again. Who knew what she was capable of?

CHAPTER FIVE

COUNCIL

A few days after what had come to be called the Battle of the Highlands, in which the Marchers and their allies routed the Armaghian host, the rulers of the Kingdoms that had participated gathered in a small, makeshift tent raised by Gregory of Fal Carrach's soldiers. The wounded had been seen to, the dead buried, and plans made for the thousands of prisoners taken when the Highland Lord destroyed the dark creature and the High King fled. Now they had to address more strategic issues, and as they worked to resolve these challenges, they understood the gravity of their discussions, for they held the fate of all the Kingdoms in their hands.

Thomas, Lord of the Highlands, had thanked his allies individually, wanting them to know how much he and his Marchers appreciated their assistance. Moreover, he wanted them to understand that the Marchers stood with them in the days to come, that the victory over the High King had not concluded matters and that there was still more to do. It had simply been a first step in a larger gambit. Thomas needed these leaders to recognize that there was a greater evil coming that would require their alliance to continue and expand if at all possible. But he could see in their eyes a reluctance to heed his words, to believe what he had to say, because to believe meant that likely sooner rather than later action would be required against a foe that had last afflicted the Kingdoms hundreds of years before. A foe once defeated, but never destroyed. A foe that for many was still little more than a myth.

"The creature that Thomas eliminated was not of Chertney's making," explained Rya Keldragan, her regal bearing dominating the small gathering. The patronymic Keldragan still had meaning for those assembled, as the ancient name still exerted an influence over the Kingdoms, and had since the time of Ollav Fola.

Rynlin sat beside her, staring into the flames of the fire that burned in the pit dug in the center of the tent. The two Sylvan Warriors were proud of their grandson and what he had accomplished, but they knew that victory over the High King was just one move in a longer, harder, deadlier struggle. A chill had settled across the Highlands, as if the dark creature that had emerged through the portal had brought with it a shivering premonition of what was in store for the Kingdoms. The cold wind that played at the edges of the tent, finding the gaps that it needed to cause the flames to flicker and dance, reminded Rynlin of a darker time. A time that he feared would return all too soon.

"True, Chertney has a strong ability in Dark Magic, in fact he's probably one of the most powerful warlocks in all the Kingdoms, but that conjuring was beyond him."

"Lady Keldragan," said Rendael, obviously struggling with the content of the conversation. "I can't pretend to understand much about the Talent or Dark Magic, or these beasts that suddenly appear out of blackness, more heinous than I could possibly imagine. But please understand, it has been three centuries since the Breaker has been threatened. Yes, dark creatures remain a problem. They always have been to a certain extent. And I understand from the young Highland Lord the threat posed by these monstrosities to his Kingdom. But believing that the dire time that preceded the Great War has returned requires a leap in logic that many of us are unprepared to take. We only just learned of Rodric's ultimate deceptions and betrayals, but to believe that the Shadow Lord is returning after so many years of dormancy? That is more difficult to acknowledge. Granted, we have some evidence that dark creatures stir in the Charnel Mountains, but where is the actual proof of the Shadow Lord? Something tangible? Something real?"

"I understand your hesitancy, King Rendael," said Rya in a soothing tone. The flames of the fire accentuated her chestnut hair and set her blues eyes sparkling. "Believing requires a change in perspective that can prove difficult. And, as you said, it means the return of dire times. But those dire times are already upon us. To ignore the signs would be folly. It would ensure the fall of the Kingdoms."

"Rya is correct," said Rynlin, still staring into the flames, his expression grim. "What's happening now is exactly what happened prior to the Great War. The chill that's settling over the eastern Kingdoms is only one sign out of many. Remember, my lords and ladies, the number of attempted incursions by dark creatures into the northern

Highlands has increased tenfold in just a matter of months. It is not happenstance. Those beasts came for a reason."

Rynlin turned his attention to Rendael first, then dragged his eyes across those of all the other sovereigns participating in the discussion.

"You ask for tangible proof," he continued, his intense gaze arresting. "You will not have it until the Dark Horde marches for the Breaker. Besides, you speak as if the Shadow Lord has been gone since we last defended against the onslaught of dark creatures that flooded down from the Charnel Mountains. Such a perspective is incorrect and naive. The Shadow Lord has always been here, biding his time. He never left. He simply was waiting for the best chance to strike once again, and that opportunity draws nearer."

"What my grandfather says is correct," interjected Thomas. "If not for the Sylvana helping to defend the northern Highlands, the Shadow Lord would have a foothold beyond the Breaker already. The fate of the Kingdoms would have already been sealed."

The Marchers assembled behind the rulers of the Kingdoms nodded in agreement, knowing that their countrymen charged with defending the northern passes could not have succeeded so far without the assistance of the Sylvan Warriors. And then when Thomas called Nestor and his Marchers south to aid in the fight against the Armaghian host, several more Sylvan Warriors arrived in the Highlands to take their place, working with the wolfpacks led by Beluil, the pony-sized wolf who grew up with Thomas and took particular pleasure in killing dark creatures, to prevent the servants of the Shadow Lord from achieving their goal of making the Highlands their own.

"What happened to the Shadow Lord after the Great War?" asked Rya, continuing her husband's argument. "We defeated but did not destroy him. We could not destroy him, in fact. He was too strong, despite everything that we tried. He's waited for another opportunity ever since. Rodric's treachery and alliance with the Shadow Lord, the increasing activity in the Charnel Mountains, the war parties coming across the Northern Steppes into the Highlands, the assassination attempts on the Sylvana, some unfortunately successful, they all point to the fact that the Shadow Lord has awakened. He is probing, identifying our weaknesses and seeking to exploit them, while massing his Dark Horde."

"We can believe what we want," said Rynlin. "We can ignore what we see going on around us. But that's simply folly. We must prepare for what is to come. To not do so will mean the end of the Kingdoms and a time of terror and subjugation from which we may never escape."

Gregory, Sarelle, Chuma, even Rendael, bore grim expressions, Rynlin and Rya's arguments having persuaded the monarchs that the threat presented by the Shadow Lord could not be ignored. All the rulers were intelligent men and women, pragmatists at heart. Their reluctance to believe wasn't so much because of what would be required of them, but rather resulted from knowing the consequences of failing to act, of understanding the pain and misery to be unleashed if these two Sylvan Warriors were correct. They had no reason to doubt the truth of their words. It simply took time for them to come to terms with what the future likely held.

"But why send that dark creature?" asked Sarelle. "It couldn't have been solely to rescue Rodric."

Remembering the beast as it burst through the black portal sent a chill down the Queen of Benewyn's spine. The demon's eyes had blazed with a blood-red fire that had terrified her, freezing her, and she knew that it had had the same effect on some of the others sitting with her now, their minds having struggled to comprehend the evil that had been unleashed. Yet Thomas had not been affected, appearing immune to the terror that had radiated from the monster. He had advanced toward the dark creature, sword drawn, seemingly unaware or uncaring of the danger. She knew that there was something unique about the Highland Lord. She was only now beginning to understand the potential significance of her conclusion.

"You are correct, Sarelle," said Rya simply. "The Shadow Lord did not send that demon to save the High King. The portal itself was all that was needed for that task. Rather, it was a test."

"A test for whom?" asked Kaylie. The Princess of Fal Carrach sat next to her father. She balanced her dagger lengthwise on her right index finger, seeking an outlet for her nerves, the conversation making her uneasy.

"For Thomas," answered Rynlin, resignation clear in his voice. "The Shadow Lord wanted to measure his greatest threat."

"What exactly do you mean, Lord Keldragan?" asked Rendael.

"Are you familiar with the prophecies?" asked Rynlin, seeing a few nod their heads, others wracking their brains to remember their lessons from when they had received their schooling. "The prophecies are very obscure. In order to understand them, you have to know what you're looking for. And even then, we miss what's important, often not able to piece the puzzle together until a foreseen event actually has occurred. Nevertheless, indulge me for a moment."

Rynlin's tone suggested that his request was anything but. He began reciting what sounded like poetry:

When a child of life and death
Stands on high
Drawn by faith
He shall hold the key to victory in his hand.

Swords of fire echo in the burned rock
Balancing the future on their blades.

Light dances with dark
Green fire burns in the night
Hopes and dreams follow the wind
To fall in black or white.

"Those are the passages that you think apply to Thomas?" asked Gregory.

"Yes, I do. As do the Sylvana. Let me explain a little more. Begin with the first line: *When a child of life and death*. When Thomas was born, he had green eyes, which throughout the Kingdoms is recognized as a symbol for life. And any birth obviously symbolizes life. On a sadder note, his mother, our daughter, Marya, died during his birth."

"That could apply to many people," said Rendael, enjoying the intellectual exercise, more than willing to challenge the Sylvan Warrior's premise. Rynlin was not the least bit offended. He always took pleasure in an opportunity to engage his pedantic nature.

"Yes, it could," said Rynlin. "But I don't think that it does. Listen to the next line: *Stands on high*. It's a very vague reference. However, we believe it speaks to two critical parts of Thomas' life. When he became Lord of the Highlands, it's traditionally been known as standing on high. And, when you join the Sylvana, you stand on high as well. In fact, he stood on the tallest peak in all the Kingdoms. I think the double reference to the Highlands and the Sylvana serves as added confirmation."

"What about the rest of the prophecy?" asked Rendael, his eyes bright, treating the discussion as a riddle to be solved.

"We just won't know for sure until each event takes place. But I believe the last six lines refer to his battle with the Shadow Lord."

"Wait a second," said Kaylie Carlomin, rising from her seat, dagger gripped tightly in her hand. "You think that Thomas has to fight the Shadow Lord?"

"We don't think," replied Rynlin with some sadness escaping from his voice. "We know."

"How can you be sure?"

The Princess of Fal Carrach glanced at Thomas in fear. No one had ever defeated the Shadow Lord in combat.

"Allow me to explain," said Rynlin. He got up from his seat and began pacing around the fire even though there was little room to maneuver within the small tent. He always thought better on his feet. "Let me repeat the lines of the prophecy that I think apply, and I'll give you my reasoning. Admittedly, the prophecies are all very obscure, and we really won't know for sure if Thomas is in fact the Defender of the Light until he faces off against the Shadow Lord. But, if he is fated to meet the Shadow Lord in combat, then it will happen. There will be no way that he can avoid it."

"The Defender of the Light?" asked Kaylie, never having heard the term before.

"Yes," replied Rya. "The one slated to contest the Lord of the Shadow."

"Also, keep in mind that the prophecies have never been wrong, and though there are several different ones that vary in certain places, they are never very far off when it comes to the important events," said Rynlin, clearly enjoying the chance to offer some instruction. "For example, all the prophecies were correct as to when the Shadow Lord first would appear in the world, and that we would defeat him at certain points in time. Now, this is the intriguing point."

Rynlin strode quickly around the fire, unable to contain the excitement that he felt when teaching.

"Before, the result of what would happen was always predetermined, meaning that the Great War was fated to occur, and it was known that the Shadow Lord's attempt to conquer the Kingdoms would fail. We would successfully push the Shadow Lord and his Dark Horde back into the Charnel Mountains. Of course, we did not know this until the Great War ended and we went back to examine the prophecies. Then we deciphered what had largely been unintelligible to us before.

"At that time we looked ahead and saw that a battle between the Defender of the Light and the Lord of the Shadow would take place sometime in the near future. Of course, when you're dealing with the prophecies the near future could be a hundred years, two hundred years or more from the present. Anyway, placing all that to the side, that's as far as the Seers of Alfeos went in their forecasts — to the actual battle between the Defender of the Light and the Lord of the Shadow. They saw nothing beyond that contest. The prophecies simply come to a close."

"What do you mean? How could they just stop seeing the future?" asked Kaylie.

"We don't know how it happened. We just know that they did. All we can surmise is that the various paths that lead to that point in time all come together, waiting for the result of that event to allow those paths to continue once more. The prophecies conclude during the battle. The seers foretold nothing more beyond that point. They just stopped, and no one can explain why. Listen to the last six lines:

> *Swords of fire echo in the burned rock*
> *Balancing the future on their blades.*
>
> *Light dances with dark*
> *Green fire burns in the night*
> *Hopes and dreams follow the wind*
> *To fall in black or white.*

"*Swords of fire echo in the burned rock.* That's a clear reference to this final battle between light and dark, a point that is no longer debated by those who have studied the prophecies, some for hundreds of years longer than I. The battle will take place, and most likely somewhere in Shadow's Reach, or rather Blackstone, as it's known today. Of that, we're fairly certain."

"So the Defender of the Light has to fight the Lord of the Shadow in his domain," said Gregory.

"Exactly. Certainly not a promising beginning for the contest. Another reference, *Balancing the future on their blades*, gives us a hint as to what we can expect to follow. The prophecies end with those six lines. Why? Because this battle will determine what will happen next. Whatever the future is to be, whatever is to become of the Kingdoms, it will be because of this contest. That's what the last line confirms: *To fall in black or white*. In the past, throughout the millennia since the Shadow Lord came to be, the victor of the struggles between good and evil was always foretold. We have always been able to hold back the Shadow Lord and stop his evil from descending upon the Kingdoms. But not this time. The result will not be known until the duel is fought. There is nothing telling us what to expect or how the contest between the Defender of the Light and the Lord of the Shadow will play out."

"So this battle will determine the future?" asked Sarelle.

"Yes, it will."

"Can the Defender of the Light win?" asked Rendael, inquiring about what the other monarchs feared to ask, all knowing the stories regarding the Shadow Lord and his deadly skills.

"Anything is possible," answered Rya, though it took a great deal of effort to offer her reply in a confident tone.

"And if the Defender of the Light loses?" Kaylie gripped her hands tightly together, having sheathed her dagger. She dreaded the answer that she knew was coming.

"Then the Kingdoms have no future at all. The Shadow Lord and his Dark Horde will reign supreme, and humanity will face the possibility of servitude or extinction."

"And you think Thomas is the Defender of the Light? Just because a few lines seem to apply to him?"

"Yes, we do." Rya nodded her agreement. Her tone was gentle, as she understood why Kaylie struggled with their conclusions. "He is a child of life and death. He has stood on high twice. Another line clearly applies as well — *Green fire burns in the night.* You know, as well as I, what his eyes look like when he's angry, and especially during the night."

"I think green fire is a very appropriate description," said Sarelle.

"When will Thomas know if he's the Defender of the Light?" asked Gregory, his practical mind having already turned toward what needed to be done to protect against the Shadow Lord and the Dark Horde.

"I know," answered Thomas quietly, finally speaking up. "I have known for some time. I am the Defender of the Light."

"But Thomas, how could you be certain that ..."

"Kaylie, I know," said Thomas in a strong but soft voice, giving her a small smile in an attempt to make her feel better, as he didn't want the fear and worry in her eyes to spread. "I can feel the pull much like I did before joining the Sylvana. It gets stronger every day. I can feel the Shadow Lord and he can feel me. He's waiting for me. It's just a matter of time. I am the Defender of the Light, and I must fight him in Blackstone."

CHAPTER SIX

DECISIONS

Corelia Tessaril stood on the balcony to her suite of rooms located in one of the taller towers of the Eamhain Mhacha fortress. Her long, blond hair blew wildly in response to the cold gusts that swept off the waters of the Heartland Lake. Normally, she enjoyed the view, especially in the early morning when the first rays of light glittered off the deep blue surface and she could see for leagues in all directions. But not today. Today, although she gazed at the rough water stirred up by the strong wind, she didn't see anything at all, and she barely felt the touch of the swirling air, her mind drifting far, far away.

She held a necklace in her right hand, the black onyx glittering like glass as the pieces of stone caught the sunlight. But she didn't notice that either as the individual pieces of the torque played through her fingers. Her thoughts were elsewhere this morning. All because of a seemingly innocuous conversation the night before with General Brennios, who commanded the Armaghian Home Guard. He hadn't revealed much in the way of detail, but then he never did, not even to her, and when it came to information, she was the ultimate safecracker. Brennios was a man devoted to his duty, his sharp features and ramrod posture suggesting that he had been born in the military. Further, he saw his duty as protecting his homeland, not necessarily serving the High King, as those two goals might not always be aligned. That approach opposed that of most every other official in the Kingdom, all of whom seemed to go out of their way to ensure that every one of her father's wishes was met regardless of how ludicrous or costly.

How General Brennios had survived so long without licking her father's boots, she could only begin to guess. But for that ability alone, she respected him. And she had learned in the court of Armagh that what was left unsaid was just as important as what was said.

She had been standing in the grand hall having just completed a brief audience with several merchants when a soldier had run in, immediately reporting to General Brennios in spite of the presence of so many others in the chamber. The soldier's report was concise, to the point.

"The barges have not returned to Dunmoor," the young soldier had said. "They're well overdue."

Brennios had stared at the messenger, not speaking for several long seconds. But Corelia knew what the soldier was talking about, the strategy that her father had employed to conquer the Highlands that relied on ferrying troops and supplies across the Inland Sea to the southern peaks of that mountainous Kingdom. Finally, Brennios replied with a simple nod of the head.

"Assemble the captains," he had ordered.

Not much to go on, Corelia had realized. But for her, it was more than enough. There was trouble in the Highlands, perhaps even disaster for Armagh. Her father's plans were not working as he had imagined, which really wasn't surprising considering her opponent. There was something about the young Highland Lord that intrigued her. He was more than competent, both as a fighter and a leader. But there was something else there. An edge. A power. A sense of control over himself and the world around him that sent her heart racing. Perhaps that's what it was that had attracted her to him.

She pulled her thoughts away from Thomas Kestrel reluctantly, instead returning to the look that she had seen on General Brennios' face. Worry. He seemed to have little faith in her father's military abilities, and she had to admit that there was some justification for that. Even with General Chengiz commanding the Armaghian army, she didn't doubt that her father would force his way into the general's decision making, perhaps creating problems that didn't need to be there. Problems that could lead to … defeat.

Abruptly she looked down at the necklace in her hand, realizing that she had been rubbing the black stones for the better part of an hour. Finally, she felt the cold air flowing across the balcony and through the open doors into her suite. Shivering, she realized that she had no choice. She needed to go. All because General Brennios had uttered three simple words: "Assemble the captains."

Perhaps she was wrong. Perhaps all went well in the Highlands. But she had learned to trust her instincts as she had maneuvered successfully through the politics of Armagh and competed with her brother Ragin for her father's favor. And her instincts were telling her that it was time to leave Eamhain Mhacha and make use of the tool that Malachias had gifted her. A tool that could give her everything that she wanted, but at what cost?

CHAPTER SEVEN

DECISION MADE

Thomas' pronouncement of his prophesied duel with the Shadow Lord had set a somber tone for the remainder of the day's discussions. But it had also suffused those monarchs who had come together to defeat the Armaghian army in the Highlands with an added urgency.

Sarelle, Queen of Benewyn, sat regally on one of the camp chairs arrayed in the tent. Always seeking to take advantage of an opportunity, she still wore her form-fitting armor despite the fact that the Battle of the Highlands had ended days before, her red hair shining as it caught the light from the fire they all sat around. Gregory, King of Fal Carrach, sat across the blaze from her. He couldn't take his eyes from her, something that she had sought and relished.

"I have sent the messages we discussed to the other rulers of the Kingdoms. But I have little confidence that they will respond quickly or as we hope."

Benewyn was known for its mercantile exchanges and traders, which made Sarelle an experienced and excellent negotiator. Though through her missives she revealed the High King's treachery and warned of the coming of the Shadow Lord, she knew that she could accomplish much more meeting face to face rather than sending correspondence. But she didn't have time for such travels. Not with the imminent threat expected to come from the north.

"It's a worthwhile attempt," said Gregory. "But I agree with Sarelle. We will receive little help from the other Kingdoms, whether because of disinterest, internal politics, or the fact that some of these other Kingdoms still might be allied with Rodric despite sharing news of his defeat."

"All the more reason to eliminate Rodric once and for all," said Rendael, King of Kenmare.

The rulers finally understood the level of the High King's treachery as the servants of the Shadow Lord massed in the Charnel Mountains. They needed to remove the High King as a threat so that he couldn't attack behind their lines while they engaged the Dark Horde at the Breaker.

"Agreed," said Chuma, chief of the Desert Clans. Short in stature, but with a large personality, he had endeared himself quickly to the other sovereigns, not only because of the competence and aggressiveness of his cavalry, but also as a result of his willingness to leave his troop of desert soldiers at the western edge of the Highlands where it bordered on the Clanwar Desert. Doing so gave them several hundred experienced fighters ready to assist the Marchers if needed while the other Kingdoms prepared their armies and then marched for the Breaker. "We can't leave a snake in the sand behind us if we're to fight on the Northern Steppes. We must cut off its head."

"I might be able to help with that."

All eyes turned to Thomas, who sat there calmly sharpening his dagger, his mind obviously already focused on the next task at hand.

CHAPTER EIGHT

WELCOMED GIFT

"Are you certain about this, Thomas?"

Rya had just stepped back after hugging her grandson, Rynlin standing beside her. All around them several hundred Marchers prepared their mounts for the journey to come.

Assuming that Eamhain Mhacha was the only place that Rodric would feel safe, at the conclusion of their meeting Sarelle, Gregory, Rendael and Chuma had endorsed Thomas' plan. He would lead a select group of fighters to Armagh, sneaking into the capital and eliminating the High King as a threat. In the meantime, they would return to their Kingdoms to marshal the remainder of their forces and bring them north, relying on the Desert Clan fighters Chuma would leave near the Breaker to provide any assistance to the Marchers if the intensity of the dark creature incursions increased.

In light of Thomas' absence, the Highland chiefs – Renn, Seneca and Nestor — would focus on defending the northern Highlands, seeking to prevent the dark servants of the Shadow Lord from using that rugged land as a staging ground for their expected attack on the

Kingdoms. Rya would continue to help in the Highlands as well, working with the other Sylvan Warriors already operating in the mountainous Kingdom and the Charnel Mountains to locate the Ogren raiding parties and then harass the dark creatures as they sought to cross the Northern Steppes. Not a perfect strategy, they all knew, and certainly not one to rely on over the long term. But it would have to do for now. If it could buy them the few months they needed to prepare, then the approach would have served its purpose.

"It's necessary," Thomas replied. "A new High King is needed if we are to gather any support from those Kingdoms that delay in responding to Sarelle's call for troops at the Breaker, and that means Rodric must go. Besides, we need to be able to defend the Kingdoms without worrying that he's lurking in the shadows preparing to stab us in the back. I have no doubt that he'd take great pleasure in that."

"Just be careful," said Rya. "After that show you put on with that dark creature made of black mist, the Shadow Lord knows you all the better now. He knows your strength. More important, he will seek out your weaknesses. He will come after you with everything that he has. He's not going to want to face you in Blackstone if he can eliminate you as a threat before that."

"I understand, Rya. We'll move quickly and keep our eyes open. Believe me, I know what I'm up against. Besides, Rynlin will be with me, so I'll have nothing to fear." The touch of sarcasm didn't go unnoticed by his grandfather.

"I know you do, but I still worry about you, particularly because Rynlin will be with you. He's not always the best influence."

"Hey," protested Rynlin. "You do realize that I'm standing right here?"

"Of course I knew you were there, my darling," replied Rya. "I wouldn't have said it otherwise."

Rya stepped forward with a smile, then a quick hug for her grandson that he returned, which was out of character for him. His grandfather, who prided himself on his roguish appearance, gave Thomas a clap on the back before Rya released him, as she saw over Thomas' shoulder that someone else wanted to talk with him before he and his Marchers headed west.

"Thomas, can I speak with you for a moment?"

Kaylie stood there, hands clasped in front of her, lines of worry creasing her forehead. Her black hair danced in the cold gusts of air coming off the Highland peaks, forcing her to push it away regularly from her elfin face. Normally self-assured, she appeared to be nervous. Rya had talked with Kaylie earlier that morning, catching up with her student on the progress that she had been making in learning the Talent. But it wasn't long before that conversation had become more personal, touching on several sensitive topics that Kaylie didn't feel that she could speak about with anyone else. With that in mind, Rya realized that now was the time to take their leave.

"Come along, Rynlin, we have much to do, particularly if you still mean to accompany your grandson. Thomas, if you have need of me during your travels, don't hesitate to reach out."

Rya fingered the silver amulet that hung around her neck, shaped in the form of a unicorn's horn. Each Sylvan Warrior wore one, and it allowed them to know when those who had earned the honor and right to wear the ancient necklaces were well or in danger and in need of help.

"If things go well, we won't have need of you."

"Let's hope that proves to be the case," said Rynlin, following grudgingly after his wife. "Just don't count on it."

Kaylie stepped forward then, initially reluctant to meet his gaze. Once again, Kaylie's beauty struck Thomas, a soft ache forming in his chest. He remembered the first time that he had seen her in the Burren. She had stood at the edge of a secluded waterfall, brandishing a dagger at two approaching Ogren. The massive dark creatures, twice the size of a man and standing at least ten feet tall, large, sharp tusks protruding from their lower jaws and curling upward, their hands shaped more like claws but still able to grasp swords or maces, had roared in triumph as they charged toward her. Her friends had stepped farther back into the pool, terrified by the monsters rushing toward them. Nevertheless, Kaylie had stood her ground, refusing to be an easy kill. Based on his experience, she was a courageous and confident young woman. Yet now, at this very moment, she seemed unsure of herself, nervous and uncertain. Thomas didn't know how to respond to the Princess of Fal Carrach's uncharacteristic behavior, so he simply stood there quietly, waiting patiently.

"Yesterday, your grandfather talked through the prophecy. Do you believe the role that he laid out for you is correct?" Kaylie finally turned her eyes to his, her fears for him now clearly on display.

"You mean in terms of having to fight the Shadow Lord?"

"Yes."

Kaylie knew such a requirement was a death sentence. No one had ever challenged the Shadow Lord and lived.

Rather than confirming her fears, Thomas wanted to tell Kaylie something that would make her feel better, that would allow her worry to drain away. But he felt that doing so would be a disservice to her. Instead, he tried to change the subject.

"Thank you for your help during the fighting, Kaylie. We couldn't have succeeded without you. You've come a long way in your use of the Talent."

"Thank you, Thomas." She smiled at the compliment, experiencing a growing pride in her ability to master the natural magic of the world. "But please don't try to take this conversation down a different road."

Thomas nodded reluctantly, knowing that Kaylie's tenacity would never have allowed him to derail her focus, though he at least had to try. "Yes, as I said yesterday, I believe that I will have to fight the Shadow Lord if we are to have any chance of surviving what's to come. That's assuming, of course, that I can make it into Blackstone alive."

Kaylie stood there for a moment, fighting back the tears that threatened to pour from her eyes. Giving in to the emotions that raged within her, she reached forward, taking Thomas' head in her hands. She stared into his eyes for just a moment, then kissed him deeply on the lips. She held him like that for a long time, and Thomas was more than happy to stay there, enjoying the private moment. But then she stepped back, letting him go. Tears streaked down her cheeks as she took one last look at him, then she turned and walked away.

Thomas watched her go, mesmerized by what had just happened. It was then that Oso appeared at his side, clapping him on the shoulder as he watched Kaylie lose herself in the preparations going on around them.

"Quite a girl," the big Marcher said.

"Yes, she is."

"A bit difficult to understand, though, don't you think?"

"What do you mean, Oso?"

"Well, the day before yesterday, after you killed that dark creature, she hit you and then kissed you. Today, she kisses you again. The next time she sees you, just to balance things out, she'll probably hit you. Do women ever act in a way that we'll understand?"

Thomas smiled. "I'm not one who can say, Oso. In my experience, women do what they want when they want. Questioning it just gives you a headache."

"I agree with you on that. Trying to figure out Anara and what she wants makes my head want to explode at times." Shaking his head in bewilderment, Oso slapped Thomas on the back a second time, smiling at his flustered friend. "No matter. That's a challenge for another day. Let's go kill a High King. That'll be much easier than trying to figure out the women in our lives."

CHAPTER NINE

ANGER AND FEAR

Rodric Tessaril, the former High King and still ruler of Armagh, galloped through the gates of Eamhain Mhacha's keep as if a demon pursued him, and perhaps one did, at least in his own mind. Pulling his horse up short, he hopped off, slipping as his worn boots hit the wet cobblestones of the courtyard in his haste, only a lucky grab for his mount's bridle preventing him from falling face first into an ankle-deep puddle of grimy water. Righting himself with a curse and not wanting to wait for the stable hand to come forward to take the reins, he walked toward the huge doors that led into the fortress, the guards pulling them open quickly, unwilling to risk the more than usually irritated High King's wrath. Rodric's anger since his ignominious retreat from the Highlands had simmered and then swelled with each passing league that had taken him farther west, finally reaching a point where it threatened to boil over.

After stepping through the spinning portal of black created by their master, he, Killeran, and Chertney found themselves at the northern shore of the Inland Sea where the Armaghians had begun their ill-fated expedition into the Highlands. The destruction that awaited him on that bleak coast had forced him to acknowledge the extent of his failure. The Marchers had wiped out the once bustling camp, the tents torn and shredded, the rickety buildings that had been constructed so haphazardly burned to the ground, the supply depot simply gone, and most likely seized by the Marchers for their own use. Only a few soldiers remained to greet him when he appeared, the rest dead or driven off to the west and obliged to make their way back to their homeland on foot. He had never considered the possibility that the Highland Lord would set his Marchers upon his supply camp. That lack of imagination had cost him dearly, and the thoroughness of the attack unnerved him. Commandeering the only serviceable boat that remained on the shore, they had traveled west across the lake and then started the arduous journey back to the Armaghian capital. The horses were lathered, half dead and starving when he finally arrived in the capital, but Rodric didn't care as he stormed into the keep, Killeran and Chertney following closely at his heels.

Rodric ached to tear into his two companions, to blame them for all that had happened, to place the fault for this devastating failure somewhere else. But his fear won out. Chertney was a tall man, almost wraithlike in appearance, with long black hair and a mustache that curled at the edges. His intense black eyes were both hypnotic and terrifying. He inspired fear and nothing more. But since his dramatic defeat to Rynlin Keldragan right before the Battle of the Highlands, the old man effortlessly combatting his conjuring of Dark Magic, Chertney had appeared diminished in some way, a shadow of his former self. Nevertheless, over the last few days, slowly but surely Chertney had regained his strength in Dark Magic, and with it that sense of menace that radiated from him had returned, aided by the look on his face that suggested that he was not one to be trifled with at that moment. Killeran, his large nose leading, and his normally pristine armor dented, scratched and showing signs of rust, trailed reluctantly behind Chertney, muttering to himself. If not Chertney, perhaps Rodric could lay the blame at Killeran's feet. Rodric knew that his real master, the one he was truly beholden to, had little tolerance for failure. The debacle in the Highlands put Rodric at risk, and he needed a scapegoat if he couldn't turn this defeat into something more positive.

He had a niggling suspicion that had blossomed into a full-fledged fear as he traveled west back to Armagh that the Shadow Lord might view his usefulness, now that the Highlands had confirmed their independence and several other Kingdoms had declared war on Armagh, as having come to an end. If that proved to be the case, then he knew that there was only one possible outcome, one that he decidedly didn't want to consider. So he had to find some way to demonstrate his continued value. He was still the King of Armagh. He would not give up his birthright without a fight. Besides, if he could hold Armagh, perhaps the Shadow Lord would have cause to view his defeat in the Highlands as only a temporary setback and something that could be turned to his advantage.

"I might have lost the battle, but they'll have to take my crown from my lifeless body," Rodric whispered to himself, his drawn features suggesting that the madness that seemed to appear now and then had found a welcome home in the High King. Having already taken root, it was beginning to bloom.

"I believe that's the Highland Lord's plan," said Chertney in a scratchy voice, having heard the comment.

Killeran glanced at Chertney with a worried expression, the rat-faced Dunmoorian lord thinking that the High King's mind, unstable to begin with, finally had been pushed too far over the edge by this latest disappointment. Chertney ignored him, no longer caring what pronouncements came out of the deposed High King, sensing the change that was coming over the land.

Yes, the cold was seeping into the Kingdoms. His master would be coming soon to reclaim what belonged to him. But that boy and his allies had slowed that progression down tremendously. At the moment, how events would play out were balanced on a sword's edge, and the next few months would determine which way that balance would shift.

Chertney would have preferred to leave Rodric and Killeran in the Highlands to rot, allowing the Highland Lord to have his vengeance. But for whatever reason, his master still had some use for them, fleeting though it may be. Therefore, he would have to continue to work with these two cretins for a while longer.

General Brennios, a tall, ascetic man, wearing the full-dress uniform of the Armaghian Home Guard, strode into the great hall just as Rodric sat heavily on his uncomfortable throne. Brennios, a protégé of General Chengiz, led the small fighting force based in Eamhain Mhacha. Rodric always worried about threats to his authority, whether real or imagined, and Brennios' army served as his primary defense to any danger that could place the capital in peril, whether from within or without. Now, Rodric realized, the Home Guard was also his last defense.

"My king, we had not expected you for quite some time. What news from …"

"We have no time for pleasantries, General," interrupted Rodric. "Thanks to General Chengiz, our army in the Highlands is lost. He was a fool and a traitor."

"My king? I don't see how that's possible. General Chengiz …"

"Enough, Brennios. Enough!" Rodric's shout echoed throughout the chamber. "We have no time for this. Leave a strong force here at Eamhain Mhacha to defend the citadel, but you are to take the remainder of the Home Guard to the eastern border and repel any invading force. I expect that it will only be a matter of weeks before the Marchers and their allies attempt to take this Kingdom from me, and that will not happen. It will not! Armagh is mine. It will always be mine! Do you understand me, Brennios?"

General Brennios had served in his position for several decades, and like General Chengiz had mastered the art of dealing with the High King, as demonstrated by his ability to maintain his position and keep his head, literally, while serving Rodric for such a long period of time. Much like his friend and mentor Chengiz, Brennios was loyal to Armagh, not necessarily to the High King. But now was not the time to consider that distinction. Now was the time to act as he had so many times before during Rodric's tirades, understanding the possible consequences of being perceived as an obstacle to the High King's wishes.

"Yes, my king. I will leave a force as you suggest and take the Home Guard to the east. We will leave by midday tomorrow."

"Make it sooner, Brennios," replied Rodric. "By tonight. It must be tonight. We don't have time. We don't know how quickly the Marchers will be able to mount their assault. Better you catch them in the open. Now off to it!"

"Yes, my king."

Bowing stiffly, Brennios walked swiftly from the throne room, happy to have escaped the High King's temper. He would need to learn more about what happened in the Highlands, but from sources that he could trust not to turn on him.

His primary task completed, Rodric started to murmur to himself once more, Chertney and Killeran only able to understand snippets of what he was saying. Clearly the High King had become fixated on the "upstart boy" who had "destroyed everything he sought to accomplish." Then, abruptly, Rodric stood and walked unsteadily from the throne room, ignoring Killeran's questions about what additional preparations needed to be made.

"If that whelp has the audacity to follow me, it will mean his head!" shouted Rodric as he exited the chamber, his shriek sounding more petulant than fearsome.

Killeran stood there for a moment, dazed, and not sure what to do next. He was certain, though, that the mental breakdown he had expected from Rodric had just begun.

"What shall we do, Chertney? We don't …"

Chertney's angry glare cut short Killeran's questions. Finally, after a week of hard travel, Chertney had the silence that he craved, and this dolt, this sorry excuse for a lord, had ruined it within seconds. Chertney struggled to control his rising temper and his coinciding desire to kill this conniving, useless Dunmoorian lord. But he couldn't. Not yet. Not until he was granted permission. There were still ways to salvage the situation. His master demanded that he try, and he would obey, understanding the consequences for failure, though he believed that it would all be wasted effort in the end.

"We have been defeated, Killeran. But we can still fight. Once Brennios assigns the Home Guard soldiers to stay here, you will assume command and see to the castle's defenses. Am I clear?"

"Yes, Lord Chertney."

For the first time, however reluctantly, Killeran offered some deference to his one-time rival. He finally understood where the real power in Armagh lay and had no desire to upset the often mercurial Chertney.

"Brennios will be taking most of the castle guard. I'll bolster those who remain with some of my forces."

"Your forces?"

"You needn't worry, Killeran," replied Chertney, a malicious smile bringing a disconcerting gleam to his eyes. "Just leave it to me. My troops will stay out of sight unless they are needed."

Killeran nodded, then walked quickly from the throne room, for the thousandth time regretting his decision to seek an alliance with the Shadow Lord. He knew that his greed had gotten the better of him. He cursed himself daily for this weakness. But he couldn't help himself, even if his life depended on it. Besides, it was too late to do anything but tread the path that he had chosen.

Chertney stood there for a few minutes lost in thought, once again enjoying the momentary silence. An uncomfortable feeling settled within him, one that he rarely experienced but had become all too common the last few weeks. Fear. That irritating whelp, the new Highland Lord, had destroyed the Armaghian host. But Chertney didn't think that the boy would be satisfied after everything that had transpired between the Highlands and Armagh during the last decade.

The Highland Lord would want more. He would want to finish this once and for all. If Chertney were in that boy's position, he certainly would. Killeran could see to the defenses, and Chertney would provide an extra layer of protection if needed. But he would also make sure that he had an escape route in place. Just in case.

CHAPTER TEN

BLOODY BUSINESS

After defeating the soldiers of Armagh and as Thomas took his raiding party toward Eamhain Mhacha, the Marchers had turned their attention once again to the northern Highlands, seeking to defend against the continuing incursions by dark creatures. The Sylvana continued to assist, as did Beluil. The massive wolf led his packs on regular sweeps through the northern peaks. Blood enemy of any dark creature, the wolves took particular delight in eliminating the Shadow Lord's servants.

Maden Grenis and a few other Sylvan Warriors working in partnership with Marchers led by Seneca, one of Thomas' Highland chiefs, had just slaughtered a war band of Ogren at the very edge of the Highlands. Leaving no Ogren alive, they had built a fire to dispose of the bodies. Once the pyre was complete and the bodies dragged into place, Maden used the Talent to set the wood ablaze. In a matter of hours, only ashes would remain.

The Sylvan Warriors and Marchers watched the fire catch, lulled by the flames, the adrenaline of the fight finally wearing off. They were proud of what they had accomplished and thankful. It had been a large war band, yet none in their ranks had been seriously injured. Nevertheless, all who now studied the flames realized just how close they had come to a potential disaster.

Maden, tall and lanky with an easy grin, frowned as he watched the pyre's black, oily smoke drift toward the south, the strong Highland winds gusting off the mountain peaks and through the narrow pass that had just served as what was likely the largest battle with the forces of the Shadow Lord the Highlands had seen in almost a decade. Yes, they had succeeded in defeating the dark creatures. But something about the events of the past few hours bothered the Sylvan Warrior. The Ogren had approached as expected, stumbling more than climbing up the loose scrabble of one of the few traversable passes in the far western Highlands. Seneca had ordered a shield wall — Marchers with shields and swords formed the wall, fighters with spears right behind to jab over the shoulder, a few dozen archers standing a bit farther back to slow the Ogren advance and pick off any attackers that might force their way past the defensive perimeter — at the point where the pass met a long plateau that extended from between the sheer sides of the two, towering mountains that tightened the approach.

A good strategy and one that he would have put in place as well if he were charged with defending the pass. The Marchers had held against the Ogren, whittling down the fearsome beasts and preventing a breakthrough, Maden and the handful of other Sylvana supporting their efforts by using the Talent to call down lightning or shoot bolts of white energy into the dark creatures to ensure the Marcher line remained intact. Yet it was almost all for naught once the pack of Fearhounds had arrived. At first blocked from coming up the pass by the hundreds of Ogren massing in front of them, the pony-sized beasts quickly lost patience. Fast and strong, their top two canine teeth extending beyond their lower jaw, the Fearhounds dug their sharp claws into the steep hillsides that funneled the Ogren toward the Marchers, threatening to sweep around the Marchers' flanks and attack them from the rear.

Maden feared that if the Fearhounds succeeded in getting behind the Highland men and women defending their homeland, the battle would be over. The only sure way to kill a Fearhound because of their thick almost armored hide was with an arrow through the eye. The huge beasts could shrug off almost any other blow from a sword or battle axe. Maden had no doubt that some of the Marcher archers would strike true, respecting their skills after having seen the damage that they could inflict from a distance. But the Fearhound pack numbered more than a hundred. There was no way the archers, even with the help of the Sylvan Warriors, could keep the dark creatures from tearing into their compatriots from behind.

Initially, afraid that the Ogren might break through the Marcher defensive line if he turned his attention and that of his fellow Sylvan Warriors toward the Fearhound pack as the frighteningly fast dark creatures scrabbled along the steep canyon walls with ease, he realized immediately upon judging the speed of the Fearhounds that he had no choice. The risk had to be taken. Calling out to the other Sylvan Warriors, they split their attention between the two sheer slopes that narrowed toward the Marcher defensive line. Maden and Daran Sharban, a tall Sylvan Warrior with curly red hair and beard, eyes always twinkling with mischief even in the direst of circumstances, focused on the western slope. Elisia and Aurelia Valeran, twin Sylvan Warriors from Kashel, one with midnight black hair, the other with shocking white, took the eastern slope.

Their approach was a simple one. The Fearhounds were too fast and too many to try to slow down with individual bolts of energy. But the pack was tightly bunched together along both slopes, so the Sylvan Warriors decided to use that weakness to their advantage. Calling upon the Talent, the Sylvan Warriors released the natural magic of the world in the form of shards of white light well ahead of and above the charging Fearhounds. At first nothing happened other than several large holes appearing in the mountainsides where the bolts of energy had struck. But then a rumbling began along the slopes as small stones started to shake loose and then slide down the steep hillsides, followed by ever larger rocks until boulders the size of small houses began tumbling down the mountains from where they had perched for millennia, undisturbed but for the wind and the rain.

In just a matter of seconds, it was over. The landslides on both slopes crushed the Fearhounds under hundreds of tons of rock and took the bulk of the Ogren still stuck in the pass as well. The Marchers only had to finish off a few dozen of the dark creatures that had escaped the falling rock and debris. Maden should have been pleased. They had succeeded in stopping another raid by the Shadow Lord's servants into the Highlands. But that nagging concern remained with him, dampening the relief that he felt. This Ogren raiding party was larger than any other that they had faced during the long weeks they had been fighting in the Highlands. And for the first time the Shadow Lord had sent more than Ogren and Shades at one time with the pack of Fearhounds following in the wake of the other dark creatures. The new strategy suggested that time was growing short. That the Shadow Lord was growing stronger and preparing for a larger attack, perhaps one that the Marchers and Sylvan Warriors would struggle to contain. If a pack of Fearhounds or, even worse, Mongrels, got past the Marchers, they would be hard-pressed to regain control of the countryside. Maden shook his head in frustration, unable to put his fears to rest. There was nothing to be done at the moment. He would need to talk with Rynlin. Maden sensed that it was time for the Sylvan Warriors to play a larger role in the affairs of the Kingdoms if they were to have any chance of keeping the Shadow Lord and the Dark Horde to the north of the Breaker.

"A bloody business," said Maden, still shaken by how close they had come to a devastating defeat.

"Aye," responded Seneca. "And a close thing. Our thanks to you and your friends. Without you, I don't know that we'd have been able to hold."

Maden nodded his acknowledgement, not feeling the need to say more. The taciturn Marcher had grown on Maden during the last few weeks. They had partnered well together, and he appreciated a man who only spoke when necessary, something that Maden valued all the more because of his own natural loquaciousness.

As the blaze sizzled and crackled, the flames reaching for the sky, howls echoed off the surrounding peaks. Both men turned their heads toward the east.

"Probably two leagues off," said Seneca.

"It seems that Thomas' furry friend has found more prey," replied Maden. "Shall we try to catch up to him?"

Not bothering to answer, Seneca started to trot to the east, Maden falling in beside him, the other Marchers and Sylvan Warriors following suit.

"More and more of these bastards are coming," said Maden. "Despite our best efforts, we can't seem to stop the flow."

"It's to be expected," said the grizzled Marcher.

"Yes, if they can establish a foothold in the Highlands, they can bypass the Breaker."

"We'll just have to make sure they can't get through. How long do you think before the Shadow Lord attacks?"

The Sylvan Warrior glided silently through the forest for a few moments before replying.

"Judging by the number of attacks and reports of increasing activity in the Charnel Mountains, probably a few months at most. Not much longer than that."

"We'll be ready," assured Seneca, rubbing his palm across the haft of his war axe, relishing the opportunity the future would offer. "Have no fear of that."

CHAPTER ELEVEN

SIMPLE TASK

Burnt ash and crushed rock swept through the abandoned promenades and streets, swirling into small tornados that appeared and disappeared at the whim of the wind. Grey clouds remained fixed over the city, a dark, misty fog seeping in between the deserted and decrepit buildings as the dim glow of the sun that fought the murk with surprising success began to dip beneath the western horizon. The only sound came from the scraping of loose and broken stone pushed by the frequent gusts of cold air across the cracked stone of the streets.

A tall, cowled figure stood on the western battlements of the circular fortress that rose in the very center of the city. Covered in black robes that mixed with the oncoming night, the figure blended with the rapidly descending darkness. As night fell, the only way to see the man-sized shape at all were its blood-red eyes that blazed brightly within the encroaching gloom. The Shadow Lord had remained among the gargoyles and other gruesome creatures carved into the stone of the keep's parapets for several hours. Not moving, his wispy robes even ignoring the demands of the wind. Simply staring to the south. Thinking. Planning. Seething.

He could feel the boy. Somewhere in the Highlands. And that connection was growing stronger day by day as the boy gained strength, becoming more than just a nuisance. Becoming a threat. At first a thorn in the Shadow Lord's side, the boy had morphed from a small prick to a weeping dagger thrust as this newly proclaimed Lord of the Highlands threatened centuries of carefully laid plans.

Fools! Incompetent fools!

So much was at stake, yet his servants had failed him time and time again. They had been given a simple task. Killeran. Rodric. Chertney. Even loyal Malachias. All their schemes. All their intrigues. All their machinations. All had failed. For the boy still lived.

As the days passed into weeks and the weeks into months it seemed more and more likely that the requirements of the prophecy would have to be met. The Shadow Lord had never been defeated. Even during the Great War, despite the fact that the Sylvan Warriors had forced him and the Dark Horde back into the Charnel Mountains, no one had stood against him and lived. That should be no different now, for his knowledge of and power in Dark Magic had only increased as the centuries passed while his enemies had become weaker. Then why was he worried? Was the boy more of a danger than he had judged originally?

The Shadow Lord didn't know, and that's what bothered him the most. He was used to certainty. He preferred absolutes. Yet this boy had changed the game and added unpredictability to the mix. As a result, the expected result that the Shadow Lord had seen with unwavering clarity for so long had now become hazy and unclear. To regain that desired certainty, he needed to kill the boy. Yet even the Shadow Lord's own efforts, distinct from that of his servants, had failed to lead to any success. The Nightstalkers he had sent after the boy had never returned. Would the traitor succeed? Would the Wraith? Both had already failed once. Could he count on his servants after so many had floundered in their many attempts to complete what should have been a simple, straightforward task?

Would it come down to single combat as the prophecy suggested? And if it did, with the puzzle having changed, could the Shadow Lord be certain of the outcome?

The Shadow Lord stood as still as one of the gargoyle statues for several more hours, his rage fueling his brightly burning eyes that blazed in the darkness.

CHAPTER TWELVE

THE CAVES

Before Thomas, Rynlin, and Oso led several hundred Marchers south from the Highlands toward Eamhain Mhacha and their ultimate prize, the former High King Rodric Tessaril, they had agreed on a route that they hoped would allow them to avoid the trouble that they expected would come their way. Skirting the eastern shore of the Inland Sea into western Fal Carrach, they then located ferries to take them across the Gullet close to where the Kingdoms of Dunmoor and Benewyn shared a border for several leagues. They assumed that if, indeed, Rodric had returned to his capital, he would place the Home Guard on the eastern border of the Kingdom. Therefore, rather than tracking the Corazon River west into Armagh as Rodric would expect, they chose to take a longer route that would allow them to avoid that possibility.

Thomas had used the Talent to search as far as Eamhain Mhacha before boarding the ferries to cross the Gullet. He had confirmed that the Home Guard marched to the eastern border of Armagh, unaware of the party traveling south of them. So far, their plan was proving to be a good one. Once across the Gullet they would head west into the Grasslands and then come at the Armaghian capitol from the south with the High King none the wiser.

The ferries, more like huge, flat barges, their sides barely higher than the lapping waves of the Gullet, each carried fifty soldiers and their mounts comfortably. Yet even with the three massive sails that sprouted from the deck of each one, they were ponderous vessels that plowed slowly through the water.

Thomas, Oso, and Rynlin stood in the bow of the first ferry, their eyes on the massive fins of the Great Sharks slicing through the waves alongside them. Thomas had asked Sorrel, the captain of their ferry, if it was safe to sail when they had first arrived at the handful of ramshackle buildings that made up the small port, counting at least five large fins slicing through the water and suspecting that there were several other beasts lurking just beneath the surface. Thomas had some familiarity with the Great Sharks, having watched them from the beach while growing up on the Isle of Mist. The massive beasts could reach a size of fifty to sixty feet in length, their jaws more than capable of crushing the hull of one of the ferries that he saw lined up at the dock.

Sorrel had assured him that there was nothing to fear. "We'll be sailing in a shallow channel about a quarter mile wide," he had said in a rolling tone that seemed to mimic the movement of the waves that splashed against the hulls of the ferries. "Those monsters can't get in there. That's why the barges have such a low draft. If those water devils try to come after us, they'll get stuck on the sandbars. They're simply hoping that we miss the channel."

"What happens if we miss the channel?" Oso had asked, then instantly regretted it.

"Then we die, young man," replied the crusty old captain. "A painful, horrible death." The seaman had then turned with a laugh, stomping off to make sure that his sailors stowed the Marchers' gear and horses properly for the voyage across the river.

"That filled me with confidence," the large Highlander had said, his face turning a pasty white at the thought of coming face to face with one of the massive beasts swimming not too far from the channel. Oso had only stepped onto the ferry when Thomas had assured him that he and Rynlin could offer some protection against the Great Sharks if it proved necessary. But so far it had not. Though the wind proved erratic as they made their way slowly toward eastern Benewyn, their ferry and the other vessels had stayed to the center of the channel, well away from the Great Sharks that stalked them from afar.

Rynlin used the quiet as an opportunity to explain the naming of Eamhain Mhacha, and what he viewed as their best chance for success.

"Eamhain means brooch, a large wheel of gold or bronze crossed by a long pin. The great circular ramparts surrounding the fortresses of old might well be likened to a giantess' brooch guarding her cloak, or territory."

Thomas smiled, remembering that just a few short years in the past, he would have endured a lesson such as this in his home carved from the trunk of a heart tree. On a cold day like this, Rya would have had a fire going in the kitchen, preparing dinner, Beluil curled up as close to the flames as possible without getting singed. And Rynlin would be in his element, weaving story after story into a vivid history, leaving Thomas with the task of identifying the point to his teachings. Rynlin's pedagogical process often devolved into a dialogue, sometimes a debate, his grandfather thriving on the intellectual exchange.

The tall Sylvan Warrior continued. "Mhacha married Brian, one of the early High Kings who assumed power after the death of Ollav Fola, who at the time ruled as the lord of all the land. It was very different from the way it is now. All the other monarchs were vassals of the High King, serving at his pleasure. The histories say that it was a peaceful and prosperous time. That is, until the High King died. Brian and Mhacha didn't have any children, but Brian had two brothers, and traditionally the throne would have passed to the oldest surviving brother. In this case, Tergon. But there was a problem …"

"Mhacha wanted the throne," interjected Oso, remembering some few pieces from his history lessons.

"She did."

"How did Brian die? Did they suspect Mhacha of foul play?"

"An excellent question, Oso," said Rynlin, warming to his role. "No one knows for sure. The only thing certain was that Mhacha craved power. Perhaps she tired of ruling next to Brian, who was said to be a strong High King, or perhaps Brian died of natural causes and she saw an opportunity. No one really knows how Brian died, but they do know what happened next. Before the oldest surviving brother, Tergon, could assume the throne, Mhacha challenged him to single combat, claiming that the brother had besmirched her honor and that she had a right to defend herself and her reputation."

"How did Tergon respond?" asked Oso, clearly taken with the tale.

"The stories say that the duel took place. At first, Tergon expected an easy victory. But then as the combat stretched on from one hour to the next, and then from morning into the late afternoon, he realized that he had made a mistake. A grave mistake. Mhacha had greater skill as a fighter than he did. As the duel continued, he grew tired, weaker, while Mhacha appeared to become stronger. Nevertheless, Tergon fought on even though his suffocating exhaustion slowed his movements. Mhacha's blade finally slipped through his defenses as his weariness became too much, Brian's queen driving her sword through Tergon's chest with the sun disappearing below the western horizon, killing the heir to the throne and winning the duel after almost a full day of combat."

"Quite a woman," said Oso.

"Indeed, Oso," replied Rynlin. "And a dangerous one."

"Yes, but there was a third brother, you said. Wouldn't he be next in line to the throne?"

"There was. He had watched the combat. Whether he was enamored of Mhacha or fearful, the histories don't say. But what we do know is that in the end she married the youngest brother, allowing him to be High King in name, while she exercised the real power as queen from behind the throne. However, that youngest brother was a widower — I believe his name was Reynal – and had five sons from a previous marriage. Some say that Mhacha could harness the natural magic of the world, having the ability to ensorcel a man. Some say that's what she did to Reynal. As his sons grew older, they saw what she was doing to their father. He was not the man he used to be, not the father that they knew, appearing to be just a vessel for the commands of his beautiful queen who remained strangely young."

"What did they do?" asked Oso, enthralled by the story.

"They attempted to assassinate her, believing that despite her power, she could not do to all five what she had done to her father. But she was stronger than they imagined. Despite their best efforts the uprising failed. Mhacha captured the five brothers in a battle that raged for five days and five nights on the fields upon which Eamhain Mhacha now rises. Feeling some small pity toward her husband, and perhaps fearing that putting the five sons to death would break the spell that she had woven over Reynal, she decided to keep them alive. Using her brooch, she marked the ground to show where the walls of what was to become the capital of Armagh should be. And for the rest of their lives, the five brothers were forced to build the fortress that is now Eamhain Mhacha."

"Did they not try to escape?" asked Oso.

Rynlin smiled at the brawny Highlander, clearly enjoying this opportunity to instruct once more.

"The stories say that it was never far from their minds. Yet they feared for their father's life. Upon capturing them, Mhacha threatened them with his death if they did not do as she commanded, and they believed her. But they also knew that their father was an old man, and who knew how long he would continue to live."

"And now we've reached the point of the tale," said Thomas with a grin, knowing his grandfather's ways.

"Correct," said Rynlin, ignoring his grandson's smug smile. "The five brothers continued to plot as they built the walls and then lay the foundation for the citadel of Eamhain Mhacha, wanting to be prepared for two eventualities. Either the opportunity to rescue their father or, sad as it may be, his eventual death. So it's said that as they built, they also dug."

"The caves," offered Thomas.

"Yes, the caves," said Rynlin. "Caves and tunnels that run through the foundations of Eamhain Mhacha. The five brothers never had the opportunity to employ the hidden passageways that they constructed beneath the fortress. When their father died, supposedly of natural causes because Mhacha did, in fact, love Reynal, she put the brothers to death, as she was finally strong enough to rule on her own. So even though the five brothers never achieved their goal, we will use their work to overthrow the High King."

"Let us hope," said Thomas, "that we succeed where they failed."

CHAPTER THIRTEEN

OBLIVIOUS

Upon crossing the Gullet without incident, and then cutting through northern Benewyn west into the Grasslands, Thomas and his raiders began to travel at night, seeking to avoid any seeking eyes. He or Rynlin regularly used the Talent to search around them and ensure that no hazards lurked. Satisfied that no danger threatened at least for now, and bored with the journey, Thomas decided to have a little fun at his friend's expense as their Marchers led their horses through the long grass, using the bright moon, full in the night sky, as their guide to the Heartland Lake.

"You know she wants to marry you, right?"

"How can you know that?" demanded Oso. The large Highlander had been thinking of Anara, now charged with coordinating the Highlander defense against the Ogren and other dark creatures during Thomas' absence. She had taken a liking to Oso after the destruction of the Black Hole and had made her intentions quite clear since then. On the one hand, Oso was pleased to be the object of Anara's attentions and apparent affection; on the other hand, what that could lead to frightened him.

"How could you not?" replied Thomas, enjoying his friend's discomfort. "Whenever you two are together, she's no more than a step away. You do whatever she asks. It's like she's made a claim on you, as no other girl will look at you when she's around."

"Yes, but …"

"You know I'm right, Oso. She's already made you her own. You just don't know it. The smiles. The touches. The whispers."

Oso was glad for the dark of night. It hid the flush of the heat rising on his face as he spluttered a response. "Yes, but that doesn't mean …"

"You better be careful, Oso. Anara's good with a blade, and she always seems to have a dagger at hand. I know she likes to whittle, but there might be more to it than that."

Oso didn't know what to say. Was Thomas right? Was Anara hoping and planning for a future together? And if she was, did that thought please him?

He thought he was saved from this uncomfortable conversation when Rynlin appeared next to them, moving Militus, his roan-colored unicorn, up the Marcher column so that he could join the conversation.

"Yes, that young lady certainly has her mind set on you, Oso," interjected Rynlin. "But I wouldn't worry too much about it. If she wants you, you're hers. If she doesn't want you, she'll find someone else."

"What does that mean?" asked Oso.

"It means that you should just accept it, and life will go easier on you."

"Is that the approach you took with grandmother?" Thomas asked innocently.

Rynlin ignored his grandson's jibe and immediately turned his attention to Thomas, giving Oso some time to recover from his discomfort.

"And you, Thomas. It seems that you're in the same situation as Oso and are just as oblivious. But your situation is more time sensitive."

"What do you mean?" asked Thomas, somewhat perplexed and decidedly uncomfortable that this conversation had now turned toward him.

"The Highland Lord must be married and quickly. The Highlands need an heir. That's the only way to ensure your Kingdom's long-term security."

Rynlin's devilish grin suggested that he very much enjoyed making his grandson nervous. Thomas couldn't tell if his grandfather was serious or simply poking fun at him. He tried to sputter out several protests, but each caught in his throat.

Rynlin chuckled at his grandson's unease. "Don't worry, Thomas. At the moment I can't think of a single person who might want to marry you." Though his grin said otherwise.

Oso let out a deep laugh. "I can think of someone."

CHAPTER FOURTEEN

MONGRELS

Thomas and his Marchers were almost through the Grasslands, having just a few leagues to go until they reached the forests that blanketed the land closer to the Heartland Lake. They had made excellent time, avoiding Armagh's Home Guard and any dark creatures sent to thwart them. Until now. The skin on Thomas' neck prickled, which for him was a tell-tale sign. Evil approached, of that he was certain. Taking hold of the Talent, he extended his senses, quickly pinpointing the darkness that steadily advanced toward them from the east. He stopped Acero abruptly, Oso and Rynlin following suit with their mounts. Thomas looked at his grandfather, who soon felt it as well.

"Mongrels." Rynlin spit out the name of the fast-approaching dark creatures. "This is not good terrain to defend against them. I'd prefer a hill or some obstacles at the least, not this flat expanse."

Mongrels towered over Fearhounds, many reaching the size of draft horses, and were said to be even more aggressive, their size giving them few things to fear. Black or grey in coloring, their sharp, hardened claws could slice through rock. Their incisors, almost as long as a child's forearm, could bite through a soldier's steel breastplate with ease. Yet even with their size, they were fast and could outrun a horse.

"It's a large pack," said Thomas, as he tracked the dark creatures with the Talent. He turned Acero toward the men and women following them. "Marchers, Mongrels approach! Form a square two lines deep. Spears in front, bows behind."

The Marchers immediately moved to obey Thomas' command, assembling around Thomas, Rynlin and Oso in less than a minute. They didn't have long to wait for the Shadow Lord's beasts to make their appearance. The Marchers were lucky, in a sense. It was early morning, and the sun would be rising soon. As a result, the oppressive gloom of night had begun to lighten. So it allowed the Marchers to pick out the monstrous shadows that flowed through the tall grass toward them.

All the Marchers had battled dark creatures before, but not these beasts, which tended to prefer open spaces because of their size and rarely entered the Highlands. The Marchers quickly realized that these massive animals, streaking toward them at a terrifying pace, made taking down an Ogren seem a simple task. They knew how to defeat a dark creature of great size, but fighting one that moved faster than the eye could track was all the more daunting.

"Spears at the ready!" shouted Thomas.

He remained mounted in the middle of the square, his sword blazing with the Talent as the two dozen dark creatures approached. The first rank of Marchers lowered their spears, jamming the butts into the soft earth as a bulwark. The second rank of fighters pulled back on their bow strings, arrows nocked and ready to be launched.

"Spears, aim for the chest or the front legs!" yelled Rynlin. "Archers, it must be the eye! Work together. It will take more than one blow to take down these unnatural devils!"

Although frightened by what they faced, the Marchers' allowed their training to take over. The men and women in the front ranks gripped their spears tightly as the Mongrels sped toward them. The first dark creatures to reach the Marchers, driven on by their slavish hunger, hurtled toward the spears in front of them with a wild abandon, seemingly unconcerned by the danger presented by the sharp steel. Many of the Marchers were shocked as they watched the first few Mongrels impale themselves on the spears, the tips sinking deeply into their chests. Even then the dark creatures fought to reach their quarry, digging their sharp claws into the turf for traction. To hold off the Mongrels that still struggled toward the Marchers despite being caught on the spears, their razor-sharp teeth, dripping a thick, stringy saliva, chomping closer and closer to unprotected hands, necks and heads, the second rank of Marchers stepped forward, shooting their arrows at point-blank range into the eyes of the Mongrels.

A few Marchers weren't so lucky, missing their marks with their spears or slicing into the beasts' haunches instead. Those failures incited a desperate melee as Marchers in the second rank shot the arrows they had on their strings and then dropped their bows, attacking with their swords in an attempt to push back the dark creatures before they could break through the Marchers' defensive line.

For several minutes the fight teetered on the edge of a blade. Several Marchers died as they strove to plug the gaps that appeared when a Mongrel surged through the line. Though the Marchers' swords were ineffectual, the steel blades simply bouncing off the Mongrels' armored hides, the attacks did serve a purpose by distracting the dark creatures. Thomas and Rynlin used these opportunities created by these brave Marchers to full effect. Thomas, having infused his blade with the Talent, charged forward, his brightly glowing steel slicing deftly through the Mongrels' toughened flesh and forcing the dark creatures back beyond the Marcher shield wall. Rynlin joined the fight as well, protecting his grandson's back by using bolts of white energy to incinerate the Mongrels' that threatened to get behind the Marchers. Acero and Militus assisted their riders by driving their spearlike horns into any Mongrel that escaped the attentions of the two Sylvan Warriors. Although the ferocious skirmish seemed to drag on for hours, it actually barely lasted a few minutes.

Just as quickly as the initial charge by the dark creatures started, it ended. A dozen Mongrels lay dead in the grass, a similar number of Marchers with them. The remaining Mongrels, less willing to sacrifice themselves on the Marcher spears, observed their prey from a safe distance, often trotting in slow circles around the square, searching for weaknesses in their quarry's defense.

"Marchers, form square!" yelled Oso, who wiped black Mongrel blood from his blade on to the grass. Wanting a clear battlefield, the burned and hacked bodies of the Mongrels potentially impeding the Marchers' during the next charge that he expected was soon to come, Oso issued his next instructions. "Marchers, wheel right one hundred paces."

The best trained of all the fighters in the Kingdoms, the Marchers performed the maneuver perfectly, shifting their position while maintaining the integrity of their defensive line, so that the ground they now defended was clear of the remains of the first attack.

"Will they come again?" asked Thomas, watching the Mongrels feint toward his fighters, then draw back, continuing to hunt for a weakness and almost taunting the Marchers to break ranks and come at them. "They seem to be playing with us."

"Aye, they will," replied Rynlin. "They're not ones to step away once a fight has started."

Rynlin counted a dozen Mongrels left, but Thomas was right. The dark creatures were acting strangely, and that worried him. The beasts had tried their standard approach of taking their prey by surprise with little success and had now adopted a more cautious strategy. That didn't fit with what he knew of these monsters. Mongrels tended to be overly aggressive and impatient with their attacks. Their circling rather than charging a second time suggested that this group could be just the vanguard of a larger pack.

"We can't stay like this," said Thomas, thinking much the same as his grandfather. "The forest is only a few leagues away, and that's a place the Mongrels won't want to go. It's too constricting and it works to our advantage. They're trying to keep us here for some reason."

"Aye. That could mean either more Mongrels following or something worse on the way."

"What could be worse than Mongrels?" asked Oso, not sure if he was more curious than afraid, which worried him.

"You don't want to know, lad."

"Then it's time to change our strategy," said Thomas. "Marchers, form wedge!"

Instantly his fighters obeyed, shifting the square into a battle wedge, spears forward and to all sides, archers staying to the middle. The Marcher wedge started at a walk, then the Highlanders urged their horses to a slightly faster gait as they advanced at a steady pace toward the forest that beckoned to them in the distance.

"Thomas, the Mongrels will figure this out."

In fact, the Mongrels had already identified the weakness. The very point of the wedge. If the beasts attacked from both sides at once in heavy numbers, they could crush the point of the wedge and drive into the center of the Marcher formation, which would mean the end of the Marchers and easy pickings for the dark creatures.

"I know, Rynlin. That's what I'm counting on. I want them to attack. Otherwise, they'll harry us all the way to the woods, and by then we may be too weak to hold them off."

"Then what are you suggesting we do, Thomas?" asked Oso, brandishing his sword as he scanned in all directions, tracking the Mongrels as they circled the wedge.

Just as Thomas expected, many of the Mongrels sprinted to get ahead of the wedge on both sides of the point. More important, the Mongrels that had trailed behind the wedge had now moved to the front, leaving the Marchers positioned at the back of the formation with no dark creatures to defend against.

"Oso, take the spears from the back of the wedge. Form them into two lines of cavalry. When I call spears to the front, get there as fast as you can. If you're late, we die."

Oso instantly set to his task, quickly understanding what Thomas had in mind. He grinned in anticipation, always preferring an aggressive approach.

The Marcher wedge continued toward the west at a steady pace, the Marchers keeping their mounts at a fast walk, each step bringing them closer to the safety of the forest, the dark smudge of green now visible as tall trees that were spaced so closely together that the Mongrels would find their movements hindered if they followed their prey into the dense wood.

"Rynlin, would you care to join me?"

Thomas led Acero forward, his Marchers parting like water as he moved out in front of the wedge. Rynlin nudged Militus to his side, a scowl on his face.

"I hope you know what you're doing, Thomas?"

"I hope so, too."

As the two unicorns advanced toward them, the Mongrels howled, bloodlust surging through the dark creatures. The beasts, which had moved to the front of the wedge, leapt forward, charging from both sides, seeking to take the two Sylvan Warriors and crush the point of the wedge at the same time.

Thomas waited to make his move until he judged that the Mongrels had gotten too close to change direction.

"Rynlin, take the right. I'll take the left. Spears to the front!"

Oso had waited on edge for Thomas' command, his fighters impatient to charge. Thomas and Rynlin galloped in their respective directions, their unicorns lowering their spear-like horns. The Marchers followed, surging toward the dark creatures from each side of the wedge, spears at the ready. The Mongrels stopped short, or tried to, surprised by the actions of their prey. The Mongrels didn't realize the danger until it was too late. Oso and his Marchers, having split into two separate groups at Thomas' call, slammed into the dark creatures' flanks at exactly the same moment Thomas and Rynlin's columns thundered into the dark creatures.

What for the Marchers had become a desperate moment quickly became a slaughter, as they ripped through the Mongrels, Thomas and Rynlin leading the way. Acero and Militus drove their spiraling horns into the chests of two of the massive beasts, killing them instantly, the Marchers following after trampling over them. In that single charge more than half of the remaining Mongrels perished, and then the Marchers who had remained with the wedge crashed into the remaining beasts. With clinical efficiency, the Marchers completed their gruesome work, spears disabling and arrows finishing. In less than a minute, it was over. The large Mongrel pack lay strewn about the long grass with no survivors.

"A good victory, but this isn't over," said Rynlin, trotting up to Thomas, a tired but satisfied smile on his face.

"This pack was not acting as I would have expected," said Thomas. "Something follows in its wake. I can feel it."

"Dragas are known to track the Mongrel packs looking for an easy kill," offered Rynlin.

"That gives us good cause to be away," replied Thomas.

Thomas charged Oso with caring for the wounded. He would lead the Marchers tasked with burying the dead. Then the men and women of the Highlands would move into the forest quickly, now less than a league away, mourning their lost comrades later.

CHAPTER FIFTEEN

ULTIMATE GOAL

Ragin Tessaril, heir to the throne of Armagh, stood on a windswept balcony looking out over what had once been a great city, but was now a ruin. The stone was worn and rotting, at least the stone that he could see as most of it was covered in a light, black ash. For the thousandth time, he thought the name of his temporary home, Blackstone, quite appropriate.

Before the coming of the Shadow Lord, the city was a major metropolis that connected the Kingdoms with the lost lands to the north, a region known as the Free Cities of the North, though supposedly these great cities existed in a world of perpetual ice and snow. But no more. The Shadow Lord had chosen this city for his capital, and it and the surrounding countryside had paid the price over the millennium. Once a vibrant landscape of farms and industry situated among the peaks, it was now nothing more than a dead land, the blackened peaks of the Charnel Mountains dominating the Northern Steppes, their shadows extending almost to the Breaker during the late hours of the day. And with the Shadow Lord came the dark creatures, searching for a way to conquer the Kingdoms to the south as their master demanded.

That's why Ragin was there now, and why he had survived the Dark Magic encircling the barren city. He had sold his soul to serve the Shadow Lord. For only with the Shadow Lord's help could the Armaghian prince achieve his ultimate goal. Revenge. He knew his enemy and had paid a terrible price for confronting him. And his failure, his weakness, gnawed at him, burning a hole in his gut that had filled with self-loathing. When Malachias, the Shadow Lord's right hand, presented him with a way to gain unheard of power, a power that would match that of his archrival, he jumped at the chance. He had to have his revenge. It was the only thing that mattered to him. It was that driving obsession that kept him sane. But he had never considered that the gift of Dark Magic came with a price, and that cost was only now becoming clear to him.

He felt a strange itchiness just beyond his senses, as if something crawled beneath his skin, eating him from within. But whenever he looked or scratched or rubbed his arm or between his shoulder blades or his belly, there was nothing there but unmarked skin. Yet, as his strength in Dark Magic increased, so did that sensation, sometimes his entire body feeling as if he'd fallen into a patch of pricker bushes. In addition, he found that he was becoming more short-tempered and unable to control his emotions, as if the Dark Magic that now coursed through him magnified the less pleasant aspects of his personality.

Physically he was changing as well. The scar that Highland whelp had given him, running from his eye down to his jaw, would never fade, the ragged, weeping skin burning incessantly. But even worse his once handsome features now had turned more sallow, almost pasty.

It seemed as if his attributes were becoming more malleable, as if the Dark Magic was reshaping him both physically and mentally, making him into whatever it wished. Or whatever his new master required.

He should have been worried. Perhaps even frightened. But he didn't care. When he was younger, he cared about his looks, about what the girls he pursued thought of him. He cared about his place in the world, and the role that he played as son of the High King. But no longer. None of that mattered. Now he cared for only one thing, and one thing only. And he would do whatever was necessary to attain it.

"It's time," whispered a raspy voice.

A wispy black shadow that towered above him appeared at his back. Two eyes, burning with blood-red fire, stared down at him, giving the shadow surrounding him its only substance.

"You know where he is? You will let me do this?" Ragin tried to speak with steel in his voice, but even his fervor failed to keep a tremor of fear from trickling into his words.

The shadow continued to stare at him silently, weighing him, judging him. Hopefully not finding him wanting.

"You are stronger, more skilled, but the boy still has the advantage of you. You could be going to your death."

"I don't care!" screamed Ragin.

He realized the price of his insolence instantly as a fiery pain shot through every nerve in his body, forcing him to the ground. He curled into a ball, weeping, as the agony intensified. Just as quickly as the pain began, it came to an end.

"Remember your place, boy. Remember what I have given you. I do not throw my tools away uselessly."

Ragin pulled himself to his knees, then bowed deeply, bringing his head to the stone. The burning was gone, but the memory of that fire remained.

"Yes, Master. Forgive me. I've just been waiting so long, Master. So long. If you give me this chance, I know I will not fail you."

The Shadow Lord stared down at the cringing Ragin for what seemed like hours, but was only seconds.

"You will not fail me, Ragin Tessaril. For no matter what your enemy could do to you, I can do much, much worse."

Ragin nodded his head, still keeping it close to the stone.

"Yes, Master. I will not fail you. I will not fail you!"

Ragin tried to contain himself, but he couldn't. The madness that seemed to be just a breath away had gained a foothold within him. The Shadow Lord didn't appear to notice or care.

"So be it," said the Shadow Lord. A portal of spinning blackness opened up before Ragin, and through it he could see a different room, a brighter room of light and air. "Find your quarry, Ragin. Destroy your enemy. If you don't, you will answer to me."

Before the Shadow Lord could change his mind, Ragin leapt through the portal, a look of manic glee illuminating his face. Finally. Finally he could hunt the one who had done this to him. The one who had caused all his misery and pain. The one who had taken so much from him. Finally, he could kill the Highland Lord.

CHAPTER SIXTEEN

GENTLE REBUKE

"I should have gone with him," repeated Kaylie for the hundredth time. "I could have helped."

Gregory tried to avoid rolling his eyes, having had to hear the same from his daughter for most of the morning. He looked to Sarelle, who rode her horse next to him, his eyes pleading. The Queen of Benewyn, normally so sure of herself and never afraid to make a hard decision, could only shrug. She didn't think that her initial instinct for addressing the Princess of Fal Carrach's sulkiness would prove useful, so she kept her thoughts to herself and her mouth shut.

The council had come to an end the morning Thomas and his Marchers left on their raid into Armagh. Chuma, chief of the Desert Clans, had headed west shortly thereafter, first to position his troop that would support the Highlanders from any incursions by dark creatures near the Breaker, and then to call the other Desert Clans to war. Rendael had gone with him, his Kingdom farther west. The monarch of Kenmare enjoyed the company of the gregarious desert chief, and it would give him an opportunity to see the sands for himself. Despite his long rule and the fact that his Kingdom abutted the Clanwar Desert, he had never traveled deeply into the sandy, arid, dangerous land. This would be his chance to do so.

Gregory and Sarelle had decided to travel together, heading south out of the Highlands and then east, and they were now no more than a day from Ballinasloe. From there Sarelle would send word through one of her ship captains — there were always Benewyn traders in the Fal Carrachian port city — to her ministers in the capital city also named Benewyn with instructions to bring her small army north in support of the Highlands.

"We've been over this before, Kaylie," replied Gregory.

"It's still not fair," declared the Princess of Fal Carrach.

"Life isn't fair," her father countered. "You should know that by now. Besides, you have duties to fulfill in Fal Carrach. I'll need your help to prepare the army to move north. It's something you need to learn how to do."

Kaylie huffed in response. "You don't need me for that." She nodded behind her, toward the Swordmaster of Fal Carrach who rode just a few paces away from Gregory. "Kael can manage that. I would simply get in the way."

"Yes, but you need to learn …" Gregory didn't have a chance to finish his thought, his daughter cutting in.

"You know I can fight," she said. "Kael can confirm it. And you've seen what I can do with the Talent. Rya says that I'm one of her better pupils and that it won't be long before I'm called to become a Sylvan Warrior."

"I understand that, Kaylie. I'm not disputing Lady Keldragan's assessment, but …"

"I should have gone with …"

"Are you done, child?" asked Sarelle, interjecting herself into the conversation with a voice that suggested that she, indeed, was speaking to a child. The Queen of Benewyn's tone stopped Kaylie short. "We've had to listen to the same complaint all morning. You don't seem to realize that there are more important things to deal with right now than what you want."

Kaylie opened her mouth to reply, but nothing came out. Though Sarelle had delivered the rebuke gently, it was a rebuke, nonetheless. Something that the Queen of Benewyn had never done to her before, and that made Kaylie think for a moment before responding.

"I understand, Sarelle. It's just …" She knew what she wanted to say, but she didn't know how to say it.

"You worry for him," said Sarelle, offering a commiserating smile.

Kaylie slumped in her saddle, all her energy leaving her. "Yes," she mumbled.

"What's that saying the Lady Keldragan uses, the one you like to quote so frequently?"

"You must do what you must do."

"Yes, that's certainly appropriate," said Sarelle. "We all must do what we must do. Right now, Thomas must do as he must, taking on the task of rousting the High King from Armagh once and for all. No one can question your ability with the blade, and your growing skill in the Talent is impressive. I have no doubt that you could be of assistance to Thomas. But have you thought of the other side of the coin?"

"What do you mean?" asked Kaylie, not understanding what Sarelle was suggesting.

"You just said that you worried about him. Don't you think that if you were on this mission with Thomas that he might worry for you as well? Perhaps that worry would get in the way of what he must do? Distract him at a critical moment?"

Kaylie stared at Sarelle, never having considered that possibility. After almost a minute, she took a gulp of air, not realizing that she had been holding her breath.

"You're right, Sarelle," Kaylie whispered, her cheeks turning red. "I hadn't considered that. Do you really think Thomas ..." She left the rest unsaid, afraid to put it into words.

Sarelle gave Kaylie a warm smile, nodding her head. "Of that I have no doubt, Kaylie."

"Then what would you suggest that I do?" asked Kaylie. "I feel the need to do something. To help Thomas in some way. But how am I to do it from here?"

"Do as your father suggested, child," said Sarelle, this time her use of the term warm. "Help Kael. Learn what needs to be done to put an army into the field. Be ready for when Thomas needs help, because he will need help soon. He'll need as many swords at his back that we can muster."

Kaylie nodded, a look of determination fixing upon her face. "Thank you, Sarelle. You're right."

Gregory looked across at the Queen of Benewyn once again, mouthing his thanks. He received a knowing smile in return, as if Sarelle fully understood the service that she had just done for him and expected something in return. A stab of worry settled in his gut, fighting the competing feeling that perhaps he wouldn't mind what Sarelle might have in mind. He didn't have time to dwell on those thoughts, however, as his daughter urged her mount to a faster pace, forcing the rest of the party to match the gait as well.

"If we hurry, we can get back to the Rock by mid-afternoon," Kaylie said, calling back over her shoulder. "The sooner we're in Ballinasloe, the better."

Gregory chuckled. "You've created a monster," he said to Sarelle.

The Queen of Benewyn could only shrug her shoulders in response.

CHAPTER SEVENTEEN

DRAGAS

Having escaped the Mongrel pack, the Marchers kept moving once they reached the densely packed trees. Even with the sun high in the sky, rather than find a place to hide away as had been their habit once they entered the Grasslands, they wanted to put more distance between them and whatever else might be following, Thomas' premonition of approaching evil gaining greater solidity as each hour passed. With the day almost done and darkness falling, Thomas called a halt, allowing the Marchers to set up camp for the night.

Several of the Highlanders were wounded, and all were tired and grieving their lost comrades. Nevertheless, the Marchers went about their tasks with a will as they used the ingrained movements of establishing their encampment as a way to turn their minds away from fear and loss, if only for a short time. They built several small, hidden cook fires, and Oso sent the first watch of sentries well into the trees in order to ensure sufficient warning could be given if intruders approached, even though Rynlin or Thomas would warn of impending danger well before the sentries were aware. It was simply a habit. And right now, Oso knew that relying on good habits and maintaining their routine was important.

It was close to midnight, the sentries having just changed and the small fires having burned out hours before, when terrifying shrieks ripped through the quiet night. Resembling the calls of the banshees from the stories that Highlanders told their children to frighten them into behaving, the Marchers sensed that whatever hunted them now would be much, much worse than a specter from a child's fable. Although the Marchers couldn't see the sky clearly because of the dense foliage, they could identify shadows darker than the night gliding above the branches and boughs.

"You were right, Rynlin. Dragas."

"I hate when I'm right."

"Since when?" countered Thomas. "If we fight without the Talent, can we win?"

"If it's only one or two of the cursed beasts … yes, but at great cost," answered Rynlin after giving the question some thought. "And if we fight with the Talent, we lose any chance of surprising Rodric and Chertney at Eamhain Mhacha and we'll have dark creatures on our trail harrying us all the way there."

"Suggestions?"

Rynlin stood there for a moment, pondering, then nodding his head as if he had just agreed with himself.

"Yes, gather all the Marchers and mounts into a circle, and bring in the sentries. Make sure those fires are completely out."

Thomas and Oso hurried to obey, and the Marchers quickly took their positions with their horses, moving silently despite the blackness of the night. The shrieks of the hunting Dragas continued, increasing in intensity, suggesting that they were homing in on their prey.

"Do what I do," said Rynlin.

Using the Talent, the Sylvan Warrior wove himself into the forest surrounding them, but in a way so subtle that the natural magic of the world was virtually undetectable. Any dark creature looking from above would not see man or mount, but rather just undisturbed, pristine forest. Thomas followed Rynlin's cue, remembering that he had done something similar the first time that he had used the Talent during his escape from the Crag. Now, working with his grandfather, they extended their natural camouflage over their troop of fighters. Then they waited. As time passed, the tension among the Marchers almost became palpable. It was much like the wait before a battle, nerves on edge, which could result if the ruse engineered by Rynlin and Thomas failed.

The shrieks continued for more than an hour, but as time passed the banshee-like calls came from farther and farther away. The Dragas continued their search, but the deadly dark creatures were no longer interested in the section of the forest in which Thomas and his raiders hid.

"Well done, lad," complimented Rynlin.

"Thanks. I have some experience with that particular skill." The last time Thomas had camouflaged himself in such a way, he had made it appear as if he had become a part of the Southern River, which helped him to evade the reivers sent after him when the Crag fell.

"That's good to know," said Rynlin. "I expect that we'll need to do much the same again before we reach the Heartland Lake."

The Marchers, spurred on by the knowledge that the Shadow Lord's servants continued to hunt them, traveled quickly through the thick forest on a northwesterly course. Several times Rynlin and Thomas made use of the Talent to mask the Marchers' passage, the Dragas returning every night, gliding across the treetops as part of their search but never locating their quarry. When the Marchers finally broke through the trees and gazed upon the eastern shore of the Heartland Lake, the sky was still dark although a hint of orange was just beginning to appear on the eastern horizon.

Before leaving the Highlands, Thomas had spoken with Sarelle of Benewyn, who had explained that not all the traders of her Kingdom always followed the traditional rules of commerce. In fact, several might take on work that required more secrecy or discretion than was standard when carrying certain goods.

With that in mind, she had suggested that Thomas and his band make their way to a hidden cove on the eastern shore of the lake well south of Eamhain Mhacha to see if they could locate a particular captain who could assist them in their travels to the Armaghian capital. In case he actually found the suggested captain, she provided a letter of introduction to smooth the way, explaining that something else would likely be required to ensure a quick passage. But he could worry about that when the time came.

Using the Talent, Thomas had found the hidden cove along the edge of the lake, confirming that several sleek ships, built for speed, were berthed in the protected anchorage. With the sun coloring the morning's low-hanging clouds a burnt orange, Thomas led Oso, Rynlin and several other Marchers past the still dozing sentries and down a hidden path in search of a particular vessel. Oso had felt the urge to berate the sailors stationed along the trail, appalled that they had fallen asleep at their posts. Thomas had dissuaded him, noting that the men assigned to guard the small bay were more skilled in secrecy rather than security. Oso could only shake his head in disgust as the Marchers tread silently into the smugglers' secret lough.

CHAPTER EIGHTEEN

A DEBT OWED

Kendrick Winsloe reluctantly opened an eye as the rising sun forced its way through an open porthole. Scratching his belly, he cursed to himself silently, regretting the long night of drinking that he had engaged in with the other captains moored along the lakeshore. Rolling onto his back, he tried to convince himself that he should go back to sleep, the pounding in his head only getting worse every time that he moved. But he knew that he didn't have the time. He had promised a friend that he would have the expected cargo to Eamhain Mhacha in three days, and that was a promise he intended to keep. He liked to brag that his ship, the *Windswept*, was the fastest on any body of water in the Kingdoms. Making this run would help to establish his reputation. That would mean more business in the future. And that's what he needed, because keeping his ship in the best of shape and paying his crew were expensive propositions.

Rubbing his eyes, Kendrick swept his legs over the edge of his hammock and fought back a sudden wave of nausea. When he had acquired the *Windswept*, he had made the decision to create as much storage space as possible, which meant more cargo, and, of course, more profit. But it had come at the expense of his private captain's quarters. He had instead taken a small berth in the aft of the ship, something that even a first mate would be loath to call his own. But he didn't care. He found the trade-off worthwhile. A few more profitable runs and he might be able to purchase another ship, and then he would be well on his way to building the fleet of merchant ships that remained his dream. His stomach somewhat settled, he began to push himself up onto his feet when a voice stopped him.

"I thought smugglers were early risers. I guess I was mistaken."

About to stand up, Kendrick fell back into his hammock. He reached for the knife that he kept on his hip, even when he slept, but much to his surprise he found the sheath empty. Behind the tall man with the roguish smile stood an even larger man, crowding the small cabin with his height and width. He flipped Kendrick's foot-long blade casually from hand to hand as if it were no more than a child's toy.

Despite his shock, Kendrick tried to gain some control over the situation. He didn't bother to deny that smuggling might account for a small portion of his business activities. Who in their right mind wouldn't try to avoid the ridiculously high taxes? "Might I ask why you've boarded my ship? And may I ask what's happened to my crew?"

"They're going about their business as they should," replied the tall man, his blue eyes flashing. "In fact, they're preparing the ship to catch the tide."

"What?" Kendrick shot out of his hammock, forgetting the size of his cabin and knocking his head on the thick wood beam that ran above his bunk. He tried to ignore the pain as he ran a hand over the knot forming on his scalp. "This is my ship, and I decide where we go."

"Your men were quite clear that you were making for Eamhain Mhacha," answered the tall man, his tone level. "As it would happen, we're going there as well, so ours is a fortunate meeting."

"That doesn't matter. This is my ship and ..."

"Then perhaps this will help."

Another man, smaller than the other two but giving off a similar sense of danger, stepped forward. Kendrick fell back down into his hammock again, taken aback by this new arrival. His eyes glowed green in the dim light of the cabin. The intense young man handed a folded parchment to him.

Fumbling with the document, Kendrick reached over to the small bed stand built into the side of the cabin for his reading glasses. Once in place, his expression turned to disbelief.

"Where did you get this?" he demanded.

"You know exactly from whom we got it."

"But, the Queen of Benewyn ..."

The smaller man stepped forward, while the larger intruder caught the hilt of Kendrick's dagger in his hand as if he were about to use it. It seemed that their patience with his questions was wearing thin.

"The Queen of Benewyn rarely provides such letters of introduction, I know. But Sarelle was quite explicit that you were the captain we needed for the task at hand, thus the letter."

"You know the Queen?"

"We do. She also said that this might help persuade you."

The smaller man tossed him a heavy bag that jangled when he caught it. Feeling its weight, he guessed that it contained several dozen gold pieces, more than he was slated to earn with the cargo already in his hold.

"The Queen of Benewyn has always protected her traders, so I'm inclined to assist," smiled Kendrick. The three men noticed that the bag of gold had already disappeared. "Might I ask our cargo?"

"It's something of a surprise," answered the man with the menacing glare, his blue eyes flashing in the light.

"A surprise for whom?"

"The High King," answered the green-eyed man. "He owes us something, and we mean to collect it from him."

"And if I may ask, what might that be?" Kendrick regretted the question as soon as it left his mouth, thinking that he might have overstepped. But the smuggler side of him had always struggled to control his curiosity.

"His Kingdom," answered the large man who barely fit through the door to his cabin, his muscled bulk blocking the entrance and maintaining a perpetual gloom in the tight space but for the single ray of early morning sunlight that shined through the porthole.

Kendrick started to laugh, thinking that these strange, clearly dangerous men were having fun with him. But then he realized that the other two weren't laughing. The sounds of his crew sailing the ship out of the hidden cove and into the lake filtered down to him.

That and the tread of many more footsteps than normal, as well as the hard clop of horses being led across the deck to the hold, so he could guess at what else the *Windswept* now carried. He eyed the men before him more carefully.

A hazardous task? Probably. But also a lucrative one. Besides, he'd never liked the High King.

CHAPTER NINETEEN

INTO THE GLOOM

The journey across the Heartland Lake sped by, a strong wind filling the ship's three triangular sails and blowing the swift vessel rapidly toward Eamhain Mhacha. In fact, nature itself seemed to want the *Windswept* to get to its final destination as quickly as possible. At least that was Kendrick's take on it, as during many of the previous times that he had journeyed north up the lakeshore often he had struggled to find the wind. As a result, on the third day since leaving the cove the smuggler did everything that he could to slow his ship down, not wanting to come too close to the capital of Armagh until well after dark.

All three days his guests, as he liked to call them, kept to themselves. His crew didn't seem to mind. The warriors, clearly Marchers, made his sailors uncomfortable, the premonition of barely contained violence emanating from these hardened fighters. Their grim visages and quiet words among each other portended dire things to come, a feeling that permeated the ship. Kendrick could understand, having heard some of the stories about what had occurred in the Highlands these ten years past. If this group planned to rectify matters or perhaps take their revenge, he'd be pleased to play a small part, as he had no love for the High King, a man who appeared to be more focused on meeting his own needs rather than the needs of his people.

Yet the tall one with the black beard flecked with grey didn't seem to notice the crew's hesitancy and discomfort, as he spent a good bit of time talking with Kendrick about what the ship captain had seen and heard on his travels to the various Kingdoms during the past year. He soon realized that his passenger rarely talked, rather just guiding Kendrick along with questions to learn what he wanted.

That was fine with Kendrick. He didn't sense he'd have any problems with this group. They were paying him well, their stated purpose appealed to him, they clearly had a strong connection to his Queen, and he had learned some things of his own during the last few days. That was the way of it if you were to be successful as a ship's captain and sometime smuggler.

You needed to pick up useful information whenever possible, even as you shared what you knew about the happenings to the north and west. You needed to know the lay of the land, or the flow of the water in this case, to be successful in this business. The increasing number of stories about dark creatures roaming the countryside, villages burned, the rising tension and conflict within various Kingdoms as some useless noble sought to gain advantage at the expense of some other useless noble, all could affect him and his crew. The tall man was more than willing to share a story or two himself, several of which threatened to turn Kendrick's hair white, what with his tales of Ogren and other terrifying monsters rampaging through the Grasslands and Great Sharks hunting in the Inland Sea. That last alone had convinced him to set extra lookouts across the length of his ship. No one had reported the massive dark creatures in the Heartland Lake yet, and he didn't want to be the first to do so. But better to be prepared. One of those beasts could sink his ship if he wasn't careful. If nothing else, the conversation with this imposing stranger made the time go by quickly.

Near midnight, Kendrick reefed the sails, taking the blacked-out *Windswept* quietly beyond the Eamhain Mhacha harbor toward the base of the fortress to the west. He used the torches burning along the town's waterfront to guide him along the coast, looking for the marker that required him to heel the ship sharply starboard as he approached the darkened citadel.

"How goes it?" asked the tall man, his blue eyes shining brightly in the gloom of night.

"Almost there," replied Kendrick, his attention focused on the water in front of him. "We need to find the channel, and that will take us in. If we miss it, we'll be stuck on a sandbar or rock waiting for the soldiers of Eamhain Mhacha to find us in the morning."

"Let's avoid that if at all possible."

"Aye." Kendrick kept his eyes on the water, reading the waves, knowing exactly what he was looking for having made this run several times before. "I'd hate to be found with your group. The High King likely wouldn't look kindly on my participation."

"That would be an understatement," grinned the tall man, flashing a smile, apparently amused by the thought.

Kendrick continued to watch the waves, then found what he sought.

"Hard port," he called quietly, the helmsman turning the wheel sharply.

The *Windswept* glided between two large rock formations that rose sharply out of the water, finding the narrow channel that required a gentle starboard turn halfway along to avoid crashing into the rocks upon which the Eamhain Mhacha fortress had been built, and then another gentle turn back to port. Sailors scampered around the ship, taking in the sails to slow the speed of the vessel and allow the light wash of the water running through the tapered neck to take them beneath the keep, which rose several hundred feet above them.

As they approached, the sound of the waves crashing against the rocks drowned out any noise. The Marchers moved to the bow of the ship and the sides to track their progress through the channel, several growing apprehensive as the ship drifted closer and closer to the jagged rocks. Right before they expected to hear the sound of splintering wood and water rushing into a cracked hull, Kendrick called out again quietly.

"Hard starboard." The helmsman responded immediately, having expected the command.

The *Windswept* turned sharply once again, drifting between a ragged break in the rock wall, so tight that the Highlanders on either side of the ship could reach out and scrape their fingers along the rock that ran past. In just a few seconds, they were through, arriving in a large, sheltered bay underneath the citadel, the calm water slapping quietly at the shore. Just ahead a small pier jutted out from the darkness of the beach. The *Windswept* glided toward it, the sailors moving quickly but silently about their tasks as they drew up alongside the jetty to tie the vessel off.

In a series of practiced maneuvers, Kendrick and his crew slid the gangplank down to the pier and began to help the Marchers and their mounts off. Many of the crew goggled at the two unicorns, horns as deadly as a soldier's lance, leading the way. Clearly the sailors had done this before, as there was no noise but the rustling of the water lapping against the pier and the hull of the ship and an every so often clink of steel against steel as the Marchers walked down the jetty into the massive cave that beckoned just ahead.

The three men who had first visited Kendrick in his cabin that night less than a week before were the last off the *Windswept*. The two taller ones nodded their thanks as they stepped down the ship's ramp. The smaller one, his eyes glowing a bright green in the darkness even with the bare illumination provided by the single lantern hoisted on one of the masts, nodded with a smile.

"My thanks, Captain." He handed over a bag that jingled with the rest of the promised gold, in fact more than Kendrick had expected. "I hope we weren't too much trouble."

"No trouble at all, though I think my boys are glad to see you go. Marchers put them on edge."

The smaller man chuckled as he walked down the gangplank. "Marchers tend to do that to most people."

"Indeed they do. Thank you for the generous payment, my lord. And remember what we discussed. The passages to the left will take you higher into the fortress through the basements that are no longer used, except by those seeking to do some illicit trading. The tunnels to the right go deeper into the foundation and are for the most part impassable."

"I remember, Captain Winsloe."

"And that trail I mentioned for your mounts. You'll find it at the very edge of the cave. Because of the overhanging rocks, the guards on the keep's walls won't be able to see you. Assuming there are no ships patrolling along the shore this morning, you can reach the city gates before you're noticed."

"By that time we will have completed our task," said the intense young man. "Thank you for the guidance and the help. I suggest that you move away from here quickly before there's any chance of your discovery."

"Oh, I mean to, my lord. I mean to." The green-eyed man began striding down the pier, turning back when Kendrick quietly called to him a final time. "And if I may, Lord Kestrel, I wish you luck. If at any time in the future you need my assistance, you know where to find me."

Thomas Kestrel smiled, assuming that the sharp-minded Captain Winsloe would see through the ruse at some point.

"Indeed I will, Captain. Thank you again."

Kendrick watched the Lord Kestrel disappear into the gloom, then quickly whispered his commands to his men to get the ship turned around and back onto Heartland Lake. He would wait awhile before entering the harbor to drop off his legitimate cargo. He had a feeling that with Marchers prowling below the citadel the next few days would be a bit unsettled, which was fine with him. A little unrest could favor a smart businessman.

CHAPTER TWENTY

DARK CREATURES

As Thomas entered the large, damp, murky cave, Oso and his Marchers had already set about their tasks. Having three days on the ship to review their strategy gave them plenty of time to prepare for their assignments to the point where they functioned solely on instinct.

Walking deeper into the grotto, Thomas came to a small passage, a set of slippery stairs cut out of the rock that led from the small, sandy beach. Oso appeared in front of him at the top of the steps, standing at the entrance to a room that was likely once used as a torture chamber. Cells carved from the rough stone ran along one wall and receded into the darkness. Thomas noted several drains in the stone floor, which likely carried away the blood and other human debris of those unfortunate souls brought down here to die.

"The Marchers are about their work," said Oso. "The horses and unicorns have been led away on the trail. No guards as of yet, but we're keeping a sharp eye. Though I should note that the two unicorns were uneasy, almost agitated. They tried to enter the cave at first. I don't know if it was because they were cooped up on the ship for too long or there was something else to it."

The Marchers had broken into groups of ten, each squad having been assigned an objective. The goal was to gain control of the citadel as quietly and with as little bloodshed as possible. But as Thomas knew, the best laid plans usually failed to survive first contact with the enemy.

"Good," said Thomas, distracted for a moment by Oso's last comment. "Let's get as far into the fortress as we can before we're discovered."

Thomas stopped in his tracks, standing stock still. The sensation that had seized him sent a shiver through his body. He reached out with the Talent delicately. Now he understood why Acero and Militus had at first balked at going along the trail, instead wanting to enter the cave. Much like the wolves, hatred of the Shadow Lord's dark creatures ran strong in unicorns. Based on what he was experiencing now, Thomas was surprised that the Marchers assigned to care for the horses had succeeded in persuading the two unicorns to go with them.

"Thomas, what is it?"

The cloud of darkness encircling the keep made him feel nauseous, the sense of evil almost overwhelming. He should have assumed as much based on what had happened in the Highlands. This discovery would require a change in plans.

"Ogren and Shades in the deeper tunnels, a lot of them."

Although using the Talent while surrounded by stone shaped by man tended to be more difficult than when surrounded by nature, it could still be done. Much as Thomas did as a child when he sought to escape the Crag, he used the Talent to create a map of the fortress in his mind, specifically identifying a handful of passageways that led from where the Ogren and Shades hid beneath the keep to the upper levels of the citadel.

"How many?" asked Oso, worry creasing his brow.

"Too many for us to handle and still achieve our goal," replied Thomas. "A small army at the least. But there's a way around it. Let me have Aric and his squad once they've completed their assignment. I'll make sure that there's no way the Ogren and Shades can make it up from where they are into the fortress. You stay on task. I'll catch up to you when I'm done."

Nodding, Oso ran off to find Aric and his Marchers. Thomas would use the mental map that he had created, find those passageways, then ensure that if any dark creature, Shade or Ogren, tried to pass through, they would be in for a nasty and deadly surprise.

CHAPTER TWENTY ONE

SOUNDS OF STEEL

Rodric stood on the balcony of his suite, gazing out over the Heartland Lake and the waves crashing against the rocks at the base of the fortress several hundred feet below him. Over the years, the water had worn away the foundation of the keep, creating caves, crevices and crags throughout. Having learned of Armagh's difficulties in the Highlands, General Brennios worried that an enterprising attacking force willing to take some risks could find a way into the keep if they were willing to explore that option. But Rodric didn't. He knew that what lurked in the deepest reaches of the citadel would deter anyone foolish enough to make the attempt.

That thought quickly dissipated, replaced by another concern, and that one was soon pushed aside by the next. And so it went, faster and faster, his fears playing through his mind. The High King struggled to concentrate, the travails and failures of the last few weeks picking at the edges of his sanity. As his mind drifted from one memory to the next, he always came to rest on the same one. It was a night much like this one, the moon shielded by low-lying clouds and a faint fog rising over the water. His son had been a fool. He understood why Ragin had done it, the calculation of it all. But his son's decision seemed to trigger the events that followed. That cold night atop the Tinnakilly battlements had been a harbinger of what was to come. Since then, his carefully laid plans had unraveled with amazing alacrity. He should have listened to Chertney. Looking back now, that sibilant swine had been correct. He should have killed the boy when he had his chance rather than trying to make an example of him in front of the assembled lords and ladies. That mistake had cost him dearly, and now his Kingdom was at risk. But he would admit that error only to himself. He was the High King after all. The High King didn't make mistakes. But his son certainly did.

Ragin had assumed that the boy was beaten. Weak, wounded and in no position to continue to resist after fighting the Makreen. Killing the one person who had bested that fearsome beast would enhance Ragin's reputation. But Ragin's decision had rapidly become a costly miscalculation. The boy, though injured and exhausted, was more than ready to fight.

The boy left a scar with Ragin that evening. And that scar had become a symbol to Rodric, a symbol of his own disintegrating power. Before that night all his plans were moving to completion exactly as he had laid them out. But in the days and weeks and months that followed, everything that he had strived toward had devolved into a mess, one problem after another, each setback followed by another defeat.

Since he had returned to Eamhain Mhacha having escaped the Highlands, he hadn't slept. Worry plagued him. He felt as if something was about to happen, something that he didn't want to have happen, but he didn't know what it might be or when. That feeling wore on him, fraying his nerves. He had become more short-tempered than usual, his mood swings more violent. He knew what it was, but he didn't want to admit it. For the first time in his life a cold ball of fear had settled within his gut and slowly had begun to grow. Since that cursed night when his son was scarred, physically and mentally Rodric now realized, he had run across the boy that had cost him so much several times, yet in each instance the boy had escaped, either on his own initiative or as a result of his servants' incompetence.

Rodric's thoughts drifted in a direction that set his stomach churning. If he was forced to face the boy on his own, without his soldiers and his sycophants, would he be able to defeat the person who had become his greatest nemesis? He had looked into the boy's eyes, unable to hold the gaze for long. The boy had power. A strength that Rodric didn't have. Rodric hated himself for this failing, despising his weakness. If the boy had died those many years ago at the Crag as he should have, Rodric would have no problems now. He could have proclaimed himself the true High King and been done with it. But the boy had taken that from him as well, and he was un-willing to admit that his own arrogance had aided the boy several times and given him more lives than a cat.

Rodric turned around abruptly, the constant rhythm of the waves crashing against the rocks broken up by the distant clash of steel on steel somewhere deep in the fortress. Momentarily frozen, he thought that he was mistaken. He held his breath, hearing just the waves, but then the screech of metal and the sounds of battle raging within his citadel assaulted his senses. He couldn't believe it, his shock making it difficult to think. But he should have expected it. His tormentor was here. He knew it! For a moment, he felt only irrational fear and struggled to gain control of himself. By the noises streaming up from the lower reaches of the keep, screams of anger and pain mixing with grunts of desperation and struggle, the attackers had made their way into the fortress and had reached several of the higher levels already. He didn't have time to wonder how the assailants got past his army to the east or his defenses here.

Walking quickly into his chambers he went in search of his guards. He needed to find Killeran and, more importantly, Chertney. He was loath to admit it, but he knew that his only chance for escape lay with the Shadow Lord's servant.

CHAPTER TWENTY TWO

HUNTING SHADOWS

The black shadow padded silently through the darkness, easily dodging trees, fallen branches, dense, almost impassable bushes and the other obstacles that littered the forest floor. The massive conifers of the northern Highlands towered above, hiding the bright moonlight except for the few stray beams that slipped through the thick foliage to illuminate the rough terrain. His prey approached. He could feel them, trying to sneak along the narrow trails that would take them to the few passes that led from the Northern Steppes deeper into the Highlands.

Putting on a burst of speed, the shadow ran through the forest until he found the place that he sought, a narrow defile that opened up into a small glade. The rocky meadow was more like a bowl, the evergreens standing sentinel on the very edge of the steep drop down to the forest floor. In some places the sides were sheer. Definitely the right place. The shadow knew that it would be difficult to climb. It would give him space to maneuver, while limiting how many of his quarry could enter, the defile restricting the number that could pass through because of its narrowness.

The shadow slid to the very edge of the trees over-looking the bowl-shaped glade, waiting, watching, relying on his senses to track the prey coming toward him, the beasts unaware of what lay in wait for them. He sensed his brothers and sisters moving into similar positions, staying low to the ground, hidden, ready, all anxious, anticipating what was to come.

The smell grew stronger as the moon rose higher in the sky, the stench of evil wafting through the forest, deadening all the other scents common to the Highlands. It wouldn't be long now. The shadow glimpsed movement at the very edge of the defile, as one dark creature and then another began to file through. The shadow waited until the massive creatures had almost reached the far end of the glade. Some stood ten feet tall and walked like men but were molded into terrible beasts, curled tusks protruding on their shaggy, gruesome faces, sharp teeth flashing in the intermittent moonlight and strong enough to gnaw through bone.

The shadow stood, tensing its legs, knowing that its brothers and sisters were doing the same. Then in a flash the shadow launched itself into the air, snarling, landing on the back of an Ogren. Surprising the beast, the huge dark creature didn't stand a chance. The Ogren didn't know it had been attacked until it felt a set of jaws latch onto its throat. With a violent flick of its head, the shadow tore the Ogren's windpipe out. The dark creature collapsed as its blood gushed out onto the craggy ground.

The huge wolf quickly surveyed the skirmish, his pack decimating the Ogren that had unknowingly crammed themselves into the depression. Eyeing a Shade attempting to pull itself up the steep slope and gain the lip of the bowl, in a burst of speed the wolf, its fur black except for a streak of white across its eyes, leapt onto the Shadow Lord's minion, crushing the back of its neck between its teeth before it could draw its corrupted blade.

The ambush ended in just minutes, Beluil's wolf pack eliminating the raiding party efficiently and viciously. They had fought silently, the only sounds coming from the terrified Ogren as they fought helplessly against the wolves of the north. Beluil raised his head to the moon, now visible through a small break between the massive trees, and howled in triumph, his brothers and sisters following suit. The call was taken up in other parts of the mountainous Kingdom, the responding howls of Beluil's other packs acknowledging the victory as they also hunted for the servants of the Shadow Lord.

Beluil was happy with the result, knowing that his brother Thomas would be pleased. The Highlands was his home now as well, and he would defend it with his packs as Thomas had requested. But there was still more to do. His pack had destroyed this raiding party, but several other bands of Ogren approached across the Northern Steppes in the dark of the night. The dark creatures would try to creep into the Highlands before the morning light.

Sprinting off to the east, Beluil's pack followed. Wolves hated dark creatures with a vengeance. They took particular pleasure in killing the servants of the Shadow Lord, and they understood that they had more to do that night. More killing was needed. But that didn't bother them. Rather, it exhilarated them. They knew that every dark creature killed was a spark for the light and for nature, and they would do all that they could to protect their world from the touch of the Shadow Lord.

CHAPTER TWENTY THREE

REVENGE

The Marchers made quick work of the castle's garrison, the Armaghian soldiers barely putting up a fight. Rodric's hold over the Kingdom had begun to slip over the last few months, and many had no desire to die at the hands of the fearsome Marchers. The few remaining guards in the fortress and the city knew of the defeats and the mistakes, though to speak of them openly in Eamhain Mhacha could lead to imprisonment or an even harsher sentence, depending upon the caprice of the High King. They could sense the tide turning and with it came an opportunity that appealed to many of Armagh's soldiers and citizens.

Rodric ruled by fear, having created an environment of absolute control, a state designed to support the interests of the ruler rather than the people. A select few had benefited from their subservience to the erratic High King, but most of Armagh's citizens were treated simply as resources to be used in his schemes and dreams of expanding the Kingdom's and his own influence. When the disillusioned soldiers assigned to the defense of the citadel and many of the oppressed people of Eamhain

Mhacha began to notice the cracks that had begun to appear in his rule, they were more than willing to take advantage of the chance presented by the Marchers. True, many of the guards continued to fight, some simply out of a sense of loyalty to their Kingdom. But their efforts were half-hearted at best, almost as if they wanted to convince themselves that they had done all that they could to defend the citadel before surrendering.

Knowing that the Marchers would soon have control of the keep, and that Thomas still remained on one of the lower levels, working to ensure that the dark creatures hidden within the tunnels beneath the citadel could not interfere, Rynlin turned his attention to a different, alarming matter. He had sensed a strange, new evil appear just moments before, somewhere near Eamhain Mhacha's great hall. It worried him. The feeling differed from the cloud of darkness that he was so familiar with that emanated from the Ogren and Shades stationed in the catacomb of passageways snaking through the keep's foundation. There was a familiarity to this foulness, but in other ways it was distinct, more putrid, more stomach churning. A type of dark creature that he had never faced before, and that worried him. He didn't like surprises, particularly of the Shadow Lord's making. Even worse, the power that this new threat contained rivaled his own.

This new evil began to move, first apparently trying to get its bearings as it wandered aimlessly. Or perhaps its motion had a purpose. Perhaps it was trying to catch the scent of its prey. After several minutes of seemingly senseless rambling, the evil appeared to have found what it was searching for as it advanced toward where Thomas was warding the last of the passageways so that the dark creatures couldn't enter the keep from below. His grandson would be fully occupied with that task, so Rynlin ran through the hallways to intercept the approaching foulness, finding the corridor and stairs that led down to where Thomas was working. He didn't have long to wait as a shadowy figure glided into the passageway at the far end.

"Is your desire for revenge so great that you would risk your very soul? That you would give yourself to the Shadow Lord knowing the full consequences of such a witless decision?"

The cowled figure stood there for a moment, surprised that someone dared to block his way. A hoarse laugh echoed through the hallway as the man pushed back the hood of his cloak, revealing the jagged scar that ran down one side of his face.

"We all must make our choices."

"We do. In fact, our choices define us. But you continue to make bad choices, Ragin."

The laugh stopped abruptly. Ragin's face twisted into a sneer, and partnered with his scar, it gave him an even more horrifying expression. "How do you know me?"

"I don't know you, Ragin, son of Rodric. You were never important enough to know. I know of you."

"I suggest you move aside, old man. I have business to attend to, and I won't be delayed by the likes of you." The imposing figure blocking Ragin's path unsettled him, but that wouldn't keep him from his revenge. Besides, with the Dark Magic he wielded, what did he have to fear from a greybeard?

"I have business as well," replied Rynlin, his eyes blazing, seeming to light up the dim hallway with blue. "In fact, you're my business. You asked if I knew you.

Actually, I do know you. You're no different than the others. The greedy fools who have traded their souls, their spirits, to the Shadow Lord in hopes of gaining something more, only learning too late and much to their disappointment that there is never a fair trade when dealing with the master of lies."

"I have no time for your pronouncements, old man. Move aside. Now!"

"I think not."

Ragin began to laugh again, a maniacal glint seeping into his eyes, a hint of madness in his voice. "You're right, old man. There is a price to pay when selling yourself to the Shadow Lord, but you can gain much in return."

Ragin pulled on the Dark Magic the Shadow Lord had imbued within him, raising his hands and shooting streams of black fire toward Rynlin. With nowhere to go, Rynlin grasped the Talent just in time, forming a shield of white energy to protect himself. Rynlin hunkered down behind the barrier of natural magic as the Dark Magic licked at its edges, but the inky flames failed to break through.

Ragin poured more and more Dark Magic into his attack, but to no avail. The old man's shield of blazing white energy continued to hold, deflecting the tainted power thrown against it. Quickly becoming frustrated by the failure of his assault, he released his hold on the contaminated black fire. Upon arriving back in the citadel that was his home, he had not expected to be opposed by anyone but his quarry. And he could feel his prey drawing near, so close yet still so far because of this weak, foolish old man. Turning his attention to the ceiling above his opponent, Ragin shot black shards of energy into the masonry. Large granite stones crashed down as Ragin sought to bury the old man in tons of rubble. Unfortunately for the Prince of Armagh, his opponent was ready.

Releasing the shield of white light, the old man raised his hands above his head. To Ragin, it appeared as if his opponent had caught the falling stone in his palms with barely any effort, the surprise of his adversary's success startling and distracting him. The old man stared at Ragin from the other end of the passageway, his face impassive, the only emotion revealed through his blazing blue eyes. Contempt and pity. Ragin's already tenuous grip on his sanity began to loosen even more.

For just a moment silence reigned in the hall, but just for a moment. Ragin screamed in rage as the old man flung a large stone toward him, forcing him to dodge out of the way before it crushed him. He had to step out of the way again, then drop to the floor, before tightening himself against the wall. Again and again the old man threw the large stones that had fallen from the ceiling above him right back at his antagonist. Ragin quickly realized that continuing his dance of survival was becoming untenable. Grasping hold of his Dark Magic once more, Ragin shot bolts of black energy toward the stones thrown his way, the corrupted, black energy smashing the carved rock into a fine dust that filled the hallway in a gritty fog that wafted between the two combatants.

After several minutes, the old man ended his attack, having run out of projectiles. Sweat poured off of Ragin, his initial assault and then defense obviously having taken a great deal from him. Though the shape of his opponent had grown hazy because of the dust cloud that swirled within the hallway, the old man's sharp blue eyes continued to shine through. The contempt remained. The pity was gone.

"You're a novice at best, Ragin. Go back from whence you came and tell your master that he's wasted his time with you. Power can only get you so far when you don't have the knowledge you need to use it."

"And if I don't, old man? What then?" Ragin tried to demonstrate the bravado that had once coursed through him, that had once made him what he was, but his cracking voice betrayed him. "I'm younger than you. And I'm stronger than you. I can feel it. You're no match for the Dark Magic I wield."

A hard edge entered Rynlin's tone, his eyes turning to flint. "Then you'll feel real power, you foolish whelp."

Ragin's face contorted in rage as he drew in as much of the Dark Magic gifted to him by the Shadow Lord as he could. Rynlin never gave him a chance to use it, the Sylvan Warrior doing something with the Talent that he hadn't done in hundreds of years, barely recalling the long dormant skill. But remember it he did. A portal that stretched to the ceiling opened behind Ragin, revealing what appeared to be a desolate, barren hillside with a grey mist clouding the landscape.

Before the Prince of Armagh realized what was happening, Rynlin gave him a hard shove with the Talent, forcing him off his feet and backwards through the magical gateway. Rynlin then released his hold on the Talent, allowing the portal to close before Ragin could release the Dark Magic that he had been so intent on using against him. Before the Prince of Armagh disappeared when the gateway snapped shut, Rynlin watched the disfigured young man's expression of anger change to that of shock, quickly followed by disappointment and then the first twinge of terror.

Rynlin turned quickly when he sensed someone behind him, taking hold of the Talent once more.

"There's no need for that, Rynlin." Thomas stepped up next to him, sensing when his grandfather let go of the Talent. "That was Ragin?"

The man Thomas had glimpsed before Rynlin had closed the gate looked almost nothing like the son of the High King. The handsome prince of Armagh Thomas had fought on the Tinnakilly battlements looked older, more worn, as if his body was just a shell. The only distinguishing characteristic that remained was the long, jagged scar on a pasty, malleable face that Thomas had given him during his escape.

"No, not Ragin," said Rynlin. "It used to be him, but no more. He's traded away his humanity for power, and now he's no more than any other dark creature held in check by the Shadow Lord's leash."

"Why didn't you kill him?"

"I couldn't kill him." Rynlin sighed, his regret plain. "I wasn't strong enough. He realized that, but he couldn't do anything about it as his training is lacking."

His grandfather's acknowledgement of his shortcoming frightened Thomas. If Ragin had become something that his grandfather could not defeat, what chance would he have in the future? Because he knew in his heart that they would meet again, their duel incomplete. He had felt it in his bones when he locked eyes with the Prince of Armagh as he stood on the other side of the closing portal, Rodric's son unwilling to allow his latest failure to get in the way of his achieving his primary goal. As his grandfather had said, there was no humanity there. Only death and the desire for revenge.

"Where did you send him?" asked Thomas.

"To a place that likely will tip him completely over the edge if he hasn't lost his mind already," replied Rynlin. "But you need not worry about him. He won't be bothering us again."

Thomas nodded, accepting his grandfather's statement, but not really believing it. He had no desire to deal with the heir to the Armaghian throne with everything else that currently demanded his attention. But if he had to in the future, he would.

"Are the passageways blocked?" asked Rynlin, still contemplating what the Prince of Armagh had become, trying to solve a puzzle that he wasn't sure had an answer.

"If any dark creatures try to make their way into the fortress through any of those hidden paths, they're in for a nasty surprise. Just in case I've stationed a few Marchers at each one to make sure none get through. If for some reason they do, I'll know and we can take action."

"Good. Now let's address the primary reason we're here."

"His private chambers?"

"That would be my guess. When your grandmother and I visited a few months back," referencing their surreptitious mission to acquire evidence of the High King's wrongdoing, "we found all the documents we needed to confirm Rodric's treachery in a private office next to his bedchamber. I sensed a hidden passage behind the desk, likely leading into the deeper recesses of the keep."

"Then let's go catch the rat," said Thomas. "We'll find Oso and his Marchers along the way and take them with us. It's time to end this."

CHAPTER TWENTY FOUR

HALL SKIRMISH

"Any problems, Oso?" asked Thomas as they strode through the corridors, a deathly quiet having descended on the highest level of the citadel.

"None at all, Thomas," replied the large Highlander. He held his sword in his hand, but he clearly hadn't had cause to use it. His frown reflected that he was none too pleased by that. "We dispatched the few guards who attempted to resist. The majority had no interest in a fight and are being held in the throne room. The Marchers guarding the passageways below report that all is quiet. Several groups of dark creatures tried to make their way through the tunnels and reach the upper levels of the keep, but your defenses held. As a result, we also now have a large number of dark creatures, or rather their remains, that we'll need to dispose of. Some of the Marchers said that even when the first few Ogren were incinerated, they kept coming. It was madness."

Rynlin nodded knowingly. "Shades were driving them. They kept forcing the beasts through, trying to find a weakness. I'm glad they didn't."

Thomas barely heard the conversation, his mind elsewhere. He desperately wanted to find the High King and pay him back for the injustices meted out on his people. Time and again he had gotten close, oh so frustratingly close, only to see Rodric slip away with the help of the Shadow Lord or his servants. When he finally laid hands on the High King, Thomas promised himself that justice would be swift.

Rounding the corner, they came to a long corridor, the doors to Rodric's private chambers at the very end. There were no guards in sight, which worried Thomas. He growled in irritation. Did the reason that he and his Marchers had come all this way escape again?

They began to walk down the hall, then stopped abruptly. Fortune looked down upon him. Thomas' smile resembled that of a cat about to pounce on an unsuspecting mouse. Rodric had appeared right in front of the doors with Chertney at his side and several fists of black-clad men trailing after, all with their backs turned toward them and not realizing the danger that they faced.

Thomas remembered fighting men such as these black-clad fighters before. Not warlocks, or at least not yet. But no better. Soulless. They had given themselves to the Shadow Lord in return for promises of wealth and power. They were shadows of themselves now, no more than slaves to whichever of the Shadow Lord's servants controlled them. Recognizing they were in for a fight, Thomas pulled his blade from the scabbard on his back, Oso and the men and women following him already having their weapons in hand. They then began walking purposefully down the hall, expressions grim but keen.

"Rodric! It's time that we ended this. Your reign is over."

The High King jumped, startled by the call much like a deer eyeing the hunter who had just stepped out from between the trees. He, Chertney and his men turned as one, shocked to see the Marchers approaching.

Realizing that Rodric was fixed in place, paralyzed with fear as his hand rested on the door handle, Chertney took command.

"Attack!"

The black-clad men charged down the hallway, swords and long knives drawn, their movements strangely coordinated. Their eyes lacked focus, yet their intentions were clear.

Thomas sprang forward, sprinting down the hall to engage and hoping to fight his way through to the High King. But he was faster than Oso and his fighters, creating a space between him and the Marchers rushing after him. Chertney noticed the gap and saw his opportunity, knowing that the Highland Lord was intent on one prize to the distraction of everything else. Grabbing hold of his Dark Magic, he almost lost control when he recognized the tall man standing with the Marchers, the Sylvan Warrior who had defeated him so easily in the Highlands. Despite the fear that surged within him, bursts of black energy shot from his hands. If Chertney was lucky, the Dark Magic would punch right through the Highland Lord's body before he realized that he was the focus of Chertney's attack.

Trusting his safety to his grandfather, Thomas ignored Chertney's assault intent only on his target. That trust was well placed. Using the Talent, Rynlin crafted a shield of white energy that formed right in front of Thomas and stayed with him as he ran down the hall. Chertney's black bolts struck the shield, the sharp flashes of light reverberating with a thunderous crack and blinding everyone in the hallway.

Chertney, forced to turn away by the blazing clash of competing powers, stepped back in fear. The Highland Lord still approached, this time more cautiously with his Marchers following behind. Chertney dodged to the side at the last second, the massive fireball that the tall Sylvan Warrior flung toward him singeing his hair, his black silk shirt beginning to smolder. His bowels threatened to release when he saw the same tall figure stalking toward him, the Sylvan Warrior's stony visage promising certain death. Rodric ducked as well, forced down by Chertney's hand on his shoulder, as the ball of energy struck the doors behind him, blasting the heavy oak shingles off their hinges and into the High King's private chambers beyond. Flames appeared just through the shattered doorway, the curtains and carpets beginning to burn, a charred smudge several feet around staining the stone on the far wall.

Thomas sprinted forward, his sword a blur as he engaged Chertney's men. Compelled by their master to fight, even after Thomas tore through three in as many seconds, the black-clad soldiers continued to resist. The Marchers leapt over the men slumped on the floor and crashed into Cherney's guard. Oso joined the skirmish with a roar that quickly became a smile. Finally, he had the opportunity he had been seeking. To take his anger out on those who had harmed his people and his homeland.

Chertney and Rodric evaded the attack, scurrying into the chamber beyond. Certain that they were making for the hidden passageway that his grandfather had mentioned, Thomas redoubled his efforts as he slipped his sword between the ribs of the soldier unlucky enough to block him from his goal. Unable to pull the blade free quickly as his opponent became a dead weight and slid to the floor, he ducked and drove his dagger in an underhanded strike into the groin of the soldier who had tried to take his head off with a wild, backhanded swing. He ignored his opponent's scream of agony. Looking up, Thomas saw that there were still several black-clad soldiers in front of him, and the tight space of the hall hindered his Marchers' efforts to push forward and break through. Although Thomas fought with a vengeance, he realized that Rodric was slipping from his grasp once again. Chertney's soldiers would fight to the death unless their commander was killed, ensuring a stiff defense. Although Thomas was more than happy to help them achieve that objective, he cursed his worsening luck as Chertney's rear guard would drain the valuable time that he needed to catch his prey.

CHAPTER TWENTY FIVE

TABLES TURNED

After the fireball blew apart the doors to his chambers, Rodric crawled on his hands and knees through his bedroom into his private office. His crown had clattered to the stone somewhere in the hallway, and he hadn't bothered to retrieve it. He pulled frantically at his tattered and smoking purple cape, almost choking himself in the process because of his clumsy efforts to release it from around his neck. Every clash of steel out in the hallway sent a jolt of fear through him as he crouched behind his desk, Chertney close behind. Pushing on the loose board by the left leg of the bureau, he released the catch holding the secret door in place. A draft of musty air enveloped him and Chertney as the hidden shingle swung open. Though a bit scorched, they were both pleased to escape the Marchers, if only for a few seconds.

"I am the High King," whined Rodric. "This is my Kingdom. My Kingdom! This can't happen to me!"

Chertney had had enough, tired of the sniveling whelp, his years of restraint finally snapping, his master's wishes be damned. Grabbing Rodric by the throat, he lifted him up and pushed him through the hidden doorway and against the back wall of the passage that led off into the darkness. Rodric's head struck a loose stone, and the High King felt a trickle of blood run down the back of his neck, soaking the collar of his shirt.

"I have thought of killing you many times," rasped Chertney, his hand tightening around Rodric's throat, making it more of a struggle for the High King to breathe. "But I haven't because the Shadow Lord wants you to live. He still thinks you might be useful. Why he would think such a thing, I don't know. But I don't question my master's decision, so I'll let you live a little longer for now."

Rodric could only stare, his mind failing to comprehend what was happening, never having been spoken to or bullied in this way before. He didn't know what to do, other than reach for Chertney's hand and try to pry the servant of the Shadow Lord's iron grip from his throat so that he could take a full breath. Finally Chertney released him, letting him drop to the ground. Rodric crumpled against the wall, massaging his bruised throat as he gasped for air.

"From now on, Rodric, you belong to me. You will do as I say when I say. Otherwise, I'll put an end to you, regardless of whatever my master might want. Now get up and get moving. I have no desire to die because of your continued ineptitude."

Chertney started down the dark path, ignoring the High King, no longer really caring if Rodric followed at all.

Rodric sat against the wall for a moment, his anger quickly growing into a barely controllable rage. Drawing his dagger, he stood quickly and threw it at Chertney's back. Sensing the motion, Chertney stopped and turned.

Rodric had expected the blade to be buried in Chertney's belly, but he was more than disappointed. He was terrified as the blade hung in the air between them, as if held by an invisible hand. Slowly the blade turned until the point lined up perfectly with Rodric. With the flick of Chertney's wrist, the blade sped back toward him, barely missing his head and striking the wall behind him instead, the spark of the steel hitting the stone eliciting a scream of fear from him.

"As I said, Rodric, you will do as I say now. And know that I can kill you with a snap of my fingers. You will live only as long as you are useful."

CHAPTER TWENTY SIX

SERVED COLD

Killeran ran through the hallways of Eamhain Mhacha, giving in to his need for haste, driven by fear, the pounding of his boots on the hard stone the only sound in the unnerving silence that had fallen throughout the citadel. His normally glaringly shiny, immaculate armor and white cape were besmirched by scratches and dents, grime and dirt, even blood, but thankfully none of it his own. When the Lord of Dunmoor learned that Chertney's Ogren and Shades could not escape their underground lair, he realized that the battle was lost before it even began. Rodric's guards would never be able to hold against the Marchers, even if they wanted to. And from what he had seen, clearly they had little desire to lay down their lives for a High King who had repeatedly betrayed their loyalty. In fact, he had barely avoided capture, running down a side corridor when the Armaghian soldiers assigned to protect him had decided that they valued their lives more than they valued his when a squad of Marchers appeared before them.

Most of the keep's defenders were dead or captured, and Killeran feared that he would join them if he ran into any of the Marchers now searching and securing the fortress. The Marchers were forcing any stragglers or those still wanting to put up a fight higher into the citadel as they swept through the lower floors of the fortress, and that was fine with him. It actually worked to his advantage. He cursed his luck, but even more so Rodric and that blasted Chertney for leaving him on his own when they became separated. But he knew where they were going, and if he couldn't catch up to them, he was still hoping to use their escape route.

Reaching the hallway that led to Rodric's chambers, Killeran stopped, the shock of his rising terror holding him in place. As he surveyed the carnage and damage, he struggled to keep the gorge rising in his throat from escaping. Chertney's black-clad men lay about the corridor, their blood seeping into the grout and staining the tiles and stone. The burnt remnants of the doors hung loosely on their hinges, small fires still smoldering in the room beyond. Some Marchers had obviously already made their way through this part of the castle, apparently having had an easy time against Chertney's soldiers, but perhaps that was a good thing. Perhaps that would allow him to slip away after all.

Forcing himself to walk into Rodric's suite of rooms, he saw that the adjoining chamber was charred to a crisp. Ignoring the stench of ash and soot, he stepped carefully into the private office and toward his one chance at survival, taking his time in order to avoid the paintings and drapes that had fallen from the walls and still burned on the scorched carpet. The hidden door was still open, so he could probably catch up to Rodric and Chertney if he moved quickly. He froze when three smoke-stained shadows emerged from the inky passageway.

Thomas stopped short, a smile playing across his face. "Rodric has escaped once again, but his rat wasn't fast enough. Perhaps my luck is finally turning."

"You!" Killeran stepped back in fear, his path to freedom blocked. His high-pitched voice failed to reflect the authority that he so desperately sought to present. "You dare to insult me? You dare! If your henchmen weren't here, I would challenge you to a duel. You got lucky that night so long ago. Luck will have nothing to do with it the next time our steel crosses."

Killeran whipped out his blade, swinging it in front of him as if he were preparing to fight, but rather hoping that with the Marcher and the tall man beside the Highland Lord, he could surrender honorably. He could not be expected to fight three adversaries at once under such circumstances.

"Yet to fight so many would not be honorable," continued Killeran, sweat breaking out on his forehead as his fear transformed into a shaking that he failed to control. "Therefore, I shall have to surrender my blade, as it is the only right-minded thing to do since we meet now as peers." Killeran twisted the sword in his hand and made to pass the blade to the large Highlander hilt first.

The Lord of Dunmoor was outnumbered. Moreover, the prospect of fighting any of the three men standing before him, particularly the boy with the brightly glowing green eyes, turned his bowels to jelly. He believed that he was entitled to the privileged treatment of a lord. Therefore, claiming the right of honorable surrender appeared to be his best option to ensure that his head remained on his shoulders. Perhaps he could then make his escape from captivity while the terms of his ransom were negotiated with the King of Dunmoor. But, apparently, the men beside the Highland Lord had little conception of a lord's right to an honorable surrender.

"They're gone, but we'll track them anyway," said the tall Highlander.

Killeran didn't recognize the sharp-eyed man whose dastardly grin made him shiver with fright. The other one was the boy from that night so long ago in the Highlands, the one who had risen so high so quickly and continued to haunt his dreams. The boy his master had wanted dead for so long. The doomed raid that he had led against the Highland village seemed to be the start of the destruction of all his well-laid plans to become more than just a Dunmoorian Lord, the boy standing before him the primary catalyst for his downfall.

The Marcher walked past Killeran with barely a glance at him or the proffered sword and then out the door. "I'll find Aric and we'll follow the trail. I expect that we'll come out wherever the dark creatures were led into the caves beneath the fortress."

"I'll help Oso," said the tall man, his hard blue eyes burning a hole through Killeran. He sensed the animosity Thomas held for the Dunmoorian lord, and he was more than willing to allow his grandson to act on it.

"Thank you, Rynlin. Could you also find the chamberlain, wherever he may be hiding, and bring him to me? Armagh needs to know that it no longer has a ruler, and the Kingdoms have need of a new High King."

"Of course, Thomas. I'll bring him presently."

In moments, only Thomas and Killeran stood in the room. His smile growing bigger, Thomas pulled his sword. Killeran eyed the words that ran down the blade of the Highland Lord, but he was unable to make them out in the flickering light.

"If it's a duel you want, then it's a duel it shall be," said Thomas in deadly seriousness. "No need to surrender, Killeran. Doing so now would be dishonorable as it appears that your odds of success are much improved. Though I would suggest that you grasp your sword from the other end. Now, shall we see if your luck will hold out for you this day?"

Killeran could only stare, unsure of what to do next. His attempt to extricate himself from the duel and gain the safety of an honorable surrender had failed. Truth be told, he knew in his heart that the boy in front of him was a better swordsman, no matter what he might tell himself. The reality of his approaching death crashed down upon him.

Yet Killeran didn't have time to think much on his likely demise. Taking hold of the hilt once more, he raised his blade just in time, catching Thomas' steel on his own as he was forced deeper into the chamber. He continued to step back quickly, trying to avoid the burning wreckage dotting the room, his opponent's blade a blur. In seconds, the Dunmoorian lord had at least a half-dozen cuts on his arms and legs, the Highland Lord deftly avoiding Killeran's battered armor as if it were a game rather than a combat to the death.

Not giving the former regent of the Highlands time to recover, Thomas tracked Killeran around the room, never allowing him to disengage. His blade was lightning fast, lunges slicing through the weak spots in his opponent's defense. Only a minute had passed, yet Killeran already was out of breath, gasping for air, with blood trailing down his arms and legs, one of Thomas' slashes having sliced a long but shallow cut in his side.

"A moment," wheezed Killeran, as he came to rest with the wall at his back.

"A moment? I think not." Thomas continued his assault, blade whipping through the air. "For ten years you murdered my people. You ravaged my land. And you want a moment? This isn't a duel, you rat-faced cur. This is your execution."

Killeran stumbled, the multiple wounds beginning to take their toll.

"Please, I could help you," he cried miserably. "I can help you get Rodric and Chertney."

"I think not. I don't work with traitors."

Killeran made one last attempt to break away from Thomas, eyeing the passageway off to his left. But he was too slow. Thomas easily met each of the Dunmoorian Lord's lunges and slashes. Then, as Killeran attempted one more attack, hoping to force Thomas away from his escape route so that he could take his chances in the tunnel, he made his last mistake. Raising his blade above his head and feinting a swing down, he hoped to gain the space that he needed to slip into the darkened passageway and slam the door closed before the boy could follow.

But instead of stepping back, Thomas stepped forward, driving his blade through Killeran's chest like a knife through butter, the breastplate splitting in two from the force of the lunge. The Dunmoorian lord remained standing for a moment, his eyes glazing over before finally sliding off the Highland blade and falling back against the wall in a puddle of his own blood. His breaths became more labored with each passing second, bright red bubbling from his lips. And then it was over. The former regent of the Highlands, the man who had inflicted so much terror and misery on the Highlands, was no more.

Thomas stood there for several minutes, looking down on the man who had terrorized the Highlands for so long, who had tortured him when he was a boy. He thought that he would feel some satisfaction for taking his vengeance on the one who had caused him and his people so much pain. But all he felt was regret, knowing that there was still so much more to do.

CHAPTER TWENTY SEVEN

BLACK GLASS

"This plan worries me, Corelia. Malachias worked with my father from the very beginning to put me on the Fal Carrachian throne. It didn't turn out as he promised. Therefore, I see no reason to trust him."

Corelia Tessaril, daughter of the High King, smirked as she couldn't help but notice the resentment dripping from Maddan Dinnegan's voice. Once Maddan's father had been the richest noble in all the Kingdoms, but that had not satisfied him. He had wanted more. So much more. In Norin Dinnegan's mind, wealth was synonymous with power, yet in his own Kingdom his riches could only take him so far. There was an obstacle that needed to be removed if he were to attain what he desired. Thus, his father's fateful decision to assassinate Gregory Carlomin, King of Fal Carrach, believing that success with that endeavor would allow the Dinnegans to take control of the throne through Gregory's daughter Kaylie. The failed assassination and collapse of the plot that included Kaylie's kidnapping had destroyed the Dinnegan house. Their properties and wealth in Fal Carrach had been seized by the crown with a price put on the heads of both the father and the son.

"I doubt your failure resulted because of Malachias' involvement." Corelia's insinuation was clear, but Maddan chose to ignore it, despite the quick surge of anger that burned in his chest. He didn't like it, but he knew his place with the High King's daughter, at least for now. Though he didn't trust Corelia, he had little choice. If he was to rebuild his family's fortunes and gain the prize that he so desperately wanted, he would need Corelia's assistance.

"That's unfair," replied Maddan, feeling the need to defend his family's honor.

"Fair and unfair are simply matters of perspective, my dear Maddan," said Corelia, her smirk only growing, though her voice was deadly quiet. "We are allies, at least for a time. You don't have to like working with Malachias. You don't have to trust him. In fact, if you did, I'd call you a fool. But that is what we have right now. We will follow Malachias' instructions for he has given us an opportunity that we must capitalize upon."

"Still, is it wise …"

Corelia continued, ignoring Maddan, his complaints having become wearisome. "We will expect him to betray us. But if he brings us closer to our objectives, then it's a risk that we will take. Now get out. I don't have the patience for you to continue wallowing in your self-pity. I need to think."

"Corelia, you must …"

Corelia slapped Maddan across the jaw, the crack echoing in the small cabin. "You must remember who is in charge, my dear Maddan."

Maddan rubbed at his burning cheek, the imprint of Corelia's hand visible. "If you ever …"

"If I ever slap you again, you will do nothing," she declared imperiously. "You'd need to grow a spine first. Now get out!"

Maddan stared at Corelia with hateful eyes a moment longer, then he heaved himself up off the floor where he had fallen more from the shock of Corelia lashing out than the actual strike and scuttled out of the room, slamming the door behind him in a final act of useless disobedience.

With Maddan's exit, Corelia's thoughts turned to her last meeting with Malachias and the question with which he had challenged her.

"Is your alliance with the Dinnegan boy worth it?" the black-robed Malachias had asked, his scratchy voice setting her teeth on edge and his putrid breath almost knocking her to the floor.

She had wondered then, doubting the value of the alliance. After the last few minutes of wasted time, her doubts had increased tenfold. But what was she to do? Maddan still had a role to play, one that could benefit her.

She pushed her uncertainties to the side, remembering her response to the cadaverous creature that terrified her, his hypnotic, black eyes seemingly burrowing into the very depths of her soul, pulling out her greatest fears and her greatest desires.

"For the time being," she had said, trying to insert as much confidence in her response as possible. "Why are you here now? I thought our business was concluded at least for the time being."

"Our business will never be concluded, Corelia, until we both get what we want."

"Then why are you here?" Corelia attempted to present an image of strength, yet Malachias unnerved her, making that task exceedingly difficult. She could barely keep her body from shaking.

"I have the information you need to begin your work," replied Malachias, grinning evilly, knowing how he made the girl uncomfortable and enjoying every second. "You will have your chance. Make the best of it. The boy needs something. He will go in search of it. That's when you can strike."

"How do you know he needs to find something?"

"Because I used to possess it. I know its value. He knows its value as well."

"That's all well and good, but how am I to …"

"There is a ship waiting for you in the harbor. It will leave on tomorrow morning's tide. I suggest that you be on it. It will take you where the boy will be. And with just a little luck, you can set your trap."

Try as she might, she couldn't escape the premonition of danger, of death, of something worse, that had settled within her after that last conversation with Malachias. She looked down at her right hand in surprise. She had pulled out the choker Malachias had given her, her thumb rubbing absently across the black onyx that glittered like glass. The necklace mesmerized her as she ran the links of burnished black stone through her fingers. The glints of bright sunshine coming through the porthole sparked off the necklace and dazzled her eyes.

Had she made the right decision? Should she have stayed with her father in Eamhain Mhacha rather than bowing down to Malachias' suggestion and her own intuition? And if she had remained in Armagh's capital, would she have had the opportunity to use the necklace to her advantage and make the Highland Lord her own?

Perhaps. But perhaps not. He would have been wary. Suspicious. She had sensed it in him when they had spoken that last night of the Council of the Kingdoms. She doubted that she could have gotten close to him if he had, indeed, decided to return to Eamhain Mhacha in search of her father. No, she had done the right thing, leaving Armagh's capital when her father sent General Brennios to the eastern border. She knew without a doubt that her father would lose the Kingdom. There was a power in the Highland Lord, a strength not seen in others, and one that she desperately wanted to make her own.

But she also knew that if she had stayed, she would not have control over the situation when the fortress fell. And she needed to have control if she were to succeed with her plan. Better to be patient. Better to wait for the perfect opportunity.

So she would bide her time until circumstances favored her. She would have one chance with the necklace, and she could not afford to fail, not with the potential consequences, both good and bad.

Besides, she was skeptical that her father even knew that she had slipped out of the fortress and found a ship to Mooralyn, and from there to where Malachias had told her to go. She had seen the madness in his eyes. He cared only for the power that he sought. He had never loved her. Rather, he had only seen her as another tool to be used.

So be it. She had learned to do the same and would continue to do so. Although the realization that her father could lose their Kingdom made her ill, she took solace in the fact that if she succeeded, she would set herself on a path to gain all the Kingdoms.

CHAPTER TWENTY EIGHT

RENEWED PURPOSE

Toreal, chamberlain of the Keep at Eamhain Mha-cha, had mastered the art of survival, which explained why he had served in his position for more than three decades despite Rodric Tessaril's violent, and often deadly, moods. Quite simply, the competent chamberlain knew when to be present and when to disappear. Therefore, when he discovered that the fortress was under attack, he did what he normally did when Rodric was looking for a target for his anger. He hid. Unfortunately, the small man with a bald pate, bushy mustache, and deep set, mournful eyes did not conceal himself well enough. The Marchers found him in a storeroom on the first floor as they swept the castle for any stragglers or would-be heroes.

"You know who I am?"

Thomas stood in front of the obscenely large Armaghian throne, Rynlin and Oso positioned behind him. Thomas refused to occupy the same seat Rodric had once graced.

"Yes, my lord."

"Good. Then you know I already rule another King-dom. I have no desire to acquire a second one."

"You don't, my lord?" asked Toreal, his surprise and confusion evident. In his experience with Rodric and the High Kings before him, they had only one desire — more power. And if you obtained more power it meant that you did so at a rival's expense, strengthening your position even more. That was the goal. The only goal in the game played by kings and queens.

"No, I'll let the Council of the Kingdoms decide who shall rule this Kingdom."

"You don't want Armagh for yourself?" Toreal was taken aback, still trying to fathom what he had just heard.

"No, I came here for Rodric. He ravaged the High-lands through a surrogate for a decade and then attacked my Kingdom." Thomas' green eyes blazed, his anger ob-vious though controlled. Toreal noted that everything about the Highland Lord was controlled. "Moreover, he's in league with the Shadow Lord. There's a price to be paid for such treachery. I owe him a debt, and I mean to repay that debt."

Toreal rose to his full though not imposing height, the stoop of his shoulders and cringing manner disappear-ing. Although he wasn't a tall man, the change in posture was an improvement, giving him an unexpected confi-dence and the appearance of proficiency. His allegiance was to his Kingdom, to Armagh, not to Rodric. If Rodric truly was gone and on the run, perhaps something could be done to ensure that monarchs such as those in the Tessaril line never assumed the Armaghian throne again.

"What would you have of me, Lord Kestrel?"

"Information first. Your service second."

Thomas, Oso and Rynlin all noted the immediate change that came over Toreal. Obviously he was a more than capable chamberlain, in that he had survived for so long under Rodric. Perhaps if the yoke placed around Toreal's neck by the former High King were removed that competence could become something more.

"Where is Corelia Tessaril?"

Toreal stared at Thomas in alarm. "She went to Mooralyn, Lord Kestrel." Before he could stop himself he blurted out what he had been thinking. "You don't mean to install her on the throne, do you?"

As soon as the words left his mouth, Toreal shuddered, taking a step back, his shoulders hunching in fear. What he had just said would have earned a lashing from Rodric at the very least, and he feared that he had overstepped his bounds with the Highland Lord.

Thomas smiled at him. "No. That would leave things no better than they are now. Probably worse, in fact. As I said, the Council of the Kingdoms can decide the next ruler of Armagh."

"That one could cause a great deal of trouble," said Rynlin. "She seems just like her father, but more confident and smarter. Describing her as cunning doesn't do her justice."

"Indeed, my lord," agreed Toreal, visibly relaxing when he realized that these Marchers, though frightening and powerful, were quite different from his former monarch. "She's more dangerous than her father, more devious. With the former High King what he wished to take was obvious from the start. With his daughter, you won't know what she wishes to take until she's taken it."

"An astute observation," said Rynlin. "How long have you served as chamberlain, Toreal?"

"More than three decades, my lord."

"Did you enjoy your service to Rodric as High King?"

Toreal hesitated. The natural inclination to guard his words after years of serving Rodric remained strong. But he chose to answer honestly, continuing to sense something different in these Highlanders. Besides, the tall one with the dark beard speckled with grey scared him. He felt certain that if he were to lie that one would sniff it out in an instant.

"No, my lord. I did not."

"And the others serving here in the Keep. Did they enjoy their service to Rodric?"

"No, my lord. They did not."

"Then why did you stay? Why not just leave?"

Toreal never hesitated in his response. "This is my home, my lord. Our home. We care about the city, about Armagh. Rodric was a difficult man to serve, but I love my city, my Kingdom, even when those ruling it are more interested in their own personal gain rather than helping and protecting the people of the Kingdom."

"Can the people here be trusted to do what is best for Armagh?"

Toreal looked at the tall man standing behind the Highland Lord. His eyes burned with an intensity that frightened him, but the chamberlain sensed no malice from him. He did sense power, real power, much as he discerned it from the Highland Lord. Still, he didn't fear these men. Despite having just met them, he respected them.

"Yes, my lord. If given the opportunity, they would do what was best for Armagh."

"And you, Toreal. If given the opportunity, would you do what was best for Armagh?" The Lord Kestrel's gaze remained fixed upon him, the question a challenge.

Toreal pushed his shoulders back, standing proudly. "Yes, my lord. I would."

Thomas nodded in satisfaction, acknowledging the truth in the chamberlain's words. "Toreal, in a few days I'll be leaving Eamhain Mhacha in pursuit of Rodric. The former High King, with the assistance of Lord Chertney, has reached a small army of Shades and Ogren that have snuck down from the Armaghian Mountains. Most likely he will be coming back here to retake the fortress. I won't let that happen. When I leave, several of the wounded Marchers will remain here to help you."

"Me, my lord?" exclaimed Toreal in shock, not understanding.

"Yes, you. You will administer Eamhain Mhacha. Make sure that the people are fed, that they receive the services they need. Make this city what it once was."

"But, my lord, I can't …"

The sharpness of Thomas' voice cut him off. "Toreal, you have been doing this for thirty years from the shadows. The only difference now is that you'll be doing it in the light. You said Eamhain Mhacha is your home. Its people are your people. Will you accept this commission?"

Slowly a smile spread across Toreal's face, the small chamberlain standing tall once more, feeling a weight lift from his shoulders despite knowing the many challenges that he faced.

"Yes, my lord, with all my heart. I will make you proud, my lord."

"Make the people of Eamhain Mhacha and Armagh proud, Toreal. That's all I ask."

CHAPTER TWENTY NINE

WILDCARD

"Can we trust him?" asked Thomas, watching the chamberlain leave with a new energy in his step, shoulders back, head held high.

"Yes, I believe we can," answered Rynlin. "He seems an honest man, and I think he wants to serve an honest ruler for a change."

"I believe him as well," said Oso, nodding his head in agreement. "His Kingdom comes first."

"Then let's turn our attention to the next task at hand," said Thomas. He moved to a table placed at the back of the throne room, a large map held down by knives, points in each corner, displaying Armagh and the surrounding Kingdoms.

"Aric led his Marchers through the tunnel Rodric and Chertney used to escape," began Oso. "When they reached the base of the keep, they were both gone, along with the small army of Ogren and Shades that had hidden there."

"How strong?" asked Rynlin.

"At least a few hundred Ogren. Aric tracked them for several leagues. They're moving to the southeast, likely toward where Brennios has placed his Home Guard in anticipation of an attack on Armagh's eastern border."

"Add that to the more than a thousand Ogren I found coming down from the mountains and heading for the same location," said Rynlin.

"And if these three groups link up?" asked Thomas, already knowing the answer.

"Then they come right back at us," replied Oso with a cold certainty. "We're too few to hold off that many for more than a few days, and it will take too long for Gregory and his Fal Carrachian soldiers to reach us."

Rynlin cut in. "So we fight here in Eamhain Mhacha, put on a splendid defense, but are gradually whittled down to nothing because of our lack of numbers. We die, Rodric has Armagh once more, and he can send his Ogren and Shades against Gregory when he brings his army across the border."

"That doesn't really appeal to me," said Thomas.

"Nor me," agreed Oso.

"All the while the Shadow Lord strengthens his forces in the Charnel Mountains in preparation for his attack on the Kingdoms," continued Rynlin. "We're already dead, and Fal Carrach and the Highlands are weakened. Not a pleasant scenario."

Thomas stood there for several minutes, studying the map in silence. The key was Rodric's army of Ogren and Shades. Remove them from the board and the game would change. He would have more options to choose from and fewer risks to worry about. So why not do just that? Why not make a move that Rodric and Chertney would not expect? And in so doing perhaps add a wild-card to the mix that could give him a much-needed advantage.

"As Rynlin noted, if we allow this scenario to run its course, Rodric wins. We lose, he retakes the capital, and then he just waits for the Shadow Lord to come over the Breaker before he ventures out to mop up whatever of the eastern Kingdoms' forces remain. That doesn't work for me."

"Then what do you suggest?" asked Oso, his hand massaging the hilt of his sword. Thomas knew it to be a nervous habit, his friend not liking uncertainty. The large Highlander preferred knowing what needed to be done, and then going out and doing just that.

"We change the game," replied Thomas.

"With our couple hundred Marchers, how do you propose we do that?" asked Oso.

"All in good time, my friend. But first, Rynlin, could you do me a favor?"

CHAPTER THIRTY

TRUE COLORS

The bedraggled, bone-tired, former High King rode his horse poorly, not paying attention to the grassy plain he and his small army of dark creatures crossed in search of the Armaghian Home Guard. The events of the last few days continued to haunt him. The loss of his capital and his Kingdom. His plans in ruin. All because of that blasted boy!

But he still could salvage the situation. He could regain what he lost. His eyes glinted with a feverish light as he struggled to maintain some consistency in thought, his mind turning furiously from one topic to the next with no semblance of order. Finally, some form of sanity returned. Mumbling to himself, he reviewed what he would do to all who had betrayed him during his ill-fated expedition into the Highlands. The pain and suffering that he would inflict on those who had failed him so badly and on those stupid enough to oppose him. Then his thoughts shifted to his new circumstances. He had revealed his alliance to the Shadow Lord prior to the battle against the Marchers and those traitorous Kingdoms that had declared their support for that upstart boy rather than him. Fools! Every one of them would pay the price for that disloyalty.

Yes, he had divulged the master he had served faithfully for more than a decade. But rather than feeling fear or worry because of that revelation, he instead felt lighter, as if a burden had been lifted from his shoulders. He no longer had to lie or dissemble. He was free to do as he wanted, act as he wanted. Besides, there were other advantages now that he had declared himself.

Rodric smiled grimly, looking at the monstrous Ogren as they trotted easily next to his and Chertney's horses, the Shades gliding in front of them. No one in their right mind would take on such a force. With his small host of dark creatures paired with the Home Guard, he could recapture Eamhain Mhacha with little effort. Then all he would have to do is wait. His enemies would come to him.

So what if that traitor Gregory crossed the border and threatened from the east? So what if the Desert Clans descended from the north? That insolent Highland pest and his Marchers had gained access to Eamhain Mhacha through stealth. That would not work again. Rodric would be prepared for any new trickery. Once he recaptured his city, he and his men would just have to wait for his master to get past the Breaker. Once the Shadow Lord did, the Kingdoms would be doomed. Rodric could ride to him in victory, earning the reward that he so richly deserved. The strategy couldn't be any more perfect. And if he could kill the Highland Lord somewhere along the way, then all the better. But if not, then not. The wretched meddler would die eventually. In the end, no one could stand against the Shadow Lord.

The only fly in his ointment rode next to him. Chertney had shown his true colors during their escape, and his lack of respect burned in the High King's gullet. That one would have to go if Rodric were to claim the prize that belonged to him. But that could wait until after he gained control of all the Kingdoms. He just needed the right circumstances to make it happen. First, though, he needed to find Brennios and the Home Guard. Then he could reclaim his capital and his Kingdom. Everything else would come together after that.

CHAPTER THIRTY ONE

DEEP COLD

Ragin Tessaril shivered, the brisk wind blowing across the top of the hill injecting a cold deep into his bones. He surveyed his surroundings for the thousandth time, hoping for some change, yet knowing that it was a useless wish.

He sat on a small hillock with a single, leafless, dead tree at its top, the branches twisted and broken. Sunlight was rare. In its place, a dismal haze covered the landscape, the greyish fog billowing and churning at the touch of the breeze. The smell almost overwhelmed him. For as far as he could see, a murky, black water surrounded the knoll and stretched off to the horizon. In some places the muck roiled, bubbles letting off a noxious, sulfurous odor that poisoned the air. In others, wide ripples would appear in an instant and then disappear just as quickly. Ragin had yet to see the creatures that disturbed the stagnant water, and he wasn't sure that he wanted to.

As the days passed, his anger ate at him, threatening to consume him, the rage roiling in his chest providing him with the little bit of warmth that could be obtained in this cursed place. Everything that he had worked for had been taken from him in a matter of minutes all because of an old man. He had prepared meticulously, accepting the demands of the Shadow Lord so that he could learn the ways of Dark Magic. Relinquishing his very soul in order to obtain the power to kill his torturer, the boy who played at the Lord of the Highlands. But all for naught, as the old man had prevented him from achieving his objective, from standing across from the Highland Lord and looking into his eyes before he killed him. And, as a result, here he sat in the midst of desolation. No food, no shelter, nothing but a frigid wind that never ceased, a cold that seeped into his very core, and a stench that made him gag if he breathed too deeply.

Ragin had thought that as soon as the old man closed the portal, he could create one of his own, mimicking what the Sylvan Warrior had done so that he could return to Eamhain Mhacha and destroy the scoundrel who had disfigured him, the boy who had given him a ragged scar on his face that had altered more than just his appearance.

But he had thought wrong. Because wherever he was, wherever the old man had sent him, Ragin couldn't touch the Dark Magic that the Shadow Lord had imbued within him. The power that had once surged through his body, that had given him hope and confirmation that he would gain his revenge, had been snuffed out like a candle's flame.

CHAPTER THIRTY TWO

NEW THREAT

Summoned by the pickets stationed on the western side of his encampment, General Brennios stood rooted in place by shock, momentarily speechless. His men had told it true, but he didn't want to believe it. High King Rodric Tessaril approached, a smile brightening the Armaghian monarch's face, and that snake Chertney rode at his side. That was not uncommon. What unnerved him was the army that followed at his back.

His friend and mentor General Chengiz had warned him that something strange was going on with the High King. Something that he feared put Armagh at risk. Killeran's influence had been bad enough, though Brennios had viewed the scheming Dunmoorian Lord as an opportunist and no more, something not uncommon in a royal court. Yet Chertney and that other counselor, Malachias, had proven much worse. There was a darkness about the two that seemed to ooze from their very pores. It had unsettled Brennios from the start, a sense of corruption and decay seeping into him every time he came into contact with the two interlopers. He had connected those two to the hidden power that appeared to be playing a role in the affairs of the Kingdom. That unseen hand had now been made crystal clear and more than justified his concerns.

Brennios watched in numbing silence as the Ogren came to a stop several hundred yards from his picket line, the Shades ordering the dark creatures to set up their own camp. For Ogren, that meant finding a place to lie down and rest, as there seemed to be little need in setting a guard. Who but a fool or a madman would attack more than a thousand Ogren? The Shades then drifted to a small grove of trees that offered some respite from the hot sun.

He had never come across dark creatures before, but he had always believed in their existence. There were too many stories from respected soldiers that he simply couldn't ignore. Ogren ate people, often indiscriminately. Shades fed on the souls of men. And all served the Shadow Lord. Much like Chengiz, Brennios was loyal to the Kingdom. He knew that Rodric was ambitious and that his morals were suspect if not nonexistent, but he had hoped that calmer, more experienced minds, such as he, Chengiz, and several others, could guide the High King and ensure a prosperous Armagh. Clearly, he had been mistaken, allowing his confidence in his own abilities to shield reality from him. He didn't understand until just then the lengths to which the High King would go to achieve his goals. Aligning with the Shadow Lord revolted him. It was a treasonous act. But what was he to do? If the Home Guard rebelled, the small army of dark creatures would make quick work of them. He needed at least five times his current strength to fight the thousand or more Ogren and Shades that had appeared before him.

Yet maintaining his allegiance to Rodric tore at his very soul. His Kingdom had to come first.

Brennios shook his head in disgust. He could do nothing now. But perhaps there would be an opportunity in the future.

"Sergeant," called Brennios.

A large man with a sword on his back and a spear in his hand hustled forward. He led the men responsible for guarding the western side of the Armaghian encampment, the soldiers now staring in disbelief at the mass of Ogren and Shades. Though the dark creatures didn't show any malicious intent toward Brennios' men, he knew what would happen if their hunger got the better of them.

"Yes, General."

Brennios looked the veteran in the eye. The Armaghian general saw that he, too, was unnerved by what he saw just a few hundred yards away. But just like Brennios, he had the wherewithal to maintain his composure as he performed the same mental calculations that his general already had completed.

"Triple the guard among the pickets. Our main concern may no longer come just from the east. We must think of ourselves first."

CHAPTER THIRTY THREE

New Story

Thomas stood in the Eamhain Mhacha citadel's main courtyard, the pitted stone walls rising above him, Coban and Oso at his side. The few hundred Marchers who had taken control of the fortress were arrayed around him. Toreal, Eamhain Mhacha's chamberlain, had suggested that the Highland Lord use the throne room for this gathering, but he had refused. Rodric's former throne, a gaudy stone monstrosity, disgusted him. And he had pledged to himself that he would not enter that room again until a new High King had been selected.

Besides, he preferred being out in the sun even with the chilly temperature that left the breaths of his Marchers frosty in the early morning light. When he raised his hands, silence descended as the Marchers' murmured conversations came to an end.

"My friends," began Thomas, his strong voice carrying throughout the enclosed space. "You have much to be proud of. You conquered this citadel in a matter of hours. You have freed this capital from a servant of the Shadow Lord. And, perhaps most important, you have taken us one step closer to ensuring that the Highlands remain free from those who have sought to enslave us."

Cheers rang out from the assembled Marchers, many raising their fists into the air. But just as quickly the roar turned to quiet when Thomas raised his hands once again.

"But we still have more to do. Though Eamhain Mhacha is now free of the traitorous High King, as you know Rodric has escaped with a small army of Ogren and Shades, a thousand or more."

Taking hold of the Talent, Thomas crafted an image that appeared above the heads of the Marchers, offering a bird's-eye view of the column of dark creatures trudging through the grasslands. The beasts were marching west, back toward the Armaghian capital, followed by Armagh's Home Guard that had been stationed originally on the Kingdom's eastern border. Clearly, the soldiers of Armagh appeared to be more than just unsettled by their new allies. They appeared terrified, maintaining a distance of almost a half mile from Rodric and his small horde with a long line of cavalry on the nearest flank to maintain some protection against any Ogren or Shades that wandered too close.

"Fal Carrach and several other Kingdoms that fought with us in the Highlands come from the east," continued Thomas. "So we could stay here within the walls of Eamhain Mhacha and do what we can to defend against the onslaught to come, knowing that our allies would not arrive for at least a week once Rodric and his dark creatures lay siege to the citadel."

Thomas didn't need to tell the Marchers what that would mean. Other than the few hundred men and women in the courtyard, there were few others in the fortress or the surrounding city who could fight against the approaching enemy. They knew that. If they tried to defend Eamhain Mhacha, many of them likely would die, as they were too few to hold such a large fortress for long. They could run, of course. But then their efforts of the last few weeks would have been for nothing. That thought obviously didn't appeal to them. Thomas could see it all in their eyes.

"What would you have us do, Lord Thomas?" asked Aric, his voice confident and calm, suggesting that he trusted and would be pleased to carry out any decision made by the Highland Lord. The tall Highlander had served as the Kingdom's flagbearer during the battle at Anselm, and he had an unceasing faith and loyalty in Thomas after the Highland Lord had saved his life in the mines.

Thomas smiled. Aric's look of quiet determination could be seen on all the men and women standing in the courtyard.

"We have been successful in our fight to free the Highlands because we have never wavered despite the circumstances we faced," said Thomas. "We have never hesitated to do what must be done, no matter the odds. But what I ask of you now you must all consider. For if we fail, our fate is sealed." Thomas waited a few moments for his words to sink in before continuing, his gaze capturing the eyes of as many of the men and women surrounding him as he could. "Rather than waiting here to fight an enemy that would eventually breach these walls, I propose that we do as we have been doing since our fight against the High King began. I propose we leave this fortress and take the fight to Rodric Tessaril. We attack."

Several shouts of support burst out from the Marchers, which quickly became a steady stream of cheers before the chant began. A chant that was becoming more and more common: "For the Highlands! For the Highlands! For the Highlands!"

The men and women standing around Thomas understood the danger presented by the High King and his dark creatures. They understood what was being asked of them by their Highland Lord, the risk involved. They also understood that Rodric Tessaril was to blame for the terror the Highlands had experienced for a decade, and they all wished to see the coward receive the just desserts that he so rightly deserved.

Moreover, many of the Marchers relished the plan that the Highland Lord laid out before them. The audacity made them think of the Marchers of old. Now they had the opportunity to create their own tale that would become a part of the Highland lore.

So what if the odds were stacked against them? So what if it seemed like their deaths could be the only result?

They were Marchers, the most feared warriors in the Kingdoms. And their young, determined Highland Lord had yet to lose a battle.

CHAPTER THIRTY FOUR

ASSURED VICTORY

Rodric had commandeered General Brennios' travel tent for his own. He sat there now within the small pavilion on a camp stool, staring at the map on the table before him, munching on the stew provided to him for dinner. The meal tasted awful, and certainly didn't meet the standards that he had grown accustomed to as High King. Normally he would have thrown a fit and then at least had the cook whipped. But his mind was elsewhere. He and his army were just a few days from Eamhain Mhacha, just a few days from retaking his capital and his Kingdom.

Rodric picked his head up upon hearing a disturbance at the entrance to his tent, then General Brennios pushed back the flap and entered. The soldier stood there for a moment, allowing his eyes to adjust to the darkness. Chertney sat behind Rodric in a shadowed corner of the tent. He appeared to be napping, but Brennios had no illusions of that. The man had powers that Brennios didn't begin to comprehend, and he had no doubt what Chertney would do with those powers if necessary.

"My king, a force has been sighted to the west," said General Brennios, bowing to the man who still believed that he ruled Armagh. "They fly the banner of the Highlands."

"How large?" asked Chertney in a scratchy voice, his unnerving eyes now open.

"Just a few hundred," answered Brennios. "And they come this way from the west. I assume that they are the ones who captured Eamhain Mhacha. They should be here by morning."

"No other threats to worry about?" asked Chertney. "Nothing strange? Nothing unexpected?"

"No, Lord Chertney. Our scouts to the east say that the Fal Carrachians are still days from our border. And there's been no sign of the Desert Clans to the north. Only these few hundred Marchers coming our way."

Chertney grunted in satisfaction, then closed his eyes once more. He sought to present an image of confidence, but on the inside his gut churned. His force of Ogren and Shades was large enough to destroy the approaching Marchers. But assuming that Highland brat was with his troops, preventing the boy from using his powers to decimate the dark creatures would fall to him. After Chertney's recent comeuppance at the hands of Rynlin Keldragan, he worried about what would happen if he were forced into a magical duel with the Highland Lord. He feared that he didn't have the strength to survive such a combat, but what was he to do? If he failed in meeting the demands of his master, his fate would be the same.

Rodric laughed with real pleasure for the first time in weeks. "The boy will make it easier than we thought with this mistake, coming out from behind the walls to challenge us. Our victory is all but assured. It shall be a battle that will be talked about for centuries in Armagh."

General Brennios stood there silently, allowing the High King his good humor. He didn't share his ruler's enthusiasm. He had heard too much about this Highland Lord to assume that any engagement with him would be an easy or straightforward one. And considering Rodric's allies, for the first time in his long career, he wondered if an Armaghian defeat now was more important to the survival of his Kingdom than a victory.

CHAPTER THIRTY FIVE

CALCULATED RISK

Deep in thought, Thomas walked the pickets that Coban had established when the Marchers first made camp for the evening. He understood the potential consequences of his decisions, the risks involved. But he also believed that those risks were necessary if his Marchers were to have any chance of success at defeating a force of dark creatures five times the size of his own, to say nothing of the potential involvement of the Armaghian Home Guard. As he whispered greetings and words of encouragement to the men and women on duty, drifting through the darkness of the night lit only by the quarter moon, he sensed a larger shadow standing behind him.

The hulking Highlander stepped forward. His steps appeared forced, his expression sheepish.

"Thomas, I need to ask you something," said Oso, concern clear in his voice. "What are you planning for tomorrow? We only have a few hundred Marchers and the Home Guard has several thousand soldiers, not to mention the Ogren and Shades. The Marchers are with you, they'll always be with you, but they're worried."

"I know, Oso. But we will not be fighting Chertney's dark creatures alone."

Thomas nodded toward the grassy plains to the northeast. In the dark, Oso could barely see anything. But then, after almost a minute had passed, he caught a dash of movement that flickered in and out in the dim moonlight. A small group of men and women rode slowly toward them.

At first Oso thought that it was a trick of the moonlight, but then he saw something that brightened his heart and made him smile. The riders sat upon unicorns, the animals' tall, sharp horns unmistakable. Though few in number, Oso knew that the Sylvan Warriors joining them would even the steep odds that they would face on the morrow.

CHAPTER THIRTY SIX

STRENGTHENING CONFIDENCE

The sun had yet to touch the eastern horizon when the Marchers began to prepare for the battle to come. Some rolled from their blankets, wiping sleep from their eyes. Others had stayed up through the night, keeping their thoughts to themselves as they sharpened their swords, spears, daggers and axes or checked the fletching on their arrows. A few stoked the embers from the previous night's fires, seeking to restart the flames so that they could prepare a warm breakfast for what promised to be a trying, potentially momentous day.

Many still wondered what the battle to come would bring, knowing the odds that they faced with the Armaghian Home Guard having joined, however uneasily, with Rodric's host of dark creatures. Yet when the sun finally kissed the sky, brightening the muted shadows of the early morning, the Marchers stopped what they were doing, awed and pleased by what they saw occurring before them.

Twenty Sylvan Warriors made their own preparations for the fight expected against Chertney and his dark creatures, sharpening blades, fixing armor and caring for their steeds. The Marchers were used to Acero, Thomas' mount, and Militus, Rynlin Keldragan's, but none of the Marchers had ever seen so many unicorns together before and were astounded by their size, the animals easily several hands taller than the draft horses that they used to plow their fields in the lower passes of the Highlands. Some found the unicorns' horns, thick at the base on the beast's head, then twisting and tapering to a sharp point, unsettling, as they imagined what that lance could do to someone unlucky enough to get in the way of a charge by the fearsome equine.

That was to say nothing of the Sylvan Warriors themselves. Thomas walked among them now, saying hello and thanking them for the aid that they offered. All gave off an air of competence and power, some menace and danger as well.

Oso recognized Thomas' grandmother, Rya, speaking with another woman of about the same size. The small woman sharpened a blade thinner than his own but just as long, then gracefully ran through a series of exercises to test its balance. Rynlin, Thomas' grandfather, laughed with a red-haired man who juggled small balls of fire in his hand, what the large Highlander assumed was a nervous habit before combat. And then his eyes took in a man larger than himself, which was saying something. Covered in leather armor, a massive battle ax on his knees as he ran a sharpening stone across the heavy blade, the warrior resembled a small mountain. Catal Huyuk. Oso remembered the formidable Sylvan Warrior and grinned when the mountain of a man nodded to him.

Oso saw that many of the Marchers watching the preparations of the Sylvan Warriors were just as enthralled by their new allies as he was, and with their smiles the Marchers' confidence grew. They knew the Highland Lord always had a few tricks up his sleeves, preferring to have options when addressing challenges so that he couldn't be forced to a single path. They also knew of his other obligation as a Sylvan Warrior, so it wasn't entirely unexpected that these Sylvan Warriors would appear in their time of need. But they had never expected to see this many legends come to life at once. For the first time since the Great War against the Shadow Lord, the Sylvana once more would ride into battle.

CHAPTER THIRTY SEVEN

CHANGE IN DIRECTION

Behind the front lines of the Home Guard, Rodric sat uncomfortably on his horse, his heavy armor weighing him down, essentially holding him in his saddle. He feared that if he leaned too far in a particular direction, he actually might slide off his mount into a heap of metal and be unable to rise from the ground without assistance because of the weight. Chertney had suggested keeping his host of dark creatures away from the Home Guard to prevent any mistakes or misunderstandings, such as an Ogren or Shade grabbing a soldier for a quick meal. Rodric had heeded that advice. So he had placed his dark creatures on the left flank and the Home Guard on the right.

He and General Brennios, along with Chertney, several aides and a small honor guard, remained between the two forces so that they could direct the battle and serve as a buffer. The nervousness of the Armaghian soldiers was obvious, most believing that they were still too close to the dark creatures for comfort. Most of the soldiers were of the same mind as their commander, wanting to have nothing to do with the dark creatures and the former High King. But they had little choice, having been informed that any who failed to perform their duty or openly disobeyed the High King's commands would be given to the Shades. That threat had immediately quelled the growing unrest.

"Brennios, stay with the Home Guard and keep them focused on their task," ordered Rodric. "They need to show some backbone and understand what can be accomplished with the aid of our new allies. Make sure the right flank holds and is prepared to sweep in as we discussed once Chertney's dark creatures have had their fun."

"Yes, my lord," replied the Armaghian general, his words clipped, his tone neutral. He struggled to keep the disgust that rose up within him from his voice. He had spoken with his officers and sergeants during the night. All had agreed that any attempt to resist the High King would lead to unnecessary bloodshed, the Home Guard too few in number to defend effectively against such a large number of dark creatures. Resigned to what was about to happen, he pulled on his horse's reins so that he could join his men. He was more than happy to distance himself from their new, unwelcome allies.

Satisfied that all was ready, as he watched the Marchers emerge from the forest a quarter mile to their front, Rodric frowned. He doubted that with so few to oppose him it would be much of a battle. Feared though they were, a few hundred Marchers stood little chance against the army arrayed against them. He chortled quietly to himself. The Highland brat, so confident, so certain, so successful, had bit off more than he could chew this time, and he was about to pay the price for his arrogance.

Rodric's confidence soared, but a tremor of uncertainty still flitted through him nonetheless. He was surprised that the Marchers had circled his host and now came at his forces from the east. With the sun rising behind the Marchers, Rodric raised a hand in front of his eyes to protect against the glare. He was having some difficulty making out what the Marchers were doing. Finally, he saw that the Marchers had formed into two lines, the second no more than a few horse lengths behind the first. Brennios had predicted that with such a small force, the Marchers would come forward in a wedge, making it harder for the Armaghians to bring their larger numbers to bear. But it appeared as if the Armaghian general's prediction had been incorrect. Rodric snorted in disgust. The man was a fool and would be removed from command once his opponents had been eradicated.

The Marchers started their mounts at a walk, then moved to a canter, then a trot as the ground in front of them evened out. The lines remained perfectly in sync as they approached the two separate, but supposedly allied, forces aligned against them. Surprisingly, the men and women of the Highlands came forward in silence, no shouts or words carrying across the open field, only the sounds of steel clattering and leather creaking carrying on the light breeze as the Marchers urged their steeds into a gallop.

"Brennios!" shouted Rodric over the rising thunder of the hooves striking the hard ground. "Release the arrows!"

Brennios was about to give the order as Rodric commanded, his archers standing ready just behind the front ranks of his pikemen and swordsmen. But he hesitated for a moment, not really knowing why. Perhaps his insubordination came from the roiling knot in his gut that had formed when Rodric had ordered him to march and fight with dark creatures. He was a man of honor. A soldier. How could he blindly follow a man seemingly intent on destroying the very honor of his homeland? As the seconds passed, Brennios breathed a sigh of relief, thankful that he had withheld the command to engage. The Marchers had turned sharply to their right, directing their charge away from the Home Guard and focusing solely on the mass of dark creatures. The Ogren noticed the change in direction as well. It excited the monstrous beasts, their prey coming within their reach that much faster. The dark creatures screamed and roared their battle cries, thinking that they would have a chance to earn some easy, tasty meat.

The shift in approach made Brennios smile in appreciation at the maneuver, understanding the value of the tactical change. As a military man he had to admire the discipline of the Marchers. What happened next made his eyes grow big first with shock and then with recognition.

Unable to see clearly beyond the first rank of charging Marchers because of the glare of the rising sun, he had failed to notice the size of the mounts in the second line of attack. But as the Marchers drew closer to the dark creatures, urging their horses to a gallop, the first line of Marchers tightened their ranks at the flanks and created more space between their mounts in the middle, allowing what looked to be twenty odd steeds from the second line to burst through to the front.

Brennios stared in awe and fear at the sight before him. The steeds were massive, dwarfing the horses of his men. And their horns! He couldn't believe his own eyes.

Unicorns! He had never imagined he would ever see such a thing. But if these beasts were unicorns, then the warriors riding upon them were not Marchers. No, they could only be something else. Something both exciting and terrifying. They could only be legends come to life.

CHAPTER THIRTY EIGHT

CHARGING FORWARD

Thomas watched with pride, the flag of the Highlands whipping in the wind, as he urged Acero, his massive, black unicorn, past the first line of Marchers. Rynlin and Rya came up behind him on his right and left respectively, and he glanced in each direction to confirm that all the Sylvana, their unicorns charging to the front and distancing themselves from the smaller steeds of the Marchers, had taken the lead.

Turning his attention to the host of dark creatures, he realized that their screams and roars had died down, replaced with murmurs of concern, the towering beasts milling about in trepidation. They still greatly outnumbered the men and women charging toward them, but they knew the stories as well, of the devastation and destruction wrought by the Sylvan Warriors, of the pain and terror to be experienced when the long horns of the unicorns slid through flesh and their hooves shattered bone. And they were now about to experience it for themselves.

Nodding toward Catal Huyuk, who rode next to Rya, the massive man, topknot streaming behind him, raised a beautifully carved horn to his lips that flashed brightly in the early morning sunlight. With a strong breath he blew a single blast that resounded across the plain. A blast that had not been heard in the Kingdoms for centuries. A blast that offered a promise. A promise of death and retribution.

WE HEAR.

Followed by another, the note clear and strong, traveling well across the grassy plains to the very edges of the Highlands and the Heartland Lake.

WE COME.

And then a third that made the ground shake even more than the charge of the Sylvana, the earth rippling as if an earthquake had struck.

WE CONQUER.

The dark creatures faltered, beginning to shove their brethren, trampling those who had fallen to the ground, many seeking a path to escape, the already tenuous control exercised by the Shades beginning to weaken all the more as the notes cascaded over them.

No more than seconds from crashing into the Shadow Lord's servants, the Sylvan Warriors who had some skill in the Talent grabbed hold, weaving the natural magic of the world among themselves, then using the horns of all the unicorns to magnify their power.

Reveling in the natural energy coursing through him, almost entranced by Acero's horn as it pulsed with a bright white light, Thomas focused his attention on the host of dark creatures swarming to his front. He released the power that surged within him, giving it a purpose, and spears of light shot from his palms to strike the dark creatures that stood before him. Other Sylvana followed his lead, though some had a clear preference in terms of their mode of attack.

Daran Sharban, the red-haired Sylvan Warrior, called blasts of white lightning down from the skies, destroying a dozen or more dark creatures with every strike and leaving nothing but blackened ground to confirm the result. His grandparents both released streams of white energy that ripped through the host of dark creatures, only charred husks remaining in the wake of their attack. Sylvana such as Catal Huyuk, who didn't have any skill in the Talent, lay about him with his massive axe, eliminating any creatures lucky enough to survive the initial onslaught.

The large host of dark creatures shattered like a piece of glass hitting a stone. Thomas and the Sylvan Warriors plowed through the horde, the Marchers following closely behind and eliminating any of the surviving beasts. As the blasts of power continued to rip through the dark creatures, slaughtering the Shades and Ogren, the angry blades of the Sylvan Warriors and Marchers extinguished what little resistance remained.

CHAPTER THIRTY NINE

HONORABLE DISOBEDIENCE

Brennios and his soldiers watched in awe and terror as the Sylvan Warriors charged to the front of the battle line, then blasted through the dark creatures with their unstoppable power. Yet despite their fear at the horrifying force displayed and the ease with which so few cut through more than a thousand dark creatures, all appeared pleased by the turn of events. They hated and feared the allies their High King had thrust upon them and clearly had no desire to engage a foe focused only on eliminating the dark creatures of the Shadow Lord.

Perhaps if those were Armaghian soldiers under attack, he would have adjusted his battle plan and come to their aid. But Brennios would not do so now, ordering his men several times to hold their position and to remain alert, in case they became the next target or, as appeared more likely, a dark creature seeking to escape the Sylvan Warriors' rain of destruction rushed toward them. If the Marchers and Sylvana wanted to annihilate Rodric's Ogren and Shades, who was he to get in their way?

"Swing your men to the left, Brennios!" Rodric rode up, Chertney at his side. For the first time Brennios saw something other than condescension or arrogance in the eyes of the High King's advisor. For the first time he saw a terror that threatened to overwhelm him. "You can take them in the flank!"

"We will hold here, Rodric," answered Brennios, refusing the command.

"You will do no such thing!" screamed Rodric, who noticed but ignored the fact that for the first time Brennios had not used his title. "You will attack immediately!"

Brennios' back stiffened. He smiled as he realized that he was about to jump from a ledge, consequences be damned. "As I said, we will hold here."

"You dare to disobey me?" Rodric spluttered out the words, rattled by his general's disobedience. He turned toward the men behind their commanding officer. "Arrest this traitor or I'll feed you to the Ogren!"

The soldiers around Brennios didn't move. They stood there in silence, anger and disappointment in their strong gazes, their expressions hardening.

"We are loyal to Armagh, Rodric." Brennios specifically dropped the titular head once again to demonstrate that their roles had now changed. "We are not allies to the dark creatures of the Shadow Lord. We have no disagreement with the Sylvana. If they want to kill your Ogren and Shades, we applaud them."

Rodric sat his horse speechless, stunned by Brennios' words, never expecting such a revolt. Finally finding his voice, he looked again to the soldiers surrounding the general, trying one more time to gain control over the rapidly deteriorating situation.

"Guards, take him!"

The soldiers around Brennios continued to stare at the former High King, fury in their eyes. A few finally moved, but not toward Brennios. Rather, they stepped toward Rodric and Chertney, swords drawn.

Recognizing the increasing danger, Chertney grabbed Rodric's arm.

"Come on, you fool! It looks like you've lost more than a battle today."

Chertney galloped away to the east, Rodric following after, despondent and in shock. The High King's reign in Armagh finally had come to an ignominious end.

CHAPTER FORTY

FREE

The battle concluded faster than anyone expected. The Sylvana wiped out the dark creatures like the surge of a tidal wave crashing against the shore, the Marchers eliminating those few Ogren and Shades that survived the initial assault. Not until they confirmed that every dark creature was dead did Thomas and Rynlin, followed by the Sylvana and Marchers, ride calmly and purposefully toward Brennios and the Armaghian army.

"General, you chose not to fight. For that decision I thank you, and I give you another choice."

"That choice would be?" The Armaghian general's eyebrows rose with concern.

"You may choose to surrender."

"And if we do not?" asked Brennios.

"Then what just happened there," said Thomas, pointing to the battleground and the more than a thousand dead dark creatures littering the ground, "will happen here."

Brennios gazed for a moment at the flag of white flapping behind the young man riding the massive black unicorn, the outline of three mountains and a raptor streaking down from the sky displayed proudly.

"You are the Highland Lord."

"I am," replied Thomas. "And you know who rides with me."

"I do," said Brennios. A bolt of worry shot down his spine at the sight of this grim-faced young man, surrounded by some very serious men and women who in a matter of minutes had destroyed an army of Ogren and Shades. He smiled in an attempt to hide his increasing nervousness.

"I never liked or trusted Rodric, but I was loyal to Armagh," said Brennios. "And I still am. I always thought that he poisoned his cousin to gain the throne, but it could never be proven. When Rodric forced his dark creatures upon us, we had little choice in the matter."

"I can understand that," replied the Highland Lord, his bright green eyes sparkling in the sunlight. "But you have a choice now."

"Yes, we have a choice now." Brennios looked at the several thousand soldiers aligned behind him, knowing that what he was about to do he did for them and for Armagh. "We surrender."

"Good," replied Thomas, a tight smile on his face, pleased that the day's carnage would come to an end. "A very wise decision."

Brennios was caught up in that smile, but he didn't take it for one of pleasure. The Armaghian general knew immediately that he had made the right decision, concluding that in the future he would never cross swords with this young Highland Lord. He had no doubt that it would go poorly for him.

Before Thomas could talk with Brennios about what would happen next, Oso appeared at Thomas' side.

"It's finished. Armagh is no longer a threat. The Highlands are free."

"The Highlands are free," agreed Thomas. "But we're not finished."

Thomas recalled the prophecy, turning his gaze in the direction of Blackstone. He could feel the pull of that dark place growing stronger by the day, but it wasn't time yet. Soon, though, he would need to make his way there. Very soon. But before that, there was still much to do. He still needed to find the Key.

CHAPTER FORTY ONE

MORNING LIGHT

On most mornings, the kestrel hunted. But not today. Today the raptor felt an unfamiliar pull. Its strong wings, spanning seven feet, propelled it a thousand feet above the ground. The white feathers speckled with grey on the bird's underside blended perfectly with the sky. When visible, the raptor was a dangerous predator. When hidden, it was deadly, shooting down through the thin air like an arrow, its sharp claws outstretched for the kill.

After ten years of oppression, the Highlands were free once more, and the kestrel sensed a new urgency. It flew swiftly, driven on by that energy, ignoring its instinct to hunt as it so easily could have done during its long flight. The world was changing and not necessarily for the better. Something was coming. Something dangerous, frightening.

After flying through the night, the raptor finally reached its destination as the sun began to rise once more in the east. Having crossed the Inland Sea and then the farms, grasslands, and copses of trees that dotted Dunmoor, it approached warily the city jutting out into the Heartland Lake, circling several times to confirm that there was no danger before drawing closer. It sensed the faint touch of darkness radiating from the citadel. But that feeling of wickedness was fading, much like when the scent of game went cold. Whatever evil had once lurked here was gone.

As the sun completed its rise, blazing across the water of the lake, the bright glare off the water lighting everything before it, the raptor alighted on the highest tower of the Eamhain Mhacha citadel. Squawking in victory, its shrill cry carrying throughout the keep and the city below, the kestrel turned its attention toward the northwest.

Many of the residents of Eamhain Mhacha saw the massive bird, believing that its appearance was appropriate, giving them hope. The kestrel served as a symbol of the role that the Highlanders had played in liberating them from the High King. But they didn't know that this was simply another beginning, not the end. They didn't know that the next step needed to be taken. War was coming from the north, a final battle looming. The kestrel knew, and it would be ready.

CHAPTER FORTY TWO

NEXT TASK

Thomas had learned a hard lesson during his first Council of the Kingdoms. With the passage of the centuries, many of the rulers had forgotten or gave little credence to the suggestion that the Dark Horde would once again threaten the Kingdoms. They preferred to think in terms of what was, not what could be, conveniently ignoring what could happen if the Shadow Lord's dark creatures once more marched from Blackstone and made it past the Breaker and into the Kingdoms. In fact, some viewed the Dark Horde and its master as nothing more than a myth, a story from the past to frighten children.

And those who did believe in the truth of that myth assumed that they had time before the Shadow Lord attacked. They understood that the pace of the incursions by dark creature raiding parties continued to increase, that it was a sign of things to come, but they hadn't quite gotten comfortable with how quickly the danger was proliferating.

Thomas knew better. And he sensed that now was the time to take the initiative. For the last decade the Shadow Lord had directed events from behind the scenes, using proxies such as Rodric Tessaril and Johin Killeran to advance his plans. Those proxies had been discovered and eliminated. But those efforts to reveal the truth had taken time, and time now was running short. That reality led to an inevitable, chilling conclusion. The time when Thomas was slated to face the Shadow Lord was fast approaching, faster, in fact, than he would like.

Thomas had resigned himself to the fact that he must fight the Shadow Lord, but to have any chance of success the prophecy decreed that first he must find the Key. Rynlin had spent centuries looking for clues as to where to locate the Key, redoubling his efforts the last few months, even breaking into the citadel in Eamhain Mhacha with his grandmother, but with nothing to show for that work. His grandfather had found traces, insinuations, new paths to follow. He pursued those lines diligently. Frequently, those trails proved to be dead ends. Or those roads led to other roads, and then to new trails and lanes, but never revealed a clear path that led to the Key, whatever the Key might be. What frustrated Rynlin all the more was that he had actually been there. He and Rya, as well as several other Sylvan Warriors, had fought against the Shadow Lord when he first appeared, answering Athala's call. But none of them had been privy to what she had done with the Key, as she was the first to learn of the prophecy and use its limited guidance against the Shadow Lord. An argument had raged among the Sylvana ever since the prophecy had first been revealed as to whether the Key was an actual key. It could be something else, some other type of artifact, or perhaps simply a concept or idea, for the ultimate purpose of the Key was to provide access to Blackstone, giving the bearer a way to work their way past the many deadly traps and dangers crafted from Dark Magic and laid out by the Shadow Lord to prevent his enemies from entering his city. For the prophecy said that the final battle with the Shadow Lord occurred there, within the charred remains of a once vast metropolis which now hid the Ogren, Shades and other dark creatures that made up the Shadow Lord's Dark Horde. Thomas believed that the Key had to be something tangible, something that could be found. Why he thought that, he couldn't say. It just seemed right. But what was it exactly? And where could it be?

Thomas and Rynlin had found a quiet place to talk, wishing to relieve the stress of their recent battle against Chertney's host of dark creatures. Moreover, they needed time to map out their next steps. Rynlin, as was his wont, had happily assumed the role with which Thomas was so familiar. That of pedantic teacher, as his grandfather spoke of the history that was most relevant to the challenge that they faced.

As Rynlin explained, Ollav Fola, the first High King, was also a Sylvan Warrior and had fought the Shadow Lord and his minions. Knowing the threat that the Shadow Lord presented, Ollav Fola gathered all the Kingdoms and led them into the Charnel Mountains, taking advantage of the time Athala, the first leader of the Sylvan Warriors, gained for him thanks to their dogged fight against the Dark Horde when it first emerged from the Knife's Edge and sought to cross the Northern Steppes into the Kingdoms, delaying the monstrous host, even pushing it back into the Charnel Mountains for a time.

The Kingdom armies and the Dark Horde fought among those cursed peaks for more than a decade, the Kingdoms often close to defeat. Yet each time it seemed that the end neared and the Shadow Lord was close to triumph, Ollav Fola led the Kingdoms from the brink of disaster to continue the struggle. Finally, the tide shifted. The soldiers of the Kingdoms destroyed more and more of the Shadow Lord's dark creatures, whittling away at his Dark Horde patiently and systematically. Ollav Fola proved victorious, defeating the Shadow Lord, but he wasn't strong enough to kill his foe.

The Shadow Lord's power was too great at what was then called Shadow's Reach, his last bastion, now appropriately named Blackstone. In fact, the stories said that the Shadow Lord could not be killed there unless the Well of the Souls, the supposed source of his Dark Magic, was also destroyed. Therefore, rather than seek what would likely be a pyrrhic victory that would severely weaken the Kingdoms more than they already had been after a decade of warfare, Ollav Fola and the Sylvana created a prison with their Talent, weaving their natural magic in a way that contained the Dark Magic of the Shadow Lord within the Charnel Mountains. And it was all centered on the Key. Though what the Key was the histories never said, Athala crafting the magical artifact and Ollav Fola employing it, both taking its secrets to the grave. Once used, the Key had been taken to the capital of Armagh for safekeeping but never revealed.

The Shadow Lord remained imprisoned in the north for centuries, and as a result Shadow's Reach became tainted by his evil, the once beautiful mountain city transforming over time into a wasteland of burnt ash and cinder as the Shadow Lord's Dark Magic poisoned the land. As the years passed, though the Shadow Lord was not forgotten, passing time softened the harsh memories of the past, and the reality of the evil of the north drifted into tales and fables.

So much so that even as the Northern Peaks gradually transformed into the Charnel Mountains, inhabited only by the remnants of the Shadow Lord's Dark Horde, the vigilance of the Kingdoms waned. As a result, only the Sylvana kept a sharp eye on the happenings in the north, ensuring that the Breaker, the Kingdoms' sole defense against an invasion from the north, remained strong, the First Guard standing atop the massive wall at least for a time.

It was because of the Kingdoms' short memory and indifference, the rulers of the various monarchies once more focused on fighting one another rather than the real threat, that one of the Shadow Lord's servants stole the Key with an army of Ogren and Shades slipping past the Breaker and sacking Eamhain Mhacha in the process. The creature, known as Malachias, returned to Shadow's Reach and attempted to free his master.

Led by the Sylvana, the Kingdoms quickly massed their armies and entered the Charnel Mountains once again, that event the beginning of what was to become the Great War. Knowing the urgency of the situation, the Sylvana forced Malachias out of Shadow's Reach and prevented him from achieving his goal. In the end, the Sylvana and the Kingdoms crushed the Dark Horde against the Breaker, gaining the Kingdoms a respite that had dragged on for centuries, but it had proven to be a close thing and had come at great cost.

Nevertheless, Malachias' efforts were not for naught. He succeeded in weakening the Shadow Lord's prison, allowing his master to once again touch the world. And the prison continued to weaken over time as the bonds of natural magic frayed with each passing year, the Dark Magic of the Shadow Lord's lair growing stronger in turn. As a result, it was only a matter of time before the Shadow Lord would be free once more and able to take revenge against those who had denied him the power that he had craved for so long. Judging by what was now going on in the north and the constant incursions of dark creatures into the Highlands and sometimes beyond, that time of darkness was almost upon them. The Dark Horde would march once more with the Shadow Lord in its vanguard.

It was also said that during the final battle of the Great War, right before Malachias escaped when the Dark Horde was crushed against the Breaker, he lost the Key. The Key that was the only opportunity the Kingdoms had to defeat the Shadow Lord and his Dark Magic. But who had pilfered the Key from Malachias and where it had been taken no one knew. Although the Sylvana had searched for the Key for centuries following the conclusion of the Great War, it had never been found. And with the deaths of Athala and Ollav Fola, they had little information on what the next step might be.

Following the lecture, all of which Thomas already knew, Rynlin continued his pacing, deep in thought. As he considered the challenge before them, the Sylvan Warrior recited the prophecy in an absent murmur:

> *When a child of life and death*
> *Stands on high*
> *Drawn by faith*
> *He shall hold the key to victory in his hand*

Swords of fire echo in the burned rock
Balancing the future on their blades
Light dances with dark
Green fire burns in the night
Hopes and dreams follow the wind
To fall in black or white

"Drawn by faith," Thomas exclaimed, his smile breaking out. "We have been worrying about it for no reason."

"What did you say, Thomas?" Rynlin had stopped, recognizing that his grandson pondered something, trying to put together a puzzle that offered more in the way of mystery than fact.

"Don't worry. I can find it."

"Find what?"

"The Key. I can find the Key."

"And just how do you expect to do that?" Rynlin asked skeptically. "I have researched countless tomes, visited dozens of libraries, spoken with every Sylvan Warrior who answered Athala's call, with little to show for it. Even what sparse information I pulled from the library at Eamhain Mhacha took me down a useless rabbit hole. I have still not given you the knowledge you need to …"

"I can feel it."

Thomas quickly explained that it was much like before he became a Sylvan Warrior. The pull that he felt toward the Pinnacle in the Highlands that served as the Sylvana's meeting place kept getting stronger when it was time for him to take the tests to become a Sylvan Warrior. So much so that he knew exactly the direction he needed to go, even if he wasn't quite sure where he was going and when he would get there. If he turned in the right direction, the one facing the Pinnacle, the pull grew stronger. The same feeling slowly had come over him again, but this time whenever he turned his mind toward finding the Key. It was faint, he admitted. Barely a touch on his consciousness, but still there nonetheless and gradually increasing in intensity. The mistake in examining the prophecy was to not connect the preceding line *Drawn by faith* to the one that referenced the Key. Finding the Key required faith.

"I know what we must do. What I must do," he corrected.

"Where is it pulling you?" asked Rynlin. His initial reaction was to be critical of his grandson's conclusion. But Thomas' logic made sense. And in all honesty, they had little else to go on. All his previous efforts at finding an answer had returned nothing of value, and he had no good leads to pursue now. So perhaps it was time to take a risk, to allow faith rather than logic to guide them as the situation became more urgent and the stakes increased.

"To the west. I'm not sure where, but I know I can follow it right to the source. Right to the Key. Whatever the Key might be. What do you think?"

"The prophecy points to you, so it makes sense," shrugged Rynlin. "Obscure just like any other prophecy, but it's all we have right now. Besides, time is not our friend."

"Whenever we spoke about this you said you believed that I would have to find a way to get into the Shadow Lord's domain and fight him there. The prophecy demanded it. Yet there was no known way to enter

Blackstone without being detected or killed. But there must be. So why not an actual Key, magical or otherwise, that would give me admittance? If I'm supposed to fight the Shadow Lord in his city, I must be able to find the Key in order to meet the requirements of the prophecy."

Rynlin nodded noncommittally, knowing that such conjecture was possible. Still, he was not entirely convinced. The Sylvan Warriors had bandied about the same concept for centuries, never reaching a conclusion that satisfied anyone.

Thomas saw that his grandfather remained skeptical. "Think back to some of our history lessons together, to what some of the other names were for the Charnel Mountains before they were called what they are today."

Rynlin rattled off as many of the names that he could remember while certain that he had missed a few.

"There was another," interrupted Thomas. "It wasn't an actual name, but comes from a myth you once told me about the Shadow Lord and how he supposedly first came to the world of man in the Burnt Peaks."

"Yes. Yes, I remember. Rising up from the *burnt rock* to announce his arrival to humanity."

Thomas repeated the lines from the prophecy. "Swords of fire echo in the *burned* rock, balancing the future on their blades, light dances with dark, green fire burns in the night, hopes and dreams follow the wind, to fall in black or white."

Rynlin quickly became angry with himself. It had been under his nose all these years, yet he had failed to put it together. Finally, he had confirmation of what he always suspected, that in order to fight the Shadow Lord, the Defender of the Light must do so in the Shadow

Lord's domain. He had suspected as much, but was still wary of stating it for a fact because of the lack of corroborating evidence. So why wouldn't the Defender of the Light have some sense of how to get past the barriers that might prevent others from entering that corrupted city? It was so obvious that he had just skipped over it. Rynlin mouthed several oaths, including many that Thomas suspected were so old that few had heard them before, except perhaps for Rya. Rynlin came back to himself, regaining control of his temper.

"It's a paper thin argument," said Thomas. "But perhaps for this to succeed, we must all demonstrate a little faith."

"Now we know what must be done."

"Yes, we do. I must find the Key."

CHAPTER FORTY THREE

SURPRISE

Gregory Carlomin, King of Fal Carrach, had prepared for the likelihood that the Home Guard would stand against his small army when it crossed Armagh's eastern border. During their travels from the Highlands across the Inland Sea and then through Dunmoor, tracking the southern bank of the Corazon River, on a regular basis Kaylie made use of her growing skill in the Talent to search the land for leagues around them. Each time, she found the way clear, Loris of Dunmoor apparently turning a blind eye, until they approached Armagh and discovered the troops arrayed against them. Several tense minutes had given way to smiles and handshakes. He had not expected a welcome from General Brennios and an honor guard to escort him to the capital. But once Brennios explained what had happened, it all began to make sense. His worries were put to rest when he saw that several Marchers were there as well to greet him and confirm the events of the last few weeks. For the most part Gregory was quite pleased. Thomas had achieved the overall objective with little loss of life or injury; nevertheless, once again Rodric had slunk away with Chertney with the assistance of the Shadow Lord.

Despite that frustration, any potential threat that the former High King presented to their efforts to defend the Kingdoms at the Breaker had been removed once and for all. Moreover, following Thomas' instructions, Brennios had moved the Home Guard farther to the east, in preparation for a move toward the Breaker at the appropriate time to join the other Kingdom armies.

All in all, the young Highland Lord had proven quite successful and efficient. Gregory had been less so in his attempts to convince his daughter to return to Ballinasloe. He had argued that he needed her there to rule Fal Carrach while he went to Eamhain Mhacha to settle matters with Rodric. His logic and contentions, though certainly legitimate and forming what he believed to be a strong argument in his own mind, never gained any traction with his enervatingly stubborn daughter.

Kaylie, sharp as a whip, knew that there was nothing that demanded her attention in Ballinasloe and that her father simply wanted to remove her from any potential danger, probably because of her penchant for ignoring his requests, such as her going off on her own without his permission to the Highlands to help Thomas defeat Rodric and the Armaghian army. As a result, her obstinacy and refusal to follow her father's instructions had led to several heated discussions between the two, all while Kaylie continued with Gregory toward the capital of Armagh, the capital that was now coming into view over the undulating flow of the surrounding hills.

Gregory understood that he could no longer treat his daughter like a child. He knew as well that with her training, both in the sword and the Talent, that she was in a much better position to defend herself. But still he worried, just as any father would. He acknowledged, if only to himself, that Kaylie's stubbornness could serve her well when she finally took the throne of Fal Carrach, assuming that she knew when best to apply it for her benefit and that of the Kingdom. But at the moment, it rankled him. Even the conversation Sarelle of Benewyn had attempted to engage him in regarding his concerns failed to assuage his worries. Gregory shook his head in resignation. There was nothing to be done now. They were approaching the city, and several officials stood in front of the gates waiting for them.

"Greetings, your majesties. I am Toreal, chamberlain of Eamhain Mhacha, and I welcome you to the city in the name of the Highland Lord." Toreal bowed deeply from the saddle, acknowledging each ruler individually.

"Well met, Toreal," answered Gregory, as they entered beneath the portcullis and made their way toward the fortress.

Sarelle took in all the activity of the residents. The last time that she had been here during the Council of the Kingdoms a pall had hung over the city. The streets had been empty, the few visible residents somber, as if they had been beaten down by poverty and despair. Only a handful of merchant vessels were docked at the waterfront. But no longer. Lively markets had sprouted in the squares. More traffic was coming through the front gates as farmers and merchants sold their goods and wares, and as they passed the harbor she saw much the same, many-masted trading ships carefully navigating the breakers that lined the entrance to the port. A once stagnant economy and people had become reenergized in a matter of just a few weeks.

She grinned at all that went on around her, seeing that Rendael had noticed it as well, and was also pleased by the transformation that had taken place so quickly in the Armaghian capital. Benewyn remained strong because of trade. If Eamhain Mhacha and Armagh once again had an open market, then her Kingdom stood to benefit, as did Kenmare.

"May I ask where the Highland Lord is?" Kaylie asked in a tight, much too pleasant voice. She had expected him to be here to greet them, but apparently not, and her pique at that discovery was quite obvious.

"He remains in the countryside, Princess, with his Marchers and some of our soldiers," replied General Brennios. "Although he destroyed Rodric's host of dark creatures, there are still a few strays that he's ferreting out."

"And you allowed him to do that?" she asked, her irritation plain. She would have thought that following their discussion after the battle in the Highlands, Thomas would be exercising better judgment now. But clearly not. "It's quite dangerous."

Brennios led his horse into the castle courtyard, hopping off as groomsmen ran over to take the reins. The chamberlain leapt to the ground as well, a spring in his step, and offered his hand to the Princess as she stepped down from her horse.

"A valid concern, Princess," answered Toreal. "But having met and seen what the Highland Lord is capable of, I'd suggest that his activities are only dangerous to those horrid dark creatures that continue to plague our lands. The sooner they're killed, the better."

"Besides," offered General Brennios. "Though I don't know the Highland Lord very well, from what I've experienced, once he sets his mind on doing something, he does it, regardless of what others might think or say."

CHAPTER FORTY FOUR

UNWANTED ACCOLADE

Toreal led them to a private chamber where they could wash away the dust and grime of their journey and then partake from a large buffet set up so that they would have space to talk. For there was much to discuss. Clearly, Rodric was no longer a threat. But what of his daughter Corelia?

Would Corelia remain in Mooralyn or would she attempt to stir up trouble? What of the Sylvana? They had played a major role in destroying the dark creatures. What could the Kingdoms expect from them in the future? Would they continue to assist in the northern Highlands and the Charnel Mountains?

What could they expect from the western Kingdoms? Would any answer the call to arms against the Shadow Lord? The consensus seemed to be no, but who could say. Perhaps some of the more ambitious western lords, in the less stable Kingdoms, would see this as an opportunity. Or in the alternative, perhaps they would remain focused on their own Kingdoms and objectives now that Rodric's sway had been broken and seek to fill the power vacuum themselves.

And what of Armagh itself? It served as a linchpin between east and west, but all agreed that the reign of the Tessarils had come to an end. Who would take charge? And what of the need for a High King? No doubt several current rulers would seek the honorific, if for no other reason than the desire to add to their own prestige.

"I think the answers to those last few questions are quite obvious."

The assembled rulers jumped a bit in surprise as Thomas walked silently into the room followed by Oso.

"My lords and ladies, welcome. My apologies for not being here to greet you."

"Thomas, you're covered in blood!" exclaimed Kaylie.

Thomas looked down, then glanced at his friend, realizing that they both wore dirty, worn, blood-spattered clothes, the dust of the road having covered them in a brown muck.

"Yes, but none of the blood is mine," replied Thomas with a smile, much to the delight of Rendael and Gregory, who both chuckled softly.

Thomas' comment only served to irritate Kaylie all the more. "Thomas, you cannot take such risks. You have a Kingdom to rule and ..."

"Kaylie, please, could we discuss this later?" asked Thomas. The smile on his face remained, but his green eyes were hard and flinty. "There are other things that we need to deal with first."

"Quite right," said Sarelle, patting Kaylie's arm to show her support for the girl, but acknowledging the necessity of addressing more consequential items first. She would need to have a conversation with Kaylie and perhaps help her better understand when such battles as she was about to fight with Thomas should indeed be fought and where. "You were saying that the answers to our questions were obvious?"

"Yes, the last few questions, at least in my opinion," he replied.

Oso had stepped over to the buffet, piling food onto a plate. He would leave the politics to his friend after several days of hard riding and fighting, only interested at the moment in filling his stomach.

"We had been considering the appointment of a temporary High King until a Council of the Kingdoms could be called," said Rendael. "Someone we could trust who could handle those matters that a single Kingdom couldn't and provide a strong face in the hopes of pulling some of the western Kingdoms to our cause."

"An excellent idea," said Thomas. "Though I believe the choice is fairly obvious."

"What do you mean?" asked Gregory, an unsettling feeling beginning to bloom in the pit of his stomach.

"It should be you, King Gregory, at least in my humble opinion."

Gregory stammered, trying to get his protest out but failing, never having considered the idea and not knowing what to say. But all the other rulers quickly agreed with Thomas' suggestion.

"I'm sure you can work out the details," said Thomas, in between bites from the buffet. "Most of the Marchers will be returning home to prepare for the Shadow Lord's expected invasion and continue to fight the dark creatures making their way across the Northern Steppes. With Gregory as High King, if only temporarily, then our individual armies can be merged into a single fighting force under his command to begin preparations to defend the Breaker."

"Where will you be going?" asked Kaylie, her gaze as sharp as a kestrel's, stopping Thomas in his tracks as he tried to take his leave.

Kaylie had listened closely to Thomas, understanding how his mind worked. She knew that Thomas had something up his sleeve.

Thomas sighed, turning back to the group. "I need to complete another task before going to the Breaker."

CHAPTER FORTY FIVE

HARD CONVERSATION

The conversation among the rulers continued for several hours, Gregory still reluctant to assume the position of High King but the other monarchs giving him little choice in the matter. Once that was finally decided despite Gregory's objections, it didn't take long to put the final issues to rest. Tired from his last few days in the field, Thomas bid them all good night, heading for the small room that he had been using since freeing Armagh from the Tessarils. Oso followed after, thankful to have finally extricated himself from the discussion.

"What is it that you need to do, Thomas?"

Kaylie had followed him out. He had hoped to make a clean escape, but should have known better. Kaylie was tenacious and would not let go what he had let slip.

"It's just something that needs to be done, and it's something that I must do."

Thomas didn't elaborate, much to her irritation. Noticing the keen intensity in her eyes, Oso decided to make himself scarce and go to his sleeping quarters on his own. He quickly bid them both good night and hustled down the hallway, glad to free himself from what he thought could become an extremely uncomfortable conversation.

"Perhaps you need some assistance? You know I'm good with a blade, and you saw what I could do with the Talent in the Highlands."

Thomas smiled at the princess, taking in her determination and courage. He was drawn to Kaylie, dangerously so, but didn't want to get too close. No one had ever survived a duel with the Shadow Lord, so allowing her beyond the emotional barrier that he had constructed around himself would simply put her in danger, something that he sought to avoid. He also needed to steer clear of anything that could distract him from meeting his responsibilities, and every time he gazed on her elfin face and dazzling eyes, his mind automatically wandered down a path from which he was finding it more and more difficult to return to the matter at hand.

"I appreciate the offer, Kaylie. I do. But this is something that I must do alone. And you have other duties to Fal Carrach." He turned to continue down the hallway, but stopped after a few steps.

"Thomas, if this is about Tinnakilly, I'm sorry. I've tried so many times to show you how I feel about you, how sorry I am for what happened, but it just doesn't seem to come through the right way."

Thomas' shoulders sagged as he faced her. He smiled sadly. "That's over and done with, Kaylie. You've proved your mettle several times over, the battle in the Highlands just one example. This has nothing to do with Tinnakilly. But as I said, this is something that I must do. It's a task that I've been given that only I can complete."

"You must do what you must do," said Kaylie, repeating the saying Thomas' grandmother Rya had used so often during her training and had become a favorite of her own.

219

Thomas smiled and nodded. "Yes, we must do what we must do." He spun and began to walk silently down the corridor.

"You know you can't keep trying to protect me, Thomas. No matter how hard you try. We must all take risks."

Thomas stopped suddenly, but didn't turn around, his chin dropping to his chest. "I'm not protecting you, Kaylie. I'm protecting myself." Then he stepped deeper into the shadows that danced in the hallway in time to the flickering flames of the torches lining the hallway until he finally disappeared from sight.

Kaylie watched him go, her gaze narrowing. His last words sent a flutter through her heart, and it took several minutes for her to regain her composure. She promised herself that he wouldn't get away from her so easily. Whatever was going on between them, it would not end before it had been given a chance to become something more.

CHAPTER FORTY SIX

SEARCH BEGINS

The night was colder than expected for this time of year. Then again, considering the stories that his grandfather liked to tell regarding the glacial cold during the Great War, a cold that froze exposed body parts to the point of shattering in just minutes, perhaps it wasn't unexpected with the Shadow Lord stirring. Of course, his grandfather did like to embellish. He always explained that it was a key part to telling a good story.

Thomas walked quietly through the halls of Eamhain Mhacha, not needing the dim light of the few torches lining the hallways to find his way to the stables. Acero had returned with the other unicorns to the Highlands. He would have preferred to take this next journey with his powerful, intimidating friend. But doing so would not allow him and his party to travel unnoticed, as the massive unicorn attracted too much attention and too many questions. Rather than a secret expedition, the journey would become a spectacle.

And attention was what Thomas wanted to avoid. The sand was running quickly through the hourglass, the urgency of completing this next task pressing upon him.

He had to find the Key, now somewhere to the west, the pull growing stronger, more insistent, every time he thought of it.

Thomas understood that fighting the Shadow Lord in a military confrontation only delayed the inevitable and led to countless, needless deaths. Better to do what he could to limit the pain and suffering expected when the Dark Horde descended on the Kingdoms. The only way to stop the Shadow Lord, assuming the prophecy spoke with any semblance of truth, was for Thomas, the Defender of the Light, to defeat the never defeated Shadow Lord in combat, destroying a creature that had existed for more than a thousand years.

Thinking about his small chance of success against the Shadow Lord threatened to paralyze him. Yet, even though he had resigned himself to his likely fate, as his grandmother Rya liked to remind him, and as Kaylie had noted earlier that evening, "You must do what you must do." Consequently, though his fear crystallized into a constant tremor in his gut every time the thought of his future confrontation played through his mind, he locked it away and sought to distract himself with his current challenge.

Taking a ship to the west offered the fastest way to get to the far side of the continent, but it would also be the most dangerous. Most ships avoided the Winter Sea this time of year. The seas were high and rough, often cresting over the masts of any vessel foolish enough to attempt a crossing. The cold added to the danger, as it could crack a ship's hull. To say nothing of the Whorl, a huge whirlpool that moved with the currents of each season. If caught by the Whorl, the ship would be pulled to the bottom of the ocean in minutes, and once in the

Whorl there was no escape. No one knew how to brave the Whorl, as no one had ever survived once captured within the swirling, watery maw. Yet there was nothing to be done but take the risk. Traveling overland would take too long and time was already short. But they still had a long way to go before they set their sights on the Winter Sea.

When Thomas entered the stables, he nodded, pleased to see that his group was ready to depart. A small band of Marchers led by Oso discussed final preparations while Rya and Rynlin stood to the side waiting for him.

His grandmother stepped forward, giving him a hug. "We wish we could go with you."

Even his grandfather, normally gruff in demeanor, grabbed Thomas into a bear hug. "We would, indeed, but we have other tasks to complete." He stepped back, looking down at Thomas with pride. "But we do have a friend here who has decided that you could use some additional help."

A black blur burst into the stables, leaping onto Thomas and knocking him to the floor. Scaring many of the horses, the Marchers rushed to calm the frightened animals. They likely would get used to the massive black wolf, a streak of white fur across his eyes, in a few days, but until then they would be skittish if not openly terrified.

"Beluil!" exclaimed Thomas, grabbing the wolf around his large neck for a hug, his massive furry friend licking his face in welcome and leaving a string of saliva across his cheek. "Tired of chasing after dark creatures, I see."

Thomas rose to his feet, running his hands through the wolf's thick fur. Both Rynlin and Rya felt better knowing that Thomas' boyhood friend would be with him on this endeavor. The two were inseparable growing up, and they knew that the wolf would do anything to protect the young man he viewed as his brother.

Rynlin watched the interchange between Thomas and Beluil with an amused grin. He desperately wanted to help his grandson, yet no matter what path he followed he was stymied. But that didn't mean he wouldn't keep trying. "I've been looking for any new clues on the Key, how to find it, more importantly how to use it, but no luck so far. If I learn anything, I'll let you know."

"Thank you, grandfather. I appreciate the help. But I doubt we'll learn any more than we discussed the night before."

Rya thought that she might have seen a small tear run down Rynlin's cheek. Thomas rarely called the dour, intimidating Sylvan Warrior grandfather, and it clearly had an effect on her grouchy husband.

Rynlin nodded, almost sheepishly. "Focus on the task at hand and you'll be fine. Leave the politics to Gregory. We'll meet you in the Highlands upon your return."

CHAPTER FORTY SEVEN

FOLLOWED

Thomas and his small band of Marchers made good time the first night upon leaving Eamhain Mhacha. Heading northwest toward Mooralyn, a port serviced by the Crescent River, they reached the sparse forests along the shore of the Heartland Lake before daybreak. After a short rest, they continued through the woods during the day, avoiding any well-traveled tracks or roads.

Thomas used the Talent to check around them multiple times during the day, finding nothing of interest or concern other than the odd woodcutter's hut. But as the sun began to set, Thomas took Oso aside.

"Can you sense it?" he asked his large friend.

"Yes," he said, looking back the way that they had come but not seeing anything hiding among the trees. Beluil sat there with them, staring intently into the woods. "But I don't get the feeling that whoever is following us is a threat. I think that they're just tracking us. Mimicking our movements and keeping their distance."

"Why do you say that?"

"Just a feeling," replied the big Highlander. "The back of my neck isn't prickling like it does when there's something dangerous around, like Ogren. Whoever it is, they're no more than a mile behind, but they're not trying to get closer. They've stopped just as we have."

"That's what you rely on to determine whether or not something's a threat?" chuckled Thomas, somewhat incredulous but trusting his friend's intuitiveness. "Whether the skin on the back of your neck warns you?"

"It's worked so far," shrugged Oso.

"Maybe so," answered Thomas dubiously, though he did agree with Oso's assessment. Whatever followed after them didn't fill him with an overwhelming dread as was the case when he searched for Ogren, Shades or other dark creatures. "But I still don't like the idea of someone coming after us and the fact that even though I can locate them, I can't tell who it is. Why don't you go ahead another league or so and then set up camp for the night. Beluil and I will catch up once we deal with whomever is tracking us."

CHAPTER FORTY EIGHT

MOVING PIECES

"This has been confirmed?" hissed the raspy voice.

"Yes, master. This comes from Chertney, who was loath to reveal the news but had no choice. Rodric has been defeated in Armagh, his army of Ogren and Shades destroyed by Sylvan Warriors, and he rides across the Northern Steppes now seeking refuge."

Malachias, no more than a shadow among the flitting wisps of darkness in the throne room of the Shadow Lord, avoided at all costs giving his master news of defeats or setbacks. He had seen the price that many of those messengers had paid in the past for being the bearers of bad tidings. But since this latest failure came at the expense of a direct rival, he felt more protected as well as an overwhelming need to drive the knife in a bit deeper. Besides, he couldn't resist the opportunity to put himself in a better light. He had served his master since well before the Great War, coming to his service not long after the Shadow Lord had appeared in the Kingdoms, and he had little patience for a rival such as Chertney or Rodric seeking to displace him.

The Shadow Lord, as was his habit, stood on the large balcony looking out on the deserted central square of Blackstone. Not a sound emanated in the dead city, other than the incessant wind disturbing the fine layer of black ash and cinder that covered the crumbling stone and ground.

"There is more, master," continued Malachias, trying to come across as disappointed rather than elated. "I'm afraid that Gregory of Fal Carrach now serves as High King. And our young Highland Lord is nowhere to be found."

The first was not unexpected, but the last worried the Shadow Lord, though his fleeting tremor of anxiousness could not be detected by his servant. His plans, centuries in the making, were not progressing as he expected or as they should. There were only a few more hands to be played in the game that he had started so long ago, and he could not allow the boy, the boy Rodric should have murdered a decade ago, to continue to unhinge his schemes.

Moreover, with this latest news about the Highland Lord, he had an inkling of what the boy might be doing. Looking for something that had been stolen from him that even his minions had failed to find despite having centuries to complete the task. That's what truly worried him. Not the fact that Rodric and Chertney had failed again. Not that a new High King had been selected. Those issues could be dealt with. No, his concern lay with this surprisingly resilient Highland Lord. The boy was too full of surprises and more often than not had turned difficult situations or expected defeats into victories. Would such be the case once again? Would he find what had been lost for centuries?

The Shadow Lord had tried to remove the Highland Lord as a piece in the game, employing the time-honored tactic of assassination. But to no avail. His Nightstalkers, though specifically bred for such a task, had failed miserably. As had the other servants he had sent against the boy. Therefore, he had felt the need to try something different. So he had placed an adversary in front of this young upstart that he thought even the boy, slippery as an eel though he may be, could not escape. Yet the Wraith had failed, at least initially. Although that dark creature had been defeated, it would continue its efforts. It was much like a Nightstalker in that respect, hunting its prey until it proved successful. But knowing the history of these failed attempts, he decided that something more was necessary. He was not yet ready to admit that the prophecy spoke true, that the inevitable would occur and that the boy would stand in the hall stretching out behind him, sword in hand, to engage in the last battle. No, he was not yet ready to accept that conclusion. If he could eliminate the boy before the prophesied combat, then all the better. It would make the prophecy moot. And if not, perhaps one of the attempts on his life would weaken the boy and ensure that the duel was a foregone conclusion.

"Thank you for the news, Malachias, disappointing though it may be." The Shadow Lord turned toward his servant, his blood-red eyes, burning harshly, infecting Malachias with a fear that he rarely felt. "And next time, try not to be so jubilant at the failures of your rivals. All of my servants will get what they deserve in the end."

"Yes, master."

Malachias bowed, keeping his eyes on the tiled floor, massive white stones abutting black, much like a chess-board. He chose not to consider the full implications of the Shadow Lord's last comment.

"We will focus our attention on the Highland Lord. Visit with our friend once more and impress upon him the need for swift and certain action."

"Yes, master."

"But before you go, tell me again," demanded the Shadow Lord, the harsh whisper of his voice alarming Malachias, sliding into him like a knife into the gut. "Tell me again of when you lost the Key."

CHAPTER FORTY NINE

DISCOVERED

Kaylie was pleased with herself, certain that she had gotten off to a good start in her efforts to follow Thomas. She had escaped her rooms without her guards any the wiser, despite her father asking them to keep a close eye on her. Not even Kael Bellilil, who had sniffed out her plan when the Fal Carrachian army marched toward the Highlands just a few months before to support the Marchers against Armagh, had caught wind of her latest attempt to escape her responsibility and connect with Thomas. She saddled her horse and exited the stables, and then the city, with no one aware of her subterfuge, except perhaps the soldiers at the gate. But at that time of the morning, the sun still a distant thought, they likely had no clue as to the identity nor cared about the doings of the cowled noblewoman seeking an early start to the day.

Breaking free from the confines of Eamhain Mhacha, she had led her horse quietly through the forest. Although Kaylie knew that her education in the use of the Talent was far from complete, she had learned many useful skills thanks to Rya Keldragan's assiduous training. One such ability that Rya thought necessary for her to learn after her attempted kidnapping by Norin Dinnegan was how to infuse a small stone with the natural magic of the world, an almost imperceptible amount that someone versed in the Talent would not be able to identify unless they knew to look for it, but could be used as a tracking device.

In effect, Kaylie could follow her quarry at a safe distance and not have to worry about discovery. Actually depositing the stone in one of Thomas' pockets had been easier than expected when she confronted him in the hallway the night before. She had used his distraction with what he needed to do to her advantage.

Yes, indeed, she was quite pleased with herself as the afternoon's shadows began to lengthen in the woods, signaling that the day was coming to an end. At least she was until her horse reared up unexpectedly, whinnying in terror. She struggled to stay on, holding desperately to the high horn of her saddle, before finally regaining control of her mount after several frantic seconds. A massive black wolf barred her path, teeth bared, a growl emanating from deep in his throat.

"Beluil, what are you doing?" she demanded, her voice cross. "You have no right to scare me like that. Bad wolf. You're a very bad wolf."

Kaylie's admonition didn't seem to faze the huge wolf, its black fur fading in and out of the early evening shadows. He sat on his haunches, a sly grin displaying his sharp teeth. The wolf seemed to relish watching her scramble to maintain control of her frightened horse.

"He's doing what he's supposed to be doing," said a quiet voice that came from among the trees behind her. Thomas stood there deep within the gloom, the tone of his voice suggesting that he was clearly displeased. "What are you doing here, Kaylie?"

She didn't respond for almost a minute. Not because her horse continued to fight her, trying to get as far away from the black wolf as possible. But because she didn't know what to say, never having expected to be caught so soon and not yet having prepared for this moment. She thought that she'd have at least a few more days to work out her story. In the end, she decided to tell Thomas the truth.

"I didn't think you'd let me go with you from the start, so I thought that I'd join you later," Kaylie said, trying to infuse as much of a sense of command in her voice as would be expected of a Fal Carrachian princess, but finding the task difficult as her horse continued to struggle against her attempts to calm it. "When you couldn't stop me." That last came out as a reluctant mumble.

Thomas stepped out of the shadows and grabbed hold of her mount's reins, placing a hand on the frightened horse's neck. In seconds, the horse settled, its terrified, rolling eyes now calm, placid.

"How did you do that?" asked Kaylie.

"A topic to discuss at another time," replied Thomas. "We're only a day from Eamhain Mhacha. I could send you back."

"No, you can't. I am the Princess of Fal Carrach, and I will decide where I go and when."

"Princess you may be, Kaylie, but do you understand the consequences of this decision? Do you have any idea what we're doing? The danger involved?"

"Well, no. I don't really know the details," Kaylie admitted sheepishly. "But Thomas, I need …"

"You need? What you need is of no consequence. You have no understanding of what we're seeking to accomplish, yet you feel the need to force your way into our group?"

"Thomas …"

"To say nothing of your father. He knows what we're about. He knows the threats and dangers we face. I have no doubt that he doesn't want you anywhere near us."

Kaylie dismounted, grabbing her horse's reins from Thomas and stroking its face gently to keep the mare calm. She turned her beseeching eyes on the angry Highland Lord.

"Thomas, please. I understand. I do. It was unfair of me to think that you'd welcome me with open arms. And you're right, I don't know the full extent of what you seek to do. I haven't been privy to those conversations. But please. I need to do this. I need to prove to myself that I can do this. I was raised a princess. I will always be a princess. Some day I will be a queen. But I cannot lead my people, I cannot do my duty to Fal Carrach, if I can't first prove to myself that I can do this. That I'm more than just someone born to privilege. I can't ask the people who will rely on me to do what's needed if I don't first prove to myself that I can do the same."

Thomas bit back his sharp retort, not expecting such honesty or earnestness. He examined Kaylie, his eyes flinty. To her credit, she refused to wilt under his gaze, her eyes fixed on his, her back straight.

"That I can understand," he sighed, shaking his head, in resignation or exasperation Kaylie couldn't say.

It might have been both. "Come on. We'll let the others decide."

Thomas was about to step back between the trees to get his own horse when a growl from Beluil stopped him in his tracks.

"Thomas, what is it?" asked Kaylie, noticing the unnatural darkness that had settled over their section of the forest, a darkness that had nothing to do with the oncoming night.

"I'm not sure," he replied. "But it's nothing good."

The rumble of Beluil's growl grew deeper, the large wolf rising from where he sat and taking a few steps to the west, his hackles raised. Taking his friend's lead, Thomas took hold of the Talent, searching in the direction upon which Beluil had focused his attention.

There. Just a few hundred feet in front of them and getting closer. The faint stench of evil approached, but so imperceptible that Thomas feared that if he turned his concentration elsewhere even for just a second that he would lose it altogether.

"Kaylie," he said quietly. "Whatever it is, it's coming from the west. Check around us and make sure nothing else approaches, particularly from behind us."

Kaylie nodded, but she wasn't sure that Thomas could see her acknowledgement in the encroaching dark. Reaching out with the Talent, she scanned the surrounding forest for several leagues around them. There was nothing there, at least nothing to worry about. She couldn't even detect whatever danger Thomas and Beluil had identified, though she had located the Marcher camp a league to the west.

"Nothing," she said.

"Good. Well done." Thomas kept his attention fixed on the west. "I don't know what's coming toward us, but it will be here soon. Take your horse over there and stay among the trees. Be ready for when I need you."

Kaylie did as Thomas requested, leading her horse between the trees to the east. She maintained her hold of the Talent, hoping that she interpreted correctly what Thomas had in mind. Thomas and Beluil remained where they were in the center of the small clearing, seemingly rooted to the ground. An unnatural silence had fallen over the forest, the noise of the nighttime animals disappearing as the evil approached.

They didn't have long to wait. After just a few minutes more passed, Kaylie picked out a cowled shadow emerging from the strange gloom. She could sense the evil that issued from the figure that stood facing Thomas and Beluil, but only just. It was muted for some reason, barely registering compared to what she experienced when opposing Ogren, Shades and other dark creatures.

"After our last encounter," began the cowled figure, it's voice cracked, apparently masked, so that it wouldn't give away its identity, although it was clearly the voice of a man, "I didn't expect to catch you unawares a second time."

Thomas nodded, one hand on Beluil's shoulder as if to hold him back, the large wolf growling deeply, its paws poised beneath him so that the massive animal could leap at the intruder. "The Crag."

"The Crag."

The silence deepened, Thomas and the shadowy form staring at one another. Then in a flash of black deeper than the night, shards of energy blasted toward Thomas. In response, Thomas immediately formed a shield of white light that was large enough to protect him and Beluil, the deadly slivers glancing off the barrier harmlessly, the bright brilliance of the Talent illuminating the surrounding forest and turning night into day. But that was only the beginning of the attack. Following the shards of black energy came bolts of Dark Magic which elongated into spears. The warlock threw so many at Thomas at one time that the spears appeared to be a single streak of black surging toward him. None were able to break through the barrier Thomas had constructed, so the cowled figure finally settled on two streams of midnight-black power shooting from his hands.

Kaylie watched in amazement. Thomas appeared calm and collected despite the onslaught, maintaining his hold on the Talent to defend against the Dark Magic thrown against him. But she could see that he had to split his focus between his attacker and Beluil, who was intent on launching himself at their assailant but was unable to do so because of the shield. Despite the black wolf's strength and courage, she had no doubt about what would happen to Beluil if he slipped by Thomas' defense and was struck by their attacker's Dark Magic.

She had to do something before that happened. But what? Then she remembered her most recent lesson with Rya. In an instant the forest grew even brighter as spears of white light shot from Kaylie's hands, aimed toward the cowled figure who was so intent on Thomas that he didn't bother to check the surrounding woods for any threats.

Their attacker rolled out of the way, shocked, barely escaping Kaylie's unexpected attack. The robed assailant formed a shield of black energy just in time to stop a stream of white light that flowed from Thomas' hand from burning him to a crisp. Kaylie continued her assault as well, spears of white energy joining Thomas' flow to slam against their attacker's shield. The blinding power was so strong and intense that it began to eat away at the shield's edges, forcing the assassin deeper among the trees.

Recognizing the untenability of his position, the cowled figure pulled in more of the Dark Magic gifted to him by his master, using some to maintain his shield, but applying the bulk toward what Thomas had expected to see. In a recurrence of what had happened at the Crag, the cowled man formed a portal of spinning black mist. Once it was large enough, he stepped through, then released his hold on the Dark Magic so that the gateway snapped shut behind him, and with it went the unnatural darkness that had covered that part of the forest.

Both Thomas and Kaylie released their holds on the Talent, Beluil charging forward to where he had last seen their attacker, turning his nose up in disgust as the reek of corruption lingered.

"Well done," said Thomas.

Kaylie could only nod, never having experienced such a rush of adrenaline before. She struggled to control the fear and excitement that mingled and danced within her.

"You see the danger that we face now," said Thomas, his voice firm. "The Shadow Lord will do all that he can to stop us. You can still head back."

Kaylie stared back at Thomas, his green eyes unyielding and glowing brightly in the night. "No. No, I want to do this. I need to do this."

"I thought as much," said Thomas with a tight grin, nodding. "Let's go."

After remounting, they caught up to Oso and the other Marchers at the camp they'd established for the evening. Oso seemed to have expected who their guest might be, but he chose not to say anything. Thomas circled his Marchers around and explained the situation, allowing them to make the final decision regarding the runaway princess. He would fill in Oso on the excitement of the evening later.

It proved to be a short conversation. All had fought in the Highlands against Rodric and the Armaghian army. All had seen Kaylie's skill with the blade, and they appreciated the fact that two of their party now had some skill in the Talent. Hard men and women they may be, but they were not fools.

The decision made, Thomas stalked over to Kaylie, not sure how he felt about his Marchers' decision, but accepting it. Wringing her hands with worry, Kaylie could tell that he wasn't happy.

"You shouldn't be here," said Thomas. "But we won't send you back. Your decision is your own. But if you're going to be with us, you need to be one of us. You need to carry your weight just like any other member of our group."

She nodded quickly. "Of course."

Thomas continued before she could say anything else. "And to be clear, I lead this band. If I give an order, you obey it."

Kaylie started to protest, but held back the sharp response that naturally rose within her, recognizing that the harsh glint in his eyes brooked no argument. "Understood," she answered quietly.

"You shall do everything that is required of you without complaint. You will follow instructions and you will be expected to perform any task that any one of us can do. If you can't, you will return willingly to Fal Carrach without dispute."

Kaylie looked into Thomas' eyes and saw how serious he was. She realized then that this opportunity to prove herself was perhaps more important than she had first imagined. She steeled herself to that realization quickly.

"Agreed."

"So be it," said Thomas. He walked out toward the forest that infringed on their small clearing. "Get some sleep. You'll have the third watch tonight."

Kaylie watched him go, pleased that she had won this battle, but regretting how she had upset Thomas. She walked toward her horse, which one of the Marchers had groomed for her while she had spoken with Thomas. Rummaging through her saddlebags, which the kind Marcher had left near her horse, she pulled out a thick blanket and stepped toward the small fire. Third watch was the hardest, from three in the morning until dawn. But that was fine with Kaylie. If Thomas wanted to test her, she could take it. And she would do so without complaint.

CHAPTER FIFTY

STALKED

As Thomas and his small band of Marchers moved north toward the distant mountains that marked the border of Kenmare and the Clanwar Desert, they stayed within the small forests that rose up before them, trying to avoid any unwanted attention by keeping clear of the farmsteads and small towns that sprung up along the way. During those quiet days, Thomas spent little time with Kaylie, treating her as he would anyone else in their group of travelers.

She assumed that he avoided her because he was angry with her for joining them uninvited. She didn't realize that his behavior really resulted from his fear that she had placed herself needlessly in danger because of him and that there was little that he could do about it.

One evening with the sentries set and the fires hidden from any prying eyes, she managed to corner him. As was Beluil's habit, the large wolf had trotted off into the darkness to scout the surrounding terrain on his own, more often than not finding a wolf pack to run with for a time.

"What was it that attacked us?" she asked.

Thomas didn't need Kaylie to clarify, knowing what was on her mind. The cowled figure had been in his thoughts as well.

"Honestly, I don't know. Clearly a servant of the Shadow Lord, what with his ability in Dark Magic."

"Yes, but I could barely sense him," Kaylie protested. "Ogren. Shades. Warlocks. They give off a signature, a stench, that's hard to forget when they get close."

Thomas nodded in agreement. "I know. That's why once I located him I didn't want to take the chance of losing him. It was difficult to find him in the first place."

"But how could he do that?"

Thomas mulled her question for a few minutes, not liking the direction his thoughts were leading him. "Perhaps he's like Chertney or Malachias," he suggested. "They both seem to have the knowledge to mask their ability like we do. Or perhaps it could be something else."

"What do you mean?"

Thomas was reluctant to share just a guess, barely a suspicion in fact, but there was no reason to hide anything from Kaylie. It could prove important if they faced the cowled figure again. "There was something about our attacker that was familiar."

"He said something about the Crag."

"Yes, he did. I faced him there months ago. He ambushed me when I came down from the Roost and escaped just as he did when we battled against him a few days ago, stepping through the portal. But there was more to it than that."

"Thomas, you need to be more specific if I'm going to understand."

Thomas shrugged, suggesting his uncertainty about what he was going to say next. "When I say he was familiar, I mean I recognized him. Rather, I think I may have met him before. I may know him."

"Where did you meet him?"

"The Pinnacle."

It took Kaylie a moment to understand the implication of what Thomas had just said. "But isn't that where …" She was afraid to complete her thought.

Thomas nodded. "The meeting place of the Sylvana."

"Is that even possible?"

"Why not?" asked Thomas. "Everyone has their weaknesses and desires. If the Shadow Lord can identify them, make use of them, why couldn't he corrupt a Sylvan Warrior? Maybe our attacker could mask his ability in Dark Magic. That, of course, is the most likely explanation. Or maybe our attacker's ability in the Talent prevented us from realizing that we faced a servant of the Shadow Lord until it was almost too late."

Their conversation ended, both staring into the fire. Thomas' suspicion chilled her to the bone. They did not talk much after that, though Kaylie kept a close eye on Thomas.

Every so often Thomas rode ahead on his own, returning several hours later. Or he stopped the group at odd times, sitting his horse stock still, eyes closed, appearing to be asleep in his saddle. She knew that he was using the Talent to scan all around them in search of any potential dangers.

During their breaks, she extended her senses as well, something that Thomas obviously noted but never commented on. She found the skill to have become a part of her after her extensive training with Rya, as easy to do as blink her eyes.

A few nights later, as the Marchers finished their meal, Thomas doused the small fire, something that he hadn't done before. He then doubled the guard. Kaylie could tell that something bothered him, but he made no mention of what it could be. Instead, he walked a few dozen feet into the woods, settling himself against a tree, Beluil in front of him as the large wolf apparently felt the need to stay close to Thomas rather than go off on his nightly survey of their surroundings. Beluil appeared to be watching and listening for something, but what it could be she didn't know. She could see the moonlight reflecting off the large wolf's eyes. Though he had lain down next to Thomas, Beluil was very much alert, ready to rise in an instant if a threat appeared.

The Marchers picked up on their leader's concerns, becoming more wary. She had the third watch again, this time with three other Marchers. When she rolled from her blanket to take her post, she saw that Thomas still sat against the tree, apparently asleep, but she doubted it. She shivered, but not because of the early morning cold. She could feel it now as well. An approaching darkness, almost an innate feeling of terror. Something evil stalked them. The feeling flitted about at the very edge of her consciousness. What it was and where it could be, she didn't know. But it was close.

CHAPTER FIFTY ONE

PAYING THE PRICE

Gregory paced the throne room of Eamhain Mhacha, unable and unwilling to sit in the same chair once occupied by Rodric Tessaril. Named High King, but only temporarily he liked to keep telling himself, he had taken on two important tasks. First, rooting out any Armaghians who remained allied or sympathetic to Rodric, and second, getting the city to function once more as a center of commerce. Both tasks hadn't proven difficult.

Toreal, chamberlain of Eamhain Mhacha, now freed from Rodric's decrees and tantrums, knew exactly who continued to harbor a loyalty to the former High King. Once identified, Brennios sent his Home Guard soldiers to explain the change in leadership in the Kingdom and to suggest that if they could not adapt peacefully, they should leave. They had one day to decide. So far, the approach had worked in part because there were so few who saw the value of staying aboard a sinking ship.

The second task had proven even easier, as the merchants and farmers flocked back to the capital the day following news that Rodric had been deposed. The economic revival, which had begun slowly, quickly gained steam, the harbor now overflowing with river barges and larger ships, some waiting in the Heartland Lake for a berth to become available so that they could unload or acquire their cargo.

So Gregory's worry had nothing to do with the tasks to be completed. Nor did it come from his knowing that Thomas had gone after the Key. He understood the importance of that mission and fully supported it. No, his worry, not surprisingly, was for his headstrong daughter, who had once again taken matters into her own hands without consulting him.

Sarelle watched Gregory with some amusement, though she did understand his concern. As Queen of Benewyn, after assuming the throne upon the death of her sister from a wasting disease, she had never married nor had children. She found that being an eligible queen had proven quite useful in her negotiations with other Kingdoms. Benewyn had never had a large military, barely having an army and navy large enough to defend their borders and protect their commercial fleet, which was the Kingdom's lifeblood.

"I understand your worry, Gregory. Truly I do. But you have other matters to attend to."

"She's my only child, Sarelle. Obstinate, pugnacious, pig-headed, yes, but still my only child."

"Those qualities have proved useful and will continue to serve her well. I have no doubt that she will do Fal Carrach proud as a leader."

"Agreed, but running off in the dark of night following after Thomas? That is not acceptable. I'll send Kael after her. He'll bring her back."

"You can't send Kael after her." Her tone was one of resignation, that she had to explain something to him that he should understand already.

Gregory stopped right in front of Sarelle, his simmering anger and worry threatening to ignite. "Why not?"

Sarelle assumed the posture and tone that she had used so often when sitting the throne in Benewyn and jousting with ambassadors and merchants. "Two reasons, High King. First, you'll never catch them. Not with Thomas leading them. He won't be found unless he wants to be. Second, she needs to do this for herself."

Sarelle's use of his new honorific irritated Gregory, who was still not comfortable with the title or the responsibility. But the wisdom of her words broke through his emotions.

"Your daughter is headstrong and everything else you said. And she's more like you than you probably care to admit, as you're just as stubborn and difficult to deal with at times."

"I don't think that …"

Sarelle carried on over his protest. "She's also intelligent, brave, clever, and she knows what's coming her way as your daughter, the responsibilities she'll need to assume. You need to give her the space to make her own mistakes. More important, you need to give her the space to learn and succeed on her own."

Gregory sagged in defeat, then chuckled softly. "You have quite the way with words, Sarelle. You're right, of course. I just hate not being able to protect her."

Sarelle stepped forward, taking Gregory's hands in her own. He felt a warmth wash over him at her touch, quite pleasant in fact, and also a bit disturbing.

"Believe it or not, that young lady can protect herself. I've seen what she can do with a blade, as well as the Talent. Besides, she's with Thomas. He's probably the only person in all the Kingdoms more protective of her than you. And you know how he tends to respond to threats."

"Indeed I do," said Gregory with a laugh.

Sarelle's hands began to stroke his softly, and she gently pulled him closer. Her eyes sparkled with purpose.

"Then perhaps we could discuss a few things while we have the time, things of a more personal nature?"

Gregory flushed, realizing her intent. He wasn't sure how to extricate himself, or indeed if he wanted to escape. Much to his relief — or was it displeasure? — Brennios entered the throne room and saved him, coughing to catch their attention. Sarelle blushed, stepping back from Gregory, but still holding on to one of his hands. Apparently she wanted to make a point to the Armaghian general and to Gregory himself. Brennios didn't miss it, a mischievous gleam in his eye.

"High King Gregory, I can report that Armagh is now secure. I have stationed several regiments of the Home Guard throughout the city and the fortress. The number is more than sufficient to protect Eamhain Mhacha and ensure that Toreal can continue to manage the city effectively. Truth be told, they have little to do. Those few who profited during Rodric's rule have wisely chosen to leave the capital, the residents having taken it upon themselves to cleanse their city of those still desiring the ways of the former ruler."

"That's good to hear, General. Thank you for your efforts with this task. And as I've said before, you do not need to call me High King."

"I know, High King Gregory," replied Brennios, amusement touching his eyes. "But after our previous leader, I enjoy applying the honorific to a more worthy individual. I hope you don't mind, High King Gregory."

Gregory nodded his thanks for the compliment. "I don't mind. Other news regarding the Home Guard?"

"Yes, my lord. I have stationed the remainder of the Home Guard to the east of the city. And Toreal has been busy. He has almost completed making arrangements for river barges and supplies, enough in number not only for the Home Guard but also for your soldiers."

"Good. How long until we're ready to go?"

"Toreal says five days, but knowing him it will likely be no more than three. He's taken to the task with a vengeance."

"Even better. Please make sure that the men are ready to leave at dawn on the fourth day."

"Do we go where I expect, High King Gregory?"

"We do, General. We make for the Breaker."

"Excellent," replied Brennios. "Finally something worth fighting for. Also, one other matter, High King Gregory. As part of our sweep of the surrounding countryside and towns, we made an interesting discovery in Mooralyn."

In response to a nod from the Armaghian general, two soldiers marched into the throne room dragging a struggling figure between them.

"You cannot do this! You cannot! I am a guest of the High King. I demand an audience with the High King!"

"That you have," replied Brennios. "I present you to High King Gregory Carlomin, ruler of Fal Carrach and voice of all the Kingdoms." The general said the last as if he meant it as a gift.

The man's struggles stopped the instant he heard the name of the King of Fal Carrach, his face turning white as he looked up in shock at the man who stood before him.

"Norin Dinnegan," said Gregory in a whisper, surprised to have such luck. The former lord of Fal Carrach, now a declared criminal, had had the audacity to arrange an assassination plot that, if successful, would have given his son, Maden, the throne of Fal Carrach after he forced Kaylie to marry him. A plot that his daughter and Rya Keldragan had sniffed out and quashed.

"You!" hissed Dinnegan, spitting out the words as his face turned red with anger. "You cannot be the High King. Where is Rodric?"

Brennios ignored the theatrics of the man before him, instead pulling out a sheet of paper from his coat pocket.

"Toreal was kind enough to prepare a list of the charges against Norin Dinnegan, former merchant and lord from Fal Carrach and deemed a traitor to the Kingdom, based on his discussions with your Swordmaster."

"Toreal is quite industrious," interrupted Gregory, his hard eyes never leaving Dinnegan, who sought but could not avoid the gaze of the man he had tried to assassinate.

"Indeed he is," agreed Brennios. The general pulled spectacles from a hidden pocket and made a show of scanning the document. "Fraud. Torture. Attempted murder. Murder. Slavery. Much of this occurred in the Highlands, so we could hand him over to the Highland

Lord when he returns. The Marchers have a saying that I quite enjoy, something about paying one's debts. I have no doubt as to how events would play out with Dinnegan in the Highland Lord's hands."

"Indeed," agreed Gregory. "The Highland Lord would take great pleasure in repaying the debt that he owes to this scoundrel. The Highland Lord may be young, but he is a hard man already."

"Yes, but who knows when Lord Thomas will return," said Brennios, once again scanning through the document. "I could go on for several more minutes it seems, but the last item on the list certainly stands out. Attempted assassination of the King of Fal Carrach and kidnapping his daughter, the Princess Kaylie Carlomin."

"Those are lies! All lies! It was not my doing. It was all Malachias. I had no choice. Gregory …"

The soldier standing behind Dinnegan knocked him in the back with his halberd, forcing him to his knees in response to the undeserved familiarity.

"My apologies," hissed Dinnegan through clenched teeth. "I was not aware of the change in leadership. High King Gregory, please understand, these are all lies. There is no truth to any of those charges. I was forced to do as I did. I'm sure that we could reach some accommodation. There is no reason for you to …"

"Enough, Dinnegan." Gregory stared down at the man with nothing but contempt. "Your begging and lies will get you nowhere. You will pay the price for your treachery and betrayal." The High King's hand drifted to the hilt of his sword.

General Brennios stepped forward. "High King Gregory, if I may. There is much you still need to do. In fact, I believe Queen Sarelle would like to continue the conversation I so rudely interrupted. But I digress. Going back to the matter at hand, I would argue that this man before us has done as much to harm my Kingdom, financing Rodric's disastrous schemes, as he's done to yours and to the Highlands. Perhaps I could ease your burden and take care of this matter to the letter of the law."

"What do you mean by that?" demanded Dinnegan. "There has been no trial. I demand …"

"You demand nothing," interrupted Brennios, having lost patience with the man who once claimed to be the richest in all the Kingdoms. "You have been condemned by the High King. His word is the law."

"But that can't be possible. It can't. I deserve so much more than this. I have been promised so much more than this. It's owed to me. I …"

"High King Gregory, with your permission may I carry out the sentence?"

Gregory looked at Dinnegan a final time, seeing how a man once defined by his wealth and craving for power, both earned at the expense of others, had fallen so quickly and so far when his hidden schemes came to light.

"Thank you, Brennios. With all speed, please."

"As you command, High King Gregory."

With another nod the soldiers grabbed Dinnegan by his arms and dragged him from the throne room, ignoring his screams and threats as they quickly turned into sobs of terror.

CHAPTER FIFTY TWO

LESSON

"Are you still worried?" asked Kaylie. "You've been much quieter than usual."

The Marchers had settled in for the evening, the mountains to the north, signifying the border between Kenmare and the Clanwar Desert, visible in the distance as the last rays of the sun touched the sky.

Thomas sat down next to the Princess of Fal Carrach, watching Oso put the finishing touches on that night's stew. He felt some trepidation as he glanced at the bubbling pot. Oso tended to experiment when it was his turn to cook, and not always with the best results. Many of the Marchers watched as well, their concern plain, but none offered to help knowing that doing so would only irritate the large Highlander and thus seemed willing to take the risk.

"Worried about what?" His innocent expression made her smile at first.

Kaylie then sighed in exasperation. "Come on, Thomas. Doubling the guard at night. Your sitting against a tree or rock and then going into your trance, looking for who knows what. Your riding off on your own for hours on end, or your sending Oso or some other Marcher on some task that takes the better part of a day. I'd be a fool not to notice."

Thomas smiled. Kaylie definitely was not a fool. "I don't really know what's bothering me," he sighed. "It's a feeling at the very edge of my awareness. A darkness that comes and goes, but quite distinct from what I feel when I locate Ogren, Shades or other dark creatures. Sometimes whatever it is gets quite close to us. Other times it tracks us from afar. It's like an annoying itch between your shoulder blades that you can never scratch."

"Do you have any idea what it might be?" asked Kaylie with some concern.

"I don't know, and that's what bothers me. It's a blackness, a void that seems to have no shape or substance, an evil that I can't identify. This is something altogether different from anything that I've experienced before. It's like a fog, and every time I reach out and try to identify it, the mist slips through my fingers."

"How close is it now?"

"I can't sense it right now. It's moved off." Thomas lay his head back against the tree, shaking his head in frustration. "But I'll know when it's back. Can you sense it?"

Kaylie shook her head. "Your grandmother has taught me many things, but our lessons were interrupted. She never really showed me how to identify Dark Magic or dark creatures from afar, though I can sense them when they're fairly close."

Thomas jumped up from where he sat. Smiling, he offered Kaylie his hand to help her to her feet. "Then I'll show you."

Surprised by Thomas' interest, she gladly walked after him as they went deeper into the woods. Much to her delight, he held her hand a bit longer than necessary. They greeted Aric who was set out as a picket before they found a small clearing just a hundred yards away from the campsite. Thomas would have been more than happy to teach Kaylie by the cooking fire, but he worried that making use of the Talent there would prove a distraction to his Marchers. They were used to what he could do, but if anything he and Kaylie tried didn't work as expected, it might set their nerves on edge and perhaps keep them from maintaining the security of their perimeter.

Satisfied that they enjoyed some privacy, Thomas began the lesson. "Do you remember when I showed you how to extend your senses when we were in Tinnakilly?"

"Yes." Though Kaylie would have preferred to forget much of what had happened after that. "I've worked on this quite a bit with Rya."

"Good. Show me now."

Taking hold of the Talent, Kaylie harnessed the natural magic that flowed all around her. She felt as if she had exited her body and now looked down into the clearing where she and Thomas stood.

"Excellent," said Thomas. His voice startled Kaylie, as she heard him speak right next to her consciousness, floating above the glade. "We're going to do this the way my grandfather taught me the first time I extended my senses."

"Okay," agreed Kaylie, realizing that they were now communicating in one another's minds, much as they did when she relayed Thomas' instructions to his chiefs when they fought the Armaghian army in the Highlands.

"Gradually begin taking in more of the Talent. As you do, push your senses out, but in a controlled way, not too fast."

"I already know how to do that, Thomas," Kaylie said with some exasperation. "Your grandmother was quite thorough with her instruction."

"Right, sorry. That she is. Take us to the northeast to the very fringe of the Charnel Mountains."

Focusing on her assignment, she felt herself moving, Thomas riding along with her consciousness, as she pushed her senses out in the direction Thomas had suggested. She picked up more speed, moving across the top of the forest, identifying a few farmsteads, before the vegetation grew sparser. Finally, she reached the lower sands of the Clanwar Desert, massive sand dunes, some rising hundreds of feet into the air, dotting the horizon.

"Excellent," said Thomas. "Do you think you can go farther?"

"Of course," she replied. "I just wanted to take a look."

Kaylie sped forward, flying across the Clanwar Desert until she reached the forbidding presence of the Breaker. She marveled at the awe-inspiring wall, which rose three hundred feet into the air and stretched from the northwest Highlands to the coast and the Winter Sea. Taking just a few seconds to examine the manmade barrier, she continued on, swiftly crossing the Northern Steppes until the Charnel Mountains, their sooty, blackened tops rising into the sky, appeared just a few leagues distant.

"Well done," said Thomas. "Do you recall the premonition you get when Ogren are near? Do you remember what it feels like?"

"I do," she replied in Thomas' mind. "It's a foreboding. It makes me think of decay. Corruption. Rot. I can't explain it any better than that."

"You don't need to," Thomas said. "Focus on that feeling. Ogren are always exiting the Charnel Mountains to cross the Northern Steppes. So I'm certain a war party is close by. Concentrate on that premonition, until it's the only thing in your mind, then see if it will lead you where you need to go."

Kaylie did as Thomas suggested, fixating on the reek that she associated with Ogren when these monstrous dark creatures came close. At first there was nothing as she hovered over the grasslands. Then, after what seemed like hours but was only a few minutes, she felt a faint pull to the north. She shot forward toward the lower foothills, where the Northern Steppes gradually rose into the towering peaks of the Charnel Mountains. Slowing down, Kaylie descended, following the stench that grew stronger and stronger with each passing league. After a few more minutes, she stopped, the reek of decay almost overpowering. She gazed down into a hidden glade not far from the Northern Steppes. More than fifty Ogren had made camp for the evening among the twisted and stunted trees.

"Well done, Kaylie."

She couldn't help but smile at the praise.

"You have the scent, or the signature as you called it, firmly in your memory. As your skill in the Talent increases, with that recognition a part of you now, you'll easily locate Ogren from afar anytime you have need to do so."

"But what about whatever is tracking us?"

"Do you remember what you felt when you sensed it, despite how faint its signature was?"

Kaylie took a moment before responding, trying to latch onto the rancidness that had curdled her stomach the few times that she had sensed the darkness that haunted them. Then she had it.

Immediately Kaylie surged back to the southwest, streaking through the Northern Steppes, ignoring the Breaker and speeding across the sands of the Clanwar Desert, when she abruptly came to a halt. Shocked by a touch of darkness at the very edge of her senses, she abruptly released her hold on the Talent. Once more she was back in the clearing, Thomas holding on to her arms so that she didn't collapse to the ground. She was exhausted, her legs rubbery and barely able to keep her standing. She leaned her head against Thomas' chest to rest for a moment and regain her strength and balance. Smiling to herself, she filed away the fact that he didn't seem to mind the close contact, his grip becoming even a bit tighter.

"That's not the best way to end that particular exercise."

"I know," Kaylie replied. "I didn't plan to do it that way."

"But you felt the darkness? You'll sense it again now if it approaches?"

"Yes," said Kaylie, picking her head up off his shoulder. Although the foul signature was more difficult to locate compared to the Ogren. Fainter. More subtle. Almost as if it was designed to get past your defenses before you realized it.

Thomas still held her, wanting to make sure that she could stand on her own without falling. "Good. I felt it, too. Still just as nebulous as before. And as you suggest, something perhaps a bit more calculating than most dark creatures."

"How dangerous is it?"

"My best guess? Based on how it flits in and out of our senses, very dangerous. Perhaps even more so than any other dark creature that we've faced so far. And that darkness seems to be right where we're going. But it's not a threat right now."

Thomas gently removed his hands. Kaylie wobbled, but stood on her own.

"Feeling all right? What you just did takes a good bit of energy?"

"Yes, just a little tired now. I just need a few minutes to recuperate."

"You're much stronger than the last time we worked together." Kaylie smiled broadly, pleased by the compliment and silently thanking Rya for taking the time to teach her. "Would you mind if I showed you some other things you can do with the Talent? When you feel up to it, of course."

Kaylie almost screamed with delight. "Absolutely. I want to know everything there is to know."

Thomas laughed, caught up in Kaylie's exuberance. "Then let me show you how you can apply the Talent to see through Dark Magic that's being used to hide someone's true self."

The lesson continued for several hours, both Kaylie and Thomas missing dinner, but not caring. They didn't have a lot of confidence in Oso's cooking. And in the days following, Thomas continued to instruct Kaylie as much as he could, often from the saddle.

The darkness waiting for them up ahead worried Thomas, and he wanted to make sure that both he and Kaylie were prepared. He knew that steel blades would have little effect on what tracked them. They would need the Talent to combat it, assuming that they could identify it before it struck.

CHAPTER FIFTY THREE

PERFECT VESSEL

The Wraith drifted through the night, appearing to be no more than a flitting shadow as it made its way through the last slice of forest before the terrain shifted to the soaring sand dunes of the Clanwar Desert. Silent, disturbing nothing around it, the dark creature sensed its prey just a few leagues to the north.

It had almost found what it needed to kill its victim, but the Wraith had been too slow to act. Maybe that was because its target had a skill that few others did. Unlike its many other victims, this one knew that it was being stalked. The boy was wary, as he should be. That would make the Wraith's kill more challenging, perhaps more exciting. But it would not matter in the end. Before the boy realized that the assassin had gotten so close that he could feel its breath on his cheek, it would be too late.

The Wraith had faced this target before and barely escaped. That failure irritated the dark creature, because it forced the Wraith to have to wait for what it lived for. What it truly wanted. The Wraith could feel the power its prey contained. The dark creature wanted that power. Craved it. Wanted it for its own. But it knew as well that because of that power its prey could sense it. That was uncommon. Even worrisome, as the Wraith relied on stealth to claim its victims. But it could deal with that threat if it could find the tool that it needed to get close to its quarry. If it did, then the Wraith had nothing to fear. Its prey would be living on borrowed time.

Therefore, better not to rush. Better to wait. The Wraith would take its time and ensure that the circumstances were right. It had located the perfect vessel once but lost the chance because of the boy's pet wolf. The large beast had sensed its approach, appearing right when the Wraith was about to strike. The Wraith had no choice but to retreat.

Now the wolf was vigilant. It sensed things that even its master could not. As the Wraith drifted between the trees, it thought that perhaps another strategy should be employed. A strategy that, much like a spider and its web, would require the victim to come to it.

CHAPTER FIFTY FOUR

FOLLOWING DARKNESS

Thomas was on edge. They had left the forest as they approached the border with the Clanwar Desert. The direction that they headed took them on the fastest route to the north and the Winter Sea. But it was also the most obvious. Nevertheless, he had no desire to curl around the mountains of Kenmare. That would add weeks to their journey, time that they could ill afford to lose. Moreover, he had no wish to have this unidentifiable darkness stalk them all the way to wherever the Key might be located.

The creatures of the Shadow Lord had tracked him before. Nightstalkers seemed to be the preferred method. But this was something new. Something more dangerous. Something that would appear unexpectedly at the very limit of his senses, and then it would disappear just as quickly. Almost as if the trailing evil sought to goad him. Therefore, better to address it head on if he could. Kaylie had agreed when they had discussed it, as had Oso.

As the landscape changed, the temperate forest and then grassland receding to scrub, the dunes of the Clanwar Desert rising before them, all the Marchers watched their surroundings closely, eyes sweeping the landscape constantly, looking for any sign of movement, even with Thomas and Kaylie using the Talent regularly to ensure the way was clear of any direct threats. The tension continued to build. Thomas could feel the darkness tickling at the edge of his awareness. Teasing him. Taunting him. Playing with him.

Kaylie could feel it now, too, having fixed the faint taint of corruption in her memory. To her it felt like a ghost, ephemeral, always there, but just off in the distance. Beluil sensed it as well. Several times the large wolf had run ahead, loping forward at an impressive pace in hopes of catching up to whatever threatened, but to no avail. The darkness simply moved farther into the distance, faster than even the massive wolf could follow.

Yet, even with the darkness plaguing his senses, with each step Thomas took toward his ultimate goal he knew with greater certainty that he moved in the right direction, the pull of the Key becoming stronger by the day. More urgent. The Key called to him, as if the very prophecy knew that time slid quickly through the hourglass, time that they could not afford to waste.

CHAPTER FIFTY FIVE

SMALL CHANCE

The Clanwar Desert amazed Kaylie. It was an environment that she had never experienced before. She quickly learned to cover her head to protect against the hot sun, which beat off the fine sand beneath them and often reflected a sharp glare depending on the angle of the light. Yet even here on the very border of the desert, where the glimpse of green grass and small copses of trees was never too far away, there was an unexpected chill mixed in with the ceaseless breeze.

As they traveled deeper into the desert, Thomas chose their route carefully, avoiding the loose sand and the massive dunes that surrounded them as much as possible. He had a knack for finding hardened ground between the dunes that offered good shade and hidden oases, where they could rest under the clumped palm trees and refill their canteens and water bags before continuing on their journey. To Kaylie it seemed almost as if he had been here before and that he had some destination in mind and knew how to get there. But when she asked him about it Thomas was noncommittal, simply saying that he had a general idea of the direction that they needed to take.

Her mind drifted to other things as she took in the stark and beautiful scenery. She was transfixed by the small, whirling dervishes of sand that spun up unexpectedly at the touch of a gust of wind. Even the snakes, scorpions and other slithering and skittering creatures that hid themselves under the shadows of the rocks, waiting for darkness to emerge, were of interest. And far above them, in the bright blue, clear sky, was a huge kestrel, drifting from one air current to the next as it tracked their progress between the dunes. Clearly it was a rough land, but there was a beauty as well, and a quiet, a peacefulness to it, that she enjoyed. That sense of calm and peace didn't seem to extend to the people who inhabited this arid land.

When they first entered the sands, Thomas had explained a bit about the Clanwar Desert and how it got its name. By how he talked about this rarely visited Kingdom, Kaylie thought that perhaps Thomas' knowledge was based less on books and more on experience, but she couldn't be sure. As Thomas recounted, there were four clans: the Ashanti, Tuareg, Berber and Massaii. They were once one tribe and ruled the trade routes through the desert, taxing the caravans that sought to connect the Highlands and the Northern Steppes with the trading cities of the northwest — Faralan on the Winter Sea and Laurag on the western coast just south of the Distant Islands — before the construction of the Breaker.

For centuries the arrangement worked quite well. But the Desert Kingdom disintegrated a thousand years before the Great War when a younger brother of the Desert Chief assassinated him and tried to take the throne for himself. This started a vicious civil war that lasted for hundreds of years. Over time, as allegiances shifted, the desert peoples finally concluded that any hope for rebuilding the Kingdom had come to an end. In the interest of establishing a lasting peace, the four clans had divided the former Kingdom into four territories.

Each clan still raided the others, but it had evolved into a regular competition rather than endless skirmishes. Blood could not be drawn by a blade unless it involved a duel agreed to by both warriors. Even then the fight was to first blood and not to the death.

Like the Highlanders, the Desert Clan warriors were few in number compared to the other Kingdoms, and they didn't want to waste the lives of their fighters in such a way. To make certain that these and other customs continued to function effectively, and so that the four clans would coexist as they had learned to do over the centuries, twice a year the four Desert Chiefs met and dealt with any disputes or opportunities, negotiating such matters as water and grazing rights. It was much like the Council of the Kingdoms, just more frequent and on a smaller scale.

Thomas noted that the Desert Clans had their problems, feuds popping up from time to time between them that threatened the peace that had held since the Great War. But the Desert Clans all agreed on one thing. They didn't want anyone not of the desert entering the sands without the permission of at least one of the Desert Chiefs. At first Kaylie had hoped to meet some of these desert dwellers. But now, upon listening to Thomas, she wasn't so sure that she wanted her wish to come true.

Their second evening in the desert, Thomas had found a small oasis with an abundance of water and shade. Kaylie and Thomas still sensed the darkness tracking them, but it was leagues away and barely tickled their senses, as it had not yet entered the desert itself. Oso set the guard schedule, and this time, much to Kaylie's surprise, she didn't have the third watch as had been her plight since she had forced her way into the small expedition. Oso had given her the first watch. She smiled to herself as she sat down with her evening meal next to Thomas so that she could eat quickly before she went off to take up her post.

It seemed that the Marchers were beginning to accept her, and that filled her with a sense of accomplishment. Perhaps now she could also learn a bit more about what they were trying to achieve. Having focused on working to make herself a part of the group, as she was doing that she didn't feel that she had the right to demand to know their intentions. And before that she had only pried a few pieces of information from her father before slipping out of Eamhain Mhacha to follow after Thomas. So she decided that if she was well and truly a member of this ragtag bunch, she deserved to know the extent of the challenge that they faced.

"Thomas, I've learned in speaking with Oso and some of the other Marchers that we're in search of a key. But why? Obviously it must be important, but what exactly does this key do?"

"Your father didn't tell you?"

"No, he was very circumspect when I spoke to him about it. I think he was afraid that I might want to go with you if I knew the purpose of the venture."

"Apparently his fear was well founded."

"Be that as it may," replied Kaylie, her face flushing scarlet despite her efforts to ignore the jibe, "why is this key the objective?"

"The Key provides access to the Shadow Lord's lair, Blackstone. It's the only way to enter that dead city and escape the traps crafted from Dark Magic laid for those who may try to enter who have not pledged themselves to the Shadow Lord."

"My father spoke of the Shadow Lord," Kaylie said. "But how could the Shadow Lord remain such a threat after all this time? I thought the Kingdoms defeated him during the Great War."

"Defeated but not destroyed. He survived, and he has but one goal. Subjugation of the Kingdoms and all who live within them. Ogren and Shades and all the other dark creatures that plague the Kingdoms exist but for one purpose. To serve the Shadow Lord. They do not have free will. Consider Chertney."

Kaylie shivered at the thought. There was something off about Chertney, something unsettling, and at times terrifying because of the power that he controlled. "What about him?"

"As you know, Chertney has the ability to control Dark Magic. You can obtain that power only one way. By giving yourself, heart and soul, to the Shadow Lord. Remember as well the black-clad men we've run into who have pledged themselves to the Shadow Lord. They sought a power that only the Lord of the Shadow possesses, and he guards it jealously. Chertney and these other fools, all desperate for power, are playing a shell game that's fixed. No matter which shell they turn over they won't find the prize that they're seeking. In the end, the only thing they'll find is suffering and death."

"But what makes you think that the Shadow Lord is returning? Even with his dark creatures, nothing has been heard from him in centuries."

"True. But remember that every dark creature is tied to the Shadow Lord. Ogren, Shade, Fearhound, someone like Chertney. That's how the Shadow Lord expands his power, regenerates his strength. The more creatures that he commands, the more people he seduces and turns to his own purposes, the more power he obtains and the more substance he achieves. And the more powerful that he becomes, the better his chances of breaking out from the Charnel Mountains and taking the fight beyond the Breaker."

"The Sylvana are expected to hold him back from the Kingdoms. Isn't that what happened during the Great War?"

"It did, but the Sylvan Warriors are fewer in number now, and many of the Kingdoms have ignored the signs. They care nothing about the increasing number of raids by dark creatures beyond the Breaker. In fact, Rodric as High King was the perfect proxy for the Shadow Lord."

"Rodric divided the Kingdoms," said Kaylie, her natural political acumen coming to the forefront. "Some Kingdoms allied to him, seeking to gain by his actions. Others opposed him, trying to prevent him from attaining more power. Regardless of where the various Kingdoms stood, it directed their attention away from the Shadow Lord."

"Correct," smiled Thomas, unsurprised by the acuity of Kaylie's analysis. "And that's the worry. As you know, some of the Kingdoms, such as Fal Carrach,

Benewyn, Kenmare, most likely the Desert Clans, will heed the call to the Breaker. But the others? I doubt they'll make any effort to assist when the Shadow Lord attacks. With our current numbers, who's to say whether we can hold the Dark Horde at the Breaker?"

Kaylie recognized the term for the Shadow Lord's host not only from her history lessons but also the old legends and tales. Parents liked to call on the Shadow Lord and his Dark Horde, threatening an obstinate child with a visit from an Ogren or Shade if they failed to heed their demand that they go to bed.

"But isn't there some way to defeat the Shadow Lord?"

"There is. I need to kill him."

Kaylie stared at Thomas in silence for a moment, remembering when he had mentioned something similar prior to the start of this journey while meeting with the assembled monarchs. When her father, Sarelle and Rendael had discussed next steps with Thomas, he had said it seriously then, taking her by surprise. Now she burst out laughing. Her laugh died in her throat when she saw the earnest expression on his face.

"You're not kidding?"

"No." She looked around the campfire, realizing that Oso and the other Marchers not on guard duty had been listening. They wore somber expressions, confirming what Thomas had just said. "That's why we're here in the desert and moving to the west. In order to fight the Shadow Lord, I need to get into Blackstone. The only way to do that is with the Key. If I find the Key, I have a chance."

"But no one has ever defeated the Shadow Lord in single combat," blurted out Kaylie, then immediately regretted the outburst.

"True. It's a small chance. But you have to take what you can get."

Thomas rose from the ground, brushing off his breeches. As was his habit, he wanted to wander the surrounding landscape for a time, using the Talent to ensure that all was quiet and calm in the still of the desert night, the stars shining brightly in the clear sky.

"I don't want to die, and I'll certainly try my best not to, but as my grandmother Rya likes to say and as you've heard so often, 'You must do what you must do.'"

Thomas walked off in silence into the growing darkness, his steps silent in the soft sand. Kaylie remained where she was, not knowing what to say. She looked at Oso in consternation.

"Some are simply required to do more than others," said the large Marcher, a sadness in his eyes. The other Marchers remained quiet around him. "But if any can survive, he can."

CHAPTER FIFTY SIX

CHICKEN

The next day the Marchers journeyed even deeper into the desert, the towering sand dunes rising around them often blocking out the sun altogether and leaving the path Thomas selected wrapped in a perpetual gloom. Kaylie was quiet that morning, thinking about what Thomas had told her the night before. His burdens seemed to be getting bigger. Her thoughts threatened to become a maelstrom in her mind. As a result, she struggled to maintain her focus. Thomas had warned them that they were entering a dangerous section of the Clanwar Desert, one known for what Thomas described as dry quicksand, which differed from the quicksand common to other climes in that the sand was so fine that large deposits of the granular material could still prove deadly to those unlucky to step into the unseen trap. If the layer of dry quicksand ran deep, the victim would be sucked down, often buried alive beneath tons of feathery crystals in a matter of seconds. Therefore, Kaylie and the others followed Thomas' instructions, leading their horses and watching where they placed each step.

Nevertheless, despite Thomas' warnings, the natural danger of the desert revealed itself. Not too long after starting out that morning, an asp had startled one of the horses when it got too close to the rocky outcropping under which the snake lay in wait for its next meal. Stumbling to the side, the horse's hind legs had left the path that Thomas had proscribed and slid into dry quicksand, which appeared to be no different than the sand that could be seen for leagues around. The Marchers close to the horse had succeeded in calming it and then pulling its legs free from the wispy, grasping particles. But it proved to be a lesson that none of the Marchers forgot. Before the Highlanders even could react to the horse's plight, half its body had slid beneath the feathery sand. From that point forward the going was slow and deliberate, but it couldn't be avoided.

"Stop," Thomas said quietly, but loud enough for all to hear. Kaylie was lost in her thoughts, so he reached for her arm, gently pulling her back toward him.

Thomas held his hand up for silence, his Marchers quickly quieting their mounts, so that the only sound came from the soft breeze dusting across the top of the sand, pushing the tiny crystals to and fro. The Marchers stood there for several minutes, no one saying a word, their eyes tracking their surroundings in all directions as if they expected dark creatures to emerge from beneath the sand.

"Thomas, what are you …"

Before Kaylie could finish asking her question, Thomas whipped his sword from the scabbard across his back and slammed the point down into the sand just a few feet in front of where they stood. When he lifted up the blade, the head of a large snake came out of the sand with it, revealing a thick body at least thirty feet long. The snake's brown and tan coloring helped it to blend in perfectly with its environment.

"A sand viper," explained Thomas. "A distant relative of the blood snake. This one isn't that big, maybe just a juvenile, but the full-grown ones are known to eat unwary travelers. They lie in wait for their prey, barely moving. When whatever they're hunting gets close enough, they strike."

Beluil stepped forward to smell the sand viper, never having seen a creature such as this before. The large wolf filed the scent away so that he could be better prepared in the future.

"The sand viper hunts by sound," said Thomas, turning the brief dialogue into a lesson for the Marchers, many of whom marveled at the size of the snake. "If you hear a rustling across the sand that sounds like the wind and lasts for more than a few seconds, but you don't feel the wind, stand still for a moment. If the rustling continues, but there's no wind, it's likely a sand viper. Once it finds prey, the snake will mimic the movement until it's close enough to attack. If it bites you, you'll be dead in minutes. The toxins contained in its venom will stop your heart and there's no known cure."

Using his foot, Thomas dislodged the head of the sand viper from the tip of his sword. Kaylie jumped back in surprise as Thomas drove his blade through the snake's neck, removing the head, then did the same in several other places along the snake's body until he had almost a dozen large pieces of the snake to carry.

"Of course, though the sand viper is deadly, it's also delicious. So we're in for a treat tonight."

Oso stepped forward, grinning at Kaylie, then several other Marchers moved to assist so that they could strap the butchered pieces of the snake to their horses.

"What does it taste like, Thomas?" asked Oso, always interested in what he put into his stomach.

"Chicken. We can make a light gravy and you'll love it."

Kaylie stood there unable to speak, a green look on her face as the Marchers completed their work. She decided instantly that she would be taking the first watch that night as she had little interest in dinner.

CHAPTER FIFTY SEVEN

TWIN DAGGERS

Anara's long dagger slid deeply into the Ogren's side, but it was more an annoyance than a mortal wound to the massive beast. The keen steel, honed after hours of sharpening, missed the important internal organs and cut instead through thick, ropy muscle. She ducked and rolled backward, avoiding the Ogren's backhanded swing of its rusted battle axe, the huge blade singing through the air above her head. She was irritated with herself at having missed her primary target. Nevertheless, her strike had caused some damage, as the dark creature was bent at the waist, a clawlike hand pushing at the wound in its side as a steady stream of dark blood leaked onto the tall grass.

Coming to her feet, she pulled the other long dagger that she kept hidden in the back of her belt. A blade now in each hand, she sprinted toward the Ogren before it could turn. Leaping through the air, she placed a foot on the Ogren's rump, propelling herself up into the air so that she came down hard on its upper back with her knees at the very same time that she drove both razor-sharp blades into the base of the Ogren's skull. With a sigh rather than a scream, the Ogren collapsed to the ground, the wound in its side forgotten as the light left its eyes.

Anara, slim and petite, sweat-soaked, red hair plastered to her pixielike face, pulled her bloody daggers free and surveyed what was left of the battlefield. All the Ogren that had attempted to break through the Marcher line were dead or soon would be, the last few that still lived attempting to escape back down the rocky slope toward the Northern Steppes that beckoned far below. The beasts wouldn't make it far. She had ordered a troop of Marchers to swing around from the west to ensure that none of the dark creatures broke free, and if those Marchers didn't catch the fleeing Ogren, the wolves would. She could already hear the howls in the distance, a warning of what was to come for the servants of the Shadow Lord.

Wiping her bloody blades on the dirty cloth that passed for Ogren clothing, she sheathed both and climbed to the top of the wooded crest from which the Marchers had initiated their ambush.

"I'm glad you were here, Anara," said Nestor, the grizzled Marcher responsible for protecting this section of the northern Highlands from infiltrating dark creatures. "Without you, I don't know that we could have held."

"You would have held," replied Anara with a grin. "You're too stubborn not to."

Nestor huffed, a chuckle escaping, as he nodded reluctantly in agreement, secretly pleased by her confidence in him. She was young and tough, having proven her mettle many times over upon escaping the mines. He had had his doubts about Anara taking on the responsibility that Thomas had given her, but no more. Not after seeing what she could do with her ever-present blades. And not after benefiting from her excellent work to ensure that the Marchers had what they needed to protect their homeland.

When Thomas, Oso and a small band of Marchers had left the Highlands for the west on a mission deemed more important than anything else, even such work as shoring up the Highland defenses and rebuilding the Crag, he had given Anara responsibility for making sure that Nestor, Renn and Seneca, with their separate Marcher commands, had the support and resources required to keep their territories free of dark creatures. She also needed to coordinate with the dozen or so Sylvan Warriors who, at Thomas' request, had come to the aid of the Marchers and were helping to protect the northern Highlands. The survivor of Killeran's Black Hole had taken to her assignment with a focus and intensity that Nestor could only describe as exceptional and somewhat terrifying. Though she was slim and barely came up to his shoulders, that belied an inner strength and determination that he had yet to find in another person. If she had to move a mountain in order to achieve her task, she would do so, whether you helped or not. But better that you helped, because her daggers were never far from her hands.

Nestor had to give the young woman the credit that she deserved. Thanks to her leadership, he, Renn and Seneca had the tools that they needed to keep the dark creatures out of the Highlands, at least for now. The frequency of Ogren war parties coming across the Northern Steppes had increased once again. Even worse, these bands of dark creatures were growing in size. The fifty Ogren and handful of Shades that the Marchers had grown accustomed to had blossomed into several hundred beasts on occasion, which stretched the Marchers to the very limit if not for the timely assistance of the Sylvan Warriors, who often made use of the Talent to even the odds.

"Maybe so," he replied. "But from the looks of things, we didn't take many serious injuries. That wouldn't have been the case if you hadn't brought reinforcements and shifted our positioning."

"I had information that you didn't. Besides, I needed to see this for myself."

Anara had arrived at Nestor's camp with fifty additional Marchers well before the sun was supposed to rise that morning with word from a Sylvan Warrior that a larger than usual Ogren war party had almost reached the passes that led up into the northern Highlands. Rather than meeting these invaders at a lower elevation, she had suggested that Nestor allow the several hundred dark creatures to climb a bit first, tiring the Ogren and giving her the few extra hours that she needed to pull more Marchers to their position from the scouting parties that scoured the Highlands for signs of incursions.

At first, Nestor had balked at her suggestion, not wanting to give up the ground. But somehow she had convinced him so thoroughly that in the end he thought the change in strategy might have been his own idea. The extra time allowed the Marchers to prepare their defenses, setting boulders and logs at the top of the crest, the men and women of the Highlands remaining hidden among the evergreens that stood at the lip. Once the dark creatures appeared, Anara and Nestor had waited until the Ogren were almost to the crown of the slope before releasing the surprise they had waiting at the top, which swept away a good portion of the beasts. The Highland archers did what they could against the Ogren that avoided the landslide and continued to claw their way to the brink. The few dark creatures that did make it to the crest were of a number that the Marchers could manage without great difficulty. But that wasn't to say that the next time wouldn't be different.

"They're growing bolder," said Nestor. "Taking more risks and sending more Ogren at us. It's almost as if they're on a schedule and we're keeping them from it."

"You might be right, Nestor. Thomas insinuated as much the last time I spoke with him. He thought the attacks along our northern border would increase, the dark creatures seeking to avoid the Breaker and instead cut through our land to make their way into the Kingdoms."

"Our young lord could be right," agreed Nestor. "The Ogren war parties are twice, if not three times, as large as they used to be. And our scouts or the Sylvan Warriors are finding at least two bands of dark creatures a week now coming across the Northern Steppes. If this continues, or the size of the Ogren packs increase, a fight like this one might be our last."

"I know," said Anara, her sharp gaze studying the Highlands for miles around from her perch at the crest of the slope. "I've been thinking about that."

"I assume you have something in mind?"

Anara nodded. "As I said, I had wanted to see this for myself, just to make sure. Now that I have, I don't think that we have a choice. I'll speak with Renn and Seneca and move them and their Marchers farther north. Renn on your left flank, Seneca on the right. You'll lead the center. I'll have a Marcher reserve of several hundred a league behind you. With a consolidated defense and the Sylvan Warriors and wolves continuing to aid us, hopefully we can keep the dark creatures out of the Highlands for a while longer."

Nestor nodded. With the Sylvan Warriors and wolves, the Ogren and other beasts had no way to sneak into the Highlands. They were always discovered well before they even set foot in the lower passes, giving the Marchers the chance to adapt their strategy as needed. Consolidating the Marcher forces made sense and would allow them to fight more effectively against the more frequent and stronger attacks.

"I like it," he said. "I'll let my Marchers know and start pulling in the scouting parties. That alone will give me a third more fighters. With that and the new approach, we'll have a better chance of holding."

"We have to hold," said Anara. "We have no choice. We have to give Lord Thomas the time to do what he needs to do."

CHAPTER FIFTY EIGHT

CAUSE FOR CONCERN

"Thomas," Kaylie whispered into Thomas' ear. He had been enjoying a dream focused on spending time with Kaylie at a watering hole that would have left him red in the face if she had not woken him. Though he had dozed for only an hour, he was wide awake as soon as Kaylie touched his shoulder.

The Marchers had reached a rocky region of the desert, the relentless sands dissipating for a time although the towering dunes remained visible all around them. Even with the rougher terrain, Thomas saw signs of movement. Much of it looked like that of Desert Clan warriors, none recent, so it didn't worry him. But with his sharp vision he picked out other markings and cues, pointing out a few to Kaylie and Oso, which did give him cause for concern.

Oso had spread the word so that all the Marchers would keep a sharp eye as they traveled farther north. Thomas continued to use the Talent at regular intervals, asking Kaylie to do so as well. They were coming to a part of the desert that contained a network of hidden crags and caves that stretched for leagues underground, thus the need to be even more vigilant. Something the Marchers had already become, as they sensed the potential danger of the new environment as well as the unease of the Highland Lord.

The Marchers were subdued as they set up camp for the night. Thomas found a large, open space with a single, flat rock in the middle that rose to a height that was just a bit higher than Oso's shoulders. Although neither he nor Kaylie detected any dangers around them at the moment, both felt uncomfortable, as if something were lurking at the very limits of where they had searched. The cloud of evil that had played continuously at the boundary of their senses had disappeared unexpectedly, replaced by a persistent but ephemeral warning that something was amiss and that a threat was near. Preferring to be cautious, Thomas doubled the guard. He then climbed the rock in the center of their encampment, which let him look out over the desert in all directions for miles around. His worry only increased. The landscape was pocked with crevices, rock slides, and narrowing gorges that resembled a maze for as far as he could see. Such a landscape could hide unseen threats and hinder the Marchers' attempts to defend themselves. As his worry increased, Kaylie joined him, laying her bedroll next to his, as they settled in for the night. It wasn't long before his fears were confirmed.

"Trouble?" he asked quietly, his green eyes blazing in the dark of the night, the full moon and bright stars playing off the sand and illuminating the campsite in an eerie, dim glow.

"Ogren from the south," Kaylie replied.

As Thomas had requested, his instincts suggesting that danger was close, during the first watch every quarter hour Kaylie had used the Talent to scour the surrounding area for any threats. She had detected the dark creatures as soon as they came streaming out of a dark, deep fissure to the south and began to make their way toward their intended victims in a roundabout route through the uneven terrain.

"Keep an eye on them," Thomas said as he grabbed his sword and jumped down into the Marcher camp.

Waking Oso and explaining what approached, they moved quickly among the Marchers and set them in a defensive perimeter, the horses placed closest to the rock rising in the center of the depression. A handful of Marchers scrambled up the rock to join Kaylie, bows at the ready. Dark creatures rarely entered the desert, but clearly this Ogren war party, led by a Shade, had a specific target in mind.

Thomas climbed back up onto the rock to stand next to Kaylie.

"How many?"

Kaylie closed her eyes for a moment as she directed her use of the Talent to the approaching band of dark creatures.

"Fifty."

Thomas grimaced. "Almost twice as many. This is going to be a hard fight. Remember to use the Talent only if absolutely necessary. It will serve as a beacon for any other dark creatures, drawing them like a moth to the flame. If there is one troop of Ogren looking for us we should assume that there are others." Surveying the southern approaches to their campsite, Thomas developed his strategy in a matter of seconds.

"Oso," he called down. "Fifty. We'll use the three narrow defiles on the southern side to limit access. Archers will allow the first few in, then we'll improve our odds."

Oso didn't bother to acknowledge what Thomas had said, understanding what his friend had in mind.

"Spears to the front," the large Highlander ordered. "Be ready. Swords in the gaps and on the flanks."

The Marchers immediately moved to obey.

"Only from the south?" asked Thomas, not wanting any surprises.

Kaylie used the Talent to search the encircling desert once again, pushing out for several leagues, even trying to extend her search deep beneath the pockmarked landscape.

"Yes, just this war party for now."

"Good," said Thomas. "So long as we can't be surrounded we stand a chance."

Using the Talent, Thomas reached out to Beluil, who had wandered off into the darkness in the late evening to scout on his own. He found the large wolf almost two leagues distant, near where the dunes began again, and sent an image of an Ogren to his friend. Beluil immediately began sprinting back toward the Marchers, eager to join the fast-approaching skirmish.

"Thomas," Kaylie called, drawing him back. "To the front!"

Thomas turned in the direction Kaylie pointed, watching as the first Ogren ran out from the gulches to the south, their bloodcurdling roars echoing off the rock enclosing the naturally formed pit.

"Archers, on my command!" Thomas cried. "Let a handful in. Focus on the pathways on the southern side."

The five archers raised their bows, sighting on the few narrow passes that led toward the waiting Marchers.

Thomas allowed five Ogren to enter the killing ground before giving his next order. "Release!"

Five arrows shot above the onrushing Ogren and slammed into the dark creatures just behind those that had made it into the open. Barbed steel tore through eyes and brains as the Ogren in the three defiles collapsed in the rocky soil, their blood seeping into the stone and sandy soil.

Pleased with his archers' shooting, Thomas continued the onslaught. "Release!"

Arrows flew once more through the night to strike the Ogren seeking to join the fight. The narrowness of the open-aired ravines, which in some ways resembled horizontal chimneys, impeded the dark creatures' movements and made them easy targets. More Ogren fell again, collapsing onto those that had already died. But the archers weren't done.

"Release!" Thomas ordered a third time.

The steel-tipped shafts flew through the night, the sharpened tips gleaming when touched by the bright moonlight, before slicing into Ogren seeking to scramble over the ones that had already died and as a result had created a bottleneck that Oso quickly used to his advantage.

Startled by the cries of pain and terror from the Ogren following them, the handful of Ogren that had emerged from the flumes had stopped their charge, watching their brethren collapse behind them, the bodies piling up at a shocking rate.

"Spears attack!" Oso commanded.

The Marchers responded instinctively, charging forward in a wedge formation and driving their spears into the backs or legs of the Ogren that had made it through the narrow pathways that led to the open bowl. The Marchers with spears then stepped back quickly, allowing their compatriots with swords to lunge forward and finish the job, and then all the Marchers immediately fell back to their original position around the rock once more.

"Be ready, Oso!" Thomas called. "More are coming."

The Ogren blocked by the bodies of the dead beasts screamed in rage, pulling the corpses from the paths, then sprinting forward, brandishing swords and axes above their heads.

Thomas employed the same strategy once again, archers targeting the Ogren behind the first rank of dark creatures, allowing them to enter the killing ground and then cutting off access and giving the Marchers with spears and swords the opportunity to eliminate those caught in the open while the remaining dark creatures struggled to join the fight.

Having finally pushed its way to the front, the Shade watched the Marchers' deadly attack with growing anger. Recognizing the limitations created by the narrow defiles, he forced the Ogren in the passageways forward, over the bodies of the slaughtered dark creatures, flooding the open space with the massive beasts at a rate faster than the archers could take them down.

After repulsing the first attack, and then a second, having used long spears and then swords to maim and then kill the beasts not feathered with arrows that tried to break through their defensive perimeter, the skirmish devolved into smaller combats. Thankfully by then the Marchers had killed more than two-thirds of the monstrous dark creatures. Unable to hold their line against the rush of Ogren, the Marchers employed the tactics that had proven so effective when taking on these dark creatures in the Highlands. Marchers broke off into pairs, working together to overwhelm individual Ogren.

Following well-honed practices, the first Marcher challenged the Ogren, then skipped away, staying just out of reach of the massive axe or blade the beast often wielded with such great effect. The lead Marcher sought to tire out the dark creature, or force it into making a mistake, allowing the second Marcher to slip in and hamstring the beast. Once on the ground, the two Marchers could finish the Ogren with less danger to themselves. No Marcher wanted to face an Ogren on his or her own, knowing that the likely result would be their death.

Thomas wanted to protect Kaylie, hopeful that she would be safe atop the rock. But what he really wanted was to go after the Shade. It was much like killing a snake. Take off the head, and the snake, no matter how large, died. In this case, kill the Shade, and its hold over the Ogren would disappear, increasing the Marchers' chances of driving off the Ogren, which would continue to fight, no matter the odds, if the Shade demanded it.

About to jump down from the rock and attack the Shade that had finally stepped out from a gully to urge its Ogren forward, Thomas noticed that an Ogren had snuck up behind two Marchers already engaged with another of the towering monsters, unaware of what came at them from their blind side.

Leaping from the stone, Thomas called out to Kaylie, "Cover my back!"

Taken by surprise, Kaylie hesitated for just a moment, unsure of how to handle the melee playing out below her. Pushing away her fear, she drew her sword from the scabbard across her back and jumped down, following after Thomas.

Thomas waited until the Ogren sneaking up on the two Marchers was almost upon his fighters. He saw the bloodlust in the eyes of the creature, thinking that it had two easy kills. Thomas pulled his sword lightning fast from the sheath on his back, stepped forward and rolled under the Ogren's huge axe, slashing the beast's hamstrings from the back before it could strike the otherwise engaged Marchers. With the muscles on the back of both of its legs severed and useless, the beast fell forward, its howl of pain echoing off the surrounding rock. Before the Ogren could attempt to rise from its knees, Thomas whipped his blade down, detaching the creature's head from its shoulders.

Kaylie watched, transfixed by the ease with which Thomas dispatched the massive creature. Thomas then ignored the Ogren that continued to fight the two Marchers that he had saved and approached the Shade, sword at the ready. Understanding his goal, Kaylie trailed in his footsteps, sword in hand, eyes scanning in every direction for an attack. The reality of what she faced settled within her as she struggled to tamp down her fear. Fighting dark creatures such as this was much different than her experience during the battles against the Armaghians in the Highlands. Tightening her grip on her sword, Kaylie told herself that she would do as Thomas asked, protecting his back, keeping an eye out for any Ogren that attempted to break away from a Marcher and attack Thomas while he was engaged with the Shade.

Rather than taking the time to measure his opponent, Thomas charged the Shade ferociously, sword slashing down and across, then whipping back in an upward slash, as he sought to eliminate the creature quickly. The Shade's glazed, milky eyes showed no emotion as it defended itself, locking its sword in place just in time to block Thomas' strike. Though Thomas wanted a quick victory, he remained careful, never overextending himself, knowing that any touch by the Shade's blade, even just a nick, would send a black poison coursing through his body that would lead to his death in a matter of minutes.

A howl blasted through the rocky bowl as a dark shadow leapt onto the back of an Ogren, crushing it to the ground with its front paws as its jaws bit into the back of the dark creature's neck. Beluil had arrived. With his friend now with them, Thomas was certain of the Marchers' success, but first he had to remove the Shade from the skirmish.

Thomas continued his attack, his steel a whirl of motion, as he probed for any weakness that he could exploit. Finally, Thomas found a hole in the Shade's defenses. With a lightning quick thrust he knocked the Shade's sword away, driving the point of his blade into the creature's chest. As the black blood of the Shade drained onto the rock, staining it, Thomas spun around at the sound of a roar no more than a few feet behind him.

An Ogren lay there, face down on the sand and loose stone, its hamstrings sliced cleanly through. Kaylie had just driven her sword into the back of its skull. He caught Kaylie's eyes, watching the green cast creep over her face.

He wanted to go to her, to comfort her for what she had been forced to do, understanding that this was the first time that she had used her blade to kill another living creature. But he stayed where he was, knowing more than anything that Kaylie wanted to be considered a part of the group, and that now she needed to stand alone. Thomas smiled and nodded his thanks before examining their small battlefield.

Doing a quick count, Thomas was pleased to see that all his Marchers had survived the fight intact, just a few having minor wounds. All the Ogren lay dead, scattered around the rocky soil. Beluil trotted among the bodies, sniffing, making sure that none would rise again. Many of the Marchers nodded to Kaylie appreciatively, acknowledging her impressive precision. Killing an Ogren on your own was no easy task, and often proved to be a death sentence. In the Highlands hers was an accomplishment to celebrate, as it normally took several men to kill an Ogren without risking serious injury.

Kaylie caught Thomas' stare, and at first she thought that he was going to lecture her about staying out of danger. Instead, he bent down and wiped his blade on the Shade's dirty clothing, removing the blood so that it didn't pit his hereditary blade. He then looked her straight in the eyes.

"Thank you," he said simply. "That was well done." Thomas then walked off to help tend the Marchers who had been injured.

Pride swelled in Kaylie's chest. It felt like a burden had been lifted. She knew then that the Marchers had accepted her. She was no longer the Princess of Fal Carrach who had forced herself upon them. She was simply

Kaylie, focused on accomplishing the same task as they were. Focused on aiding the Highland Lord in his quest for the Key.

CHAPTER FIFTY NINE

DESERT MEETING

The night still upon them, the Marchers dragged the Ogren and Shade into a pile that blocked the narrow paths the dark creatures had used for their approach, then reestablished their defensive shell. Thomas and Kaylie resumed their positions on the flat rock, but they did not sense any other encroaching danger. Though Thomas could see just as well in the dark as he could in the light, his Marchers could not. So they would continue their journey across the rocky, uneven terrain when the sun rose.

But as Thomas expected, just as the Marchers were about to set fire to the bodies of their attackers so that they could move on at first light, warriors from one of the Desert Clans appeared. Drawn to the fighting, and having followed the dark creatures since they first entered the Clanwar Desert, but unable to engage them during the day because the beasts disappeared into one of the many caves or crevices liberally spread about the surrounding landscape, they were surprised to see what had befallen their prey. The smaller, wiry men, wearing loose, light-colored clothes and sporting long moustaches and beards, sometimes bedecked with jewels or bells, rode their sturdy desert horses easily, as if they were born in the saddle.

These desert fighters had heard stories of the Marchers, their prowess in battle, but they had never expected to see it for themselves, the small group of Highland warriors having dispatched, apparently with ease, such a large war party of Ogren. As these desert fighters, outnumbering the Marchers three to one, surrounded them, Thomas commanded the Marchers to form into a wedge, but to keep their hands off their sword and axe handles to demonstrate their peaceful intentions. Beluil remained on the very edge of the formation, a low growl issuing from deep within his belly.

"Are these the same men who fought with us in the Highlands?" Oso asked.

"I don't believe so," replied Thomas. "But even if they were, that wouldn't matter. They'll view us as trespassers here. No one is permitted in the Clanwar Desert unless given express permission by one of the Desert Chiefs."

The Marchers' nervousness increased as the men encircling them spoke rapidly in an ancient language known only to those born in the desert. Unable to follow the rapid-fire exchanges, the Marchers didn't know that after discussing how claims of Marcher martial prowess seemed to be true, one of the fighters suggested they kill them now rather than bring them to their tribal chief. That resulted in a heated argument among a select few of the men that continued for several minutes.

"Hauk tu la norsan."

The leaders of the desert troop fell silent, staring at Thomas, shocked that someone not of the desert had spoken in their tongue. After a few moments of silence, bedlam ensued as all the desert fighters began to shout and argue at once.

Kaylie watched with growing consternation as the men on horseback became more animated with their apparent argument. "What did you say?"

"I told them that what they were thinking was a bad idea."

"What were they thinking?"

Thomas smiled at her. "They were arguing about whether to kill us all now so as to save them the trouble of having to bring us to their chief."

One of the desert fighters urged his horse forward, apparently the leader of this group. Thomas guessed that a decision had been made. Before the fighter could get a word out, Thomas stepped forward.

"Barak do haram su rey."

The approaching soldier stopped, staring sharply at Thomas. He then smiled, though it seemed a reluctant grin, bowed his head slightly, and then rattled off several long sentences that the Marchers couldn't understand.

"What just happened, Thomas?" Oso asked, his nerves on edge. Not knowing what was being said made the large Highlander more uncomfortable than when fighting a band of Ogren.

"The Desert Clans don't look kindly on strangers entering their lands. Even the caravans and merchants that still make their way across the sands get permission first to ensure that they can travel through the desert without being harassed by Desert Clan warriors. Since we don't have permission, I claimed the ancient right of acknowledgement, requiring that we be brought to the chief. Such a demand can't be denied by an honorable desert warrior. And Farou, who sits his horse right in front of us, has granted us that right. He and his men will take us to their chief."

"And what happens when we meet the chief?"

"I don't know," Thomas said, a wistful smile appearing on his face. "It's up to the chief."

Oso looked at Thomas as if he were hiding something. He had known Thomas for years, yet he was still full of surprises. How had his friend learned to speak in the desert tongue? That question would have to wait for now. "So we could have died just now or we could die where we're going depending on the whim of the Desert Chief?"

"Yes, that's about right."

"Wonderful."

CHAPTER SIXTY

OLD FRIEND

After less than a day's ride, the Desert Clan warriors brought the Marchers to a large oasis nestled between several towering sand dunes that extended for almost a mile. Off in the distance at the far end a small waterfall fell into a lake with plentiful shade provided by a large swath of palm trees. The desert people had taken up every inch of available space on the grassy tufts beneath the trees, pitching silk tents and digging campfires in the sand, as well as corrals near the lake for their mounts. The tent city gave off a feeling of permanence. Clearly, they had established their camp near the water and under the shade some time ago and had no immediate plans to leave.

Dismounting from their horses, the Marchers were led on a haphazard path that wound through the tents toward a shaded part of the lake. The tents were pitched with little semblance of order, a controlled chaos ruling the camp. The men and women of the desert, particularly the children who stared at the strange warriors, stopped whatever they were doing to watch the strangers pass, silence following them through the settlement. The Marchers soon emerged in front of the largest tent of all, one that dwarfed the throne room of Eamhain Mhacha, with guards positioned around it, curved swords hanging at their sides, eyes wary, expressions hard.

It wasn't long before the Chief of the Desert Clan emerged from his palatial tent, surveying the Marchers. His expression was grave, his eyes hard. Not a tall man, he was stout with broad shoulders and scarred arms that showed he knew how to use the twin sabers strapped to his belt. His long beard, which came halfway down his chest, was braided with bells that jingled softly as he walked. Coming to a stop, he stood face to face with Thomas, their noses no more than a few fingers apart.

"So, you are the leader of these thieves and beggars. A stunted shrub as ugly as a mule who needs the protection of a woman." The Desert Chief gestured to Kaylie, who stood a few feet behind Thomas, hand on her sword hilt.

The Desert Chief had spoken in the language common to the Kingdoms, so the Highlanders understood the insult, and they were quick to take offense. Their hands moved to the hilts of their swords, Oso even faster as his blade was halfway out of its sheath. The warriors surrounding them quickly raised their throwing spears, ready to strike at anyone who made a sudden move. Thomas made a calming gesture, and the Marchers wisely withdrew their hands, Oso allowing his sword to slide back into its scabbard. But the Highlanders' harsh glares and angry scowls bore down on the desert fighters.

Speaking in the language of the Desert Clans, Thomas responded. "I do not have time to listen to the useless prattle of an old hag who has the breath of a goat and the intelligence of a rock."

Many of the surrounding fighters lowered their spears in surprise, shocked by what this boy had just said to their chief. The Marchers looked around in an attempt to read the situation, somewhat bewildered and unable to decipher what Thomas had said. Thomas repeated it in the common language so that they could understand, Oso gulping and wondering if Thomas had been wise to respond with an insult of his own.

The Desert Chief stared at Thomas, a sharp look in his eyes. Thomas stared back defiantly, his eyes blazing. Kaylie was convinced that Thomas had just doomed them all to a painful death. Then much to her surprise, the Desert Chief let out a huge bellow of a laugh, lunged forward and gripped Thomas in a bear hug.

"It is good to see you again, Thomas," said the chief, speaking in the common tongue. "You are away for far too long, and now I see you twice in a matter of months. How fortuitous. You know you really should visit more often. When you were younger you moved through the sands with the grace of a desert cat, putting some of my best warriors to shame."

"It is good to see you again, Chuma. I have been away too long from the sands. I forgot how beautiful they are."

Thomas turned to Kaylie and Oso, introducing them both. "Chuma is a Desert Chief of the Ashanti Clan," he explained. "He was with us in the Highlands when we defeated Rodric." Neither had met Chuma during the short time that he fought with the Marchers, though Kaylie now did recognize him from the council that had occurred after the battle. The Desert Chief had said little then, spending most of his time listening to the discussion.

"Yes, that was a good day," the Desert Chief said. "A good day indeed to put that fool to flight. But better to kill him. Have you killed him yet?"

"Not yet," replied Thomas. "But it won't be long. He owes me a debt."

"He owes many debts, but you have the right of first claim," Chuma nodded agreeably. "My apologies for your treatment on the way here. These men were not with me in the Highlands. I left those fighters in the eastern sands, closer to the Breaker, to give us warning in case events moved faster than we expected."

"It was nothing," replied Thomas. "I would expect nothing less entering the Desert uninvited."

"Once these men find out you are the Highland Lord you won't be able to escape them. They are greatly impressed by your escapades thanks to the stories I've shared."

"Nothing too outrageous, I hope?"

"Of course not, my young friend. Of course not. I save most of my exaggeration for my own stories," he laughed. "Come, let us talk." Chuma pulled Thomas after him while instructing his men to find places and food for Thomas' party. "Marchers, welcome to the Clanwar Desert. I am Chuma, chief of the Ashanti. You will be well taken care of."

Over his shoulder, Thomas relayed his own instructions. "Oso, make sure everyone has a place. They'll have an opportunity to get cleaned up before we eat."

Just then servants appeared to direct the male Marchers to the bath set aside for the men, while a servant came to Kaylie's side and directed her and the female Marchers toward the bath for women. Because there was so little water in the desert, it was a precious commodity.

To show respect for visitors, no matter how unwanted or unexpected they may be, they were given the privilege of bathing before dinner.

Chuma put a familiar arm around Thomas' shoulders as he guided him toward his tent. "So, how are your grandparents?"

Before allowing the servant to guide her toward the baths, Kaylie watched as Thomas walked off with Chuma. Once again Thomas had surprised her, not sharing everything that he knew. And if he didn't reveal his friendship with Chuma, what else had he kept to himself? She promised herself that she'd find out more when she had some time with Thomas on her own, hoping that she had finally gained his trust. And if he was reluctant to share his secrets, she'd pry them loose one by one.

CHAPTER SIXTY ONE

COMPETITION

As the sun began to set, the sharp red hues of the bright light dancing off the gentle waves of the small lake, the Marchers settled around the blazing cook fire situated in front of Chuma's tent. After weeks of travel, Oso was thrilled to see that it was more of a feast rather than a light supper as course after course came forward.

"You should try this," suggested Chuma, as a large platter was placed before them. Kaylie examined the dish skeptically.

Famished, Oso was ready to dig in. "What is it?" he asked as he reached for what looked to be skewered meat roasted over the fire.

"Baby sand snake broiled in goat's milk."

Oso stopped for a moment, rethinking. Kaylie recoiled, remembering how much she disliked her one bite of sand snake that she had nibbled on a few days before.

Oso shrugged, grabbing one of the foot-long pieces of crispy snake as his hunger got the better of him. "No harm in trying it."

"That's the way of it," commented Chuma. "You're just as adventurous as your young friend here," patting Thomas warmly on the back.

"You seem to know Thomas rather well, Chuma," suggested Kaylie.

"Ah, Princess, the stories I could tell about this one. He visited us many times with his grandparents, and each time he became engaged in some escapade that set tongues wagging. I would hate to embarrass him."

Ignoring Thomas' look of thanks for demonstrating some level of discretion, if only for just a few seconds, Thomas sighed in resignation as Chuma began to regale his friends with tales of his youth here in the desert. He had expected no less. Much like his grandfather, Chuma loved to play the role of storyteller.

The Desert Chief proceeded to do so with vigor. "When Rynlin and Rya first brought Thomas here, he was an enigma. He didn't talk much. But he watched everything and seemed to learn from all that he saw. Moreover, this was a child with no fear. The first day, he sent our entire camp into a tizzy. We thought that he had wandered off into the desert and gotten lost. Rynlin said not to worry, so I didn't, at least initially. But when it started to get dark and he still hadn't appeared, I decided to send out search parties. The desert is not the place to be alone at night. That's when the really dangerous predators emerge.

"Right when a group of soldiers was about to set off in search of Thomas, there was a ruckus at the edge of the settlement. People were screaming and shouting, scrambling among the tents, trying to escape something. I thought we were under attack. But who should appear walking calmly through the camp, apparently ignorant of the commotion that he had caused, but Thomas."

Chuma chuckled softly, his memory of that moment obviously still strong. He continued his narration.

"Walking by his side was the biggest desert cat I have ever seen. This beast was almost the size of that monster wolf that follows Thomas around. These desert cats are solitary animals. They go to great lengths to avoid people. And usually if an unlucky person runs into one, they don't survive. Yet Thomas had found this one skulking in the sand dunes off to the west, injured, and befriended him. The cat was hungry so Thomas thought to get him something to eat.

"The remainder of the time Thomas was with us, the two were inseparable. The cat had been hurt, so Thomas made it his mission to help the animal heal and regain its strength before it went back off into the desert. It was the most remarkable thing. Even when Thomas returned to the Highlands, for weeks after that the desert cat snuck into the camp as if it were his home.

"In fact, one night I got up because of a strange noise outside, not paying attention to much of anything, when I fell flat on my face as soon as I exited my tent. I learned much later that Thomas had asked the cat to look after me, to protect me, so the massive feline would slink in at night and stretch out in front of the entrance to my tent. I had tripped over him. When I picked myself up from the sand and saw that huge beast, teeth shining and its yellow eyes glowing in the night, I almost pissed myself right there!"

Chuma's raucous laughter rumbled over the oasis, Marchers and desert warriors laughing alike, as many of the desert people did, indeed, know the common tongue, and those who didn't obtained a translation from those who did.

"That cat stayed with us for many seasons, following us around the desert. My daughter even named him Mischief, as he enjoyed sneaking up on me and scaring the living daylights out of me. When Thomas visited again, he thanked the cat and said that he was free to move on. Being the Highlander that he is, I believe his exact words were: 'Your debt is paid.' Nevertheless, I should note that the desert cat still appears from time to time, seemingly checking up on me as Thomas requested so long ago."

"Thomas spoke to the cat?" asked Kaylie.

"Indeed he did, but you shouldn't be so surprised knowing that Thomas can speak to that big black wolf of his. I knew quite early that Thomas could communicate with any animal that he desired. It's a skill that's valued here in the desert, though perhaps not in every Kingdom."

"You're right, I shouldn't," agreed Kaylie. "Beluil has a mischievous streak in him as well."

"I meant to ask, where is that huge beast of yours? Is he traveling with you?"

"He is," replied Thomas. "And I'm sure he'll turn up eventually. He wanted to wander near the mountains for a bit, see if he could find any wolf packs."

"Ah, yes. There are, indeed, wolf packs there. Several that are even coming down into the desert, something that has happened rarely in the past."

"Why would the wolves enter the desert?" asked Oso, taking another bite of baby sand snake and clearly enjoying a meal that he had doubted at first. "I would think that they would find more and better game in the mountains."

"Dark creatures," answered Thomas.

"Exactly so," confirmed Chuma. "As you probably know, wolves are natural enemies of Ogren, Shades and any other spawn of the Shadow Lord. If they scent those depraved devils, they'll track them to the ends of the earth to destroy them. And as you've confirmed not too far from here, unfortunately these dark creatures are becoming more of an affliction here in the sands, just as I've heard has been the case in the eastern Kingdoms."

"It's to be expected," said Thomas.

"It is," replied Chuma. "After the council in the Highlands, I've been paying attention to the signs, and I've met with your grandparents privately. The Desert Clans meet in a fortnight. We will be with you at the Breaker. Of that, have no doubt."

"Thank you, Chuma."

"It is no more than what is required," replied the Desert Chief. "To not be there would be a stain on the honor of every desert warrior." The many desert fighters arranged around them murmured their assent or nodded their heads.

Kaylie sat there surprised. Normally the serious business between kings and queens was rarely straightforward, often requiring diplomacy and negotiation during which the parties tried not to say what they actually meant. But in less than a minute Chuma and Thomas had completed important business. Perhaps it was a lesson to be followed when she assumed responsibility for Fal Carrach.

The conversation turned once more to stories of Thomas. To Kaylie it appeared as if Chuma treated Thomas as the son he had never had, regaling his visitors with a tale about the time Thomas won a horse race against his best riders followed by one when he saved his daughter's life after she fell into a den of sand vipers. Kaylie was enthralled, absorbing as much as she could, though at times, thanks to Chuma's penchant for exaggeration, she found it difficult to separate fact from fiction.

As the evening turned to night, she became more aware that several of the Marchers had become intrigued by the desert women, who wore flowing skirts and tops that left their midsections exposed.

"Careful, Oso," said Thomas, tracking his friend's wandering eyes. "Anara might not take it well if she knew that you were paying so much attention to these young ladies. She always seems to have a hidden knife close at hand."

Oso almost choked on his food, sputtering a few pieces of sand snake out of his mouth.

"I was not …"

"Don't worry, Oso," Thomas laughed. "I'm just playing with you."

But Kaylie wasn't amused, and she saw how Thomas' eyes wandered as well. Particularly when a beautiful girl with dark, flowing hair, a wisp of a figure, a twinkle in her eye and her midsection bare, approached.

"Hello, Thomas," said the young lady.

"Asmera." Thomas rose quickly with a huge smile on his face. He lifted her off the ground and twirled her around, missing Oso's warning gesture, who had caught a glimpse of Kaylie's pained reaction that she tried to hide. "It's good to see you."

"You've never been away so long, Thomas," said Asmera, her voice teasing. "I was afraid you'd forgotten me."

"I could never forget you, Asmera."

Kaylie stood up, walking toward Thomas and Asmera. She had a smile on her face, though it obviously was forced. She was angry with herself, realizing that she really had no claim on Thomas, yet she felt jealousy building within her.

"Aren't you going to introduce us, Thomas?" Kaylie asked sweetly, too sweetly in fact as Thomas caught the edge in her voice and stepped back from Asmera.

"Yes. Yes, of course. I'm sorry about that. Asmera, this is Kaylie, daughter of King Gregory, heir to Fal Carrach. Kaylie, Asmera, Chuma's daughter."

"An honor, Princess," said Asmera, giving her a respectful nod.

"It's nice to meet you, Asmera."

Asmera sat down next to Thomas, on the side away from Kaylie, and immediately engaged him in conversation. Kaylie tried to enjoy her meal, but much of it now had no taste in her mouth. She became angrier with herself as the feast continued because of her souring mood. She tried to force her way back to the role of pleasant hostess that she had perfected after having had to attend so many feasts at her father's request, but it was proving more difficult than she had expected. As Thomas and Asmera laughed, Kaylie tried not to appear wounded by the lack of attention. Her face brightened when Thomas said that they'd be leaving in the morning.

"A good idea," agreed Chuma. "Time is of the essence. Asmera has spoken to me. She'll be going with you."

"What?" Thomas' smile turned into a look of concern. "Chuma, we have a dangerous task. You know what it entails."

"Thomas, you know the law," said Chuma.

"Thomas, it's my choice," countered Asmera. "I've been trained as an Ashanti warrior. You needn't worry."

"She'll get you through the desert without any trouble," confirmed Chuma. "Besides, I cannot refuse her. You will need her if you wish to navigate the Pits safely."

CHAPTER SIXTY TWO

LACK OF UNDERSTANDING

Early the next morning the Marchers prepared to leave, saddlebags packed and restocked thanks to the generosity of the Ashanti Clan. Kaylie was in a foul mood, her temper threatening to get the better of her as she checked her saddle for the third time. Thomas and Asmera had not appeared yet, and although she refused to admit it, the seed of jealousy continued to spread within her. Adding fuel to the fire, Oso seemed nervous as he tiptoed around her, almost as if he were afraid of her, which only set Kaylie more on edge.

"I don't understand why she has to come," said Kaylie, finally revealing the source of her increasing exasperation.

"Thomas explained it to me last night," Oso replied with some trepidation but in a level tone. "Asmera's of an age to be married. As Chuma's daughter, there's a great deal of interest among the Desert Clan nobility. In fact, several young men from other tribes have asked for her hand. But she hasn't accepted. Thomas doesn't think she's ready, or perhaps she's waiting for someone in particular to ask her, but he hasn't spoken to her about it yet. Anyway, according to desert custom Asmera can choose to wander for a time instead of getting married. It's common for the men, not so much for the women. But she's Chuma's daughter, and she's known for being strong-willed, perhaps to a fault, so no one in the Ashanti Clan is surprised."

"Who's she waiting for?" asked Kaylie, trying to sound casual.

"What do you mean?"

"You said someone was waiting to ask her for her hand in marriage?" Kaylie had crossed her arms, her gaze challenging.

Oso hesitated before answering, not sure why Kaylie had become so intense so quickly as she bit off her words.

"I didn't say that. I said that was a possibility. I don't know if she's waiting for someone to ask her. Thomas just said that might be why she wants to go with us."

Oso breathed a sigh of relief as Kaylie seemed to be satisfied with his hurried response. But she quickly moved to another topic.

"What do you mean by wander?"

"Thomas explained that in the desert once you reach the age for betrothal, if you're not ready to get married or don't have a suitable match, you can wander, or rather go on a journey to learn more about yourself. It's a custom that's geared to enhancing accountability and maturity. The only rule is that it can last for no more than one year, and then you must return and meet your responsibilities. He said that many of the young men, and a few of the young women, often move among the different Desert Clans during their time away. Some of the braver ones will leave the desert altogether and explore other Kingdoms, but that's rare apparently."

"But why did Thomas give in to her so easily? I can understand why Asmera would choose to avoid marriage, but Thomas made my efforts to join this group exceedingly difficult in comparison."

"I don't know," said Oso. "I'm sure he has a good reason. Besides, they've known each other a long time. Apparently, they spent a good bit of time together growing up."

Oso stopped talking, recognizing that he may have said too much. He realized quickly that he had made a major mistake. Kaylie looked crestfallen. He concluded that whatever was going on between Kaylie and Thomas, he'd best stay out of it.

Kaylie's fears with respect to Asmera immediately went to the worst possible scenario, which made it all the more difficult for her to release the anger and doubt that simmered within her and threatened to boil over. What she saw next didn't help matters. Thomas approached, having just exited Chuma's tent with Asmera a step behind her.

"Ready to go?" asked Thomas pleasantly, his saddlebags draped over his shoulder.

"I've been ready," Kaylie responded sharply. "If we're going, let's go."

Kaylie stalked off to her horse with barely a glance in Thomas' direction. Thomas stood in place, eyebrows raised, feeling as if he had just slammed into a wall and not understanding what had just happened.

"What was that about?"

Asmera stepped up next to Thomas, sizing up the situation with a twinkle in her eye. "I'll explain it to you later."

Thomas watched Chuma's daughter follow after Kaylie toward the horses. He glanced toward Oso, who stood there sheepishly shrugging his shoulders.

Thomas followed the two young women to the horses, wondering what dangers the next part of their journey might hold. Yet this time, the dangers he worried about had shifted to his travel companions rather than the dark creatures that he feared would continue to plague them.

CHAPTER SIXTY THREE

WRAPPED AROUND

The small party traveled for several days, first between the sand dunes and then winding their way along the eastern edge of the mountains that bordered the Clanwar Desert. Asmera served as guide, stopping at every oasis and watering hole along the way, while Thomas focused his attention on the surrounding landscape. There were no signs of dark creatures anywhere near them. But the darkness, the faint stench of corruption, that he and Kaylie couldn't identify, continued to flit in and out of his awareness, enervatingly so.

Kaylie was quiet for much of their journey, keeping to herself. She was frustrated with herself for how she felt, especially when Thomas rode near Asmera, the desert princess' smoky laughter making her teeth hurt. Asmera was beautiful and obviously someone Thomas knew quite well. Yet even though Thomas made several attempts to talk with Kaylie, she remained distant, trying to keep her feelings from getting the better of her. She thought that she and Thomas had a connection, but neither had ever expressed anything beyond friendship. Moreover, she realized that there were many aspects of his life that she knew nothing about. Obviously, Asmera was important to him.

Although Kaylie knew it was childish, she avoided Asmera as much as she could. Following almost a week of clipped and often tense interaction, Asmera tried to coax the Princess of Fal Carrach into a conversation. That night after dinner, as Thomas checked the sentries and wandered the perimeter of their camp with Beluil in tow, trying to get a feel for the land, Asmera sat down next to Kaylie, much to her annoyance.

"It must be difficult," said Asmera, direct as was her nature. "To love someone who must fight the Shadow Lord."

For a moment Kaylie's breath caught in her throat. "I don't love Thomas. I ..."

Asmera's look cut through Kaylie's attempt to deflect. Apparently she wasn't very good at hiding her feelings.

"It's that obvious?" she asked, deflated.

"To me and a few others, perhaps, but not to most. And clearly not to Thomas."

"I'm sorry, Asmera. I've been acting poorly." Kaylie shook her head in embarrassment. "It's just that when I see you and Thomas talking, you two look so happy together. And I feel like a knife has been driven through my heart. But I have no claim to Thomas."

"So you love him?" asked Asmera, a worldly look on her face, though it was more a statement than a question.

"Love him?" Kaylie was unable to keep the shock from her voice, though her saying it out loud made it ring true in her mind.

"Yes, you love him," said Asmera, her tone firm, now certain of her assumption. "I love him, too."

Kaylie's stomach lurched, the bile rising in her throat. She'd been right.

"And I hope Thomas loves me, too," continued Asmera, unconcerned by the impact her words had on Kaylie. "When we were younger, we performed the rituals of the marriage contract. We were foolish children, not knowing what we were doing. But you must understand, Thomas didn't have any friends our age, nor did I, being the chief's daughter. Perhaps it was the same for you as Princess of Fal Carrach, but when I was growing up the children my own age viewed me as a prize to be won, a way for them to gain what they wanted."

Kaylie nodded her head in understanding, thinking back to Maddan Dinnegan and some of her other so-called friends. Friends in name, perhaps, but no more than that based on their actions. She could certainly sympathize with Asmera, realizing that they had faced similar challenges during their childhoods.

"It is the way life is in the Desert Clans," continued Asmera. "Thomas saved my life once from sand vipers. He is a special person, and I do love him. I would do anything for him, but he is not for me."

A well of relief surged through Kaylie as she took in Asmera's words, surprised and thankful for the desert princess' honesty. Her insecurity had been unnecessary, and she had allowed herself to be dragged down by it.

"He's not?"

"No, he's not," confirmed Asmera. She leaned into Kaylie, as if she were confiding a key point. "If you need advice on how to get closer to him, I have a few ideas that might help. Thomas is slow to trust and afraid of what is to come."

"I'll keep that in mind," Kaylie replied. "Thank you for your honesty, Asmera. I do appreciate it." For the first time in a week Kaylie felt as if a weight had been lifted from her chest.

"We are direct here in the desert, Kaylie. We don't have the time to be otherwise. So you needn't worry. Thomas and I are only friends. Maybe even like the brother I never had. Yes, I will admit that at times I have thought of him as something more. As the daughter of Chuma, I am supposed to marry into another Desert Clan. It helps to maintain peace among the different tribes. But I wanted to see what the other options might be. So I visited a seer to find out if Thomas would be in my future. I must admit, I found it a very appealing idea. But the seer said it was not to be. That he would marry another and unite the Kingdoms. In fact, I have already met another I would like to marry, but he has yet to make his interest known. Hopefully at the next meeting of the Desert Clans I can choose him."

"You can choose your husband?" asked Kaylie, somewhat surprised.

"Yes, of course. You can't?"

"I don't know," answered Kaylie thoughtfully. "Traditionally the man has asked for the woman's hand in marriage. But as a princess, I have responsibilities to Fal Carrach. My father may want me to marry for the good of the Kingdom, rather than for my own good."

"Yes, I've heard of that," said Asmera. "A poor way to do things. Anyway, I hope you believe me when I say that I would like to be your friend, and that I will not be competing with you for Thomas. I have spoken to him, and he seems to like you very much."

"He said that?" asked Kaylie, a small smile breaking out on her face for the first time since they left the Ashanti camp.

"Well, his exact words were, 'Like her? Of course I like her. But half the time she says or does something just to irritate me.'"

Kaylie blushed, remembering several examples that Thomas could likely call to mind as part of his argument. "I guess I have done that."

"That is love in a man who does not know it yet," said Asmera confidently.

"Are you two taking a turn at sentry tonight?" As was his habit, Thomas had walked up silently to where they sat at the edge of the oasis under a cloudless night, the bright moon and stars lighting up the evening.

"Yes, we will," replied Kaylie. "Do you always have to sneak up on people?" she added a bit sharply, fearing that he had heard their conversation.

Surprised by Kaylie's tone, Thomas raised his eyebrows and chose to move on and find Oso, not sure if it was good or bad that Asmera and Kaylie finally seemed to be warming to each other.

Asmera laughed softly, "You two need to stop hiding your feelings. You are making all of us suffer as you dance around each other."

CHAPTER SIXTY FOUR

THE PITS

The Marchers continued to follow Asmera for several more days along the base of the mountains, moving from one hour to the next from sand that sucked at the hooves of their horses with dunes towering a hundred feet or more above them to terrain that resembled the lower Highlands, if a bit drier and hotter, the land rocky and rough, brown rather than green, and often requiring the riders to walk rather than risk injury to their mounts, then back again to the imposing dunes.

All had been quiet as they journeyed to the north, which bothered both Asmera and Thomas. Thomas used the Talent regularly to extend his senses for leagues around, often asking Kaylie to do the same to ensure that he didn't miss anything, yet no signs of danger or dark creatures appeared.

That, in itself, didn't worry them. They viewed that as a blessing. Rather, it was the lack of travelers in this part of the desert that suggested that something was amiss. Having come to the end of the rocky terrain after walking through a gulch that opened up to a broad expanse of smooth white sand that Asmera explained ran all the way to the coast and the Winter Sea, the last few mountains in the range rising to their left and stretching farther to the north, the Marchers halted to rest.

"This is strange," said Asmera, scanning the smooth sand, hand blocking the glare of the sun from her eyes.

"How so?" asked Kaylie.

"The way we came is a trade route. Merchant trains are always coming from the other direction."

"Kaylie and I have searched regularly, sometimes well into Kenmare to the west and toward the Breaker to the east," said Thomas. "There was no activity at all. Nothing."

"Strange, very strange," Asmera murmured. She continued to examine what lay before them for several long minutes, as if she were trying to perceive something that only she could see. "This is Berber territory. We should have at least run into one of their patrols before reaching the Pits."

"Pits? I don't understand." Kaylie looked out across the broad expanse of desert, the soft sand giving off a shimmering sheen under the harsh brightness of the sun. It was perfectly flat. No sand dunes, no obstructions. It appeared to be no more than white sand going on to the horizon.

"Looks can be deceiving," said Asmera, coming to stand beside her. "It looks flat, but littered throughout are the Pits. The shifting sand covers them, holes that could swallow a horseman whole. Some are even larger. It's like falling into dry quicksand. Once you tumble in, you don't make it out. You'll be covered by tons of suffocating sand in seconds. Because of this, the Pits are known as the graveyard of the desert. Anything could be buried out there."

Kaylie shivered at the thought. "Then how do we make it through?"

Asmera smiled at Kaylie. "That's why I'm here. To lead you through the Pits."

CHAPTER SIXTY FIVE

SAND AND GLASS

"There, up ahead," pointed Kaylie, catching the flash of the bright sun on what she assumed to be a piece of metal. As she and the Marchers approached it became more than that.

Having traveled through the Pits for almost two days, Kaylie had become used to the harsh environment's deceptiveness. Though the landscape appeared flat and unchanging, it was anything but. Undulations and troughs in the land gave the terrain an unevenness that could not be discerned from afar. It made travel all the more difficult, as some of the dunes rose higher than a man riding a horse, or the sand fell away into shallow trenches that could pull the unwary several feet below the surface in seconds.

Kaylie had to admit that having a guide who not only knew the path through this treacherous land, but also how to avoid its dangers, was essential. Otherwise, she doubted that any of them would make it out of the Pits alive. Asmera had led the Marchers unerringly north, not put off by the difficulty of navigating what to the naked eye appeared to be a flat, sandy plateau that merged into the horizon. For the most part, she was able to avoid the Pits. Only once did a Marcher stray from the path that he was told to follow. Before anyone could take a breath, he and his horse were up to their necks in loose sand that sought to pull them deeper.

Quick thinking had saved him, as Asmera showed the Marchers how to rope both the Marcher and his horse and pull them out without risk of them sinking to a level when extricating both man and animal became impossible. The experience led to some good-natured ribbing of the Marcher by his compatriots and a new-found respect for the dangers surrounding them.

Worried about their isolation, Thomas and Kaylie used the Talent to search around them every hour, seeking any signs of movement beyond that of a sand snake. Halfway through the Pits, Kaylie had found something unexpected.

A Berber warrior, wounded and unconscious, lay half in a Pit, having succeeded in keeping his upper body out of the grasping sand but exhausting himself in the process.

"I know him," said Asmera, an unexpected catch in her throat, as she leapt from her horse to help him. "Denega, son of the Berber chief."

"Would he be out here on his own?" asked Thomas, glancing around warily as Oso and Aric helped Asmera gently pull the wounded desert fighter from the Pit and begin to minister to his wounds. The Marchers recognized immediately what had caused his injuries as they began to clean and bind the slash across his shoulder and his chest.

"No, no sane man would come here by himself."

"That's what I thought. Marchers, battle formation!" The Marchers instantly moved to obey the command.

Thomas had guessed at what Asmera was finally realizing, distracted as she was by the wounded desert fighter. If Denega was here, where were his comrades? He would not have been left on his own unless something terrible had happened, and in the Pits it was a distinct possibility as there would be little to no evidence of what may have occurred.

Grasping the Talent, Kaylie extended her senses, wanting to know for herself. Her fears were confirmed just a few hundred yards to their west.

"Thomas! Ogren and a shade. Coming fast from the west."

"How many?"

"Several hundred. They just emerged from where they were hiding."

"There are crevices in the earth there closer to the mountains that run for leagues beneath the desert," explained Asmera. "Some that go several hundred feet deep."

"They were waiting for us," muttered Thomas. "Oso, Aric, get that man on a horse. There are too many for us to fight. Asmera, continue leading us north."

"But Thomas, if we do that the Ogren will take us," the desert princess replied. "The way through the Pits is winding and will force us to double back in some places."

"Don't worry about that, Asmera," said Thomas. "Take us straight north, Pits or no. I'll make sure the way is safe and clear."

"As you wish, Thomas."

Asmera was worried, but she trusted Thomas and would do as he requested. She immediately urged her horse to the head of the Marcher defensive formation, relieved to see Denega protected in the middle of the column.

"Kaylie, stay with the rear guard. Do you remember when I was showing you how to fight Ogren with the Talent?"

"Yes, Thomas," she said, recalling the lessons clearly, as well as their difficulty.

"Then consider this your opportunity for real practice. If any Ogren get too close, do whatever you can to keep them off of us."

Kaylie nodded, finding her place in the back of the formation as he had asked.

Thomas then took his place at the head of the column, nodding to Asmera to begin the march. She turned due north, grimacing with reluctance as she knew that several massive Pits, some large enough to swallow small towns, lurked just ahead.

Giving his horse his reins, and confident that his well-trained mount would follow the other battle steeds, Thomas took hold of the Talent and focused on what lay ahead. Drawing on the natural magic of the world, Thomas directed the energy to their front, applying it to the sand their horses now trudged through. In seconds, the soft sound of hooves gliding through the loose, granular flakes became a hard pounding.

Thomas had applied the power that he controlled to the sand, hardening it instantaneously into glass, knowing that the heat of the Talent would transform the fine crystals and leave the Marchers with a solid, cool surface upon which to make their escape.

Asmera noted the change in their path immediately, at first surprised, then she smiled to herself. She should have remembered that Thomas always had a trick or two up his sleeve. She increased the speed of the small party to a trot, then a steady gallop, confident that their way out of the Pits would remain clear so long as Thomas could create the track upon which their lives now depended.

Kaylie glanced back repeatedly, worry troubling her. She knew Ogren were near. She could feel them, the familiar cloud of darkness drawing inexorably closer. And then the massive beasts appeared, roaring and shouting their war cries. Although the Marchers had gained some distance on their pursuers, the Shade driving the Ogren quickly realized that the Marchers' escape path would benefit his beasts as well.

The long strides of the Ogren allowed the monsters to gain quickly on the fleeing Marchers as they raced across the glass track in pursuit. In just minutes, several of the dark creatures were no more than twenty yards behind, screaming in rage as they waved their weapons above their heads, anticipating the feast that they would have upon catching their quarry.

Grasping hold of the Talent, Kaylie tried to concentrate and remember what Thomas had shown her just a few days before. But riding a galloping horse and maintaining control of the Talent proved more difficult than she had expected. Fear coursed through her as she saw one Ogren outpace the others, now no more than a yard or two behind. The dark creature would be on them in seconds. The Marchers in the rear guard were preparing to turn and fight, but Kaylie couldn't allow that as she knew the likely result. There were simply too many

Ogren. That fear helped her hone her control, and she decided to use what Thomas had created for their escape to her advantage.

Directing the Talent onto the path behind them, small spikes of glass began to appear. At first the pursuing Ogren didn't slow, simply crushing the small outcroppings with their feet. But as Kaylie became more confident in what she was doing, the sharp glass spikes grew larger, the needle-sharp points shooting up from the path and curling back toward the hunters. Quickly reaching knee height, the Ogren could no longer ignore the shards of curved glass, the thick, spiked stilettos forcing them to slow down and swing their battle axes in front of them to clear the way.

That bought the Marchers a precious few more seconds. Now confident in her ability, Kaylie refined her touch. Knowing that the Ogren could simply knock down whatever she created, she realized that timing was all important. She waited for the Ogren to once again gain speed, allowing their path to remain clear for the moment. Free from any barriers, the dark creatures drew closer once more, and this time Kaylie knew exactly what to do.

Applying the Talent, massive spikes of glass grew behind the Marchers in less than a second, the glass spears sloping toward the oncoming Ogren, the massive beasts unable to slow in time. The dark creatures' momentum forced the spikes through their chests and guts, the shards of glass puncturing whatever few pieces of stolen armor they may have worn and their hardened skin. As the bulk of the Ogren caught up to those most anxious for the kill, the few Ogren that had succeeded in escaping the trap were shoved forward by the approaching beasts, forcing them onto the rapidly sprouting glass spikes.

The Ogren advance came to an abrupt halt, as the Shade had the dozen Ogren impaled on the glass thrown off the shimmering path into the sand. Knowing now what it faced, the Shade brought some semblance of order to its beasts, having the dark creatures start off again after the Marchers at a slower but steady pace.

Looking back over his shoulder and impressed by Kaylie's handiwork, Thomas kept his attention focused on his task of creating their escape route.

"Asmera, how far out are we?"

Asmera knew that Thomas referred to the Great Pit, their galloping mounts having taken them out over the largest Pit in the desert, one that could swallow a small city. She had told him about it the night before, the last major obstacle before they'd be free of the Pits.

She understood what Thomas was thinking. "We're far enough."

Thomas nodded then stopped his horse, the Marchers streaking past him. Kaylie looked at him quizzically as she rode by, wondering what he was about to do next. The Marchers stopped a few hundred yards ahead, still in battle formation.

Thomas took his place in the middle of the glass path. He watched the Ogrens' unwavering approach, just a hundred yards away now. The front ranks, unable to control their blood lust upon seeing their prey having come to a stop, sprinted forward, seeking to close the distance. The Shade, in the middle of the beasts, hesitated, perhaps sensing that something was off.

He should, thought Thomas. Keeping his hold on the Talent so as to maintain the glass path that he had created for the Marchers, he took a small sliver of the energy he controlled, turning it over and over in his hands. The small sliver grew into a ball of white flame, spinning faster and faster, increasing in size every time it rotated. When the first Ogren was only yards away, sword raised high to cleave Thomas in two, the Highland Lord threw the ball of energy down onto the path the Marchers had used, the track upon which the Ogren now sprinted.

The energy burst through the glass, the tremendous heat melting the bindings that held the sand crystals together. To the shock of the Shade and Ogren, the glass disintegrated. The once solid path transformed once more to sand, the sand of the Great Pit, which hungrily reached for the Ogren that now stood upon it. The massive bulk of the Ogren gave the beasts little chance. With no solid ground for miles around, many of the Ogren disappeared in the blink of an eye while others continued to struggle for as long as possible, not knowing that their efforts were in vain and that their movement actually quickened their deadly descent into the Great Pit.

Thomas watched for a moment, unmoved by the cries of distress and fear as the beasts disappeared below the sand, not leaving a trace. When the Shade finally sank beneath the feathery crystals, its head covered by the soft sand whipped up by the breeze, Thomas turned his mount back to his Marchers and trotted slowly toward them.

CHAPTER SIXTY SIX

MINE

The remainder of the Marchers' time in the Pits proved uneventful. Wanting to avoid any repeat of Ogren streaming out of one of the many crevices that dotted the landscape to the west, Thomas continued to use the Talent to create a solid, glass path for them across the sandy waste. Although any dark creature near them that had mastered Dark Magic could sense such continuous use of the Talent and use it to track them, Thomas wasn't concerned as he broke the trail behind them once they had traveled a good distance so that there could be no easy pursuit.

A day later, the Marchers had reached the northern edge of the Clanwar Desert, the eastern peaks of the mountains of Kenmare off to their west.

"I would like to continue with you, Thomas. But I can't. It seems that I will have to end my wandering before it has barely begun."

The daughter of the Ashanti chieftain had gratefully accepted supplies from the Marchers and was filling her saddlebags, preparing to make the long trip back through the Pits.

"What of the dark creatures?" asked Kaylie, worried for her newfound friend.

"Thank you for your concern, Kaylie. But it's nothing to worry about. Denega and I can avoid them easily."

"You'll be all right with Denega?" asked Thomas. The desert warrior had recovered some of his strength, although his wounds would continue to pain him for several weeks until they healed.

"More than all right," replied Asmera, a suggestive twinkle in her eyes. "Besides, the Desert Clans must know of the Ogren incursions. We must take action and clear the Desert, then turn our attention to larger worries."

Thomas nodded in understanding. "I can offer you several Marchers if you think they would be of assistance."

"Thank you, Thomas, but no. Your need is greater."

Asmera hugged Thomas before mounting her horse and making sure that the Marchers had gotten Denega in the saddle as well. The desert fighter seemed to be doing much better — smiling every time Asmera looked at him, which was frequently — but his face was still wan and drawn.

"Remember how I left because I wasn't ready to marry?" asked Asmera, speaking directly to Kaylie. "That wasn't entirely correct. I was ready, but I was still mulling my options. Although several young men had declared their intentions, the one who had mattered most had not."

"Denega?"

"Yes. We met several summers ago, and since then he's made it a point to visit every year since. He's a brave warrior and a good man. And the fact that he's son of the Berber chief won't hurt matters either."

"What are Denega's thoughts on the matter?"

The Berber Clan warrior had benefited from the aid offered by the Marchers and was able to sit a horse so long as the travel was slow. But he still struggled with the pain of his wounds and tired easily. It would mean a slow return with frequent stops.

"It's a long trip back. I'll make the most of it and find out."

"Of that I have no doubt," laughed Kaylie.

"Remember my advice, Kaylie," whispered Asmera, reaching across her saddle and pulling the Princess of Fal Carrach into a hug. "At some point you must share your feelings."

CHAPTER SIXTY SEVEN

MOUNTAIN MAN

"They're not really mountains," objected Oso, surveying the smaller peaks that rose before the Marchers and comparing them to the towering spires of the Highlands. But he was pleased nonetheless because of the familiarity of the terrain. The cooler, crisp air that became thinner as they climbed up to and through the first pass into the Kenmare Mountains raised the Marchers' spirits. That and the fact that there had been no sign of dark creatures since the attack in the Pits. Thomas regularly used the Talent to search the area, asking Kaylie to do the same, so that she could hone her skill and ensure that no surprises lay in wait.

Mid-morning approached, the Marchers leading their horses down a small, steep path, when the group came to an unexpected stop. Kaylie peeked around the many large Marchers assembled in front of her, then stepped back in surprise. A massive warrior stood in front of them, blocking their way. Wearing leather armor that barely fit his broad, hulking frame, the fighter wore a huge sword on his back and carried a wickedly curved axe in a hand that seemed large enough to crush a small boulder.

Thomas stepped forward, a smile on his face. Kaylie was worried for a moment. She trusted in Thomas' fighting skill, but she feared for him if he were to challenge the man who stood calmly barring the tortuous path. She soon realized that her concern was unnecessary. As Thomas approached, the warrior's stoic expression broke into a grin, and he pulled Thomas into a hug that likely would have crushed a bear. Releasing one another, Thomas and the hulking warrior talked for a few minutes, the small band of Marchers behind them forgotten for the moment.

Oso watched the exchange, exhaling what appeared to be a sigh of relief. "I'm glad he's a friend, as I would not want to get on that man's bad side. He could probably cut me in half with that axe of his."

"It seems that everywhere we go, Thomas has a friend or two stashed away that we know nothing about."

Again Kaylie realized that she had no knowledge of a large part of Thomas' life. He had traveled to many of the Kingdoms, having all manner of friends and acquaintances, while for the most part she had remained in or near Fal Carrach. To say nothing of what he had experienced as a Sylvan Warrior.

"Better a friend than an enemy," stated Oso. "I didn't have the chance to speak with him, but I remember him from our fight against Rodric in the Highlands. He's a Sylvan Warrior, and he's been helping Anara and the Highland chiefs clear the northern range of dark creatures."

"Yes, another Sylvan Warrior," said Aric, stepping forward to join them. The Marcher was pleased, captured by the mystical nature of the small band of warriors charged with protecting the Kingdoms from the Shadow Lord and his servants.

"How do you know he's a Sylvan Warrior?" asked Kaylie.

"The necklace with the unicorn horn," replied Aric. "It looks just like the one Lord Thomas wears."

"I need to speak with him," said Oso. "Any man with an axe like that could likely offer some good advice on how to fight Ogren."

Thomas concluded his conversation a few minutes later. The tall warrior, who resembled a walking mountain, slapped him on the back, then trotted down the path with an unexpected grace and dexterity, disappearing among the crags and fissures along the trail.

Thomas approached the Marchers to share what he had learned from Catal Huyuk, the Sylvan Warrior charged with protecting these mountains.

"The Ogren we met in the desert are nothing compared to the raiding parties here in the Kenmare Mountains," he explained. "Apparently the dark creatures have been infiltrating these peaks for some time, but even more so during the last few weeks, likely taking advantage of our focus on the northern Highlands. Kenmare doesn't have a fighting force like the Marchers, so they're struggling to keep the dark creatures in the mountains and away from the farmsteads to the west. Catal Huyuk will accompany us through the mountains, as he's seen more and more activity by the Shadow Lord's servants with no good cause behind it. Once he gets us through the peaks, he'll return to the northern Highlands to help Anara."

"Could all the dark creatures be here because of us?" asked Kaylie. "Are we being tracked in some way?"

"You could be right, Kaylie," admitted Thomas. "Remember, use of the Talent, as we've been doing, can be detected by some of the Shadow Lord's creatures. So they could be using that to find us, though we didn't have much choice in the Clanwar Desert. I have no doubt that the Shadow Lord does not want us to achieve our objective, and I wouldn't be surprised if he has a general sense of the direction that we're going, but it's a risk that we can't avoid. We'll just need to be careful in the use of the Talent and keep our eyes open. How fast we travel might be our best defense against further attack."

"Well, if that's the case, then let's get moving." Kaylie pulled on her horse's reins, leading the way down the path, the Marchers falling in line behind her.

"Catal Huyuk? Wasn't that an ancient city that disappeared a thousand years ago?" asked Oso, mulling the name of their new friend and remembering how easily he tore through Rodric's Ogren in the Highlands.

"It was," replied Thomas, surprised by the large Highlander's knowledge.

"It's fitting, then. He's about as large as a small city."

"I wouldn't tell him that," laughed Thomas. "He doesn't always have a sense of humor."

"Don't worry about that," replied Oso. "I know when to keep my mouth shut. I don't plan on irritating him. I just have a few questions for him. Besides, I'm just glad to have another blade with us."

CHAPTER SIXTY EIGHT

LEAP OF FAITH

Upon making camp in a hidden glade along the crest of one of the Kenmare peaks that provided a view for several miles around in all directions, the Marchers banked their fires, wanting to keep their presence hidden from any searching eyes as a moonless night fell upon the land. Catal Huyuk did not return to the site until just past midnight. Thomas had been waiting for him. Kaylie had first watch, and she observed them talking for several minutes in hushed tones before they both walked off between the surrounding trees. When Aric came to relieve her and she settled under her blankets she found it difficult to fall asleep. Something clearly had worried Thomas and the broad, imposing Sylvan Warrior, which meant that she had cause to worry as well.

The next day began with quiet efficiency, the Marchers breaking camp quickly and heading deeper into the Kenmarian heights. As the day wore on, however, the small group became edgy, even with their massive guide calmly leading the way. He had warned of the many Ogren raiding parties apparently wandering in the mountains with no apparent purpose and their resulting need to remain wary. Though dark creatures had not been sighted, the Marchers expected that if only by chance it would likely only be a matter of time before the Ogren found them. Circumstances changed for the worse shortly after midday.

"Ogren. Getting closer," said Thomas.

"Agreed," replied Catal Huyuk, loquacious as ever.

"I don't think they know where we are specifically, but it won't take them long to locate us."

For a moment, Thomas wished that Beluil had continued with them beyond the Clanwar Desert. His senses and ferocity, as well as his ability to find the wolf packs of Kenmare, would have proved useful. But Thomas had given his friend another task that would take him back to the Highlands.

"Then let's move," rumbled the huge Sylvan Warrior.

Catal Huyuk increased his pace, the others following after, all becoming more tense and wary as the sense of approaching danger became more concrete. The Marchers remained alert, Thomas and Kaylie using the Talent from time to time to confirm what they suspected, though it wasn't until late afternoon that their fears were made real.

"They know where we are," said Thomas, having stepped his horse off the trail and taken a moment to use the Talent to search the surrounding area. "Three large bands are coming toward us."

"How long?" asked Oso.

"Half hour at most."

"Everyone, then, quickly," said Catal Huyuk. "Follow me."

Catal Huyuk broke into a run. The Marchers hurried after, urging their mounts after the formidable Sylvan Warrior. In minutes they had to pull up short. Catal Huyuk had led them to a ravine about twenty feet across that led out onto a small plateau. A drop of several hundred feet to the easternmost branch of the Crescent River threatened at the verge of the ravine.

"Quickly. Everyone across. We can defend ourselves on the other side."

Catal Huyuk bent at his knees and in a single leap from a standing position easily launched himself across the open space, landing deftly on the far side.

Oso shrugged his shoulders, then circled his horse back around before urging his mount into a gallop. They jumped the ravine with a few feet to spare. The other Marchers quickly followed Oso's lead.

In no time at all, Kaylie was left standing on the far side of the ravine with Thomas. Kaylie looked at Thomas with some trepidation, but she caught his small smile and brief nod. She took confidence in that. Giving Thomas a small nod as well, as if what she was about to do was a common occurrence for her, she pulled her horse back, then touched her heels to its flanks, urging the mare to a gallop.

Her horse easily vaulted the ravine, landing comfortably on the other side, which brought a huge smile to her face.

Just as Thomas' horse prepared to leap the gap, a single Ogren burst from the brush behind them. The dark creature charged toward him, sprinting over the short distance so quickly that Thomas feared the beast would catch them before they made it across. Giving his horse its reins, he turned around in the saddle, pulling a throwing knife from his belt. Taking the tip of the blade between his fingers, with the dark creature about to lunge for him, he threw the blade behind him with a flick of his wrist. With the Ogren roaring in victory as it reached for the flank of Thomas' horse, the dagger struck true, taking the huge beast through the right eye. As Thomas' horse soared through the air and he grabbed frantically for its mane, the dark creature tumbled over the edge in silence.

Thomas still hadn't gained control of the reins, so he wasn't prepared for the jolt of the landing. The jarring impact rattled him to his bones, and he unwittingly pulled back on the one rein he had managed to grab a hold of. In response, his horse reared, and he fell off its back. He realized how close he was to the edge when his legs hung out over the open space of the ravine. As he felt himself beginning to slide backward, he scrabbled in the loose dirt with his hands, desperately seeking some kind of purchase but finding none. But before he could slip further over the edge, Catal Huyuk reached out with a giant hand just in time to grab his arm and pull him to safety.

"Probably a scout," growled Catal Huyuk. "You need to be more careful." With a grin, the large Sylvan Warrior helped him to his feet and patted him on the back.

"Not a word," said Thomas, nodding his thanks to the mountain of a man who stood beside him. He took a few deep breaths in an effort to calm his nerves. "Not a word."

"What do you mean?" Kaylie asked, a spark of false innocence in her eyes.

CHAPTER SIXTY NINE

OVER THE GAP

The Marchers dismounted, allowing their horses to move away from the expected battlefield, as an occasional growl or snarl carried up from the lower heights in the direction from which the Marchers had just come. Oso hastily formed the Marchers into a battle line, bows at the ready, arrows stuck point first in the soft earth at their feet to speed each shot. Catal Huyuk stood at one end of the formation, massive axe in hand, staring intently at the forest on the other side of the crevice. He was calm, apparently unconcerned, yet his eyes danced with anticipation.

All was quiet, almost unnaturally so, as the constant chatter of the animals living in the sparse forest that blanketed these mountains slowly died away. There was nothing to see but the Marchers' breath frosting in the cold air. Then the pounding began. Softly at first, then louder, the ground beginning to shake on the other side of the crevice. Then louder still, the rhythmic quality resembling the beat of the drum, as the steady tread of the approaching enemy came closer with each passing second.

When the first Ogren stepped from between the trees on the far side, the Marchers raised their bows, ready to release. Only Oso's shouted command to hold fire stopped them. More Ogren began to appear, then even more, spilling out onto the small clearing. Soon several hundred of the dark creatures milled around uneasily, corralled by the split in the earth and the trees to either side. Many of the terrifying beasts roared in anger or frustration, seeing their prey just beyond the crevice, so close but still just beyond their reach. Surprisingly, none showed any inclination to attempt a crossing. In fact, with so many Ogren in such close proximity to one another, a few fights broke out, the massive beasts, aggressive by nature, not caring what they killed.

That changed when the Shade appeared. Gliding out from between the trees, the Ogren parted as it stepped gracefully to the gap. It stood there arrogantly, examining its quarry on the other side of the fissure. Behind it the Ogren grew quiet, compliant, clearly cowed by this dark creature that led them in the name of their master.

Catal Huyuk had guessed at what would happen next, and he knew that if the beasts were successful the odds of survival would be stacked against them. "Thomas, the Shadow Lord knows exactly where we are. There's no need for you to restrain your use of the Talent."

Thomas nodded, glancing at Kaylie to make sure that she understood. In response, she sheathed her sword, just as Thomas did. With a great deal of concern they realized now the expected severity of the coming skirmish.

Apparently satisfied with the circumstances of the current situation, the Shade issued a silent command. The first rank of Ogren, only ten in all because the rocks and trees lining the glade constrained the small space where the monstrous dark creatures now stood, ran toward the crevice, attempting to bridge the gap.

Screaming their war cries, some slavering in anticipation of the meal that stood right in front of them, the Ogren leapt through the air.

Massively strong across the shoulders because of their tremendous size, this now proved to be a disadvantage for the beasts. The Ogrens' great weight made jumping long distances a challenge, and this proved to be the case now. A few Ogren failed to make it to the other side, just missing the edge and slamming into the cliff face, their clawlike hands hopelessly scratching against the sheer stone before the beasts plummeted to their deaths in the river hundreds of feet below. Several of the other Ogren that failed to reach the other side likely would have made it if not for the Marchers showering them with arrows as soon as their feet left the ground.

Those that did make it across did so just barely, and in spite of the arrows jutting from their immense frames. These beasts met their demise at the hands of Thomas and Kaylie. Both having drawn on the Talent, Thomas crafted shafts of blazing white light that he shot at the Ogren lucky enough to span the gap but unlucky to have to face him. Following his example, Kaylie did the same with the Talent, sweeping the crest of the gorge clean of dark creatures.

It proved to be an effective and necessary defense, for the Shade had Ogren to waste and the dark creature didn't hesitate to use them. Intent on its goal, the Shade sent one wave of Ogren after another leaping across the crevice. With the sun just about to hit the western horizon and darkness quickly descending, the Marchers stood their ground resolutely as the dark creature attack continued unabated. When the arrows ran out, the Marchers relied on Thomas and Kaylie, stepping in with Catal Huyuk to help dispatch the larger number of Ogren that were making their way successfully across the crevice. The Marchers silently thanked Catal Huyuk for selecting this battleground. They knew that without the rocks on the other side that hemmed in the dark creatures, and thereby restricted how many Ogren the Shade could launch at them at one time, they faced certain death.

Nevertheless, though the Marchers put up an effective defense, Catal Huyuk reluctantly admitted to himself that with the Marcher arrows gone, it was just a matter of time before there was a breakthrough. The Shade seemed to have reached the same conclusion, halting the attack as darkness descended over the mountains.

The Shade recognized that the Marchers had nowhere to go, and that if its quarry attempted to escape during the night, it would simply mean that its Ogren could cross the crevice with impunity and catch up to the Marchers the next day in a less defensible position. The Ogren, having watched the Marchers destroy half their number in less than an hour, appeared to welcome the chance to step away from the crevice and wait for the following day to continue their attack. Staring at the Marchers for a few moments more, finally, with the settling darkness almost complete, the Shade left several Ogren to stand guard at the edge of the crevice during the night, then pulled his remaining dark creatures closer to the trees at their backs, satisfied that regardless of whether its enemies remained where they were or fled, the Shadow Lord's servant could destroy them whenever it so desired.

CHAPTER SEVENTY

DIFFERENT PATH

Aric and Oso stood guard by the crevice, ready to shout a warning if the Ogren attempted to cross at night, though that possibility appeared to be unlikely. The Shade didn't seem to feel the need to rush, and Thomas soon understood why as he made use of the Talent to search the mountains around them. The Ogren on the other side of the fissure were no longer their only concern.

Catal Huyuk and Thomas had reached the same conclusion as the Shade, and they soon fully understood the dire nature of the threat they actually faced. With their arrows gone, tomorrow would prove more difficult. Even with Thomas and Kaylie's use of the Talent, each attack across the gap during the morning likely would wear down the Marchers until their numbers dwindled to the point where resistance would prove untenable. But that was no longer the only worry as a new danger approached.

"I can sense several more bands of Ogren making their way toward us," said Thomas, munching on the bread and watery stew that they had prepared for the night. The fire gave away their position to the Ogren across the crevice, but at this point it didn't matter. "One on the other side of the crevice, two on this side and coming up behind us. They'll be here by morning."

"Any more bad news?" asked Kaylie, who sat next to Thomas, their legs touching. Kaylie told herself that it was because the rock they were sharing required it. But she admitted to herself, however reluctantly, that she hoped that there was more to it than that.

"Indeed I do," he sighed. "A pack of Fearhounds are following behind the Ogren. They're farther away, but they're making up the ground quickly. I expect that they'll be here in time to join in the morning fun if not before based on their current pace. And those dark creatures will have no problem at all leaping the gap, especially with our lack of arrows. The Shadow Lord seems quite intent on making sure that we don't reach our destination."

"Though this has the makings of the ending of a great tale, a last-gasp fight to the death, we cannot stay here," grumbled Catal Huyuk. The mountain of a man sounded almost disappointed.

"Can we make it down the cliff face?" asked Kaylie. "If we can find some handholds and footholds ..."

"It's a good thought, Princess, but the cliffs are sheer. Even with the rope you carry, you would never reach the bottom safely."

"You know these heights better than anyone," said Thomas, fairly confident that his friend had another option in mind. "Any ideas other than a defense that would be remembered by the bards?"

Catal Huyuk grinned. "I do. Gather your Marchers and horses quietly, but leave the fires burning. Let the dark creatures on the other side think that you remain here. Then follow me."

Thomas immediately set off to obey. In a matter of minutes he had the Marchers ready and moving silently behind Catal Huyuk as the Sylvan Warrior led them deeper among the large rocks on the northern side of the crevice. For several minutes the Marchers followed in almost complete darkness, only the moon, often shrouded by clouds, offering some illumination.

As they moved farther away from the Ogren, Catal Huyuk explained. "Just a bit farther down this trail is a path barely wide enough for a man on horseback, though in some places it might be a very tight fit and you'll want to walk your mount. The path switches back dozens of times and will be treacherous because of fallen stones, but it will take you down to the river. You can follow it west to Great Falls in Kenmare."

"The Ogren can't follow?" asked Oso.

"No, they are too big. It will force the Shade to take his beasts back down the mountains to try to catch you. By the time the Shade makes it to the river, you should have a day's head start. If you keep a fast pace, you should gain the city walls before they catch you."

"You said the Ogren can't follow," confirmed Kaylie. "But what of the Fearhounds?"

"Alas, Fearhounds will have little difficulty on this path," said Catal Huyuk, who stopped then stepped out of the way.

He had reached the hidden track, a small sliver of space that rose up between the cliffs just wide enough for a man on horseback as Catal Huyuk had promised. Thomas' gaze followed it up the cliff face, noting that the higher up he looked, the tighter the space, as if the cliffs were trying to once again join together.

"You won't be coming," said Thomas matter of factly.

"No. I will wait until morning and then make sure that the Fearhounds don't follow. There is a good spot a little farther down the trail where I can hold any pursuers as long as necessary. It's a natural bottleneck."

Thomas didn't like the idea of putting his friend in danger. "Come with us. We can get down the path before the Fearhounds pursue us."

"It is not a risk worth taking," said Catal Huyuk. "Remember, Thomas, the primary objective is finding the Key. That is what truly matters."

Thomas growled in resignation, knowing that he wasn't the only one who had to make sacrifices if they were to be successful and hating the burdens of his responsibility all the more.

"Don't stay too long. I expect to see you in the Charnel Mountains."

"You can count on it, Thomas."

CHAPTER SEVENTY ONE

TAKING A RISK

Making their way down the hidden path as quickly and safely as possible, the twists and turns and loose rock forcing them to an agonizingly slow pace at times, Thomas and the Marchers still reached the branch of the Crescent River with the sun just rising in the east. Nevertheless, the dim light stayed with them for several hours as the mountains blocked the sunlight from reaching them and kept them in a hazy gloom, caught between morning and night until they had ridden several leagues to the west.

Their stops were brief over the next few days as they tracked the river. Thomas and Kaylie regularly used the Talent, extending their senses in search of any danger as they feared that the Ogren and Fearhounds would make up the ground the Marchers had gained thanks to Catal Huyuk's heroic efforts. But the dark creatures remained behind them by at least a day or more and the demanding pace they traveled was designed to keep it that way. A pace that wore on them and their mounts but proved necessary. Difficult travel and little sleep were less of a concern than having to stand and fight against what chased after them. Finally, after three days of hard riding, their horses spent, the walls of Great Falls rose above them.

Capital of Kenmare, the hustle and bustle of the city that spread across both sides of the Crescent River could be heard for leagues around. Any merchants traveling the Winter Sea and seeking to bring their goods to the east, or for that matter merchants from the east seeking to bring their goods to the north and west, inevitably stopped in Great Falls on their way to or from Faralan, Kenmare's primary port city located a dozen leagues to the north where the westernmost branch of the Crescent River emptied into the Winter Sea.

Traveling from Faralan south down the Crescent River to Great Falls was an easy journey, except for one major obstacle. Just to the north of Great Falls at the edge of the city limits, a massive waterfall, actually several connected waterfalls, broke out over the length of the mile-wide river. Every second, thousands upon thousands of tons of water fell from the rim of the falls to crash almost a mile below where the Crescent River flowed swift and strong to the coast. There was no way around, as the lip of the cliff that the Crescent River dropped from stretched out in a semicircle, its central point at Faralan, so that the land between Faralan and Great Falls appeared to be a gigantic half-crescent-moon-shaped canyon surrounded by sheer cliffs that ran for leagues until the heights met the Winter Sea in two places. Thus the importance of Great Falls.

The incessant pounding of the falls added to the noise of the busy river city, as goods were winched up and down the mile-high cliffs on cranes that dwarfed the largest merchant ships. Because of the size of the drop, the cranes were situated at several strategic points along the cliff face, so that each huge bundle of goods could be lowered or raised on their massive pallets, carefully and slowly, then transferred from one crane to the next.

Though it often took a day or more for the cargo of one ship at the top of the falls to be transferred to a ship at the bottom, the delay was worth it, as traveling by land added weeks or more to any journey, for there was nowhere else but Great Falls to travel up or down the Cliffs of Kenmare. For Rendael of Kenmare, this fact proved to be a boon, as the taxes and fees he levied for moorings and the transfer of cargo kept his treasury well stocked and his Kingdom solvent.

As the Marchers entered through the main gates of the port city, swallowed by the mass of merchants and travelers who had made Great Falls a stopping point, Thomas ignored the stalls and vendors selling everything from Distant Island spices to Ferranagh tobacco. Instead, he studied the walls that rose behind him, satisfied that Ogren could not breach them easily, though a Shade might attempt to make its way into the city during the dark of night.

Thomas felt the pull of the Key more intensely as he traveled steadily to the northwest. At first just an itch between his shoulder blades, now he could feel the tug in his gut. And with each passing day that pull grew stronger. He couldn't explain why, but he knew that they needed to continue toward Inishmore and then the Western Ocean. Therefore, they had to find a ship below the Falls that would take them to Faralan, and then from there to Laurag, the capital of Inishmore, all while avoiding the Whorl. That deadly obstacle, at least, should be well to the northeast this time of the year and less of a threat.

Thomas turned back around as Oso led them through the throng in search of an inn in a quieter part of the city. He breathed a sigh of relief, letting go of the tension that had been building up within him during the last few days. They would be safe here, at least for the moment. For several days he had not sensed the darkness that had trailed them through the Clanwar Desert, nor had Kaylie, almost as if it were allowing the Ogren and Fearhounds to do its work for it. Perhaps the pursuing evil had been put off by the natural defenses of the city.

Heading away from the river, Oso and the Marchers pushed their way through the crowds until they found the Hunter's Rest, a small inn tucked up against the city's northern wall and away from the controlled chaos of the market squares. Clean and quiet, with a great room for meals, the Marchers settled in easily to their new surroundings. Exhausted by their escape from the Ogren, the Marchers ate first, then enjoyed baths before finding themselves back in the great room for drinks and stories. Oso and Aric in particular were eager to find out as much as they could as to what might be happening to the west and in Inishmore, a Kingdom known for its instability, and their next destination. Therefore, they spent a good bit of their time talking with the merchants and other travelers sprinkled about the room to acquire what gossip that they could.

Kaylie enjoyed the opportunity to relax, letting her fears and concerns go at least for a time. Though Kaylie wasn't so sure about Thomas, who had settled his chair against the wall of the great room so that he could see all that was going on around them and anyone entering the inn. He appeared to be dozing, but Kaylie knew better.

"You can't relax, can you?"

Thomas didn't even bother to open his eyes. "What do you mean?"

"I can feel it, you know. You're extending your senses even now."

Thomas opened his eyes and smiled. He leaned forward, bringing the back of his chair off the wall. He glanced around the common room briefly, glad to see that his Marchers were enjoying themselves, and pleased even more that they all remained sober and watchful, wanting to be prepared in case anything unexpected happened.

"It's a habit I find difficult to break."

"Do you ever just let go? Or are you always so tempered in your approach? So controlled?"

Thomas took a moment before responding. "I haven't had much practice in letting my worries go. It seems that whenever I try to do so, it proves to be a mistake."

Kaylie winced on the inside, thinking that Thomas might be referring to when they had first spent time together at the Eastern Festival, and what had happened when he had perhaps done just that to meet her for their picnic. She didn't want to remember the cost that he had paid for that decision and the angst and guilt that she had finally released after months of anguish.

"But don't you often feel the same, Kaylie?" Thomas continued. "Raised to rule a Kingdom, forced to take on responsibilities and burdens that weigh you down and bring you nothing but boredom or grief?"

"It's not always like that," she protested.

"True, but much of the time …"

"Much of the time it feels exactly like that," Kaylie confirmed with a sigh. She grinned as she thought about it a bit more. "I do have to admit, though, that even with all that we've been through, the last few weeks have been a great deal of fun."

Thomas chuckled. "You mean riding in a saddle for days on end, being chased by and having to fight Ogren, cold food, the stench of Marchers too long without a bath …"

"And the opportunity to make my own decisions, feeling like I'm a part of something important, that I'm contributing. That I'm accepted for who I am and what I can do, not because of the title that I bear."

Thomas smiled, staring into Kaylie's eyes. She felt as if he were taking in everything about her. As a result, her cheeks flushed, her body growing warm.

"I understand that completely," he replied.

Enjoying each other's company in silence a few minutes more, the warmth of the room built on their exhaustion. They decided to turn in, Thomas stopping to talk with Oso and Aric for a few minutes before following Kaylie upstairs to the sleeping rooms. The Marchers were sharing rooms. Thomas and Kaylie had their own chambers. Though smaller in size, they appreciated the privacy.

Kaylie opened the door to her room, then turned back toward Thomas. He stood there quietly, a small smile playing across his lips.

"Thomas, tonight was a welcome change …"

Before she could say anything else, he leaned forward, kissing her softly on the lips. Surprised for just an instant, Kaylie quickly responded, and the gentle kiss became stronger, lasting for what seemed like a much longer time than it really was. Finally, breathless, Kaylie pulled back, her face flushed red.

Kaylie smiled.

Thomas nodded. "Good night, then. Make sure you lock your door." He then turned and entered his room, closing the door softly behind him.

Kaylie stood there in the hallway for a full minute, not moving. Finally, she stepped into her room, closing and locking the door. She normally didn't like surprises, but that one had certainly appealed to her.

CHAPTER SEVENTY TWO

TRAILING SHADOW

The next morning Thomas and Oso went out to the docks before the sun rose, seeking a ship anchored below the falls that could take them west. The pull from the Key had grown more insistent, a slowly building ache. Thomas was convinced that his final location was beyond Laurag now, somewhere in the Distant Islands. But he wouldn't know for sure until they headed in that direction.

Much to their irritation, despite several hours of effort, they couldn't locate a ship that would take them all the way to Afara as all of the captains sailing in that direction were unwilling to brave the mercurial waters of the far northwest. The best that they could do was a merchant vessel bound for Laurag. Wanting to keep moving and be on their way as soon as possible, they reached terms with a captain who had come to the bottom of the falls to ensure his cargo was handled properly.

Looking a bit rough about the edges but appearing to be exceedingly competent, Torlan, captain of the *Waverunner*, told them to have their party at the bottom of the falls by daybreak. Oso and Thomas then jumped onto the lifts that would take them back to the top of the falls and walked in the direction of their inn, satisfied that their work for the day had been a success. As they made their way through the crowds, markets and squares that dominated the city's business and cultural activity, Thomas tried to take his time and experience what was going on around him as Kaylie had suggested. Rather than rushing from one point to the next, he and Oso stopped to watch the various street performers or examine some strange and exotic good that they had never seen before. For a time, Thomas enjoyed himself, but as he approached the inn his unusual calm was shattered when his senses prickled, a feeling of danger sweeping over him.

It wasn't Ogren or Shades. The war party that had tracked them from the mountains had stayed away from the city, obviously hoping to pick up their scent once they left the safe confines of Great Falls. No, this feeling differed. It was more subtle, but just as dangerous. Several times Thomas looked back over his shoulder, sensing an imminent threat, expecting an attack, but finding nothing to suggest that his concern was justified, as there was nothing around him and Oso but the regular ebb and flow of too many people crammed into too small a space.

Nevertheless, the feeling continued to plague him. It felt like the shadow of darkness that he and Kaylie had identified as they traveled from Eamhain Mhacha into the Clanwar Desert, always on the very limit of their senses, then slipping away for a time before coming back to tease him.

Reaching the inn as night fell, Thomas explained the next step in their journey to the Marchers. All were satisfied with the arrangements, as they, too, wanted to keep on the move. Resolved to an early start, after dinner they all retired to their rooms to prepare for the journey, while Oso and Aric went to the horse traders by the main gates to the city, seeking to make accommodations for their mounts, which wouldn't be accompanying them.

When Thomas reached his room, Kaylie stopped just behind him, her hand resting on the doorknob to her room.

"Thomas …"

"Yes, Kaylie?"

There was a hopeful yet hesitant quality in Kaylie's voice. There seemed to be something that she wanted to say or do. An awkward silence settled between them as Thomas was still distracted by the sense of evil that had touched him earlier in the day. Just as Kaylie was about to say something, Thomas spoke.

"Kaylie, yesterday I …" He knew what he wanted to say, but didn't know how.

Noting his discomfort, Kaylie found the courage that Thomas seemed to lack.

"You feel like you made a mistake last night. That you shouldn't have kissed me." Her voice was quiet, disappointed.

Thomas looked at her in surprise. "No, not at all," he stammered. "It's just that …"

"Thomas, you'll confront an Ogren, a Shade, other dark creatures without fear. Why is it that I scare you?"

Thomas bowed his head and sighed. "Because I care about you. When I look into your eyes, I lose myself in them. When I kissed you last night, it felt right. I wanted to kiss you again and again. But I don't want to hurt you."

"How could you hurt me?" asked Kaylie. "Last night I seem to recall kissing you in return."

"Yes, I know." Raising his head, her warm expression made it difficult for him to think clearly, the urge to reach for her growing stronger. But he fought the impulse. "We both know what will likely happen when I face the Shadow Lord."

Thomas saw the change instantly come across Kaylie, her eyes turning hard, her expression determined. "You need to give yourself more credit, Thomas." She spoke in a voice that reminded him of her role as the Princess of Fal Carrach, strong, clear, with authority that could not be ignored. "And remember, what happens between us, it's something that we both decide. Both of us. Are we clear?"

Thomas nodded, at a loss for words.

Then Kaylie nodded. Leaning forward she kissed him gently on the cheek before she stepped quickly into her room, locking the door behind her.

Thomas stood there for a moment, staring at the rough wood of the door. Not sure what had just happened, he felt as if he had failed an important test. And not knowing what else to do, he walked into his room, cursing silently for not being able to express himself well or clearly, something that certainly couldn't be said of Kaylie.

CHAPTER SEVENTY THREE

WRAITH

Thomas had a hard time sleeping that night, tossing and turning, his mind never turning off. The conversation with Kaylie continued to play through his mind, and each time it did it didn't improve. Moreover, the feeling of approaching evil kept getting stronger, stalking him, but despite the handful of times that he sought to use the Talent to pinpoint the location of the threat, he failed. The darkness was too amorphous, always moving, always shifting, always just a touch beyond his grasp. Struggling to identify the evil that plagued him, that kept getting closer and closer, he leapt from his bed, pulling his sword from its scabbard. He stood there in his underclothes, the early morning chill no more than a minor distraction. His senses were on edge, and he strained for any hint of what to expect. As the minutes passed, he felt the evil continue its slow advance, now no more than a few feet away. But he still couldn't pinpoint it. Although every fiber of his being told him that he was in mortal peril, nothing seemed out of place. All was quiet in the inn. There was nothing to suggest that danger was close. Still, a shiver went up Thomas' spine as the approaching evil crept closer, the miasma of wickedness almost sickening him.

A slight knock at the door startled him. Sword at the ready, the sense of wrongness flooding the room, Thomas extended his senses, prepared to strike at whatever threatened. Kaylie stood in the hallway. Worried for her safety, Thomas opened the door quickly, pulling her into his room as he looked up and down the hallway. Seeing that all was as it should be, he closed the door behind him.

"Can you feel it?" Thomas asked Kaylie. "That cloud of darkness that was always just on the edge of our senses? It's close, very close."

"I don't feel anything, Thomas."

"It's here. Somewhere. Closer than it's ever been."

Thomas crept to the window, peering out at the street below, careful to make sure that he wasn't seen by anyone who might be watching his small chamber. Their rooms were on the top floor with no easy way down. But perhaps there was a way up if they needed to make their escape, thinking that he could use the ceiling overhang if need be to pull himself up onto the roof. He debated rousing the Marchers, the sense of evil clouding his senses, consuming him, when a quick movement at his back diverted him from his thoughts.

"Thomas, stop for a moment," said Kaylie, her hand gliding softly across his back, stopping to trace the scars that crisscrossed his skin from his time at the hands of the High King. The marks of the whip had faded, but the furrows into his flesh had never left him.

Thomas stepped away from Kaylie, his back to the wall. He hadn't really noticed Kaylie when he pulled her into his room, more worried about what danger might be lurking in the hallway. He was shocked by what he saw now, his eyes wide and mouth open.

Kaylie stood there in her shirt and nothing else, the top open, buttons undone to reveal soft, white skin. Her toned legs were hard to miss. She had a hand on her hip, jutting a bit to the side, to accentuate the curves of her body. If he stared hard enough, he could make out the slopes of her breasts. Her eyes were sultry, mouth pouty. Thomas had no idea what to do. He had kissed her the night before, yes, but that just felt like the right thing to do at the time. He had never expected that this would be next. What had come over her?

Caught by her eyes, Thomas stood frozen against the wall, his sword threatening to slip from his grasp. Kaylie approached him, hips swaying provocatively, her movements inhumanly graceful and sinuous. Kaylie raised her hands to his shoulders, then ran them softly up and down his chest. His sword barely remained in his hand, the tip digging into the wooden floor, forgotten, as he watched Kaylie's soft lips approach his own.

"We've danced around this long enough," she said, her breath hot in his ear. "It's time. It's time that you became mine."

Kaylie raised her lips to his, pressing her body against him as her hands sought to cup his face. His eyes closed in anticipation, what he had dreamed of about to become reality. But the mood was broken when the door to his room slammed back against the wall and tilted at an angle, its top hinge broken.

"You cannot have him!" screamed Kaylie.

What! Two Kaylies? Thomas tried to move away from where he was pinned against the wall, but the Kaylie who held him there kept a firm grip on him as she turned to face the one who had just entered his room. "Too late, Princess. He will be mine, and then I will take you as well."

The Kaylie holding him up against the wall turned back to him, but this time her eyes were different. Darker. Harder. Predatory. When she leaned in toward him, mouth open, he saw a forked tongue slipping out, her teeth now sharp, pointed, like those of a shark.

Thomas finally recognized the danger and tried to get away from this creature that had taken on Kaylie's appearance. But he couldn't. Her eyes still held him. He couldn't break away. He couldn't turn his gaze from the dark pools of shadow no matter how hard he tried, the soft blackness that played within, the orbs mesmerizing him. It reminded him of his encounter with the dark creature that attacked him in Eamhain Mhacha after the Council of the Kingdoms. The logical part of his mind considered the issue, remembering that the thing that he had fought that night had first appeared as Sarelle, Queen of Benewyn, before changing to Rendael, King of Kenmare, then finally Oso. The part of his mind that focused on survival screamed at him to move, to break free, but he couldn't. Those spinning spheres of black kept him there, his muscles locked in place.

Knowing that time was of the essence, Kaylie leapt forward, dagger outstretched. Sensing the threat, the creature holding Thomas whipped around, raising its arm to block the blow. But its arm had changed, as had the rest of its body. No longer resembling Kaylie, the dark creature's skin had mutated into grey scales, its hair midnight black, just like the swirling pools of darkness that formed its eyes.

Kaylie's dagger strike glanced off the creature's hardened forearm, but she maintained her attack as best she could in the confined space. Her flowing movements and quick jabs kept the creature off balance as it dodged and deflected Kaylie's attacks. Yet Kaylie could not break through no matter what she tried. Even when her dagger struck the creature's arms or penetrated its defenses to hit the creature's chest, sparks flew as the steel slid across the scales, but her steel barely slowed down the dark creature, leaving no mark. The creature's shifting scales were impenetrable, and Kaylie was tiring. Moreover, Thomas remained fixed against the wall, nothing but his eyes moving as he tracked the fight. All it would take for him to die would be a single swipe of the dark creature's claw against his exposed throat. Kaylie couldn't allow that. She had to keep the dark creature occupied, off balance.

Sensing that its opponent was flagging, the dark creature attacked with an almost animal ferocity, forcing Kaylie back toward the broken door. Soon it was all that Kaylie could do to protect herself, as the dark creature's hands had transformed into sharp claws that scraped time and again against her blade, the sound setting her teeth on edge.

"You have meddled where you shouldn't, girl," whispered the dark creature, its voice sibilant, reminding Kaylie of the sound a snake might make. "And your time has come. Once I take you, I will take the boy as …"

The dark creature never finished its comment, as the tip of a sharp blade, pulsing with white light, appeared in its chest. For a moment everything was still, the dark creature staring down at the hard, shining steel running through its body, the blade pulsing brighter and brighter as it appeared to pull the life from the dark creature before it finally slid off the blade and collapsed to the floor, the light in its eyes drifting away and a black ichor seeping from the wounds in its back and chest to stain the wooden floor.

Thomas stood there, still appearing a bit confused, but sword in hand, the sharp blade covered in a slick black blood. Kaylie's intense attack had forced the dark creature to turn its attention away from him, giving him the time to fight and then finally break free from the Dark Magic that had been used against him. He knelt down, making sure that the dark creature was dead, then released his hold on the Talent and wiped the blade on the washcloth by his water basin.

"What was it?" asked Kaylie, finally noticing that Oso, Aric and the other Marchers stood in the doorway, drawn by the noises of the struggle. Swords and axes at the ready, they realized that they had arrived too late and that all the excitement had come to an end.

"I've never seen something like this before," answered Thomas. "But Rynlin told me what he thought might apply after we left Eamhain Mhacha. I think it's a Wraith, a dark creature that can change its shape and appearance into whatever it wants. It's supposedly one of the Shadow Lord's most effective assassins, not only because it can get close to its targets with impunity, but also because it has the capacity to immobilize them. I think that cloud of darkness that's been tracking us emanated from this creature. It might explain why it was so hard to determine what it was."

Kaylie stared nonplussed at the body, nodding her head.

"That makes sense," said Kaylie. "That would explain what I saw, how it affected you. Why couldn't I harm it?"

"You were using a steel blade," answered Thomas. "You can't get past a Wraith's natural armor unless you use the Talent."

"Which explains why your blade …"

"Yes," said Thomas simply.

"Your grandmother showed me how to do that," said Kaylie. "But I'd like to practice it a bit more, just in case."

"We can, just as soon as we're out of this city and aboard ship."

"Good," said Kaylie, sheathing her dagger and walking from the room. "Between now and then," she called back over her shoulder, "try not to be caught by a pretty face."

The Princess of Fal Carrach walked across the hall and into her room. Before she shut the door many of the Marchers nodded to her in respect, several catching the end of her duel against the lightning-fast Wraith, all smiling at her quip.

Oso looked down at the body on the floor, taking in the black hair and grey face, the forked tongue lolling to the side with its sharp teeth evident. Then he turned to his friend, somewhat worried.

"You found that attractive?"

CHAPTER SEVENTY FOUR

A FEELING

Rya stared absently into the small fire, her mind wandering as she watched the flames dance in front of her, sparking every time a gust of the cold northern wind blasted into the small clearing the Sylvan Warriors had occupied for the night. It had been a difficult day, but in the end, it had proven to be a good one. Their work had paid off, the results of which could be seen at the bottom of the gulley just a few hundred yards away. They had dragged the Ogren that they had not incinerated fully with the Talent to the lip of the small gorge, then pushed the bodies over, creating a pile of at least four score dark creatures. Rynlin had then set the pile alight and even now, several hours after the skirmish, it continued to burn, the glow of the flames, rising to the top of the crest, visible in the distance. They had selected that location for a reason, thankful that it was downwind so that they could avoid the terrible smell of burning flesh.

Rynlin sat next to her on one of the logs that they had pulled closer to the fire, poking at the flames with a stick, his mind clearly elsewhere. Maden Grenis and the twins, Aurelia and Elisia Valeran, sat across from them.

Brinn Kavolin had eaten his fill from the stew they had made, then wandered off into the night to check their perimeter. They had little concern of dark creatures sneaking up on them, as all were skilled in the Talent, but the tall, thin Sylvan Warrior preferred to know the surrounding terrain like the back of his hand, and this was his opportunity to do so.

Normally, Rynlin and Maden Grenis never stopped talking, whether with or at one another. It was in their nature, they simply couldn't help it, and the other Sylvan Warriors often enjoyed the give and take. But not tonight. Tonight a feeling had overcome them all. An inevitability of what was to come, leading to the quiet that had draped itself over the Sylvan Warriors like a funeral dirge.

Perhaps it was because Catal Huyuk had not yet come back from the Kenmare Mountains, mused Rya. Rynlin had asked that he return to his protectorate and keep an eye out for Thomas, expecting that his grandson would head in that direction in search of the Key. The hulking Sylvan Warrior who rarely spoke exuded a calm that they all missed in that moment, to say nothing of the terrifying effect that he had on dark creatures when he wielded his war axe with such great skill.

But she didn't think that was really the reason for the quiet. Rya expected that they would be moving on in the morning, another Ogren war band probably already coming across the Northern Steppes and trying to sneak into the northern Highlands. Such was the reality of their existence at the moment. The friends and warriors gathered around the small fire knew that a critical time was approaching with the fates of all those living in the Kingdoms hanging in the balance. The Shadow Lord was testing them, and it was only a matter of time before he set his Dark Horde upon the Kingdoms once again. Time was running out and Thomas would soon play his role as set out in the prophecy. That's likely what had captured their thoughts, just as it had hers, she surmised. Her mind was rarely far from musings about her grandson and the task that he had charged himself with completing.

Unexpectedly she jumped up from her seat and turned toward the northwest, her hand holding tightly to the amulet she wore around her neck. The sharp point of the unicorn's horn dug into her skin, drawing several drops of blood. Rynlin had stood up with her, his hand reaching for the amulet that had gone ice cold against his chest.

"What's the matter?" asked Maden Grenis, startled by the actions of his two friends. His worry only increased when they ignored him for several minutes, Rya and Rynlin still staring to the northwest as if in a trance, their bodies rigid. Elisia and Aurelia had risen from their seats as well, thinking first that danger approached, but then they realized the cause. The twins waited calmly as the minutes passed, which only served to irritate Maden. He wasn't known for his patience, and clearly something was wrong. But he didn't know what.

Finally, Rynlin and Rya released their grips on their amulets, both breathing a sigh of relief.

"He's all right, Rynlin," Rya whispered, unable to keep the tremor from her voice.

"He is," confirmed Rynlin.

"What was it?" asked Maden, barely able to contain himself.

"Thomas," replied Rynlin, who pulled his wife into his chest, Rya burrowing into her husband and closing her eyes in thanks that her grandson still survived. "We were thinking of him and our amulets went ice cold."

"He was in danger," Elisia and Aurelia both said in musical voices at exactly the same time so that it seemed that they had spoken with one voice.

"But he's all right?" asked Maden just to confirm. He had known Thomas ever since the boy had come to live with Rynlin and Rya, and he had liked the quiet, focused child immediately. In fact, Maden had come to think of him as a nephew.

"Yes, he's all right," nodded Rynlin. "He was in danger. A darkness that I couldn't identify had almost descended upon him. For a moment we feared that his spirit was taken. But the darkness is gone now. Our amulets are warm once again. He's safe, for the time being."

"The Shadow Lord?" asked the twins again.

"Or his servant," answered Rynlin.

"He must be getting close," offered Maden.

"I think he is," said Rynlin. "Now that I can feel Thomas again, I can sense his urgency through the amulet."

"If he gets the Key …," started Maden.

"When he gets the Key," corrected Rynlin, his eyes blazing with certainty, "we must be ready. When he gets the Key, the Sylvana must be prepared to ride to war."

CHAPTER SEVENTY FIVE

GROWING CLOSER

Thomas stood at the bow of the ship, watching as the sailors scampered up the masts, unfurling sails, tying off lines, and preparing to exit the harbor. His Marchers had all found berths in the stern, the captain offering his small cabin to Kaylie during the passage to Laurag. The massive merchant vessel, five masts in all, resembled a floating city, as it carried both cargo and passengers to its various ports of call. Card games already had broken out on the parts of the deck not used by the sailors, something his Marchers had quickly come to appreciate and enjoy since they had left Great Falls a few days before.

Initially Thomas thought that it would take a month or more to reach Laurag, after the *Waverunner* made a quick dash down the Crescent River from Great Falls to Faralan, taking on a few more slats and bins of cargo before leaving that same day and entering the Winter Sea. But Torlan, the amiable captain of the ship, explained differently. Normally, at this time of the year, yes, it would take five or six weeks, as the winds generally came from the west with unexpected gales and squalls running rampant through the Winter Sea. Thus, the decision by most experienced shipmasters to stay near the coast, settling for the slower, safer passage of following the shore, rather than risking what would be a more dangerous but potentially faster route in the open water. But not this time.

For the first time in centuries the Whorl, the massive whirlpool with a width of several leagues that drifted around the Winter Sea, and the primary cause for the unpredictable and dangerous currents and rogue waves common to this ocean, had shifted from its traditional location for this time of the year. Normally farther to the north, near the Charnel Mountains, it had strayed to the south earlier than expected, its southern edge curling dangerously just a few leagues from Faralan.

As the *Waverunner* broke from the port and quickly picked up speed, the sails on its five masts caught the wind, snapping into place as it sped out toward open water. Once the ship had settled into the waves, Torlan came to the bow, his sharp eye observing everything going on around him. He was just as quick to praise his crew for their good work as he was to spit out a blistering string of curses when a sailor failed to meet his expectations. The crew seemed to appreciate it, even when they felt the brunt of his wrath. There were no surprises with Torlan, so the crew knew where they stood with him. He was fair but strict, and most sailors believed that they couldn't ask for more than that from a captain.

Thomas looked to the east, seeing with his sharp eyes the very edges of the Whorl. In that direction the sea spun in a frothy, clockwise direction that ignored the pull of the moon and the currents, sucking down to the bottom of the sea in a matter of minutes any ship unlucky enough to be caught within its currents.

"Aye, it has a mind of its own," said Torlan, resting his muscled forearms on the railing as he looked out over the sea. "We're lucky, young master. A few days more and we might not have made it out of Faralan."

"Because of the Whorl?" asked Thomas.

"Aye. Right now we're enjoying the benefits of that blasted blight of the Winter Sea. I can't tell you how many ships have been lost because of it. But now it's aiding us. The Whorl moves, yes, but it always spins in the same direction. The winds that are filling our sails right now," gestured Torlan, pointing to the thick, white sailcloth that strained against the strong blast and had the huge ship cutting through the waves as if it were just a skiff, "are coming from the Whorl. If we had been just a day or two later coming out of the port, we might not have made it."

"How so?"

"The Whorl tends to be to the far north this time of year, so why it has come down this close to the coast of Kenmare is a bit of a mystery." Torlan glanced over his shoulder, shouting quickly to a sailor to tie off a line that had broken free from the forward mast, before turning back to Thomas. "But I'm not complaining, mind you. I'm just surprised that the Whorl is still moving toward the coast. It's almost as if it's going to settle right in front of Faralan, which means no shipping in any direction until it moves again. We never would have been able to make it to Laurag if the Whorl had gotten ahead of us. Its winds would have been too strong, and no one would have risked its currents. But now we should get to Laurag in half the time."

Thomas nodded, his sharp eyes picking out the signs of life in the ocean. Off in the distance, he saw a pod of dolphins playing in the water, and every so often a flying fish leaping out from the water before diving gracefully back into the crest of a wave. He had been taught that the Whorl was a natural occurrence, that nothing controlled it. It moved as it wanted when it wanted, though it tended to follow a fairly regular pattern during the year, which allowed for fairly consistent commerce across the Winter Sea during certain seasons.

But could there be something more to it? Could it have moved early in the hopes of keeping him from going west? As Torlan had said, where it had placed itself now went against what they knew of the Whorl. Did the Shadow Lord have that much power over the happenings in this world?

Thomas pushed these depressing thoughts from his mind. Taking that path led only to fear and uncertainty. He could afford neither at the moment. He gazed back out over the waves. The pod of dolphins, off their port side, had disappeared. Then he realized why.

"Is it common for Great Sharks to be in this part of the Winter Sea this time of year?"

The huge fins of three sharks, fully eight to ten feet above the water, sliced through the waves. Thomas was familiar with the beasts, having grown up on the Isle of Mist. The massive sharks, fifty to sixty feet in length, were the apex predator of the ocean. Nothing could challenge them.

Thomas had gotten a close view of the monsters whenever he sailed his small skiff through a narrow canal from his home on the island to the Highlands. He always stayed in that shallow channel, which prevented the Great Sharks from attacking, knowing that if he strayed beyond the boundary to deeper water he would pay with his life. Great Sharks were known to track larger ships, and captains of smaller ships feared them. There were so many stories of Great Sharks attacking and destroying vessels that ship captains always kept a close eye. But Torlan didn't appear worried because of the size of the *Waverunner.*

Torlan followed Thomas' gaze, cursing under his breath. "Blasted monsters," grumbled the ship captain. "No, those beasts rarely visit these frigid depths. They stay to the coastal waters off the Charnel Mountains. Why they came this far southwest, I can't say."

The captain watched the fins cutting through the waves a bit longer, noting with some disgust that despite his ship's speed they followed the *Waverunner* easily. The size of his ship gave him comfort, but he was a cautious man by nature, and he liked to prepare for the worst.

"Tell me, young master. Those Marchers of yours. Good with their bows?"

Thomas smiled. "The best."

"Would you mind if I made use of a few? Nothing strenuous, you see. Just a few always on the rails watching those damned creatures, ready to take action if need be."

"I'll see to it, captain."

"My thanks, young sir. Nothing to fear, I'm sure, but better safe than sorry." Torlan turned to go, wanting to check on the rest of his ship and crew. "Good afternoon, miss. I trust all is well?"

"Yes, Captain Torlan, thank you. And thank you for the use of your quarters."

"No thanks necessary, miss. No thanks at all."

Torlan walked off, releasing a constant string of praise or curses depending on the quality of work he saw as he went on his way. Kaylie stepped up and took his place, standing close to Thomas, her shoulder touching his. Thomas felt a warmth spread through him, though he tried to ignore it as it threatened to muddle his thoughts.

Thomas closed his eyes for a moment, enjoying the companionable silence and proximity with Kaylie. But it lasted only so long. He could feel the Key, its pull stronger by the minute as the *Waverunner* skimmed through the waves to the west.

"I know that look," said Kaylie, nudging him with her shoulder. "Do you know where it is exactly?"

"I have a good guess. In a few days I'll probably know for sure."

"Laurag as you thought originally?"

"I don't think so. A bit farther to the north, most likely."

The silence returned, Kaylie looking at her hands. Thomas kept his eyes on the Great Sharks, which continued to trail the *Waverunner*, maintaining their distance but never straying too far behind.

"Thank you," said Thomas. "For what you did in Great Falls."

Kaylie nodded. "You seemed quite taken with her," said Kaylie, a small smile touching her lips.

"It wasn't a 'her,'" protested Thomas.

"True, but that's what got that thing into your room."

Thomas sighed, knowing that it would be awhile before he could live down what had happened. "I felt that darkness, that cloud that seemed to be following us from Eamhain Mhacha. I knew it was in the inn, but I didn't know where. When you appeared at my door, I pulled you — I mean I pulled what looked like you — into my room, because I thought that you could be in danger. I didn't realize that I was pulling the Wraith right where it wanted to be."

"Are you sure that was the only reason?" asked Kaylie cheekily.

Thomas blushed, remembering the image that had confronted him when he had shut the door, the Wraith standing in his room. It had taken on Kaylie's appearance, using its Dark Magic to assume her shape, features, gestures, voice, everything about her. But the revealing nature of its clothes and steaminess of its manners were distinctly not what Thomas had come to expect from Kaylie. The Wraith had put him off guard, and that had helped the creature's Dark Magic work, freezing him in place, much like a fly caught in a spider's web. Only the real Kaylie's appearance had saved him.

"I didn't really see what you, what the Wraith that looked like you …" Thomas gave up. "I admit I was a bit surprised …"

"It's all right, Thomas," said Kaylie, patting his arm. "You can admit that you liked what you saw."

"Kaylie …"

As Thomas grew more flustered, Kaylie broke out laughing. "I'm sorry, Thomas. I couldn't resist teasing you a little."

Thomas leaned back against the railing, surveying all the activity on the ship's deck and trying to figure out what to say next. He needed to talk to Oso and set a guard schedule as Torlan requested.

"If you want me to say that I was … pleased by your appearance, or rather the image of you the Wraith had taken, then yes, it was quite eye-opening. I …"

"That's all right, Thomas. You don't need to explain."

Thomas stammered for a moment, then finally blurted out what was on his mind. "It's just that you're really beautiful and …"

"Thomas …"

Kaylie cut him off, not wanting the conversation to go any farther. She had intended to have a little fun at his expense, and she had achieved that goal. But she didn't want to go down a road that might increase her own embarrassment.

Thomas' eyes captured hers, the green intensity burrowing into her heart. Before she knew what she was doing, she had stepped up close to Thomas, leaning her arms against his chest, and kissed him lightly on the lips.

At just that moment, the ship hit a deep trough in the waves, dropping down into it. The jolt pulled Kaylie away from Thomas as she grabbed for the railing. Her cheeks burned a fierce red and her eyes struggled to meet his. She scrunched her hands together, discomfited. She had not planned on doing what she had just done, and she realized that several of the Marchers had seen it, though they had the intelligence to stay silent and avert their eyes when she peered out across the ship once more.

"Well, good. That's kind of you to say. Thank you, Thomas."

Kaylie quickly escaped to her small cabin, locking the door behind her. She berated herself as she sat on her bunk, not knowing what had come over her. Her anger initially came from her decision to kiss Thomas, as the urge to experience again what she had felt in the inn at Great Falls had dominated her thoughts. She told herself that she needed to stop acting like a foolish girl. She needed to act like the princess that she was. Yet each time she tried to regain her composure, the memory of Thomas' lips touching hers set her face blazing, a small smile lifting her flushed cheeks.

CHAPTER SEVENTY SIX

STRANGE BEHAVIOR

"Thomas, Torlan's asked for you. Something strange is going on."

Oso stood in the doorway to Thomas' small cabin in the early morning hours. The tall Marcher appeared agitated, worried, which was out of character for Thomas' normally imperturbable friend.

Rising quickly, Thomas threw on a shirt, pulled on his boots and out of habit grabbed his sword. He followed Oso up the tight stairway, the sharp, cool breeze of that time between morning and night clearing the cobwebs of sleep from his mind. Oso led him to the port rail near the bow of the merchant vessel. His Marchers, set to watch the waters around the ship, had their bows drawn, arrows ready to shoot.

"They're not acting as they should," said Torlan, who gazed out over the water. The fins of the Great Sharks that had trailed them for the better part of a week had drawn closer than ever before. Rather than following, they had picked up speed and now were circling the merchant vessel, much as they would if they were hunting prey. "Smaller ships, yes, I wouldn't be surprised by this behavior. To them a small ship is simply a possible meal. But not the *Waverunner*. We're too big a ship."

"There might be more to it than that," said Thomas, watching the massive sharks.

The beasts had no trouble staying with the vessel, which continued to benefit from the strong westerly winds generated by the Whorl. But the circles the Great Sharks were swimming were becoming tighter. Despite the darkness, with Thomas' sharp vision, he could see the malevolence in the red eyes of the Great Shark that had just swam by the ship's port side, its sharp teeth visible.

"That's just an old wives' tale," sputtered Torlan. "It can't be true."

Thomas turned toward the captain, a hard gleam in his eye. "In every tale, there's a kernel of truth. That's what my grandmother likes to say. There's more truth to this tale than anyone would like to admit."

"The Shadow Lord! Blazes, how are we to defend against these behemoths?"

"As best as we can. Captain, get your men to the rigging. Oso, wake any Marchers still in their bunks."

"What do you mean to do, Thomas?"

"We're not going to wait for them to attack. We're going to turn the tables. I want to get as many strikes in as we can before they decide to come at us."

"Music to my ears," said the tall Highlander, who raced below decks, bellowing for the Marchers to arm for battle.

Torlan sprinted off as well, showing remarkable speed and agility for a man of his size. Sailors began pouring up onto the deck, ready for their orders.

"What would you have us do, my young friend?" asked the captain. He had already decided that if they were to survive this engagement, he needed to cede command to the young Highlander with the green eyes that blazed brightly in the early morning murk.

"We continue a bit farther on our course," said Thomas, watching the Great Sharks closely. "If we're going to survive, we need the light of day."

"That's no more than an hour off," replied Torlan.

"Then let's hope we can make it that long."

CHAPTER SEVENTY SEVEN

SHARK ATTACK

Hearing the shouts and commotion on deck, Kaylie flung herself out of her bunk, dressing quickly. Buckling her sword on her back, she sprinted up the steps. Sailors and Marchers created what appeared to be a tapestry of chaos on the main deck of the *Waverunner*, yet there was a purpose to it all. Picking out Thomas, Oso and Torlan at the bow, she dodged across the rough wood in their direction.

"What's going on?" she asked, noting the tense expressions that greeted her.

"Great Sharks preparing to attack," answered Torlan. "Perhaps you should go below decks, young miss."

"I will not, Captain," replied Kaylie, the fire rising in her voice. "I can fight just as well as any Marcher."

"That she can," said Oso.

"We need her, Torlan." Thomas turned, looking directly at Kaylie. "We were hoping for more time, for the sun to rise before they attacked, but it looks like our time's up."

Kaylie looked out over the rail, discerning the Great Sharks circling in the dim light offered by the deck lamps, the wakes created by their fins becoming larger as their speed increased. They swam no more than fifty yards off the ship now.

"They're preparing to charge," warned Torlan, watching the Great Sharks as well. He had seen the massive beasts do much the same thing time and time again. Soon they would try to ram them, and whether his ship, large as it was, could absorb such a blow, or possibly repeated blows, he didn't know.

"Kaylie, we need light," explained Thomas. "We can't fight these creatures in the dark. Can you give us that?"

Kaylie returned his gaze unflinchingly. She had never done it before, but she had grown comfortable in the use of the Talent, enjoying her lessons with Thomas every night after dinner. She knew she could figure something out.

"Yes, I can."

"Good. Find a spot on the main deck, maybe by the helm, where you can see in every direction. When I call for it, give us the light that we need."

Kaylie nodded and ran off, knowing exactly what to do.

Torlan watched her go. "What is she going to …"

To stop what would likely be a series of questions that he didn't have the time to answer, he lifted his palm. A bright white ball of light appeared, dancing above his fingers.

Torlan stepped back in shock. "I've heard stories, but I never believed …" His eyes were wild for a moment, then with visible effort he regained control of himself. "I've heard of a Highlander with such power. I never expected it to be true. The stories you hear in the inns lining the waterfront tend to be more tall tales than anything else. Clearly, this one was …"

"True," said Oso. The tall Highlander watched the captain, waiting to see how he would respond to this obviously unsettling discovery. It didn't take long to find out.

"Then perhaps we have a chance after all," said Torlan. "My Lord, the ship is yours to command."

"Thank you, Torlan," said Thomas. "Man the helm and keep us on this course. When the first Great Shark charges, turn into the attack. Aim the bow at the beast. Make it strike the prow."

"As you command, Lord Kestrel," said Torlan, who lumbered off across the deck, yelling encouragement to his sailors as he went.

"Oso, form the Marchers into three groups. One each to the port and starboard rails, the last to the bow. Bows ready. Tell them that I might add a little something extra when they shoot."

Oso ran off, organizing the Marchers quickly. Having done all that he could, Thomas took hold of the Talent, allowing the power of nature to flow through him. Extending his senses, he saw what he had expected. The Great Sharks' presence had cleared the water around them of other sea life. Thomas glanced to the west for just a moment, somewhat surprised. A pod of dolphins still tracked them, following the progress of their ship and the three predators.

On a whim, Thomas decided to try something that he had done many times, in fact one of the first things that he had learned to do as a child when trying to control the Talent. He reached out with his mind, seeking to connect with the dolphins. Finding the dolphin that he thought was the alpha, the largest female around whom the other dolphins swam, he attempted to connect with her.

At first there was nothing. It was like he was butting his head up against a brick wall. But then something changed, an acceptance. Then a welcome. Thomas had succeeded. He had linked with the dolphin matriarch. Using images as he did when communicating with Beluil, he offered a greeting and began to explain who he was, where he was going. The dolphin quickly replied, asking why the Great Sharks had entered their territory. Thomas attempted to answer when he had to break the connection unexpectedly.

"Thomas!" shouted Oso, who had come to stand with him on the bow, several Marchers behind them, bows at the ready. "Off to the right! One of the beasts is turning."

Thomas regained his concentration, confirming what Oso had said. The first Great Shark had stopped circling, instead angling toward the ship.

"Torlan! Hard starboard!"

"Hard starboard!" repeated Torlan, turning the wheel. His sailors responded immediately, trimming the sails, taking in certain lines, letting out others, as the ship cut smartly through the waves in the desired direction. Kaylie stood just behind the captain, waiting.

"Kaylie! Give us light!"

Knowing the need would be immediate, she already had opened herself to the Talent, taking in as much of the natural magic of the world as she could safely hold. Raising her hands toward the darkened sky, she then released the power that she controlled, the stream of white blasting from both palms until a bright haze filled the sky for a league around. Kaylie had replaced the early morning murk with a brilliance as strong as the sun, giving everyone on board the *Waverunner* full knowledge of what they faced.

The Great Shark that had maneuvered to attack quickly picked up speed, the other two continuing to circle and waiting to see what the result would be. Torlan had turned the bow as Thomas requested, aiming right for the Great Shark. The beast didn't seem to care, staying on its course, its enormous fin cutting through the water faster and faster with every passing second as its massive tail propelled it through the water.

"Oso, on your command!" shouted Thomas, the pounding of the ship rising and falling through the waves almost deafening.

Oso didn't bother to respond. He knew what was needed. "Marchers, to the ready!"

The Marchers standing behind him at the bow stepped forward, bows drawn, arrows nocked. The Marchers on both sides of the ship did the same.

Oso waited until the Great Shark was almost upon them. "Release!"

The arrows shot through the salty sea air, targeting the attacking Great Shark. Thomas watched the bolts speed away, knowing that the shafts of wood and sharpened steel heads would have little effect against the thick skin of the Great Shark. But he could remedy that. Using the Talent, he focused his attention on the arrows, infusing them with power, the long shafts of wood and metal becoming blazing bolts of white light.

Amazed, but not surprised, the Marchers observed their arrows streak toward the Great Shark, then quickly prepared to shoot again. Torlan watched in shock, but he maintained his presence of mind to keep his ship lined up on the attacking beast.

The first arrow struck, then another, and another. The Marchers were true in their aim, and the power Thomas had infused in the quarrels allowed them to pierce the Great Shark's hide. At first, the Great Shark appeared unaffected, but more and more arrows struck, and the huge beast began to falter. As each shaft pierced its rough hide, tearing into it, the white energy sizzled and penetrated deeper into the beast.

When one of the last arrows ripped through the Great Shark's right eye, it finally tried to turn away, but it was too late. Torlan kept the *Waverunner* on course. Instead of the Great Shark crashing into the five-masted craft, the huge ship rammed the beast, its prow slamming into the creature's belly.

As the *Waverunner* passed the floundering beast, the Marchers fired several more arrows into the Great Shark, Thomas infusing them with energy as he had done before. The Great Shark's frantic movements slowly came to an end, its thrashing tail becoming still, and then the dark creature began to sink, its eyes unmoving as the last of its life bled into the surrounding waters.

Kaylie maintained her control of the Talent, continuing to illuminate the sky for a league around. She yearned to join the fight, but knew that her current task was just as critical.

"Hard port!" yelled Torlan, his sailors scrambling to obey his command.

A second Great Shark had turned, seeking to take advantage of the distraction provided by the attack of the first. The beast, charging toward the side of the hull, swam at a speed so great that it created a wake that threatened to swamp the deck of the ship. Try as Torlan and his men might, Thomas understood instantly that the ship would never turn in time to meet the dark creature head on. The Great Shark was too close, and the *Waverunner* would not be able to swing its bow around.

Oso recognized the danger as well, taking immediate action. "Marchers, release!"

Arrow after arrow shot from the bow and the port side, the Marchers on the starboard side sprinting across the deck to lend their aid. As before, Thomas infused each quarrel with the energy of his natural magic. With each strike, a bolt tore into the hardened hide of the Great Shark and then sizzled more deeply into its body. But the beast still kept coming, ignoring the pain, maw opened wide, sharp teeth glistening in the white light.

"Brace for impact!" shouted Torlan. Those who could did, those who couldn't found themselves tangled in the rigging or collapsed to the deck, many of the Marchers knocked onto their backs as the massive beast slammed into the merchant vessel amidships.

The Great Shark had flung itself half out of the water during its charge, its frightening snout taking a huge chunk out of the port rail, several unfortunate sailors sliding into its deep gullet as the creature's weight pushed the ship down into the waves, threatening to flood the main deck with seawater.

Those Marchers still standing continued to shoot their arrows, but Thomas knew it would not be enough. Despite the size of the *Waverunner*, it was listing severely because of the Great Shark's weight. The vessel was threatening to capsize as the masts and sails sank closer to the ten-foot waves.

Thomas sprinted from his position in the bow, leaping down toward the flooding deck and catching a rope that had come loose during the collision that allowed him to swing out across the deck. His momentum carried him toward the Great Shark, which gnashed its teeth, trying to reach more of the sailors who struggled to escape on the slippery wood. As Thomas flew through the air, he released the rope just above the thrashing Great Shark. Thomas grabbed hold of his sword, pulling it from the scabbard on his back, as he dropped back down toward the ship.

Hands clasped tightly to the hilt, he infused the blade with the Talent, its white glow almost blinding as he drove the point of the sword with all his might into the head of the Great Shark. Sliding through much like a stick through mud, the magicked blade bit through the beast's dense skull into the Great Shark's brain. That was the end.

The Great Shark's attack faltered, its life drifting from its eyes as it slowly but inexorably slid back from the ship's deck toward the ocean. Not wanting to go with it, Thomas pulled his sword free with a wrenching tug and jumped from his perch on the Great Shark's skull, his feet falling out from under him because of the water-slicked deck. He was about to follow the carcass of the beast into the frothy water when a hand gripped Thomas by the arm.

Oso had reached him just in time, grabbing hold of what was left of the deck railing to steady himself. As the dead weight of the shark fell into the sea, the ship righted itself, damaged but still seaworthy.

"The third Great Shark," said Oso. "We need to …"

"Don't worry, Oso. That Great Shark has more to worry about than us right now."

Thomas lay back on the deck, not caring that he was soon soaked through by seawater. Exhausted, he needed to catch his breath.

Oso peered out over the waves. Thomas was right. The Great Shark was retreating with several smaller fins in pursuit. Dolphins. They seemed to be hunting the monstrous shark.

"They are," said Thomas, reading his friend's mind. "Three Great Sharks are more than a pod of dolphins can handle. But one Great Shark? That's a different matter. I doubt that beast will make it more than a league alive."

"But how did the dolphins …" Oso stopped speaking, looking down at Thomas who had a wide grin on his face. Oso smiled as well, shaking his head in good-natured resignation. Even now, after all this time, Thomas was full of surprises.

CHAPTER SEVENTY EIGHT

TAKEN TO TASK

Several hours after the battle, the injured having been seen to, Thomas and Kaylie wandered to the bow of the *Waverunner,* the ship battered but still in good shape considering the assault that it had faced. They enjoyed the quiet, the privacy, needing time to collect their thoughts. The struggle against the Great Sharks had balanced on a knife's edge for a moment, until Thomas had done something that no one had expected. His actions had unsettled Kaylie in a way that she didn't like.

"Thomas, I wanted to talk to you about something." Kaylie turned from the bow, looking out over the ship as well, glancing at Thomas, who seemed a bit uncomfortable. "And just so we're clear, I'm not speaking to you as a friend right now. I'm speaking to you as the Princess of Fal Carrach."

Thomas nodded, looking at her sheepishly. "All right."

Kaylie continued. "You're the leader of this expedition. But more than that, you're the leader of a Kingdom that depends a great deal on you. To say nothing of all the other responsibilities that seem to weigh on you. You can't always put yourself in danger. We're here, your Marchers are here, knowing the dangers they face, yet they're here because of you. They're following you. And they expect to fight with you at the Breaker. So instead of thinking that you have to manage every skirmish or danger on your own, allow your Marchers to do what they excel at. Allow them to do what they came here to do. They're here to protect you and help you gain the Key. You can't place every task, every burden, on just your shoulders."

Thomas stared at Kaylie for more than a minute, the spray from the bow of the ship slicing through the ten-foot waves and coating their hair and clothes with a fine mist of salty sea.

"Point made, Princess," Thomas responded. "I'll keep that in mind going forward."

But his thoughts were elsewhere. For now he was content that his Marchers were safe and on the right path. And he felt certain that he would find the Key, giving him the ability to unlock the magical defenses of Blackstone. But beyond that he was less certain. When it came time for him to meet the requirements of the prophecy, to stand across from the Shadow Lord and fight for the future of the Kingdoms, would he survive the encounter? Would he live or die?

CHAPTER SEVENTY NINE

PRICK OF PAIN

The Shadow Lord stared down at the carving in the floor of his throne room, his burning eyes boring into the figure of the boy with the blazing sword. For an instant his rage almost got the better him, feeling the Dark Magic beginning to swirl around him as he felt the need to strike out at the boy, to smash the stone, for apparently there was no other way to harm his nemesis. Mustering all his willpower, he forced himself to release his hold on the power that surged within him.

The Wraith was dead. His deadliest assassin was no more. How it had been killed, he didn't know. But the Shadow Lord had felt the sharp prick of pain when his dark creature, bred specifically for a task such as the one given to it – to assassinate those who would oppose the Shadow Lord – had disappeared. As had the beasts in the Winter Sea. Simply gone.

He should have expected this result, though he had hoped for better. The boy was resilient, if nothing else. Dangerously so, as he had proven time after time. Once again, the boy had forced the Shadow Lord to rethink his strategy. No matter what obstacle the Shadow Lord had placed in front of the boy, he had avoided it. Perhaps he should simply assume that the boy would find the Key, that he would succeed on his quest, and that sometime soon the Shadow Lord would stand exactly where he was now, but instead of staring at a stone carving, he would instead face the boy. The prophecy spoke of it, and based on the boy's success, the prophecy seemed to require it.

But he didn't have to simply accept the reality that appeared to be trying to impose itself upon him. There was more that he could do. There was more that he could try. He had other killers that he could set in front of the boy, if for no other reason than to make the boy's life more difficult before he finally saw the ruins of Blackstone with his own eyes.

Regardless, the boy would die, whether during his search for the Key or, if he was lucky enough to survive that quest, the duel prophesied to take place in the Shadow Lord's lair. Either way, the Defender of the Light would be no more, and the Lord of the Shadow would reign supreme.

If you really enjoyed this story, I need you to do me a HUGE favor – please write a review. It helps the book and me. I really appreciate the feedback. Consider a review on Amazon or BookBub at http://www.bookbub.com/profile/peter-wacht.

Follow me on my website at www.kestrelmg.com.
You can find a link to the map of the Kingdoms, join my newsletter, access free content and keep an eye out for the next book in the series … or perhaps even a new story.

Printed in Great Britain
by Amazon